The Color of Reseda

Maria Kurtovich

DORRANCE PUBLISHING CO., INC
PITTSBURGH, PENNSYLVANIA 15222

This is a work of fiction. Names, characters, places, and incidents are either the product of the author's imagination or are used fictitiously; and any resemblance to persons living or dead; events; or locales is entirely coincidental.

ISBN # 0-8059-6115-1
Printed in the United States of America

First Printing

For information or to order additional books, please write:
Dorrance Publishing Co., Inc.
701 Smithfield Street
Third Floor
Pittsburgh, Pennsylvania 15222
U.S.A.
1-800-788-7654
Or visit our web site and on-line catalog at www.dorrancepublishing.com

To my husband, David, for his loyal support and unwavering encouragement.

Reseda (reseda adorata) (fr. mignonette): a fragrant, ornamental plant of a distinct, pale, silvery green color; native to the Mediterranean.

Chapter 1

Claire decided to leave the office earlier than usual on that balmy April day in 1943 which promised an early spring that year. She was weary of the long cold winter and longed to catch a few rays of sunshine to warm her frozen limbs. It was not only a desire for physical reprieve from the hardships of the past months she was longing for, but she hoped constantly and fervently for an end to that abominable war that had now lasted for nearly four years and which had taken such a great toll in lives and dreams.

From her office, it was just a short walk along Operngasse to the Ringstrasse, the grandest of all the lovely streets in Vienna. She liked to stroll beside the magnificent buildings along each side of the boulevard. The formidable Opera House, the statue of Goethe next to the Burg-Garten, the Heldenplatz with its monumental statues of heroes of the past, of generals on their bucking horses, of poets in thoughtful poses, and statesmen of varying fame. In the background loomed the Hofburg, formerly occupied by the Kaiser, Franz Josef, and his beautiful and unhappy wife, the Empress Elizabeth. The elegant castle now contained the Spanish Riding School, museums, and other government offices.

A fleeting memory passed through Claire's mind about the time when she had attended a great formal ball at the Hofburg and was waltzing through those magnificent halls and rooms. She had enjoyed all the glitz and glamour of times past when only the high and mighty of the Austrian empire had had access to it.

We have come a long way in our little country, she pondered; from the conglomeration of nationalities under one rule, that of the House of Habsburg for seven hundred years, to the split into many little countries, of which Austria with its seven million people, was the smallest as the result of

1

the ruling of the Treaty of Versailles after the first World War. It was to punish Austria for the sin of the war, that it was accused of having started in 1914 when it had retaliated for the assassination of its' crown prince and heir to the throne, Ferdinand, and his wife, Sophy, by a Serbian nationalist.

When the war ended in a devastating defeat for Austria, it became a republic. Claire remembered the annual celebrations of this event in school where the children learned songs in praise of the new republic. The new socialistic government was not going to allow wars to happen again, the students were told. Claire had always been chosen by her teachers to recite a poem at these celebrations, and she felt great emotion upon such occasions although she barely understood the politics involved. She knew well enough of the misery which that war had brought upon the people. So many men dead or crippled. Hunger, homelessness, and unemployment affected nearly every family. The cause of that was blamed on the imperialists; the Habsburgs in Austria, the Hohenzollern in Germany. To get rid of them all would prevent a repetition of the past. *"Nie wieder Krieg"*—never again war— was the slogan of the day, and Claire believed in it wholeheartedly. She had been luckier because her father and her uncles had returned from the war alive, and in good health, but many of her friends in school had lost their fathers, sometimes even their grandfathers. Claire's family had lost savings and investments in the reestablishment measures which the new government had to impose. She was not really aware of these things as a child, but she was fully cognizant of the lack of food and other necessities, and the mood of the people around her, and it gave her much concern about the future.

While strolling leisurely along the Ringstrasse on that lovely April afternoon, she was giving the historic past just a passing thought. The vision of her surroundings, the tree-lined boulevard with its elaborate buildings and the lovely squares and parks, made her proud of belonging, of being a Viennese, "born and raised," as the saying goes. She took pleasure in the sunshine, the young greening of the chestnut trees, the delicate first blossoms on the shrubberies beside the walkways, the aroma of the fresh soil, the scent of flowers, and the frolicsome chirping of the insolent sparrows. For a long heartbeat she even felt joy. She longed so very much to be happy. The walk home that day, instead of the ride on the streetcar, was definitely beneficial, and she decided that she must do it more often. Nature and beautiful surroundings always lifted her spirits.

Just then, an announcement came over one of the public loudspeakers which were posted all around the city. People stopped to listen, and Claire did also. "Mass murder at Katyn!" The graves of a great number of Polish officers, murdered by the Russians, had been discovered by a German troup contingent. Some gruesome details were reported, and, as usual, also some heroic victories of the German military.

Claire felt sick. She leaned for a moment against a tree. All the joy of the day had vanished. She felt suddenly hurried and anxious to get home. All that she had enjoyed just minutes ago seemed now to be painful. She wanted to be alone. For nearly four years now, she had tried to be brave and endure the war, to be part of a strong home front on which the soldiers out there in the trenches could depend, and not to succumb to defeat and despair. It became harder to do with every passing day. Sometimes, the news was almost unbearable, even when interspersed with promises of a "final victory" through the *Wunderwaffe*, which was almost ready to be deployed. She had no idea what it could be, but if that weapon could indeed end the war, it would be a *wunder*— a miracle. Aside from being a little skeptical, she was ready to believe again.

Claire's thoughts went to Stefan. Where was he now? Somewhere in Russia, he wrote her, but he could not divulge details. He was so brave and never doubted. He believed in all the propaganda and expected the same from her, although her doubts were often painfully repressed in her responses to his enthusiastic letters.

Claire and Stefan had been engaged for nearly the length of the war. It was a comfortable relationship, marred or enhanced by the long intervals between seeing each other. In the beginning, she had felt rather sad and disappointed not to have fallen head-over-heels in love with Stefan, but she learned with time to appreciate his solid and steadfast character, his intelligence, his loyalty. He loved her in his way, she thought. He would always take care of her. She could lean on him and trust him. Was this not more than one could ask for? He was quite handsome too. Tall and lean, with honey-blond hair, always carefully combed and cut to fit his military cap. His uniform of perfect cut and fit—the picture of a model officer. And that he was. Devoted to duty, believing in God, country, family.

Yes, she was lucky that he had chosen her as his future wife. And yet, she quickly buried in her mind any little doubt that their relationship might not be perfect. Indeed it was perfect, and the latest incident should not even cast a little shadow on it. It was mostly her fault anyway, and she should be glad that Stefan was the sort of man who understood her. He had not had a leave for nearly a year, when she had received a telegram from him that he would be on a military mission to headquarters in Germany. This would make it possible to take a side trip to visit his parents near Dresden for two or three days. Would she please arrange to travel there also, so they could have some time together, however short?

So many things went through her mind, when reading his message. Of course, she would love to go, but it would be difficult to arrange for the train tickets at a time when civilian travel was so limited. It was a lengthy train ride all the way to Dresden, and, services were severely curtailed after sustaining many bombings. Besides, she was duty-bound to her own job. She could not see how she could defend her absence from the office, even for a few days and such heartfelt reasons, when the business, as little profitable as it may have become, needed her attention. Stehle Company had made her manager of the Vienna office for the duration of the war, during the absence of her former boss, Georg Woerner, who also had been recruited during the very first weeks of the war. There was the anticipated delivery of goods from the factory, papers which needed her signature and merchandise anxiously awaited by the customers. Even a day or two of neglect could mean so much to them. No one at the office could substitute for her and make decisions on her behalf. The staff consisted only of a skeleton crew now. Nearly all the able-bodied men were serving in the military and other personnel had been requested by the Labor Exchange for reassigned duties in these last-ditch war efforts.

She called the home of Stefan's parents. Stefan had not yet arrived, but his mother, Magda von Brecht, was very gracious, and understood Claire's dilemma. Claire suspected that Magda was not as sorry that she could not come, as she had expressed. A house guest in these difficult times was a burden, even at the home of the Brechts, who were still able to keep a maid. Bombing raids interrupted all the ways of daily life. Even more, Magda wanted to have her son to herself as much as possible. There were so very few occasions for that now.

Stefan was the Brecht's only son and was as devoted to his parents as they were to him. They had received Claire politely when Stefan introduced her to them, but she felt some resentment. Or did she imagine it? The Brechts were too well mannered to show displeasure, but something was missing. Maybe it was just their German way. They were not as gushing as their southern cousins, the Austrians, or specifically the Viennese. Claire herself had to get used to German ways in her business, when she had decided to join the Stehle company after Austria became part of the Third *Reich* in the *Anschluss*. The influx of the cool and more reserved "northern cousins" who came to do business here was not appreciated in every corner. Yes, they brought much needed work with them to the economically bankrupt Austria, but could they not say "Please" and "Thank you" more often? Claire had heard that so often from her Viennese compatriots, but she soon found that, within their cool outer shell, these Germans were as feeling and compassionate as the Viennese considered themselves to be, just in a different way.

Claire found good friends among her new associates, but also among those at headquarters in West Germany, whom she got to know through their correspondence and from their visits to Vienna. She was happy when showing these visitors around her hometown. She heard their enthusiastic praise, and she could even tolerate it when they sometimes criticized the long-winded formalities and slower pace in Austria, or "*Ostmark*," as it was called after the *Anschluss*. This name change was another thumb in the eye for many Austrians, who were used to being citizens of a sovereign country and did not want to accept having become only a part of another. To point out that throughout history Austria had shown variations in its name, size, and rulers, did not convince those who were looking to be critical.

Chapter 2

The Woerners had introduced Claire and Stefan when inviting both of them to their house for dinner. It was obvious that they had matchmaking in mind. Claire did not mind. The Woerners had been always very kind to her, and even though Georg Woerner was her boss, in the privacy of their home they showed her only friendship, for which she was grateful. At one such occasion, she met Stefan von Brecht, who was the son of the Woerner's dearest friends in Germany before the Woerner's moved to Austria and Georg became the head of the Vienna branch of Stehle. Stefan's mother Magda was a granddaughter of the founder of the company, was still involved financially, and also had some managerial clout. When the Woerners heard young Stefan would be stationed for some time as a soldier in Vienna, they invited him frequently, and there it happened, that the young people met. Claire liked Stefan, who seemed to be the epitome of a serious soldier, handsome in his uniform, cool, and reserved. However, he also had delightful manners and could be nearly as charming as the best of the Viennese. His very precise clipped German accent seemed to complement his snappy appearance, which sounded so "educated" compared with the often sloppy Viennese colloquialism.

Although a great number of restrictions on the life of the civilian population were implemented right at the beginning of the war in 1939, such as food rationing and blackouts, civilian life could still be enjoyable to some degree for a while. There were movies, first class theater productions, concerts, restaurants, outings into the Vienna Woods, and the transportation facilities were still in full operation. September of 1939 was a threat only to those who were immediately called to arms and who participated in the invasion of Poland, which lasted just three weeks.

Stefan had volunteered for military duty, was schooled and trained in Germany, and was now a lieutenant, stationed temporarily in Vienna. He kept his political views strictly private, as was proper for a military man, but his loyalty to his country and its' government was unquestionable.

Claire and Stefan made a handsome couple, and both enjoyed the looks passing folks gave them. Claire's parents accepted the courtship with a friendly demeanor, but when after a few months they were presented with the reality of an engagement, Claire's mother, Rosemarie, was not as happy as Claire had hoped she would be. This troubled her, although deep in her own heart she had admitted to herself, that her feelings were not of overwhelming happiness, but were tinged with some sadness, which she could not really explain. On the surface, all seemed to be just perfect. Stefan was as honorable a man as she had ever met. There had been some in her past that had made their attempts to capture her heart, who would not deserve that compliment as much. He loved her—she was sure of that— although he was not a man of many words when it came to expressing his innermost feelings. If she expected an outpouring of emotional expressions, she would be disappointed. However, he did write loving letters punctually every week. Claire was grateful for that. It had made her loneliness throughout these years bearable.

Newly engaged, they had of course talked about their future plans as all young couples would. At that time they had both agreed that they would wait for marriage until the war was over. After all, that could not be so long in the future, as the German Army was victorious and everybody was convinced that the war could not last. Maybe a few months? When the war in Poland was won, and the Allies confronted the German Army in the West, the French Army, even with their famous fortification, the Maginot Line, which had been considered impenetrable, could not withstand the German onslaught, and France surrendered. Now, the war would end, would it not? The Germans had also been victorious in the Balkans—what else? The short-lived treaty with the Russians came to an end. The English began heavy bombings of German cities, and the Germans did so to England, and the war dragged on and on, bringing misery to the whole world.

Stefan was involved in the fighting in the West, and after a short time with the occupational forces in France, he then became involved in all the major battles on the Eastern front. He fought at Stalingrad, was captured by the Russians. He endured hardships beyond description; despite being in a hopeless situation, he was lucky to be freed by a German troop contingent which had briefly recaptured some areas around Stalingrad. At that time he received a medal for bravery and was granted home leave, and Claire and Stefan enjoyed a few happy days together.

In the meantime, Claire had moved into an apartment of her own. She furnished it with care and in good taste as far as the limited availability of furnishings would allow her to do. Years ago she had inherited some lovely antiques from her grandmother, including a sterling silver tea set and some Meissen porcelain. Her parents also let her take the piano and a few favorite paintings when she moved out. They felt generous towards their only child, especially her mother, who had always doted on her. Her father, Friedrich Baumann, a University professor, scholar, and writer, was not a very warm or generous person, but was content if left alone to pursue his studies. He never objected to his wife's generous gifts to Claire, as long as it was not his desk and the comfortable chaise, the places reserved for his "thinking."

The marriage of her parents had apparently not been a very happy one; Claire thought this might have been the reason why Rosemarie showed some hesitation in accepting Stefan. Her mother did not seem to trust men, but Claire did not want to be affected by that attitude. She had always had good male friends in school and later on, and never shared her mother's feelings in that respect.

By the time Stefan returned from Stalingrad, the apartment looked warm and comfortable, and Claire was very proud of it. Stefan had missed home for so long and he was happy when visiting Claire in her apartment. He complimented her good taste and spoke of the future when it would be a cozy place for them to start a new life. He would like to stay on in Vienna after the war. He had a degree in law, and was thinking of either a private law practice or a government job. There was time to ponder about that.

He never stayed overnight, even when she pointed out her little guest room, modest but comfortable, which sometimes even her company visitors used, when hotel rooms were not available. He declared he would never compromise her in that way, he loved her too much for that. Claire thought she would not have worried about that, but did not say a word. However, at times his correctness bothered her. She had happily agreed to postpone their marriage till after the war, but that was now so long ago. She felt herself getting older, and life felt emptier than ever. She envied her friends, who managed to raise children despite the difficult times and longed to have children of her own, many of them, she imagined, although she had grown up as an only child herself. Or because of it? Even as a young girl she had seen herself as a mother, surrounded by a loving brood. Maybe she was dreaming again—these dreams of a happy life, a loving husband, adorable children. It would probably be one of those dreams that would never find fulfillment. Claire believed fervently in prayers and knew they were granted, if they came from the heart, and were not striving for gold or riches or material gains. So she kept on praying. She had almost given up envisioning the "brood," but would be happy with even just one. She had talked to Stefan about it at one time. He had just smiled, and told her to be patient. Oh, she was—was there anything else in her life but patience? How could Stefan be so "patient," she wondered. When he was stationed in occupied France he talked in letters about his experiences and described the civilian life of the French at that time. He pitied their lot as a conquered nation, but found their life style decadent; the women beautiful, but of questionable morals. Claire had never worried about Stefan's faithfulness, but at that time began to wonder how he could abstain so steadfastly. She asked him about it in a roundabout way. He only smiled at her tolerantly and said that a soldier was preoccupied most of the time with just trying to stay alive when death and destruction were his daily companions. Although Claire believed him, an occasion arose where she felt wicked enough to test his fortitude.

Stefan had invited Claire to a special opera performance, and came to pick her up at the apartment. Claire was not yet dressed to go out when he arrived. She purposely wore her pale green silk dressing gown, which her mother had at one time brought for her from Italy. When she tried it on in front of the long dressing mirror, she was pleased with herself. The robe was of beautiful quality, its color enhanced the little green specks in Claire's blue-gray eyes. Her auburn, wavy hair, was cut fashionably short; the neckline bared an exquisite, slender neck with skin of porcelain luminescence; her slim figure showed well under the folds of the luxurious silk, and Claire almost blushed over her own appearance. She was not vain, often rather critical of flaws as she perceived them, but this time she approved of her appearance. It was not in her nature to use feminine wiles to lure a man, but she could not help herself to test Stefan's reaction if she would greet him at the door, just cloaked in that special green silk robe. She could almost foresee his reaction. There may have been a gleam in his eyes, when he said:

"You look lovely, Claire," but quickly added: "Hurry and get dressed, we don't want to miss the overture."

She ventured to say; "Would that be so bad?"

He did not answer. She smiled faintly and followed his advice.

It was a great performance at the opera, after which they had a cocktail at a nearby bar. Then they walked home through the dark city streets, discussing how rare it was these days to get to see and hear "Lohengrin" with such an extraordinary cast of singers. It had been a very nice evening indeed, and after Stefan kissed her tenderly at the door, he left for the officer's quarters where he was staying. He did not want to spoil the evening by telling Claire that he had orders to leave for the front again the day after next.

Claire went slowly up the stairs to her apartment, took the light green silk robe from the hook in the bathroom and put it back into her wardrobe. She thought about her soon upcoming twenty-sixth birthday, and how time was flying.

Chapter 3

During her childhood years, Claire's family spent the hot summer months of July and August in the country. Grandmother, who lived with her daughter's family after Grandfather's passing, was included, and she was often her and her young brother's only companion, when her parents traveled alone to places like Italy or Greece, where Friedrich met with scholars from other parts of the world to exchange ideas and philosophies. In the meantime, in the countryside of one of Austria's provinces, Claire and her little brother André played and frolicked and participated in the simple pleasures of the village children.

If the children, Claire and André, had foreign sounding names, it should be explained, that Rosemarie found some pleasure in adopting foreign customs and cultures. She had been raised in a Viennese environment, where French was her second language, as was often expected in educated circles of a long bygone era. Her family was one of them. Times since then had changed, everything became less formal, less gracious, she felt. She did not impose her inclinations on her daughter, but held on to them herself. Her background may have been the reason for her reservations regarding Stefan. Not that she could blame him for lacking culture, but he was, as she put it—although only to herself—too "German," too stiff, too—even too "perfect." Just like her own husband, Friedrich, who was not even German, but was Austrian by birth and heritage. Even though, he lacked the attributes so often seen in the Viennese, namely charm, she thought.

When Claire was eight years old, and little André four, he became ill on their vacation; it seemed to be more serious than a cold, so that grandmother felt it necessary to notify his parents in Florence, who immediately returned to Hartberg. By that time the little boy had become delirious, and the doctor recommended transfer to a children's clinic in Vienna. He did not want to frighten the family, but suspected that the child had Polio. His diagnosis was confirmed in Vienna, and despite attempts to prolong the child's life—a cure was not expected in such cases—little André died. It was an experience that Claire, who was only a young child herself, never forgot. The distraught parents blamed each other for possible neglect because of their absence when the child became ill, although it was quite clear, that nothing could have prevented the dreadful disease, to which many children succumbed in those times, or, if their lives were saved, became crippled. Soon grandmother passed away also.

Through the years, Claire and her parents took summer vacations in a number of resorts. Claire was especially happy in the mountains of Salzburg, where the family spent several weeks each year. She loved hiking with her father, or roaming through the nearby woods on her own, swimming in the lake, or reading in the garden of the small villa which her parents rented for the summer. It became her favorite vacation spot, and during the whole school year she dreamed of that time in the summer. If only she could have some of her friends from school there too, it would be great.

In later years, when she was about sixteen or seventeen, she missed her Viennese friends less when she met other young people at the lake. Some were summer guests like her, others were sons and daughters of the townspeople. They soon became her friends and during the school year back in Vienna, they even kept contact through letters.

Claire especially enjoyed those from Fritz Engebrecht, the "heartthrob" from the beach of Kammersee. All the girls gathered around that dark, curly-haired fellow who showed off his prowess on the diving board and in other athletic feats, where his bronze tanned physique caught the attention not only of the girls, but also of the other envious young men, whose winter-white city skin turned mostly only into a boiled-crayfish red. Fritz was a native, born in the village, orphaned and raised by a maiden aunt, who was a recognized painter, as well as a writer. Fritz had a number of uncles and aunts who also took part in his upbringing, paying for his schooling, but he nevertheless liked to play the role of one poor little orphan to the fullest. He probably truly felt that way, missing the parents he lost when he was only a baby; they had died in an accident. Fritz was an accomplished athlete, not only participating in local and national competitions but winning major ones.

Claire did not need to join his admirers since she was the object of his attention during these summer days anyway, and he kept the memory of himself alive during the rest of the year by sending his poetically inspired letters. Fritz was not shy about letting everybody know how he adored Claire, and how heartbroken he was that she did not return his feelings. He called her a "cold-hearted city maiden," and Claire admitted to herself that she took advantage of his admiration by playing the game during these carefree summer holidays, without committing herself to anything. It gave Fritz a chance to act like a character from the literature, where the lovesick, misunderstood hero laments his pain in wonderful poetic verse. It was much fun for the summer months.

Claire was probably not completely free of some theatrics of her own, posing as a lovelorn maiden. Not that she lacked admirers in school, but she felt she was incapable of a continuing interest in any of her dates. She tended to agree with Fritz's assessment of her as a "cold-hearted city maiden." She did not want to be that way. She told herself that she probably would never marry but would become a teacher like her father, and also like her father be occupied with the pursuit of the classics more than that of love. At the same time she dreamed of having children, thinking that she would make a perfect mother, a little like her own mother, but even more so, being stronger and wiser. All daughters always want to be as good, but just a little bit better than their mothers, don't they?

Claire was slow in accepting friendship, from boys as well as girls. Casual ways were not to her liking. She was looking for a true friend, and if there should be only one, it was enough for her. There were some who came close to her requirements, such as Heidi, whom she had known forever, it seemed. Their mothers had been friends in school, and had shared their experiences in their newborns of nearly the same age. Heidi was a good friend and could be trusted with all of Claire's confidences—small or big. She was always there when tears needed to be dried, sorrows shared. It was not exactly the same response to happy and joyful events, where Claire noticed a little jealousy appearing in her friend, but she liked her just as well.

Felix Sandel was a boy in school with whom Claire shared many interests. They walked to school together and took walks in the afternoons after school in the park; they discussed everything that was on their mind, be it school, friends, teachers, literature, world affairs, etc. They seldom agreed, but that made it the more challenging: the disagreement and the effort to convince the other was really the most fun. They visited the venerable National Library and some of the great museums together, and were in awe or contempt—depending on their prevailing inclination—of the great men and women of the past. Good and warm weather found them with Lixl's— short for Felix—"fold boat" on the Danube and its tributaries, where the Viennese enjoy water sports and related activities. Lixl and Claire said they truly loved each other; however, a more experienced observer would probably have called it puppy love, and its innocence was probably the reason that it fell apart once the two youngsters became adults.

Her "love" for Lixl did not prevent Claire from flirting with other boys when the occasion arose, but her interest faded quickly for often quite nebulous reasons. A big reason, in Claire's mind, was when she received a note from one of these boys where he made errors in spelling or grammar. That canceled out all his other possible virtues, such as good looks or popularity. Claire was a top student, and would have felt that it was beneath her to be in love with an inferior student. Good friends, yes, but that was all. Lixl qualified—to a degree—as good friend, since his spelling was flawless—and that did not cause their eventual break-up.

Claire was critical of herself, called herself fickle, and predicted she would never find someone she could tolerate for any length of time, therefore marriage could not be in her future. What a pity, she would have made such a good mother! Such thoughts were often on her adolescent mind. The truth, however, was that she was not at all unhappy or discontented. She was smart, had a good sense of humor, a warm and compassionate heart, and was ready for a good time whenever it presented itself. She was also serious in her studies, and in her approach to life's expectations. Her parents had good reason to be proud of their daughter. Occasionally, she had a tendency to revolt and become rambunctious, but mostly she managed to be obedient, unless challenged in her convictions. On the whole, her home life was pleasant, loving, and free of major battles.

Having digressed from describing summertime at Kammersee, other beach companions should be mentioned too. There was, for instance, Gerda, also a summer guest from Vienna, a pretty, blond, sweet girl, who certainly could have turned heads but she had eyes only for Fritz. However, it was told before where that young fellow stood. There were other young people; some of them came to the beach daily, some only occasionally, such as Burgl Mayer, the daughter of a nearby farmer. She was a student at the University in Vienna, and was therefore given a few vacation days at the beach besides helping out with farm duties as most of the other farm kids had to during their summer vacations. She was also Fritz's cousin, and there was some good-natured heckling between the two of them, and some family jokes were shared. Altogether it was great fun and Claire had always a good time.

One other young man, a little older than the rest, was also a steady sunbather. Claire wished he would participate more in the general games, but he kept himself on the sidelines, although he never failed to put his beach towel next to hers. He was a student at the Vienna Medical School, in his early twenties, and was very reserved. Claire thought he was the personification of her dreams: tall, blond, good looking like no other boy she ever knew, and when he looked at her with his dark blue eyes, she felt all wobbly and insecure. She was well aware he paid some attention to her, but she could not interpret it. They swam together, raced, or just talked a little. He never showed any prowess on the trampoline like Fritz, was not tanned "bronze" either, nor curly haired; actually, Peter Burghoff was no comparison to the popular Fritz Engebrecht. He was very special, Claire thought. After a long swim, resting next to each other on the grassy beach, he would tell her about his studies, and she was all ears. She would like to study medicine herself, she told him, although she had still a year to go before her *Matura* exams, which were a requirement for University studies. She was not sure her parents would want her to become a medical doctor; the teaching profession was what they had in mind. Peter was not encouraging either. He thought the medical profession required much physical strength, and few women were suited. So went their conversations. He was very nice, but still so distant, and although flirting with boys her own age had never been difficult, Claire felt awkward and shy in Peter's presence, and was annoyed with herself for it.

On their way home from the beach one day, Fritz and Burgl told her about Peter's background. It was obvious Fritz was not very fond of him, although they were raised in the same village. When Fritz considered himself as a poor orphan boy he talked of Peter as the conceited baron from the castle. Burgl just laughed and called Fritz jealous. Peter was not conceited, she said, but was quiet and did not make a fool of himself as the others did. As far as the castle was concerned, it was just a large farmhouse, although a long time ago it really had been a castle, sitting on the hillside overlooking the lake and the village. It still showed some remnants of a wall, a corner tower, and a moat where sheep were grazing now, as she pointed out to Claire. That's why everybody in the village and in town still called it the castle. The older Mr. Burghoff, although one of the wealthier farmers around, could be seen behind the plow himself or loading hay and cutting grain when they were short handed. Hans, the younger of the Burghoff boys, was studying agriculture at the University and was expected to take over the estate. Burgl knew him better than his older brother Peter, because he went to the school in town she also attended, as well as Fritz, she added, and Fritz nodded. Peter had gone to a private boarding school, and therefore had not had the same contact with the other local kids. Burgl, pert and outspoken, said with a sigh that she wished she could get closer to Peter, that hunk, but even when she saw him occasionally at the University in Vienna, he kept his distance. Well, that was all right, she had other irons in the fire anyway. Claire found Burgl very likable and was pleased when she invited her to come with her to her home and meet her parents; Fritz came along also, as Burgl's father was his uncle. There was a steaming pot of soup on the stove, and an invitation was extended to Claire and Fritz to stay and share their meal. Frau Mayer brought the large, freshly baked round loaf of bread to the table and with a knife she made the sign of a cross on the underside of the bread before cutting into it. Claire remembered that her grandmother on her father's side used to do that also—it was a lovely old custom—and it made her feel comfortable.

These carefree summer vacations were enjoyable not only for swimming and frolicking at the lake and walking through the forest and meadows, all real treats for a city youngster, but she also liked the country atmosphere with all its animal sounds and, yes, even the smells. It felt good. She was not quite sure, because nobody at home talked about their ancestry further than those they used to know, such as the grandparents, but she wondered if her love of that country smell was in her blood, if her ancestors had been farmers, cowhands maybe? Those she knew of were teachers like her father. One uncle was a priest somewhere, another a banker and a tradesman—no one had told her about farming ancestors.

It was a sad day when the weather did not permit recreation activities at the lake, but on one of these "sad days" Peter arrived at her door, and asked if she would be interested in going for a motorcycle ride. Of course she was, and with parental permission off they went. It was her first time riding on such a vehicle. She enjoyed the race along the country roads, the wind blowing through her hair, and most of all holding on to Peter Burghoff. It was a short ride the first time, but there were a few more occasions, and Peter showed her some of the sights of the surrounding countryside. They left the motorcycle on the side of the road and climbed over rocks and boulders to a fantastic waterfall. It was a very secluded spot, no one around, and Claire wished Peter would be a little less formal, not call her "Miss Claire," as he always did, maybe even take her hand; but he did not. He was nice, showed her plants she did not know, and flowers that only grew in certain spots between the rocks. They found edible berries, took their shoes off, and got so close to the waterfall's edge, that the spray touched their faces. It was wonderful, but he never came close unless to help her over some obstacle in the terrain.

Claire felt elated in Peter's company, but these wonderful days came to an end only too soon, when September approached and her school's beginning loomed. Her parents were anxious to return to the comfort of their home in the city, and in previous years Claire had also been eager to return to school, to her classes, and her friends. This time it was different. She knew this last year at school would be a little more strenuous, because of the preparation for the final exam, the *Matura*, but studying never scared her. She came to the beach for the last afternoon and said good-bye to all with promises for a return next summer.

Next morning at the train station, she was surprised by Fritz and Burgl and some of the others, who had come for a joyful send-off, bringing flowers, joking, laughing, and singing. In all the excitement she almost overlooked a fellow standing a little further away in the background, smiling at her. It was Peter—he had come too! She waved and walked towards him to bid him farewell also. He asked, somewhat casually, if it would be all right if he wrote to her in Vienna, and maybe they could get together sometimes during the year. Very formal again—but his dark blue eyes seemed to look quite sincerely into hers, and she blushed, which made her almost angry to be caught like that. She quickly told him her address in Vienna, hoping he would remember.

There was no time for more exchanges—the train came whistling to a stop and she had to hurry to follow her parents. There was the usual confusion finding the compartment and storing bags and suitcases, but there was still time to open the window and wave, mostly looking if "he" was still there. "He" was; he did not wave, but smiled, and she thought she still could feel his blue-eyed gaze, and it made her swoon. Her arms filled with the bouquets of autumn flowers, she fell back on her seat—happy and confused. "He" had become not only a summer acquaintance, but much more important. She would not have dared to call it a "summer romance," that would really have been an exaggeration, but maybe she could mention it as such to her friend Heidi? How soon would she hear from him? These and more questions went through her bewildered mind. Her mother, having observed her daughter's state and being somewhat amused, smiled from the seat opposite. Her father, the practical one, figuring that there was no room in that crowded compartment for all the flowers, which had already started to look a little bedraggled and would not last for the three hour train ride in the midday heat, took them out of Claire's arms, opened the window and threw them out. Normally, Claire would have protested and begged him not to do that. Today—she did not seem to even notice. She leaned back in her seat, and all she could think was: *I am in love, I am in love....*

Chapter 4

Peter looked after the train and when he could not see the waving arm anymore, he turned to go on his way. Burgl called to him, wanting to know if he would come to the beach in the afternoon, but he shook his head and said he had work to do at home. On his way there, he did think about that girl he just saw leaving on the train. Too bad, the summer was ending; it probably would be dull at the beach now. Nice girl, Claire, not loud and silly as most others her age, also quite smart and pleasant to talk to. It flattered him somewhat to see her blush when he asked for her address, which he had known already. One time he had accidentally looked at the return address on one of her letters she had mailed in his presence. He had made a quick note of it then, but by asking for it again he wanted to make sure that an attempt to get in touch with her in Vienna would be acceptable. He had noticed she had blushed—*that was nice*, he thought. Yes, he was looking forward to seeing her in Vienna. Not too often probably, because they would both be busy studying, but he did not want to lose sight of her. *Did she have a boyfriend in Vienna?* he wondered. She never mentioned her Viennese friends to him in their conversations, although they had often talked about school.

The walk home took about thirty minutes, through grassy fields where cows were grazing, some of them already resting in the warm sun of the midmorning after having had their fill of luscious grasses. The rushing waters of the Kammer brook along the side of the road were the only sound to accompany his thinking. He loved the peacefulness of the countryside he called his home, and he thought of the approaching time in Vienna. He had been in awe of the ambience of history and culture he had encountered when he had started his first years at the university there. His passion for music, developed

17

at the Jesuit boarding school, was nourished by the many offerings at the concert houses, the opera under the direction of famous conductors such as Toscanini, Krisp, and singers like Melchior and Elisabeth Schwarzkopf.

And yet, the sound of the rumbling brook was also music to his ears, as was the ever changing tune of the blackbirds, the trill of the high flying lark or the sensuous song of the nightingale. He knew he would always be torn between the lure of the big city and his roots in the country. Would he marry a girl from the city who would make the decision where he would settle in the future for him? He rejected that thought immediately. All his life he had been in charge of his own decisions and he wanted to keep it that way. Tradition dictated the role of the male in every stable family, and it was so in his father's house also. At the moment he forgot his mother's influence, her strength, her faith, her fortitude, the mother he loved above all, who had guided him through sometimes difficult periods in his growing up years and who was still influencing his life.

When Peter stepped into the hallway of his home, he heard his mother's commanding, steady voice from the kitchen, giving instructions to the maid about the upcoming dinner. As if this had been a signal to his stomach, he felt hungry all of a sudden, smelling with pleasure the aromas emanating from that direction. Another reminder of his happy life at home in the country.

Hanna Burghoff stood at the center of the kitchen, a beautiful woman in her late forties. Tall and strong in bearing, a serene face of classic lines, her blond hair in a simple braid around her head and those blue eyes of sapphire we have seen before in her son, who was now standing beside her. They resembled each other greatly; he with all the masculine overtones, and she providing the picture of Ceres, the goddess of the Earth, as the Greek sculptors of antiquity chiseled her image.

Hanna, pleased to see her son, told him his father wanted to talk to him before dinner. He was at his laboratory in the greenhouse. Peter went there immediately. He shared his father's interest in agricultural experiments. Anton Burghoff bought seeds from all over the world to search for improved plants, mostly for silvi cultural use, since he had added a profitable tree growing business to his other farming enterprises. He was also looking for unusual plants, growing in various parts of the world, still unknown to the flora of the region here despite climatic similarities.

Anton Burghoff welcomed his son with a friendly grin, but became serious immediately. At Peter's questioning look, he said:

"It's about Hans. He came home early this morning, his motorcycle demolished in a ditch along the road—I just had them haul it away."

"Is Hans hurt?" was Peter's first question.

"Luckily, he was just thrown into the recently mowed meadow and except for some scrapes and bumps, he suffered no damage beyond hurt

pride, and not too much of that either, since he seems to have been somewhat inebriated and did not know exactly what hit him. From what I could
determine, it must have been the boulder on the side of the road there, normally easily avoided."

"Thank God, he is not hurt," Peter said.

"Yes," his father said, "but I am angry at him, and will have to deal with
him some other time. For today, I do not want to alarm your mother, and will
go lightly on him, but I want you to have a heart to heart talk with him about
this and other concerns of mine. He will probably open up to you more than
to my stern approach. I am not talking about his occasional brawls at the tavern in town—my God, I remember my own youthful digressions—but his
apparent recklessness. Above all, it is the company he is keeping that worries
me a great deal."

Peter interrupted:

"Father, they are the kids from around here, all friends of ours, nothing
sinister about keeping company with one's old buddies."

"It is the new line of politics they are espousing, talking about events that
have taken place in Germany, and their admiration of the whole Nazi culture."

"Father, I think you worry too much about the influence the German
Nazis could have on our little Austria. We are not their type of people. We
do not believe in their ideals. Their problems of economic disaster may be
similar to ours, but their solution certainly is not. The Catholic Church and
its influence is very strong here and its sympathies are clearly not with the
National Socialists."

"Well, that is not how Father Grumbacher sees it according to his sermon last Sunday, but you were not there to hear that," Anton said, somewhat
accusingly.

Peter smiled—he had to admit that he missed Sunday church too
often—in his parent's view. He felt guilty of having become too cosmo-
politan not to be bored by the homespun simplicity of Father
Grumbacher's sermons. Both his parents were intelligent people; he could
not understand their acceptance of the old priest's ramblings week after
week for so many years. What Peter did not see was that they had become
so used to it, they could more or less tune out the sermon, but still participate in the religious service of the old traditional ways which were
comforting to them.

Peter's religious education came not from the village priest at
Kammerbach, but from the sophisticated priests at the convent where he had
attended boarding school for eight years. These were not especially memorable years for Peter, who resented the Jesuits' strict discipline which they
demanded not only in their practice of religious rules but in the teaching of
secular subjects and the conduct of everyday life. There never seemed to be

any tolerance for exuberant juvenile behavior. If there was ever a teacher who showed understanding, he was soon transferred to other duties.

These thoughts passed quickly through Peter's mind, while he assured his father that there was not much to worry about Hans. The brothers were very close, despite their difference in character and life style. Peter, only three years older, was the quiet, thoughtful, dependable, sensible type, who had always set high goals for himself and proceeded to follow in that direction. Hans was the cheerful, charming boy who delighted in life, enjoyed fun and games, was friend to everyone, and did not worry about the future. He knew it was already decided for him. By tradition, he would take over the farm and live his life the way his father lived, and his grandfather before him; it was good enough for him, he had no further aspirations. He studied as much as he had to at the agricultural college to learn the newest methods for improving the old farming ways and he was full of enthusiasm about new farm machinery; his father had a difficult time explaining his reluctance to throw his traditional ways overboard, although a number of tractors and labor-saving machinery had been acquired. For instance, they had just recently completely remodeled the barns, installing milking machines and running water to keep each stall spotlessly clean. Anton bragged that one could walk through his cow stalls in one's Sunday finery without getting a speck of dirt on it. However, he kept a skeptical resistance to other newfangled agricultural ideas, thinking that labor-saving devices would mean letting some farm hands go at a time when unemployment was Austria's biggest social problem. Some people at the Burghoff farm had worked there all their lives, and in many cases their fathers and mothers had also. Anton would not think of changes when they could be avoided. However, economics would force him to make decisions which he did not anticipate just then.

While they were talking, Peter and his father walked slowly towards the main house; the bell for their midday main meal had just sounded. The conversation with Peter had somewhat reassured the older man. He was always satisfied when Peter was around to consult, because he trusted his judgment almost as much as that of his wife, although it would not have been "manly" to admit that to her. It was not necessary, she knew it well enough herself.

Chapter 5

The kitchen was overseen and ruled by the matriarch in a quiet, self-assured manner. The family sat around a long dining table which was set up in the large hall and where also most of the farm workers, who made up the permanent staff, joined them. Only the seasonal helpers took their meals in another room off the kitchen. The food served at the Burghoffs was ample, nourishing and tasty, called *Hausmannskost*, or plain fare, with exceptions on holidays or other festivities when Hanna recalled the special recipes she had learned at the finishing school in Salzburg. Hanna had been sent there by her father, a wealthy farmer from Tyrol who had special plans for his only daughter. The three sons would have to be satisfied with equal division of their ancestral estate, but he was more ambitious for his very pretty and talented daughter; he saw her as the proprietor of one of the better city hotels. Her inheritance would be substantial enough to draw fitting suitors to complete the team.

Those had been Hanna's father's plans for his beloved daughter. They were not Hanna's. She loved the country, the mountains, the fields, the life in the village, the dances, and the music. She was of a happy nature, but could also display serious tough-mindedness. She was tall of stature, with classic features of rare beauty, proud and self reliant; sometimes she was called haughty by some of her peers, but she had many good and devoted friends also, and therefore never took notice of adverse remarks. During the two years at the finishing school in Salzburg, Hanna had learned many things of interest to her: fancier cooking than the simple farm fare, for instance, and special gardening secrets, as well as the social graces practiced by the city folks, and more. She loved needlework above all and was so good at it that she won much praise for it. She was open to all things she deemed to be of value, and rejected inferiority.

At eighteen years of age, she already knew exactly what she wanted: be the wife of an intelligent, capable farmer who had enough land and livestock to feed many, and everything that went with it. She was going to be the mother of children she would be proud of; she did not want to own a hotel in the city or anywhere else. She did not tell her parents of her desires when she returned from school, but kept up her life at home in a normal manner, helping her mother with running the household, often surprised that her mother knew much more than she had given her credit for before her own schooling, but also trying to introduce some changes. Child-bearing and child-rearing are no strange events on a farm, even for the youngest and only daughter in the family. They occur to married or unmarried farm folks in traditional fashion, the former more celebrated, but the latter more likely to be accepted as an act of nature than it was in the snobbish city. What Hanna had learned about the necessity of special cleanliness in handling the newborn as well as its mother, and how she tried to teach that to the working women on the farm, brought her favorable comments even from the village doctor. Her days were filled with many tasks, and she never seemed to be bored, but during the winter season, when life on the farm slows down, she was often seen with her brothers at dances in the village; she joined the choir, singing at church or at festivals. Hanna's father wished to keep her away from such simple places of entertainment; they were good for the boys, but not for his daughter. He did not see the prospective suitors in those places. Actually, Hanna herself had no interest in the male company at these dances or sing-alongs other than just for dancing or singing, which she did quite well and which she enjoyed. Occasionally, other young people from other villages and towns came to folk music competitions, or to the harvest festival fair. Then it did get a little more exciting, but Hanna was not yet looking for more.

At the latest fair, a number of people, both young and old, had come from the Salzburger county to look at and purchase some of the horses for which Hanna's home district was famous, a handsome breed called *Haflinger*. The older people, including her father, discussed business matters in the evening at the restaurant "Post" across from the church, and the younger generation enjoyed themselves at the dance hall down the road, with music roaring throughout the night.

Within a group of loudly bantering jolly young men, Hanna noticed a fellow who seemed to be somewhat special. She could not say what made him so. His appearance was pleasant, a sturdy figure, not too tall, a handsome face, a broad forehead under dark unruly hair, very attractive she thought. She liked his voice, it sounded deep and musical; not a bass, she concluded, but definitely a baritone. Then the fellow turned and their eyes met. In an instance there was a connection, which neither one could explain, even if they had been aware of what was happening. He came towards her and said, somewhat hesitantly:

"I am Anton Burghoff, I have come with my father from Kammerbach in the Salzburger County, to look at the Haflingers; are you from here?"

"I am Hanna Greiner; my father owns some of these horses, I doubt that he is in a selling mood though, but I am sure he would like to show them to you and your father. If you like, come by tomorrow—just ask for the Greiner place, anybody here will give you directions."

With a friendly smile, she left him standing there and went home. All she remembered was a wonderful voice and steel-gray eyes looking at her in a way that made her heart go a little bit faster.

Anton Burghoff thought he had never seen more beautiful blue eyes in all his life, in a face crowned by heavy braids of golden hair. He said to himself: *This is the girl I am going to marry.* He did not even wonder if she was available, or would want him. No, Anton was so sure he would take her to be his wife. He was twenty-five years old, just ready to become serious after a number of encounters with girls had left him disinterested.

Hanna went home, slightly disturbed about meeting the young man. She had never felt that way. It was not her way to blush easily, but she still felt red in her face. These eyes—that voice—would he come to the farm tomorrow, she wondered.

He came with his father the next day; Hanna's father and her brothers were there and the men talked about horses. Her mother invited them afterwards into the house for refreshments, and they chatted amiably about each other's families and farm life. When Anton said goodbye, he said he would like to come again when the mare had foaled, would Hanna let him know? She promised.

After he left, Hanna thought she knew what he reminded her of with his sturdiness of appearance, the look of his eyes that showed strength and also soul—a *Haflinger* horse!! Hanna was so fond of these horses, that the comparison seemed very complimentary to her. Hanna decided to confide in her oldest brother, Karl, that she was interested in knowing more about the Burghoff family in Kammerbach. Could he discreetly find out? Karl was a little surprised, but also pleased about her trust in him. He was going to get the information Hanna wanted.

Within weeks she had the details: a good farm family with substantial properties. Because the once large estate had been divided twice into smaller holdings in the beginning of the nineteen hundreds, it had not regained its former size. Anton was the heir to the farm in its present state of about five hundred acres of farmland and forests, including grazing land for cattle and sheep. The young man was considered to be quite capable, and had a good and solid reputation, as did his family. There was also talk of an almost forgotten aristocratic title to their name.

23

After reporting what he had found out to his sister, Karl said to her, smiling: "Why are you interested in the Burghoffs?" and Hanna answered without hesitation or inhibition: "If Anton Burghoff will have me, I am going to marry him." She knew instinctively that Anton was the right man for her. She told her brother this, but she also asked him to keep their little talk confidential.

Several weeks later she wrote to Anton Burghoff that the newborn colt was ready for inspection and he was welcome to visit. Anton came, found the colt perfect and Hanna even more so. They were so instantly in love with each other, that they felt that nothing could prevent them from marrying soon; after getting permission from each other's respective fathers, of course. Anton had no doubt about his father's acceptance of the girl of his choosing, but Hanna's father, Rupert Greiner, was not overwhelmingly pleased. Had he not had grander plans for his daughter? After he had sent her to a fine school to improve her status, she wanted to become a farmer's wife after all? And the fellow of her choosing? He liked him well enough and had a good exchange also with his father, but that was before they decided to become part of his family. Rupert Greiner had the unfounded idea that the Burghoffs were looking for his daughter's inheritance to improve their somewhat diminished estate.

In reality this was never in Anton's mind. He did not have any idea of the extent of Hanna's dowry, and would have taken her at the moment he saw her in the dance hall of the village. The young lovers did not let Father Greiner's objections spoil their happiness. He also knew his daughter too well than to expect she would change her mind.

Only three months later a wedding feast was held at the Greiner farm in Tyrol. Hanna and a lovely *Haflinger* colt followed Anton Burghoff to the Salzburger county.

One would like to add here: And they lived happily ever after, but since the story goes on for a while longer, we all have to wait for the ending. It is interesting to note, however, that Anton Burghoff, always proud of his wife and deeply in love with her all days of his life, was also very impressed with himself to have been so clever as to have chosen her above all others. He never knew—and did not have to—that it was Hanna herself who had done the choosing, and she also knew that it had been the best decision of her life.

Chapter 6

On that balmy spring day in April 1943 when Claire's hopeful spirit was dampened by the radio announcement of the terrible Katyn incident, another event was coming her way which was going to change her life dramatically. Depressed by the bad news she had just heard, she now could no longer enjoy the warm spring air and nature's promises of new life sprouting all around her, which had justly pleased her only a few minutes ago. She decided to make it straight home, take a street car to shorten her trip, stop at the grocery to redeem a few coupons so she would not lose her rations, in all, get into the routine of her humdrum everyday life. In the evening she would call her mother, who was not feeling too well. All dreariness around her again.

The next streetcar coming along was crowded as usual this time of day with elderly men and women going home from work and soldiers on leave. She could barely make it up to the platform, when a soldier with his backpack pushed his way behind her, so that she was squeezed with her back towards the other passengers. Nothing unusual about that, but when she felt a hand from behind touching her shoulder and neck, she turned her head, annoyed by such impertinence and looked into a face whose dark blue eyes twinkled with surprise and joy, and an old familiar voice said: "Hello, Claire." And, as in old times, she felt her face redden and her knees buckle; but she caught herself quickly and tried to say as coolly as possible

"Oh, Hello Peter!" Not much conversation was possible in that crowded place, but Peter asked where she was going to exit.

"At the University," she said. That was really only a few stops away, and they tried just an occasional smile towards each other. Squeezing through the passengers in front, they both finally landed on the station floor and shook hands.

"What a lovely surprise," said Peter, "I have thought so often about you."

"You have?" Claire said with an overtone of sarcasm, which was not lost on Peter. He became serious, as they walked on the sidewalk past the University.

"Where are you heading?"

"Home," Claire said, "and you?"

"I have an appointment with a colleague at the Hospital in half an hour. That leaves us little time to catch up on old times."

"I live just around the corner from the *Allgemeines Krankenhaus*, in the Alserstrasse; we can have a short walk together."

"Oh, you don't live with your parents anymore?" Peter asked,

"No." Her short answers continued, to his annoyance. He was genuinely happy to see her, but she did not seem to respond in the same vein. He could not know how difficult it was for her to pretend. When his blue eyes looked with such sincerity, she was overcome with the magic of his presence just as so many years ago.

"Are you expected at home?" he tried to ask an important question very delicately.

"Yes," she said, deliberately slow, and added " by my very devoted cat." Both laughed, which broke the somewhat icy conversation from before.

"Do you have problems with mice?" Peter asked. "I love dogs, but the cats at our home in the country are strictly there to perform their duties of keeping the rodents out of the house; I never thought of them as pets."

"Well, maybe you are never lonely and do not know how comforting sweet and warm a kitten can be."

"Are you lonely, Claire?"

"Sometimes…but here we are, this is where I live and you need to cross the street just at the next corner to the main entrance."

"I know. I used to practice here, don't you remember?" Suddenly he was very serious, that was typical Peter.

"Claire, this was just not long enough to have a nice chat. I have another meeting tomorrow morning, but am free the whole afternoon before leaving on the evening train for home. Could you get yourself free, so we could have a conversation in earnest and renew memories of old times?"

Claire tried to master all her pride, and refuse him, but there was really no use in fighting it. She wished to be with him with all her heart and to hear his voice again. She gave him her office address in the Operngasse, and he said he would be there tomorrow at two in the afternoon. She disappeared into her doorway.

He went across the street, feeling sad and lonely, and wondering if she would stroke the warm fur of her little cat. Maybe he should try that some day himself.

Claire went slowly up the three flights of stairs to her apartment. Her mind was confused; her heart partly joyful, partly scared. It was not a good time for Peter to enter her life again, even for a short afternoon. Just because she did not need to add to her troubles: the war, her mother, friends scattered, business complicated. At her door she looked first in her mailbox: nothing. For two weeks no news from Stefan. His dry letters did not exactly cheer her up, but gave her comfort because he still cared for her. Mucki, the cat, did indeed greet her affectionately, purring and snuggling around her legs. Claire quickly took care of all the kitten's needs. Then it occurred to her that she had forgotten to go to the grocery, which she had to do immediately, or she would have almost no food for herself tonight.

Herr Angerman at the corner store greeted her with his usual friendly grin. He was fond of this customer, who did not give him the trouble others often did, blaming him for the lack of this or that which was supposed to have been on the shelves, but had never arrived. Of course, Claire could put up easier with that part of civilian life these days, since she had only to take care of herself and not of children or other dependents. Feeding herself was no problem for her. It did not satisfy her taste buds, but she put that all in the category of "inconveniences," compared to the "sacrifices" that the military had to endure. Herr Angerman, the grocer, did not only like her quiet friendliness towards him, but the old man feasted his eyes appreciatively on the young woman's appearance, and in return occasionally threw something extra into her shopping bag, like a fish head for her cat or other morsels. Today's ration yielded one pound of potatoes, half a pound of rice, two carrots, and something special: one can of sardines, the lovely Portuguese variety, packed in precious olive oil. Herr Angerman also bagged one small onion with it, which was not on the ration card. Claire appreciated it all, although today her mind was occupied with other things than the mundane requirements of an empty stomach. She did not even feel hungry, although she had not eaten since the soup at noon.

At home, she changed immediately into her bathrobe and cuddled up with Mucki on the sofa in the living room. She needed time to think, to straighten out her emotions. She did not want to admit to herself that she was looking forward to tomorrow and to Peter. She tried desperately to think of Stefan instead. Where was he when she needed him? The picture of both men melted into one while she drifted off into a numbing slumber, but she awakened after a short rest because it was rather chilly in the room. To warm herself, she did what she often did during those cold winter evenings when she could not allow herself to waste precious fuel to heat her place: she immersed herself in the bathtub, filled with as much hot water as the gas water-heater would produce. That was a comfortable place. She put a few crackers and a cup of hot tea, her writing materials, and a book on a tray. She spent many evenings in relative comfort, and taking care of her correspondence in that manner before going to bed. Most often she also turned her radio on, so she could keep informed. Today she did not, but she was going to write to Stefan. She figured he must be back with his outfit at the front by now. His stay with his parents had only been for two days. He had called from there, and although the line was not clear, she could hear his reassuring voice that he was well. He also added that it had been right for her not to have come. There had been a number of air raids and bombings and she would have been exposed to unnecessary danger. He was grateful that Vienna was still spared the attacks and destruction of the magnitude the West had to endure. She had barely time to tell him how great it was to hear his voice, when the line went dead. She knew he would write soon, and she had sent off her weekly letter also. Another one from her was due that day, but she could not find words. Tomorrow, she would do so.

Tomorrow? Anxiety overtook her. "Stefan, I need you here! You have to save me!" As soon as she thought it, she was angry at such stupid emotions. She was Claire, by now an accomplished business woman, running a branch of a nationwide manufacturing company to the satisfaction of her superiors, she made important business decision daily, handled customers competently…and she needed protection to deal with an old affair of the heart, that had died a long time ago? Never!

Claire jumped out of the tub as the water was getting cold and the gas was turned off, as happened so often lately. Tomorrow. What was she going to wear? She looked through her wardrobe—nothing new in there for ages, except for the suit that her tailor had made recently from one, which her father had sacrificed for that purpose. He used to have many suits when he was still traveling, but lately he seldom needed a change in attire for his work at the University. New clothing material was not available anymore, and one had to be inventive and also have a tailor willing to rip up and cut anew. Claire's tailor had sewn for the family for many years, and the old man was quite willing to do the remaking from the male into a female fashion product, and she now had a new suit that was quite becoming. The white silk blouse was old and a little worn, but looked very nice under the jacket! What was she doing? No, there would be nothing special for the date with Peter. She would wear her navy blue standby, the same she wore today. Well, maybe the silk blouse would be a compromise. Her supply of stockings was another matter—all of the once respectable silk stockings were heavily darned at the heels, but by carefully pulling them in, one could prevent that showing. She found a suitable pair. All her shoes were a little rundown also, but the newly soled black pumps would do. Hat and gloves were just fine. It paid to have bought them when there was still a nice selection and good quality; the same could be said for the her purse of fine kidskin.

Chapter 7

Claire went to bed, but could not fall asleep for a long time. Why was she angry at Peter? She had tried to forget her disappointment, but had never really succeeded. He remained in her memory despite occasional flirtatious encounters with other men, which hardly ever stirred her soul as Peter had. When she first met him—it was nearly ten years ago—she was a young schoolgirl, struck by the one who stood out in the crowd—older, more sophisticated, more reserved. He did not court her as the other boys did; why she was drawn to him, she could not explain. Not then and also not later, when she was older and nearly grown-up. Occasional dates in Vienna at a concert, the opera, a movie—were no promise of more than that. Except once: It was in 1936, when he wrote and asked if she would be interested to go with him to a performance of "Koenig Ottokar's Glueck and Ende" at the Burgtheater. Claire accepted with the greatest pleasure. First, Peter—she had not seen or heard from him for a while, then the play at the Burgtheater—the foremost stage for accomplished dramatists and writers in the country, presented by the most important actors of the classic drama at the time. She could hardly wait. Her new light blue silk dress would be just right for the occasion, and mother's pearl necklace made her look grown-up, she thought.

When they met at the side entrance of the theater, as arranged, she could feel Peter's appreciative looks, and she felt silly, blushing again, as if she were still a schoolgirl. It was at the University across the street from the Burgtheater, where her life these days centered, and although two more years of study still lay ahead of her, she certainly could call herself mature and adult now.

Peter acted much less reserved that evening than on previous occasions. He was talkative and charming, and seemed to enjoy the excellent performance as much as Claire did. At intermission, when her enthusiasm about the presentation of the dramatic conflicts in the play overflowed, he admitted to be not too excited about theater on the whole. He preferred concerts or the opera to nourish his soul, but he had known about Claire's taste, and since he wanted to see her again, he thought of pleasing her that way. Claire was happy indeed and said so. One of the best dramas by "Grillparzer," one of her favorite poets and dramatists, played by such distinguished actors as Hoerbiger and Vesely at the lavish Burgtheater, with its marble staircases, paintings, elaborate decor with gold tapestry and sparkling crystal chandeliers! The enthusiastic and appreciative audience added to her euphoric feeling, but, of course, more than anything, Peter Burghoff was sitting next to her. What an evening!

After the last curtain call, Peter suggested they go for coffee at the Kaffee Landman next door, another Viennese landmark, where for generations the important people of Vienna had gathered; the politicians, even Stalin and Trotsky at one time did so; Dr. Sigmund Freud was a steady guest of the establishment and many of his genre. At night, the actors of the Burgtheater gathered there and other patrons of the arts.

Peter found a little table where they had their mocha and discussed the fine points of the play. Claire did at least, and with great emotion. Peter asked if she ever felt the same after a concert performance. Claire said that was different. Music entered her soul and not her mind; she could only feel it but not dissect it. Later, Peter mentioned that his medical training was coming to an end and that he would now have to think about the future in earnest.

When they left the Landman, they strolled along the Ringstrasse, passing the Burgtheater again. It was such a lovely, mild, and clear night at the end of the month of May for which Vienna was famous. Many poets and composers, past and present, have praised it in songs. Tempted by the fragrant air coming from one of the loveliest gardens along the Ringstrasse, the Volksgarten, they entered the dark park, illuminated here and there by one of the old fashioned gas lamps, which had not yet been replaced by more glaring electric lights. They strolled towards the expansive rose garden, where many exquisite varieties of roses were already blooming and their fragrance filled the air. It was too dark to distinguish their colors, but they emitted a heavenly scent, and provided a most romantic atmosphere, which apparently was not lost on the late night visitors to the park. Nearly every little bench here and there along the walkways was occupied by people. If they were young or old was not distinguishable, romance was. Peter and Claire strolled towards the marvelous white marble statue of the Empress Elizabeth, the beautiful, yet unhappy young wife of the Emperor Franz Joseph, whose tragic life and death touched every Viennese heart forever. A moonbeam crossed the face of that loveliest woman. Claire had seen that statue so many times, always at daytime, and had stood there, wondering about her lonely life. At night, it appeared to have magical powers. Claire whispered

"If I ever have a daughter, I shall call her Elizabeth," Peter had taken her hand in his with a firm grip and said solemnly:

"So will I."

Not far away there was an empty bench under a willow tree whose long cascading branches formed an arch above it, a spot as if designed for resting and meditation. Under the clear star-studded sky the balmy night seemed to promise happiness forever, and when Peter put his arm around Claire's shoulders, she succumbed to that glorious feeling of being in love. They talked little that night, in words that is, but their kisses really said it all. Tender, not passionate, as they deemed to be appropriate to start loving one another with respect and commitment. Both knew in their hearts that their love, blossoming for years, would last forever—just as all young lovers are apt to believe.

They had not looked at the clock, but an early dawn on the horizon told of a new day, where reality had to be faced and dreams to be set aside for a while. When they parted at the Wiedner Haupstrasse where Claire lived, she was getting anxious and hoped to slip into her home unobserved, otherwise there could have been trouble with her father. She had never been that late before. Everyone seemed to be fast asleep at home, and she breathed a sigh of relief. Only her mother's questioning remarks next morning made Claire tell her a little about the evening with Peter—not all of it, of course, but what she did not tell, her mother guessed, and she was happy for Claire, knowing the girl had had dreams of Peter for a long time.

Fortunately, Claire did not have any lectures at the university the next morning, so she could sleep in. When she woke, the sun was shining bright into her window, another beautiful day, but even a rainy one could not have looked brighter and sunnier to her. She thought she had never felt as happy in all her life and would now be so forever. She remembered some of their conversation at the Landman, when Peter tried to tell her about himself: that he was finishing his hospital residence requirements very shortly. Then he was going to go home to Salzburg and contemplate his options for the future. Not unlike all other professions, the outlook for medical doctors was not the best either. Unemployment in Austria had reached climactic proportions and it extended into all corners. The future was uncertain even for the best educated. Peter had been encouraged to apply at one or the other smaller clinics in Vienna, where some of his professors could help him with introductions and recommendations, but Peter confessed that despite his love and appreciation for the city which had provided him with so many cultural experiences during his schooling, he remained in his heart a "country boy" who would like to return to his roots.

Claire had listened and nodded with understanding, but had not realized that his words were also a question. This never occurred to her, and when Peter went home that night, it disturbed him. He knew that he was deeply in love with Claire, that she was the only girl he had ever felt about that way; other flirtatious occasions were forgotten almost as soon as they happened. Even when a young nurse here and there had tried to get the handsome doctor's attention, none had succeeded for more than a casual date, a movie, or less. Claire—she was the one he would always want for a wife. He could not offer it right now and did not dare to ask if she would wait for him. He knew she loved him, but she was only twenty years old—she had two more years at the University—it would give him time to establish himself. At twenty-two she would know if she, the educated city girl, could live the simpler lifestyle in the country. In one way, his heart was filled with love and joy, but unlike Claire's, who did not let any other emotions cloud that beautiful feeling, Peter's included thoughts about serious matters and responsibilities.

Chapter 8

—————

Claire remembered it all during the night, when sleep would not come early to her. She remembered her happiness, and then the waiting. Not too impatient at first, because he had told her that he needed to go home to the country and think and plan, and she knew it would be a difficult time for him. However, when time passed, and she did not hear a single word, not a post-card, nothing, she could hardly believe she had been betrayed in such a man-ner. She felt sorry—ashamed to have been so open about her feelings that night in the Rosegarden. She had thought he loved her too, but now had to admit that he had never said so in words. Neither had she—in her mind words had been unnecessary—but she had trusted him. Why, why did she not hear from him at all? The answer never came, and the years passed.

Now, seven years later, here was Peter, and he was making her heart flut-ter and pound again; he had no right to do that. She would not allow it. She had found Stefan, but Stefan was so far away. She had not seen him for such a long time that he appeared almost like a phantom. She quickly turned on the light on her nightstand to look at Stefan's photograph. There he was, the dashing officer, smiling that little ironic smile of his which had fascinated her from the first day she met him. Now she did not want him to look at her like that—"Please, Stefan, be serious, I love you, come home, I'll be a good wife to you"—and slowly she fell asleep.

When the alarm clock woke her, Claire's thoughts went immediately to the morning demands of her office. She had to call the shipping agent first, to see if the machines had arrived, and then call Pamberger, the distributor in Graz, to let him know, otherwise she would get his calls and complaints about the delayed delivery every hour. She would have to dictate to Fräulein Frank the most important letters that had to be dispatched that day, so she could still sign them before Peter's arrival. She was not going to explain to the office about her afternoon with Peter. They might just as well think he was somebody from headquarters on an inspection visit to Vienna. That happened often enough, and they would not think anything of it. She would call Lieschen Woerner, who was always informed about official visits and tell her that she would not be able to meet her later for tea, because one of her oldest friends had unexpectedly come to town just for the day, and she could not turn down a chance to see a long lost friend. Lieschen would understand. Claire would also call her mother to find out how she was, but would say nothing about Peter. He was to be her affair alone, and she could handle that well.

With so much planning for a free afternoon to spend with Peter, she forgot how uneasy the thought had made her the previous evening. Now she was looking forward to a nice chat to make up for seven years of silence. She was in control, an astute businesswoman with experience in negotiations, cool and collected—and she wished she had one of her mother's little pills to calm her down.

Peter was on time. When he asked the receptionist to see Miss Baumann, he was told that he was expected and directed to a door on which he saw Claire's name engraved on a brass plaque, and below her name it said "Director". When he entered her room, he pointed that out and said he was impressed. She laughed and said, it should really add: "for the duration of the war." He said he still admired her courage in taking on such responsibilities. Claire answered:

"The responsibilities seem to be growing daily, but the problems even more, and most of them end in frustration. One has to deal with constant changes of production at the factory, delivery schedules, irate customers, for which only one unilateral excuse can be presented: the war! But I don't want to dwell on my business affairs, I would rather leave them behind this afternoon."

The little chat had broken the ice, and conversation seemed to flow easily. Claire could not help noticing, how handsome Peter looked. During this past seven years he had grown into a distinguished looking man of thirty-four. She noticed with amusement a few fine wrinkles around his eyes; very becoming, she thought. Oh, she was not the only one aging, she felt with satisfaction. She almost considered herself an "old maid," or closely approaching it, being twenty-six, nearing twenty-seven years old, single, childless; engaged yes, but what prospects?

Peter's thoughts went in the same direction He also noticed some difference in Claire, but expressed his observation in a different way, "You have not changed, you are as lovely as I remember you." She protested:

"Peter, since when have you become a flatterer? I don't remember you as such! I have changed, but haven't we all?"

"Your loveliness has not changed, but I have to admit that you seem to be more slender than in the old days—lost some baby-fat?" he joked.

"Perhaps—thanks to the government whose caloric allotment keeps us trim these days."

"Are you suffering due to the shortages?" he asked with some concern in his voice. He knew that he himself had little concept of that, since he always had a little extra from the farm.

"No," she assured him, "I am doing just fine; maybe our diet is really healthier for us now, but I admit that sometimes the thought of a roast on the dinner table on Sunday can still make my mouth water. But that time will come again."

Peter, taking her arm, asked:

"Now, let's decide how we are going to spend this glorious afternoon; what would you like to do?"

"I am all yours," was almost on her lips, but she quickly caught herself, she had to watch her language. She said instead:

"Peter, I have not had a nice holiday or even an outing for so long, that I cannot even think, that there would be anywhere I would not want to go or be—decide for us."

"The weather is so lovely, spring is in the air. How about taking the streetcar to Nussdorf, then from there the bus to Kahlenberg. Later we can decide which way to walk back. My train leaves at nine o'clock. How do you feel about my suggestion?"

"I love your idea," she said enthusiastically, although his mention of the nine o'clock train departure gave her a little jolt. That was all included: joy and sadness, it was her lot. It still gave her many hours of happiness.

"Let's make the best of it." She did not mean to say it—but it escaped her before she could put on the brakes again. Peter squeezed her arm appreciatively.

Not much was spoken on the ride to the Kahlenberg, but as soon as they had disembarked from the streetcar, a free and happy atmosphere seemed to surround them. They had left their inhibitions behind, feeling like children on holiday. They chatted amiably; Claire stopped worrying about betraying her feelings. Peter, normally given to taciturnity, felt carefree like a young boy, and he credited it to Claire's presence. Hand in hand, they wandered through the woods, looking on the forest floor for fragrant violets, the lovely cyclamen, crocuses, primroses, the first to bloom in the woods in the spring.

The Vienna Woods contain so many marked easy hiking trails with benches in certain locations to provide a little respite to the tired wanderer. On Sundays, half of the Viennese are to be found in their beloved Wienerwald, but during the work week, and especially in these war times, few people, and mostly only the old ones, the one left behind, could be seen. The restaurant on top of Kahlenberg used to be a fine place. It was rundown now also, not many people visiting, and not much was offered to the traveler, except the lovely view over Vienna.

Peter and Claire continued on the wooded paths to the next hill, the Leopoldsberg, also with a restaurant at its summit.

Those who do not know Austria, and especially Vienna, may be surprised by the number of eating places everywhere. The smallest village may have two or three, where they also serve as meeting places and not just as food service establishments. In the countryside at large, at least a small eatery is found on every mountaintop and in every corner of every valley. The Austrians keep good food and drink on their list of priorities. Their suffering on that account in these times of war was just overshadowed by their contributions to the war effort and the resulting losses.

There is a chapel on Leopoldsberg, dedicated to Count Sobieski, the Polish general who became most famous when, in 1683, he came to help the Austrians defeat the Turkish army which had besieged Vienna several times. It was from that same spot here on the hill where the defenders assembled for the last and deciding assault on the enemy and it was successful. The Turks, under Kara Mustafa, finally left and returned to their homeland. Of course, there are many stories told referring to that historic event. The chapel was built later to honor the memory of the Polish rescue mission under its general, Count Sobieski.

Claire and Peter stepped for a moment inside the chapel, admired the paintings on the walls; many depicted battle scenes, others were portraits of various famous people of that time. It was quite a charming place to visit, not exactly a place to worship.

Outside the chapel and from the garden of the restaurant, there was a wonderful view of the City below, and no matter how many times one has admired it, it fills every true Viennese heart with pride and joy: *This is my city—the city of dreams, of music, of poets*—of a history that goes back to when the Romans settled here in the first century A.D. and called that outpost of their empire *Vindobona*.

Claire knew so many of the old stories from her childhood in school, where they had been told and retold so many times. Today her mind was not filled with history and fables. She was praying. This was not new to her, she had done it ever since she could remember, beginning with the little bedtime prayer her grandmother had taught her. She had always believed in the value of prayer, and when she was a young girl she had asked God for many things; God had been good to her. Growing up, she had realized that prayers were not to ask God for favors, but to thank him for his blessings. If God would listen to requests He would have had to hear those desperate prayers for peace from millions around the globe. Apparently God was not listening— or did not want to interfere—did not take sides. He had given people the gift of free will—so they may choose for themselves—heaven or hell. It was not God, but four powerful men who were responsible for the world's suffering right now, Stalin, Hitler, Churchill, and Roosevelt and only they could stop it. God could not be a part of it.

Not all of these thoughts were in Claire's mind at the moment, but they were often so when alone at night and ready for her daily prayer. Although she had long ago stopped asking for favors—today she made an exception. "Please, God, let this afternoon last—add a few hours, minutes even, I can't bear to think of it ending."

Claire was standing against the rocky barrier over the bluff. She seemed to be lost in thought. Tall and slim, her slender neck erect, beams of the setting sun highlighting the warm color of her hair, tousled in the gentle breeze. Peter was so moved, looking at her with eyes that wanted to capture her image forever. His heart was heavy, and his desire to take her into his arms was overwhelming. The pain not to have the right to do so, was unbearable. Claire, feeling his presence, turned fully towards him with that small and sad smile which he had observed before. She extended her hand and he took it and brought it to his face, gently stroking his cheek. Claire's eyes misted, and a single tear rolled down her cheek. Peter wished to kiss it away, yet he did not dare. There were a few moments of silence, yet so much was said.

Peter mentioned that they must make their way down before the darkness of the early spring evening would catch up with them. The trail was a little treacherous. For a while there was still sunlight shining through the trees and little benches in spots for viewing the city below invited them to stop. They sat down again and Peter said she had not told him one thing about her present life. He could see she had succeeded professionally, but what was her personal life like?

Claire answered, first haltingly, than with some relief, as if confessing. She told him how she graduated with a teaching degree, and almost got caught up in it because of her father's desire for her to follow in his footsteps. It made no sense to Claire, since she was not interested in teaching and even less in philosophical endeavors like her father. Therefore, when the *Anschluss*, the German takeover of Austria, occurred about the same time, and with the influx of German businesses employment opportunities had sprung up, she jumped right in, was really lucky to find a good place, the right people—in short, was content. About that time she met Stefan von Brecht, a native of Dresden, a friend of her director's family, related through his mother to Claire's employer, the Stehle company. They were engaged a very short time after their first meeting; Stefan was by profession a lawyer, but had volunteered for military service at the beginning of the war, and was serving now on the Russian front with the rank of major. Both, he and Claire, had agreed to wait for marriage until the war ended. That was to have been in a short time. Well, these plans had not materialized as yet, but Claire had been satisfied with their arrangement.

"That's about it," Claire said, and looked expectantly at Peter. It was his turn now. He hesitated—

"There is a little tavern at the end of the road in Heiligenstadt, let's stop there."

It was one of Beethoven's many former lodgings which had become tourist attractions, and some of them were wine taverns. Good old Ludwig had not been a favorite lodger, and had to change his domicile quite often because he was cranky, not very friendly, and his music-making at any time of day was too loud for the neighbors. He liked the area near Vienna's famous vineyards adjoining the Wienerwald, and he stayed there for a long time. In Heiligenstadt he had composed his famous Third Symphony, the Eroica, which he dedicated to his hero Napoleon, whom he admired greatly as a great freedom fighter and liberator. Of course, Beethoven changed his mind later about "Nappy," just as many Viennese had done about another "liberator" of a later time, namely "Adolf."

Over a glass of wine they talked about Beethoven and his music, a favorite subject of Peter who knew and loved all of that great master's compositions. From there it was only a short jump to talking about his other favorites, Brahms, Schubert, Wagner, and Strauss. Claire mostly listened, studying every detail of his beloved face, to bury the memory of it deep in her heart, because she felt with great trepidation that the end of that extraordinary day was approaching. To her dismay it was she who had to remind him that he had to catch a train. He had not told his "seven year life story," and she thought that maybe it was just as well. In some way she was afraid to hear what she did not want to know.

They left hurriedly. Claire wanted to come along to the train station. She thought good-byes were easier said there amidst all the other people. They had to wait a long time for the streetcar and also for the transfer to the Westbahnhof. Peter felt uncomfortable, did not find appropriate words and Claire tried to hide her feelings of almost despair, to which she had absolutely no right, as she told herself.

The station was extremely crowded, mostly with soldiers coming and going, standing around forlorn and lonely or being hugged and kissed by some loved one. It was a sad and depressing sight, despite some laughing and jesting and even singing here and there. Peter stood in a long line at the cashier's window for his ticket, but right before his turn the window closed. The last train for the night to Salzburg was just leaving, the next one was at seven o'clock the next morning. Peter looked resigned. He was going to make a few phone calls to see if he could find accommodations for the night. Claire did not say anything; she knew from her various attempts to find a hotel room for her business visitors that two or three weeks advance reservations were necessary. Peter had indeed no luck, but said he would wait in the waiting room at the station with all the other soldiers, who for one reason or the other were also left behind and had made themselves comfortable on the benches, even the floor, with their bags as pillows. There was not a single seat available anywhere. Claire said casually, so as not to be misunderstood, that she had an empty guestroom in her place, which was often used by stranded friends, and he was also welcome to use it. Peter was hesitant—would it compromise her to show up with a male guest at that time of night? Claire assured him that that was of no concern to her, even if they had to go to the air raid shelter together in the middle of the night. On the first floor of her building was a *pension*, and one guest would not look different from another.

Peter grabbed the valise that he had stored at the station in the morning, and they took the next streetcar to Alserstrasse, to Claire's apartment. Despite acting rather nonchalantly, both were somewhat tense and unsure, but when Claire showed Peter around in her small, but very cozy flat he felt comfortable and relaxed.

"As if it were home," he said, and added "only you have made it nicer, you have good taste." He admired the Biedermeier chest, the paintings on the wall, even the old rocking chair.

"It's from my childhood days, it was always in my room and therefore I had to take it with me."

Peter loved it. The pillows on the sofa were hand-embroidered and filled with soft eiderdown. Her bookshelf contained selections of her favorite classic authors, as well as contemporary writings. Peter had read some, but was not too much interested in literature. The lovely fireplace in the corner of the room was made of white, ceramic, glazed tile, now unfortunately cold, but nevertheless promising good warmth when there was enough coal to heat it up again. The gleaming hardwood parquet floor was partially covered by a Persian rug, old and worn in some places, but still quite respectable. A small rosewood desk, covered with papers and books, drew Peter's attention. Claire admitted with a shy smile, that she sometimes wrote short stories, which had occasionally been published. Nothing of special value, just a pastime when she felt lonely. One other hobby she indulged in was needlepoint. Some of the pillows on the sofa showed her work. Peter was favorably impressed.

Claire did not show him her bedroom, but when she went in to leave her suit jacket there and throw a pullover over her silk blouse, he could see parts of a brass bed, covered with white linens and pillows, and a little of a bay-window with padded seating or pillows on the other side of the room. Great taste here too, he thought. No knickknacks, no frills as there were in his home, he thought with a sigh. To his relief, he did not see a picture of the man Claire was engaged to anywhere. He did not have any right to be so, but he felt tremendously jealous, and was ashamed of it immediately.

Coming back from the bedroom, carrying a vase with a few spring flowers, which she set on the living room table. Claire told Peter to use her phone if he thought he should inform his people back home about the delay. Peter said, that was not necessary, as he was not expected. She found that strange, but did not question it.

"Make yourself comfortable, Peter. You can take your shoes off if you like, I'll make some tea for us, all right?"

Peter relaxed, sat back in Claire's old rocking chair, and closed his eyes. He did not plan it that way, he said to himself, but missing the train was another happy circumstance occurring in these last two days.

Claire rummaged through her cupboards in the kitchen, and found a box of crackers, a little stale probably, but with the can of sardines she got yesterday and the long-hidden bottle of Wachauer wine, it would make a pretty good snack. When she came back with her tray of food and dishes—she had, of course chosen the old Meissen for that occasion—Peter observed with pleasure her quiet moves and her composure. She turned the lamp in the corner low to provide a mood setting. They ate with relish, even the old chocolate cookies, saved from Christmas, still tasted delicious. The wine was of good quality, a bottle she had saved for a special occasion, not even guessing what that would be. But here it was—the occasion could not be more special, she told herself. The wine sparkled in her lovely crystal glasses—there were only two of them—which she had at one time purchased at an antique auction. They had been expensive, but was it not worth it? Her little presentation looked wonderful despite the meager tidbits. The wine—they drank the whole bottle—made her somewhat lightheaded and Peter more verbose than usual.

Claire wanted to know all about Kammersee and her old friends there. Peter told her that his brother was in the military. His induction was a great shock to his parents because usually the only son on a farm was excluded. There was a suspicion that Hans had secretly volunteered for the sake of his beliefs and ideals. Of course, that was at the beginning of the war, nobody had predicted its lasting so long. Hans was doing well and taking to military life with the same exuberance he had as a civilian. Their parents were fortunately in good health and handling their business as well as could be expected under all the restrictive conditions. A number of their farm hands had to go to the military and in their place they had been allowed some foreign laborers. It worked out pretty well, but Peter found it ironic that the Germans would send their sons to die for the liberation of other nations, and take their refugees to replace them.

"Peter, that is not fair to say," Claire said.

"I know" Peter answered." I am not fair on many subjects, I am too critical of people, of events, of politics—I want it all to go my way. Is it fair, for instance, that I have escaped the draft? I am in good physical condition—better than one-eyed Fritz Engebrecht."

"Peter!" Claire admonished him.

"Yes, I am sorry. The authorities decided I was needed as the only medical doctor in the area for civilian needs. And, believe me, I did not fight that decision. I am doing my best, my workload is tremendous, which, by the way, is good medicine for my own problems, but sometimes I question my lot, comparing it with the fighting men out there. My life is not on the line as theirs is daily—is that fair?"

"What is Burgl Mayer doing these days?"

"Oh, Burgl is married to an innkeeper and owner of a tourist hotel in Tyrol, as well as mother of a strapping little boy. She came recently to visit her parents, and I was consulted about a little ear infection of the child, nothing serious. I enjoyed seeing her. She asked about you."

"Strange," Claire said, "why would she assume you know about me?"

"Fritz Engebrecht is also a soldier," Peter continued his report.

"I know," Claire interrupted, "he came for a short visit to Vienna about a year ago, I was happy to see him, dapper in his uniform, and in good spirits. He has lost his 'I am a poor orphan boy' image that he used so well, and is in command of a military outfit."

"Well, well," Peter said "still the old charmer, and has not given up on you?"

"Oh Peter, you still don't like him, do you? Do you know that he married the blond Gerda and has a son already? That made me envious—the son, I mean."

"I have to admit he was always a thorn in my side. I don't know why, I was probably jealous. He had such an easy, uninhibited way to court you publicly, while I was unable to come up with even a few words."

"Peter, you did not have to say anything—although now I wish that you had."

While the wine had loosened their tongues, Claire felt the conversation was becoming too dangerous for her. She got up from the table and said she would quickly see to it that the guestroom was ready. Peter claimed he was not sleepy at all, he had enjoyed their conversation. When Claire returned to the living room, Peter had settled himself in the rocking chair with a book from the shelf. Claire inhaled that reposeful picture of domesticity; that's how it should be: Peter relaxing in their living room, while she happily went about her way.

Peter stood up, stretching, and asked like a little boy. "Do I really have to go to bed already?"

"Peter, tell me about yourself now, I think it is time."

"You are right, I have avoided it all afternoon."

"Why?"

"I have been rather a pessimist all my life—and I was mostly right. Today was a remarkable exception. I had come to Vienna for strictly business matters, and it magically turned out to be a most joyous day in my otherwise dreary humdrum existence. Seeing you again made me so happy, and it pointed out at the same time, how wrong I had been, how I failed during the past seven—did you say seven years?" He stopped for a moment, and with a slight sigh continued:

"Yes, it was in 1936 when I finished here in Vienna with my medical training. When I last saw you, I was in a great quandary about planning my future. I was always trying to do the 'right' thing, whatever that meant. Probably the teachings at the hand of the Jesuits had their influence on me more than I ever admitted because I had resented it mostly. It was severe schooling, responsibility for every action taken was hammered into us from the beginning when we were only ten years old. The promise of hell for every unrepented sin was obvious, but even not doing one's duty in every detail of one's life was coming close to sinfulness. The only joy I remember from those days, was the music I was exposed to, mainly church music of course, but when I was getting older I searched for other kinds and collected quite a sampling of the best of the classics.

"One other highlight of these days were the holidays that brought me back home, where I could enjoy the freedom to roam the fields and woods, climb mountains, help with the farm chores. I loved everything that brought me close to nature. Early on I decided, with the full support of my mother, who knew me better than anybody else and still does, that I would become a medical doctor. I could have attended the University in Innsbruck, but it was mother who decided it had to be Vienna, the best. And I promised in my heart never to disappoint her—as if I could! You see, I am also a rather spoiled mother's boy." Peter added with a smile:

"I was not exactly the best student at the boarding school, but once in my chosen field at the University, I was ambitious enough to stand with the best. It took my full concentration, and I was well aware I could not spend much time fooling around with my fellow students. I had a goal which I partly reached in 1936—about the time I last saw you. You may think that I had forgotten the evening at the Burgtheater and the night at the park? It was my sweetest memory. However, there were hurdles before me, plans to be made. Times were difficult, you may not remember it as well, you were so young! Yes, difficult times and your youth kept me from acting on impulse. In the first place, I felt, I had to establish my practice. I had already made up my mind, that I wanted to return to the country, despite some

42

encouraging suggestions by my professor at the University to try it in the big city. My specialty was surgery, and he thought my chances in Vienna would be greater for the future, than burying myself somewhere in the small world of a country hospital. I talked to you about that, do you remember? But you had no special opinion about it, you just said that you too loved the country. I wondered—you knew it only from the experience of a somewhat indulged vacationing youngster.

"Well, I went home with all my belongings which I had accumulated in the city as a student in the last six or seven years, not to return. The welcome was celebrated with a feast my mother arranged, and to which my father had invited nearly the whole village. I got plenty of advise—from young and old. It was well meant, but I was going to do it my way. After a few weeks helping with the harvest and roaming through the woods, even going hunting, for which I previously never had much inclination, but now enjoyed it just for the sake of stalking the prey, never for the killing. All the gory, bloody surgery experience did not harden me enough to find a thrill in that part of hunting.

"Meanwhile, my mother had subtle suggestions about finding the 'right' girl. I just laughed it off—I did not tell her I had found her already—but she needed time to grow up a little more, I could not push her into adulthood, when she was still so young and innocent. This is how I thought about you then, Claire! But I must say something here, which you may not expect to hear: I was anxiously waiting to hear from you. I had told myself, that if our last meeting meant as much to you as it did to me, you would let me know, would write to me. In that case, a hundred horses would not have kept me from going to Vienna and taking you home with me. But if you did not— then I would have to take it as a sign, that I was premature, that a romantic night of kissing in the park was not a commitment to anything for you."

Peter stopped here because he could see Claire's face pale.

"Claire, are you feeling all right?"

"Yes, please go on Peter."

"I am taking too long, you are getting tired."

"No, no, please go on, I have to know."

"When fall approached, I visited a number of doctors in the neighboring towns, as well as hospitals. I found little to choose from. I did not want to be too far away from the farm. I would have liked to find an older doctor whose practice I could share, and eventually take over, and in a town of medium size with a well run hospital. It was difficult—there were more doctors looking for jobs and fewer patients with funds or insurance to pay for services. Many doctors complained about an overload of unpaid medical services. Finally, I had a recommendation to see Dr. Krieger in St. Johann, an elderly man, very pleasant, who was ready to take on an assistant who could buy him out and in a few years take over the practice. I liked what I saw, I liked Dr.

Krieger, and could promise to have funds ready whenever he was, because my father guaranteed part of my inheritance when it became needed.

"St. Johann—you probably know it—is a lovely old town, with a direct train connection to Salzburg, which can be reached in about one hour. It has a number of smaller industries, including tourism, and is surrounded by farms, working mostly in livestock. I liked the atmosphere as well as Dr. Krieger. He suggested I share his roomy house with a large garden overlooking the Salzach River. It contained another apartment beside his medical facility. What more could a young doctor expect? Dr. Krieger was willing even to share his housekeeper for part time duties. He suggested I start by the New Year.

"In the meantime, not everything was going too well at home. My brother Hans was in some kind of trouble. Political trouble, that is. Father had foreseen it, but I had my mind closed to it. It was selfish when I could think only of my own future plans. I thought the controlled press could not be trusted to report truthfully, and in disgust I had turned myself off politics and failed to see what was brewing. More and more people, especially the young, looked across Austria's border to the big brother, who seemed to fare better and better economically. Our own government was week. But what do I have to tell you about those times, you know them yourself.

"Hans had joined an underground movement, and when he contributed an article to one of their papers containing some inflammatory rhetoric in praise of the National Socialists in Germany, he was arrested, jailed, released, etc. Father relentlessly condemned Hans's action, but more people in the community became involved in political debates and secret meetings. The authorities did not tolerate dissenters and were harsh with those they caught for even little infractions."

Claire nodded:

"I know, a boy in my class in school was prevented from graduating because he was found with a German magazine, and police found more of that kind of reading material in his home."

Peter continued:

"I remember those times especially because of my brother's involvement, and how I was in that way sidetracked about thinking of other things. I will make it shorter from here on, because it is more difficult to explain to you. In February 1938 the political situation burst. Austria was no more, we were annexed to the 'Third Reich' You must know what happened then."

"Yes, I was just graduating from the University. Various factions of student organizations had been fighting there for a long time, some confused with idealistic notions, others more vitriolic. I stayed out of it. I had friends from my days at the gymnasium on all sides; fraternities, even the Zionistic student organization, were often involved at the University in brawls with opponents from various political groups or with bystanders. Sometimes it became confusing."

Peter continued his story:

"One day, my father wanted me to accompany my brother for a weekend in Vienna, where Hans, now feeling vindicated, openly participated in one of the many demonstrations in support of our new government. I did not participate, of course, but was lucky enough to get a ticket to a concert that was given for Hitler, mostly featuring the music of Beethoven with the Vienna Philharmonic under the direction of Krisp. Musically it was a first class event, despite the political overtones. Seating next to me were two young women, apparently sisters, who expressed themselves not only enthusiastically, but with absolute understanding—at least the one next to me—of every nuance in the musical score. I was impressed. At intermission, I started a conversation, and again found the young lady's music appreciation genuine and remarkable. I thought that she knew even more about music than I and guessed that she was a student of music. So the conversation went. No, she said, she had just graduated with a doctor's degree in Chemistry and was on her way to pursue a career in that field in Germany, since we were now part of the greater world. I could see her political leanings. She said that she had received an offer of a position at a great pharmaceutical company in Berlin. I was duly impressed with that accomplishment also, and expressed my regrets that under the circumstances I would not see her again at one of these concerts in Vienna. She said that she had a few months time to consider her options, because she had not decided if she wanted to leave her beloved city of Vienna. Well, we exchanged addresses, and that was it. Not long after that I received a note from her, that she had an extra opera ticket to Wagner's Tannhauser; she and her sister had season tickets to the opera but her sister could not attend this time. Would I consider a trip to Vienna? The cast was superior. Of course, I could not resist the invitation. From then on there were a few other occasions to meet. I really liked her. She was intelligent, pretty, and charming. When the time came for her to accept or reject the job offer in Berlin, I made her another offer, namely to marry me instead. She accepted hesitantly, and only under the condition that she could travel to Vienna as often as her heart desired, because she admitted that she was not really excited about a life in the country. I pointed out the Salzburger music festival every summer, but she insisted it must also include Vienna. I could not see why I should not agree to what I would also enjoy sharing.

"Marlena's parents were nice people; her mother, who was French, was teaching language at a high school in Vienna. The father was an engineer. The girls, that means Marlena and her sister Blanca, had inherited their looks from their mother: dark, nearly black hair, a darker complexion, black eyes—exotic in some way. I was fascinated by it. My mother was not, I have to admit. Right from their first encounter there was a tension between them, but I did not want to pay attention. My mind was made up. It was the right time for me. Dr. Krieger had hinted that a lady of the house was needed, and I agreed. I had enough of bachelorhood.

"The wedding took place in Vienna. My parents felt somewhat out of place, not because of their simple country appearance, but rather because they felt closed-in wherever they went. They missed the open spaces of our countryside, and somehow so did I, although I had been living in the city for so many years. We were looking forward to going home as soon as possible; Marlena was not, and we almost had our first disagreement right then.

"Hans and Marlena hit it off well, because of Hans's carefree nature, and even more so because of shared political ideals. I had not thought too much about our different views in that respect. To me, it was not important. It soon turned out to be of consequence, but I still felt tolerant.

"Our married life did not have a good start. Marlena not only dislikes the country, but hates every aspect of it. She does not care for the people, who are too simplistic for her. She even despises good old Dr. Krieger, and this feeling is mutual. He is not impressed with her academic accomplishments; he considers her my wife, and not the "doctor" in her own right, as she complains. She could by now have been an acknowledged chemist with a doctoral degree, with a good income to boot. Her complaints never stop, and I have to admit to myself, that I have made the greatest mistake of my life. But I was determined to make the best of it. I hoped that when we had a child, her attitude would change.

"We had a child. Little Eva is now almost three years old, but it did not change Marlena. It almost made it worse. She blames me for ruining her life. She feels tied down with the child, although we hired a nursemaid immediately, because Marlena could not and would not take care of the child properly. Fortunately, the young farm girl we have is quite capable; having grown up with many siblings, she has experience in child care. And now comes the most tragic part of my woeful story: the child exhibits all of Marlena's unpleasantness. She is hostile towards everybody, even, or especially, me. She turns away from me, whenever I approach her; she barely tolerates the nursemaid. She also has no attachment to her mother, who does not seem to care. Frustrated about my whole situation, I consulted a doctor friend of mine, a neurologist, who suggested emphatically that Marlena seek professional help, a psychiatrist. Of course, Marlena refuses, she insists more and more that only a divorce could help her, so she can regain her self-worth in her academic world. I cannot give in to these demands. You know that divorce in our family, in our community, in my position, in my religion—is out of the question. I accept my cross and have to bear it. What really pains me is the hurt I caused to my dear mother. She cannot be consoled."

While Peter was talking, more and more haltingly, Claire was over-whelmed with his confession. She felt pain for him and for herself also. She got up from her seat on the sofa, came towards him, who was still rocking slowly back and forth in the chair, as if the motion would calm his emotions. Claire sank to her knees before him, put her arms around his knees, laid her head against them, and tears were flowing uncontrollably.

Peter was startled, he stroked her hair and begged her not to be sorry for him. It was all his fault, he deserved no pity, just compassion.

"Dearest Claire, I did make a great mistake for which I have to pay the consequences. I have hurt my family and now you too. What would I give if I could change these years, but I cannot. Please, please, don't cry and make me feel even more miserable."

After a few moments, Claire got up, dried her tears and said almost mat-ter of factly:

"Good night, Peter. Your room is ready, I'll see you in the morning." And then with some hesitation:

"Thank you, Peter, for sharing your story with me, I shall think of you forever with the greatest affection. I hope, some day you will be happy again, and I hope the same for myself."

Before Peter could say anything, she had left the room. He heard her open and close some doors, then the one to her bedroom, and he got up to go to bed also. It was long past midnight, the happy hours of his reunion with the love of his youth had passed so quickly. He was grateful and terribly sad about it. He hoped for the blessing of a good night's sleep.

Claire went to bed with uproar in her heart, she felt almost physical pain. Seven years of wondering, yearning, and finally resigning herself to the fact that love for her could not be the "heads over heels" variety, but just con-tentment with reality. She would try to love Stefan the way he needed to be loved, not emotionally but rationally. She would not forgo her memories of the love she had dreamed of as a girl, but be good to Stefan as a friend—and a wife, of course.

Trying to find sleep, Claire could not, haunted by Peter's revelation. She wondered if it would have been better not to have seen him again, not to have been mesmerized again by those blue eyes that could penetrate her whole being. There was no answer.

She heard the door to the adjoining living room open and through the crack under her connecting door she noticed that a light was turned on. For a moment she was startled. He would not…No, he was a gentleman, just like the other man in her life!

Then the small sound of the creaking rocking chair came through the door. She had almost stopped breathing, her mind was raging. She did not fully comprehend what overcame her, but she got up, went to her wardrobe and took the light green silk robe from the hook. While shedding her nightgown, she put on the robe. There was not one rational thought in her mind, not a plan for seduction, just an automatic giving in to her emotions. She opened the door, and saw Peter with a book in his hands. He was startled.

"Oh, did I wake you, I am sorry, I could not sleep and was going to read for a while."

Then he saw the lovely figure in that revealing gown and his pulse began to race; she appeared to him like a vision from a dream, yet he felt the reality of her presence, inhaled the fine scent of a woman in love.

He stood up—she let the silken robe glide from her shoulders to the floor, where it lay in a little insignificant pile. Peter uttered words that he had never used in all his life:

"I love you dearest, dearest heart."

When Claire woke next morning, she slowly unfolded his arms around her, looked at that beloved face, and the happiness of the last hours engulfed her with such an enormous sensation, that she almost felt faint and unable to rise. She did, gently, so as not to wake him. She slipped out of bed and, grabbing her clothes quietly from the wardrobe, she left the room.

It was her usual time for getting ready for the office. She made herself a quick cup of tea, covered the pot with a cozy to keep it hot for Peter when he woke. Her bathroom toilet had to be quick also. She had to leave before Peter would miss her. She knew in her mind, what had to be done, but Peter's questioning eyes would make her heart weaken and she could not risk that. She had no regrets about the night, no guilt or shame. She was fully convinced that God had something to do with her prayers, and had granted her a few hours of complete happiness. She had not done anything wrong, but she also knew that it had to end. She was still Claire with the self-respect and moral convictions with which she always conducted her life.

When Peter woke up alone and found that Claire was gone, his disappointment was not relieved by the note she had left. It said simply:

"My dearest Peter—I love you and shall love you the rest of my life. Goodbye—maybe we will meet again in another world—God be with you."

He understood she meant that there could be no future for them together, and with a sad heart he knew she was right. It was just like her to act with such tenderness and gentleness. Barely thirty-six hours had passed since their reunion after seven years, but it had given him a lifetime of happiness. That it had to end, was his fault alone, and he would feel guilty and sorry about that forever.

He had missed the early morning train also, therefore he had time to look for a flower shop on his way to the train station. At least there was not yet a shortage and rationing of flowers. What should he choose? The red roses were elegant and sumptuous, and the obvious choice for the moment, but then he saw a few branches of the most fragrant white lilac. It reminded him of Claire in all her beauty, innocence, and delicious sweetness. He had the florist send them to her office, including an expensive vase, and a note, saying only: "I love you."

When Claire arrived at the office, there seemed to be more mail than usual that had piled up from the day before, and she was glad she could bury herself in her work. The secretary pointed out that there was also a personal letter for her from headquarters. She took quick notice, but set it aside for later. First the most important phone calls to the warehouse where some irregularity in the last shipment was reported and had to be cleared up. Claire sighed. She also called her mother, who wondered why she had not called the night before. Claire did not make any excuses, just said that she would like to come over tonight, and maybe spend the night. Would that be all right? Her mother was delighted, they had not had a good chat for a while, and she was lonely too.

The lilac arrived and her secretary had a questioning look in her face. Claire had on occasions received flowers and had never been secretive about the sender, but today she just buried her face into that lovely bouquet and said nothing. Soon the room was filled with that delicate fragrance. *My beloved Peter* was all she could think.

Chapter 9

Now to the letter from Herr Birkenstall, the president of Stehle. The letter was very cordial, very nice, very complimentary, very personal—and very definite. She had somehow expected the unavoidable, but when it was in black and white, it was nevertheless shocking. Headquarters had decided that because of the nearly complete cessation of civilian production, several branches must be closed for the duration of the war, and the one in Vienna was one of them. She was told to take her time, a month, or two, or three, whatever was needed to shut down, close up, and store the furniture and supplies. Specific instructions would follow regarding the company cars, which had been hardly used for some time anyway because of the lack of fuel, and about the discharge of the employees as well, the required report to the Labor Exchange and other authorities. Herr Birkenstall wanted to give her a little advance notice so she could have time to decide what she intended to do herself, before the Labor Exchange got hold of her. In these times of labor shortages every able-bodied person was required to participate in the war effort, as the government put it, so she would be immediately assigned to a job, if she liked it or not.

Claire was not surprised, but nevertheless saddened. Too much emotional upheaval in the last days even for her, who normally tried to be strong and calm in adversity. She called Frau Woerner, who had already heard the news herself from her husband, who had told her not to say anything to Claire, until it came from Mr. Birkenstall. The two women were fond of each other and often consoled each other when the war news made them anguished. They did not find many comforting words today. Lieschen Woerner asked Claire to visit with her today or tomorrow. Claire promised. She proceeded to handle today's business, as if nothing had happened. She would let her crew know about the situation tomorrow. After office hours she went home to take care of Mucki, the cat, who would be lonely that night, but Claire resisted her first inclination to take her along to her mother's. Then she went to her bedroom, picked up her pale green silk gown, still on the floor in the doorway to the living room. She felt a little embarrassed about her actions of last night, which would make her out to be a scheming temptress. She knew in her heart she was not. She had been overcome with love and desire, which still lingered on. She picked up the gown and put it away, with the intention of never wearing it again. Her bed still showed the indentations of the bodies of last night. For a moment Claire buried her head into the pillow trying to catch some remaining scent of the beloved man, but it was gone. She felt alone again, and it was painful. She was also strong and determined that the memory of that night must remain just that: a sweet memory, a present from the gods to be treasured over a lifetime and which had been given under the condition of keeping it secret. Only Peter and she would ever know.

She quickly changed the linens and made up the bed. She decided that from now on she would sleep in her guestroom. She would miss her own bedroom with the bay-window looking out into the distance to the Vienna woods, but it would be easier to be distracted in the surroundings of the simpler, cooler guest room. Glancing around the room to be sure that everything was normal again, she discovered that the picture of Stefan on her nightstand was missing. What happened? She had to leave before finding it.

When she arrived at her parents' home, her father opened the door and greeted her as usual with some absentmindedness.

"Where have you been? We missed you."

"Where I always am, at the office, at home, or on the way from it or to it." Claire said in a rather crisp manner, and was immediately sorry for her stupid answer. Why was she so impatient with her father? They had never been very close. He had always been buried in his books and his writings and paid little attention to his daughter, except when they went on explorations through the woods and mountains on a few occasions during their summer vacations. Then he could be stimulating and talkative, but at home he was a recluse, not paying much attention to either wife or child. Claire had always felt sorry for her mother. Now, both her parents were getting older and it seemed by needing each other more, had also grown a little closer. Claire noticed—it seemed for the first time—her father's stooped back, his temples as well as the short stubbly beard under his nose more white than gray; her father was getting old. All of a sudden she felt moved by his appearance, and vowed to pay more attention to him from now on.

Her mother was in the kitchen preparing an evening snack and tea. She always managed to scrounge something special together for Claire's visits, despite the rationing that left the cupboard uncomfortably bare. How she used to enjoy preparing meals for family, as well as guests, that were culinary delights and expressions of her desire to please. Rosemarie embodied the gracefulness of women of a past era, who accepted their role in life as their husband's loyal companions, keeping a genteel household for them in compliance with their station in life, raising their children to be obedient and respectful to their elders, a wife who never complained or showed dissatisfaction with her lot. In her own opinion, Claire, adoring her gentle mother, had not inherited her noble character. She was not as accommodating or tolerant of people and had very different aspirations. Of course, she had grown up in a different time, after the first great war, when values had changed in the nation as well. Her contemporaries did not share the older generation's sentimental memories of the "good old days" in the monarchy of Kaiser Franz Josef. The young people's country was a republic now, and they all had discovered a "social conscience," which they thought the previous generation did not know anything about, even if that opinion was based more on socialist propaganda than fact.

While her mother had attended a fine school for young ladies of the upper class, Claire went to a Gymnasium, just converted to mixed-gender education. Most of her classmates were boys and consisted often enough of a rambunctious bunch. The new generation of young women were competing with their male counterparts, were ambitious and conscious of their self-worth. They could handle themselves just as competently in business, as in professional endeavors. They now became doctors and lawyers. Claire was one of them—capable, self confident.

Then there was last night! That "self-confident" businesswoman who could handle train loads of merchandise and negotiate with demanding customers and salesmen, had felt so insecure and weak and had wished to be taken care of, to be comforted by and held in the arms of a big, strong man; Peter?!!

Rosemarie Baumann brought a pot of steaming tea and a tray with some little sandwiches and set it on the dining room table. In the meantime Claire had put some twigs of the white lilac she had brought with her into a crystal vase, and Rosemarie made remarks about its fragrance, without asking questions. Claire had decided not to mention Peter at all. Rosemarie was so sensitive to Claire's moods, and could have guessed more than Claire was willing to share. Her father had joined them, and they chatted about everyday affairs. Then Claire took out Birkenstall's letter and gave it to her father to read. He read it aloud, so her mother would hear it also. Both expressed sadness over the ending of Claire's job, but said that it was to be expected, and she would surely find another position to suit her. Her mother added, that they must feel great admiration for Claire at Stehle's headquarters to write such a personal and nice letter. She then asked about Stefan, and Claire said that she had not heard from him for nearly three weeks. Rosemarie said that some of her friends who had sons on the front told also about how long mail took these days.

Claire turned to her father and asked about the progress of his studies. He seemed to be pleased about her sudden interest.

"I am nearly finished revising my old lectures on World History, and feel pretty good about the result. They should be published soon."

"I always wondered why you stopped with Napoleonic times; world history is made continuously," said Claire.

"It takes a long time until we arrive at some perspective on historic events. I guess one hundred years, or two or three generations, will be necessary to distance oneself from events for a more objective judgment. For instance, I despise Stalin, Communism, and all it stands for, but despite the fact that I read Marx, Lenin and all the other thinkers and writers of our time on that subject, I know in my heart that my judgment is far from being objective. I feel the same about National Socialism. You hear people say these two ideologies are the opposites on the spectrum, and that we moderate thinkers huddle somewhere in the middle. There is a tendency always to see two sides to everything and if we just compromise on a middle ground, we should have found the truth. I believe that there are never just two sides, but always many sides to a story, and to find the middle ground as if it were a mathematical problem to be solved by computing averages, makes very little sense in historic observations." Friedrich Baumann continued in that vain to talk about subjects of interest to him.

Claire felt little comfort from her visit. It was not her parent's fault for really not understanding her pain. She could not confess it, she had to carry it alone. She was very tired. Explaining she had a headache, she went to bed early. Her parents thought she was under great emotional stress because of the job situation. Friedrich Baumann could not help but to say to his wife, that if Claire had taken his advice and had become a teacher, she probably would not be in that situation right now. Both felt glad that she had come and shared her distress with them.

Rain and wind had broken the short spell of spring. Claire felt that the weather was now more in accord with her emotional state. No time for dreaming and looking forward to better times. She had to deal with the harsh present. There was a short meeting with the staff at the office. Everybody had expected it to happen and, although disappointed, took it in stride. Bad news was the order of the day in these times, so why expect anything else, Claire noted with sadness. They planned together and promised their cooperation to finish and clear out within four weeks.

This evening Claire went to visit Lieschen Woerner. After both women shed a few quickly dried tears to comfort each other, they proceeded to discuss the situation. Lieschen would be much involved, since she and her husband still had hopes of reviving the office after the war. They had lived in Vienna now since 1938, had come to know and love Austria and would want to stay on, when Georg came back from the war. Lieschen had a note for Claire from her husband, in which he expressed regret over the situation which would separate them "for a while" he said, because he fervently hoped that she would return to the company again. Claire appreciated the warmth with which the Woerners had always treated her, and even now they showed concern over her future. They knew of Stefan's long silence and Lieschen suggested Claire should call or write to Magda von Brecht. She had also been informed by other friends from Germany, that the Brecht's had a difficult time in Dresden.

Then they discussed the necessary steps that were to be taken to dissolve the office, where Georg also still had many personal items left. On her way home, Claire had to stop at a shelter because of an unexpected air raid alarm. She huddled with a group of strangers, worried and harried mothers, crying children, and lamenting old women, who had been awakened from sleep and forced to seek shelter by the block wardens. It was the law and they had to obey. Claire noticed how much easier it was for her with only herself to take care of. Once everybody was settled on makeshift provisions, calm settled over the people, and they accepted the situation stoically.

The alarm did not last for too long. The enemy bombers coming from the direction of Italy just crossed over Austrian territory for their aim at German cities. Austria had so far experienced very little inconvenience with air raids and even less bombings, but the thought of the poor people who would feel the scourge of war that night was painfully shared. Next morning, Claire placed a telephone call to Dresden, but the connection was not completed during the whole day. It was difficult these days to get a long distance call through, therefore Claire wrote a letter and asked if the Brechts had more news from Stefan than she had. A few days later she received the following letter from Magda:

"Dear Claire—we are as concerned about the lack of news from Stefan as you are, however we are informed through sources close to military intelligence that our forces on the eastern front are proceeding in a planned, great offensive, which should give us the final victory over the Russian enemy. The northern region is still hampered by cold and snow—imagine snow in May! Many of our friends are in the same position regarding mail from the front; it is coming in only slowly. We just have to understand, that our brave soldiers out there have more important things on their mind than writing love letters. If we hear anything we will let you know, and we beg you to do the same. In the meantime let us be brave, pray for our boys, for our country and for the Fuehrer. Yours, Magda."

Claire felt the letter was cold, impersonal, even a little haughty. She was hurt, but also tried to be understanding. For the Brechts, she was still an outsider, and at present, Claire felt that she did not even deserve more. The waiting continued.

Claire tried very hard to bring her own emotions into some kind of order. She had been naive to think, that she would be able to set aside her encounter with Peter, keep it just a sweet memory and go on as before, concentrating on a future with Stefan. She thought of Peter when awakening in the morning and he was her last thought before going to sleep at night. Would she have to confess to Stefan? Not now, for sure. It would have to be in person. Stefan was not a man who would be able to accept what had happened to her. Proud and honorable Stefan! But could she continue a life with him with the guilt of a lie in her heart?

It was good that work at the office kept her from too much brooding. Her duties to conclude the affairs of an orderly shutdown were constantly on her mind. It seemed she would be able to handle it all within the four weeks she had given herself, however Georg Woerner wrote admonishing her to take her time. Headquarters were not pushing. He suggested to keep on Fräulein Frank to help with all the business correspondence, as well as Bert, the office boy, who could do the packing of all the customer files which were to be kept, and the brochures which might come in handy when they started the business again, and so on. He also told her he had been writing to a friend in Vienna, the president of a manufacturing company supplying the army. Georg Woerner was not certain about details because his friend was involved in a classified project, but he knew that he had influence with the government, and therefore had asked him to find a position for Claire which would be commensurate with her abilities, so she would not be at the mercy of the Labor Exchange which could require her to accept any offer. How nice of Mr. Woerner. He had always been a friend rather than a boss, and she was grateful for his attention, but she let him know, that she had not had a vacation for three years, apart from a day here or there, and she would like to take a longer time before beginning another job, if it could be arranged. The Woerners supported her plans fully.

If her timing was right, she could still enjoy some summer days in her beloved mountains, and then, in the fall, refreshed, as she hoped to be, think of her future. She did not want to make more definite plans at this time, but was thinking that she could possibly find a teaching job. Her teaching credentials were in order and the certificates valid. It was originally a profession she had avoided, but now it seemed not such a bad idea. She loved children, a teacher shortage plagued the city because of the induction of so many male teachers into the services; she figured that she might be even needed. Her salary would not compare to what she had earned in her present position, but money was the least of her concerns at a time when there was not even anything to spend it on. It had given her a kind of perverse pleasure to see her savings grow, when hardly anything could be bought with it.

So Claire was planning her life again, and felt partially content. She wrote to her friend Heidi Bogner-Karner in Styria and announced her visit as soon as her job was finished. Heidi had so often begged her to come. She was lonely too since her husband was also serving and despite the fact that her two little children provided her with much distraction. The prospect of seeing her old childhood friend and chatting with her as in the old days was quite exciting.

The closing of the office was coming to an end. The people at headquarters had proposed a three months time limit, including the time for unused vacations, which Claire considered quite fair. She would receive a salary till the middle of August, including all benefits. Her parents thought it was generous, and that it would give Claire enough time to investigate possibilities for her future business aspirations. Maybe the war would be even over by then! But enough of wishful thinking. She put such speculations behind her, it had been so fruitless in the past. She had been disappointed so many times, when all the exulted announcements of victory on all fronts still did not bring an end to that wretched war. She continued to challenge God every night in her prayers to show his mercy for mankind by ending their senseless destruction of each other, but God did not listen. He must have other plans.

A phone call from a former classmate, who knew about the latest sacrifices her generation was continuously making, was disturbing: Karl Spitzer and Bruno Weiss dead, Lixl, wounded. Lixl had written occasionally, trying to keep their old school ties and memories alive. The lonely soldier, who had been on battlefields all over the Western front, had them more vividly on his mind than Claire. She had occasionally sent him small packages of cigarettes or sweets, just as she tried to do that to other friends who were serving in the military. These men were always grateful to be remembered by the "home front". She thought with pity of Lixl, and hoped his injuries were not too serious. Lixl had always expressed concern about that and said that he was more worried about returning from the war crippled than not at all.

Why was there no news from Stefan? That was not like him. He always wrote punctually, as if it were his duty. Finally, she found the promised letter from Stefan's mother in her mailbox, and opened it eagerly. Was it good news? The Brecht's had just been informed, that their son was "missing in action". But they remained hopeful and asked Claire to think about it the same way-. Stefan had been in such a position before in Stalingrad and had found his way back, he would do it again. They saw their son always as an invincible hero. Claire however, could not help but thinking of the proverb:

the pitcher that goes too often to the well gets broken, and she was sick with worry about Stefan.

These past weeks had put a great emotional and also physical strain on Claire, and she felt not at all well, weak and nauseous, especially in the morning, with hardly enough pep to get up, but she continued with her daily routine. Rosemarie noticed Claire's pale face with great concern and Lieschen Woerner also suggested that she see a doctor in town before going on vacation. Claire thought that rest in the country would return her old strength, but took her mother's and friend's advice, because there seemed to be something not quite normal in her body. She scheduled a prompt visit to Dr. Novak, the Baumann's family doctor since her early childhood. The old doctor seemed to be genuinely glad to see Claire, and since he was a dear old friend, she told him about the most important aspects of her present life, leaving Peter out, of course. After a thorough examination Dr Novak became serious.

"I am ordering some tests, Claire, and should have the result by tomorrow, please come by around three in the afternoon."

"Do you think that there is something serious wrong with me?" Claire asked anxiously.

"No, not serious at all, but I want to be sure to give you proper advice as to how to spend your vacation."

At her appearance the next afternoon, Dr. Novak had cleared all his other scheduled office hours, and ordered tea from his housekeeper to make Claire's visit more personal than official. He had known the family for so long, had even been the doctor who had tended to little André, when he had polio and died. After a little chitchat about the weather that had finally seemed to turn into real spring, even though late this year, Dr. Novak put his spectacles over his arched nose, and studied his notes.

"Claire, the weakness you experienced lately, may come mainly from the fact that you are seriously anemic. It seems to me that you do not pay enough attention to eating well."

Claire interrupted with a faint smile:

"Who can do that on our scant rations?"

"I know," Dr. Novak continued, "all my patients have the same, and indeed valid, excuse. Nevertheless, I maintain that you can do things to protect your health even in these times. You have to change your eating habits, not skip meals; even if they are meager they still can be chosen more nutritiously. You have to be careful how you redeem your ration coupons. If there is meat available, choose liver, e.g., if there are vegetables, try to select those which give you more iron, vitamins, etc. I'll provide a list for you. But that won't do altogether in your case. Since you are able to take time off for a vacation, I shall recommend a health spa for you where you can spend several weeks under medical supervision."

"Is it that serious?"

"Considering my next finding, yes. By the way, you told me that you were engaged for several years—why are you not married by now?"

"Oh, Dr. Novak, in the first place, we had decided to get married right after the war, and that still applies. Can you guess when that will happen?"

"Well, maybe you will want to change your marriage plans to sooner rather than later."

Claire did not understand, why Dr. Novak should be concerned about her marital plans, he was only consulted about her health. She was almost becoming a little annoyed, but quickly overcame her impatience with the old doctor.

"Claire," Dr. Novak continued " to put it bluntly—you are pregnant."

If it had been possible, Claire would have now paled even more.

"By the middle of next January you should give birth. You are otherwise healthy and I expect no problems during your pregnancy, but you have to deal with your anemia. I would be glad to talk to your fiancé should he have any concern. Where is he now?"

"Missing in action," Claire uttered, barely audible.

"Missing in action"—how that applied to both men in her life. For the moment she could not comprehend it all, but then joy took over. Very unreasonable for her to feel that way with all the problems she would have to face, but to expect a child of which s he had dreamed almost all of her adult life, and even as a teenager—was—well, a dream come true. She recovered long enough to look into the warm and understanding eyes of the old man, and said with an almost happy smile:

"I will try my very best and behave so that no harm shall come to my unborn child."

"I am not worried about the child. It will take all the nourishment it needs from your body, and not care how that diminishes you. You have to look out for yourself to regain the strength you need to go through the process and be a healthy mother once the baby is born. As I can see, you will have the additional burden of facing that whole time by yourself without the usual support of the baby's father. But if it is any consolation to you, I can tell you that you are not alone. Many women are now in such a situation, where fathers are fighting the war, and their families are on their own. At least you have your parents, I am certain they will help you."

"Dr. Novak, I have to ask you not to tell my parents. They could not bear the thought of my situation, I cannot burden them with it. Will you promise?"

"Of course, dear, but maybe you underestimate them. You know they love you and you do need assistance."

"I will think about it while I am on vacation. I will take your advice and find a place at some health spa. Will that not be difficult?"

"I may be of help to you in that respect. I have referred several of my patients to a specific clinic on the Woerthersee in Carynthia, where I know the doctor who runs it. I will give her a call, and let you know as soon as I find out."

"Her?"

"Yes, her name is Dr. Amelia Seredinsky, she is a good doctor, schooled in Vienna, I have known her for quite some time."

"Amelia!" exclaimed Claire surprised, "I used to go to school with a girl of that name, she was a few years older than I, quite an athlete, on all the sports teams, beating even the boys in competitions, a likable girl, although I did not know her too well."

"That must be it—there could not be more ladies with that same name—what a coincidence—now I can add your name to my recommendations to her. I hope to call you shortly."

With that assurance and a warm hug from old Dr. Novak, Claire left, spent the afternoon in the sunshine of a lovely spring day in the Stadtpark, watching nature around her coming to the fulfillment of its intended life cycle, and tried to listen to her own sprouting germ in her womb.

She was not naive enough to think that these coming months would be all joy and expectations. Besides that, there would be many hurdles to overcome. Instead of the usual weakness that had overcome her lately, she felt all of a sudden strong and determined, capable and—happy. If she was sorry about anything, it was that she had no one to share the news with, which is normally received with joy.

Peter—no, not Peter. She was not going to complicate his already burdened life. She thought of him with all the love she ever had, but it was clear that he wouldn't be part of her life ever again. She knew it would be easy to ask him to come again, to love her again. She would be his mistress? They would have some wonderful times together, would love each other—until that love died in the murky waters they had created. No—she felt their love had been pure and honest, and ending any future contact cleansed it of all the possible guilt or shame.

Her mother Rosemarie? How could she hurt that gentle woman with the knowledge that her only and beloved daughter had failed, at least in her mind, although Claire had not the slightest inclination to think of herself as being any less virtuous than before. Lieschen Woerner, her friend and confidant during the past few years?

No, in this matter she would have to be alone. Stefan was the only one towards whom she felt responsible, and she would have to deal with that sooner or later. She did not want to believe that Stefan's present situation was a lucky reprieve for her, such cruel thinking was not allowed into her soul, but it was lurking there. She would have to pray for guidance—it was always her way. God would tell her. God had granted her so many good things in life, even though she still did not forgive him for his tolerance of that abominable war.

It was getting late now. She tried to free her mind from all these confusing thoughts and visit her parents with whom she could at least discuss Dr. Novak's advice for recuperation from her anemic state at a health spa. That went better than expected. Her mother said she had noticed Claire's apparent weight loss with concern. That and all the worries about Stefan and the office had been just too much for a young woman to bear, and if she could find some rest in healthful country air and with, hopefully, a better diet, it would be just great. It was decided that Claire could, if necessary, board her cat with her parents for the time being, although her father was not fond of cats or any other pets which could interfere with his comforts at home. Claire assured him, that Mucki would be almost no trouble at all, although she was concerned about food for the cat. Her mother was not, and said there were nearly always some little morsels to be found for such a tiny creature.

That was one of Claire's concerns settled. Now she had to decide what she should and could pack to take along. While pretending to be away for just a few weeks, she knew that it would not be possible for her to return soon showing her condition. Claire was not afraid to tackle all the problems before her. She was self-confident enough, and was always thinking of the many other women who in these dark days had to do the same. How could she not be up to such a challenge?

One thing, however, bothered her deeply. For the next months—maybe even longer—she would not be telling the truth, she would be lying, deceiving, pretending—could she ever live such a life? She had to deal with that conflict in her soul, having drawn strength from her integrity and honesty often enough, for which she had even been praised in the last testimonial of her employer at Stehle. The world was not the same anymore; one could no longer afford to live by the old values. These days, it came down to playing the survival game. Deep in her heart Claire knew that she was rationalizing, excusing, justifying all the same. Her mind told her that she had no other choice in order to survive; maybe she had to lose some self-respect in order to save pain and harm to those she loved most.

She spent the next two days preparing for her departure, packing, talking to friends, waiting for Dr. Novak's call about his inquiry for a place for her at the health spa. She also packed some of the things which would be necessary for her to establish a small household for the next few months, linens, dishes, and such.

Dr. Novak finally called and said Dr. Seredinsky remembered her and was glad to be able to accept her at the clinic on the 15th of June if that would suit her. That would give Claire enough time for a short stop at her friend

Heidi in Bruck. Her larger containers would be sent ahead to Carynthia. There had been some concern about its shipping because transportation for civilian needs had become so difficult these days, but while at the Stehle company she had working relations with a transport agency and she could still count on these connections.

Saying good-bye to her parents was more emotional on her part, because only she knew that it would have to be for much longer than these two people thought. Rosemarie was surprised by Claire's tears and admonitions that they take good care of each other; Claire had gone on vacations before and they had also, but it was never a big deal. Was their daughter more seriously ill than she had reported? Rosemarie decided to talk to Dr. Novak, which she did a few days later. Dr. Novak was unusually short with her, said only that Claire would be fine after the needed rest, and excused himself as being busy, so that he did not have to get into an extended conversation with his old friend.

Claire left two days later, on a sunny June morning. The train ride to Bruck went through a lovely landscape and over the Semmering Pass, which separates the provinces of Lower Austria and Styria. It excited her the same as long ago in her childhood when the long family summer vacations started, traveling over the same pass. Of course, there was a difference now that showed everywhere. The train stopped often and the stations were crowded with soldiers on leave, trying to find their way home for a short reunion with their families. Nowhere was the happy noise of vacationers, but instead weary refugees from various parts of the war zones with their bundles of salvaged belongings. The conversations of the train passengers dealt with concerns as to possible bombing of the train, although at that time enemy overflights occurred more often at night than during the day, but since the Semmering Pass was on the very important North-South route from Vienna to its southern borders with Yugoslavia and Italy, it could become a target for the enemy.

No enemy action occurred that day either, and Claire landed in good spirits in Bruck, where Heidi awaited her at the station. Her neighbor had lent her a handcart, no other transportation being available. The two women loaded Claire's luggage, and made their way through town. It was the first time Claire had been faced with such hard work, but she found it challenging. The two women were happy about seeing each other again, and, chatting all the way, it did not seem too long to get to Heidi's house, located in a lovely section just outside town. The small house looked picture perfect, with a picket fence around a small garden, now planted with vegetables, where formerly the loveliest of garden flowers had their beds. The boys came running from the house, greeting their mother enthusiastically and warming her friend's heart. How wonderful to see Heidi being happy with her family.

The first evening was spent in easy conversation, neither of the two friends ready to dig deeper. Claire was to spend three days here, so there was time to become personal. She found Heidi changed in just some little ways from the carefree girl of high school days to a motherly figure, clucking like a hen over her brood. Claire immediately regretted these thoughts. Heidi was just the way a mother with two young children should be expected to be, but Claire did not want to think of herself becoming so frumpy. She vowed to stay young and fresh as her mother did. She could not remember seeing her mother looking other than refined and well dressed behind the stove even with an apron on, her hair always neatly coifed, her delicate hands well cared for.

Heidi worked in the garden, you could see that, and did many other chores that a city woman in a Viennese apartment was not faced with. Heidi said that in normal times she would have had a helper, but all girls who used to be available for such jobs were working in the factories now, to replace the men who had left for the war. Heidi's husband, Eduard, had been a high school mathematics teacher at the nearby Gymnasium before the war. They seemed to have had good reasons to look forward to a happy future, when the war disrupted their life. One little boy was just a year old, but another baby was on the way when Eduard became a soldier, fighting in a war that had little meaning for him.

Bruck was known for its surrounding iron ore mines and factories He was the son of a miner. Eduard Karner had been a good student in school, went on to the University, got his degree in mathematics and decided to teach in the same school of the same town he grew up in. He had met Heidi on a skiing vacation in the usual "boy meets girl" situation. They continued their acquaintance, married, and planned to live "happily ever after."

However, here they were now: he fighting somewhere deep in Russia, and she doing the best she could to make it on her own. She did not complain; it was the lot she shared with so many others, but it was not easy. Now and then she also worried about the future. As an important industrial town, air attacks were a looming possibility. Air raid drills were already conducted frequently. She had made a simple shelter in her own basement, with some provisions stored there, but she was always in fear for the children's well being if her home should be hit or damaged.

Then it was Claire's turn to talk about everything, the situation in Vienna, Claire's parents, and Stefan, of course. Claire thought that Heidi would be the one she could confide in. She had to tell someone or her heart was going to burst with all the kept-up and unshared emotions. So she told her story, and Heidi was in tears of sympathy. Claire had to tell her friend repeatedly not to pity her; she was in a difficult situation, but by no means unhappy or desperate. She needed a friend to share her secret with, but she was going to be perfectly fine. Heidi did not want to dampen Claire's optimism, though she knew from her own experience with the pregnancy and birth of her second child, that it was not going to be as easy as Claire imagined; but to do it all alone she could help her friend in a number of ways. For one, she told Claire, she could come and stay with her if she wanted to. Her house had an empty guestroom and she would love to become the baby's godmother also. They looked at that room with the wonderful vista of the wooded hillside behind the house and the mountains in the distance. Claire loved it, but hoped to be somewhere on her own. Her savings should carry her through for at least another year. And by then the war would certainly be over. *Here we go again* she thought, *I am doing it also, saying that phrase which has become a cliche by now. I must not do that, but can't one at least hope?*

In a chest drawer were neatly folded outgrown baby clothes, which Heidi offered if needed. Claire did not know if anything new would be available to purchase, but thanked Heidi for her offer; she would let her know. During their conversation, Heidi asked repeatedly if Claire did not think that Peter should be informed, but Claire was very determined to keep him out. Her heart might be aching at the thought, but her mind was made up.

When they were parting, Heidi thought that Claire had no idea what was ahead of her. That accomplished businesswoman was so naive compared to her who was a simple mother-housewife, and she was truly sorry for her friend. Claire, on the other hand, was buoyed by her visit. *How important good friends are for your soul,* she thought.

Chapter 10

Arriving in Velden, in Carynthia, she was met by the sanatorium's carriage which took her to her building at the treatment center, located in the midst of a large garden where patients walked around or reclined in lounge chairs. It looked friendly and relaxed at first sight. She had to go through the usual entry formalities, and then was shown her room on the second floor. Claire was pleased with its size and location and the lovely view of the mountains. She opened the door to the balcony and mild and fragrant waves of air filled the room. She was told that her program would be given to her as soon as her doctor had seen her on her rounds. Amelia Seredinsky was not running the place, she was employed as the Resident Doctor at the Spa. The director of the institution was in charge of the whole operation. Before the war, this was a first class sanatorium for the very wealthy. Now run by the government, it served mostly patients sent by their health insurance companies or by the veterans hospitals. They were often elderly pensioners, but mostly injured military men, sent here to recuperate in the mild air of this southern Austrian province.

When Dr. Seredinsky came around, they had a friendly exchange, referring with a few words to their common school experiences. The doctor reviewed Claire's medical record, and said that the nurse would be informed as how to instruct her about her treatments. No further personal comments were made, and Claire relaxed. Later, an assistant arrived to take her around to acquaint her with the facilities, the dining area, the treatment center, hot mineral spas, etc. It seemed to be a well-run place, orderly, not lacking in comforts, but not the luxury of the past either. No cut flowers in the now empty stone urns in the halls, no paintings or tapestries on the walls, except a large picture of the Fuehrer, of course. A well-stocked library was a pleasant surprise. Claire thought she could stand it to live here for a while, to relax, read, and sleep. The only things to disturb her soon enough were the loud-speakers which made the same public announcements as in Vienna. Well, we must be informed, she thought with a sigh.

The food was acceptable, not prepared to her taste, but a little more plentiful than her rations in Vienna. She did get more milk and vegetables, and when she recorded a small weight gain after her first weigh-in, she was praised by the doctor. Amelia sought her out frequently in the dining room where they shared their meals at the same table. They often talked about the old schooldays in Vienna, gossiped about the professors they had had in common, as well as some of the classmates. One of Amelia's best friends had lost his life early in the war on the Western Front in France. When she mentioned it, Claire noticed tears in Amelia's eyes, and she assumed that friend had been a special one, but she did not ask and Amelia did not volunteer it. An easy friendship grew up between the two of them, for which Claire was very grateful, but it did not extend to sharing her intimate secrets. Amelia was discreet too. She seemed to assume that Stefan, the "missing in action" soldier was the father of Claire's baby, and except for occasional questions if Claire had had further news, nothing was said.

Some other patients tried to get acquainted also, especially a lonely soldier here and there, but except for a friendly smile and inquiry about their health, Claire kept her distance. Amelia remarked on this, and Claire explained that she was here strictly to regain her strength, and was not interested in making new friends.

The weeks went by uneventfully; Claire was feeling ever so much stronger, and she was giving thought as to what to do next. She had to find a place to stay, when her term at the health spa had expired. When she was at home preparing for an extended absence, she found just enough room in one of the crates she was packing for either her typewriter or Grandmother's silver tea service. Both were valuable to her. The former might come in handy for her to continue her writings maybe even earn some money with it. The other she would not want to lose, if by chance her home was bombed; it could also be valuable as a trade-in for goods, if times should become that difficult. She had finally decided on the typewriter, and that had indeed become a good choice. She retrieved it from storage, where she had left most of her belongings which were not necessary at the sanatorium, and had started to write essays in the genre she used to before, some of which had occasionally been published in magazines. She wrote about the subjects which caught her attention in daily life, avoiding, however, always feeling that this subject should be left to people who were more knowledgeable. She had been thinking of Heidi, her struggles as a young mother with a husband in the war. She could write about the matters which faced so many women these days, and how they coped.

She sent her two-page essay to the local newspaper, not expecting too much, and was almost surprised to be invited to come and meet the editor. She was a little shy about that, because by now she could hardly hide her pregnancy. Although taking long walks along the shore of the lake by herself, she still had somewhat of an old fashioned inhibition in presenting her telling figure to the public. Dr. Seredinsky encouraged her to go and see Paul Thoene, the editor, whom she knew socially, and who was a very nice man, she said.

Claire went, was cordially received, and had a lengthy conversation with Paul Thoene. Standing behind his desk while greeting her, she saw a very handsome man, probably in his mid-thirties, and she immediately thought what everybody else was thinking these days when seeing a man of that age who was not in uniform *How come he is avoiding serving his country-what kind of deal did he make?*

He asked her to sit down in the chair in front of his desk and he began to question her in a charming and comforting manner, especially about her previous writing, and what she had published. She admitted to being strictly an amateur in that field and told him a little about her professional life before coming to Velden. She told him about the closing of her office as a result of limited civilian production for the duration of the war. She was happy to have found some reprieve here in the country from her former business activities, which had been stressful enough so that her doctor had recommended a complete rest. After several weeks she had grown a little tired of inactivity, and had started to do some writing. She said she was aware that it was not of any great literary value, but that it provided her with an outlet which she enjoyed.

Paul Thoene said she did not need to be so modest, he found her essay well written and its content meaningful, even moving; that was why he had wanted to meet the writer in person. Otherwise, he would have just accepted the essay for publication by sending her a check in the mail. Claire blushed. The conversation with that man she had just met made her feel warm and comfortable, as if he had been an old friend. Thoene told her that beside the newspaper, he published a couple of magazines, geared mostly to the interests of the farming population, but also books, novels, and the like, searching for that great masterpiece which every publisher hopes for.

The conversation went on to other subjects; he wanted to know how her stay at the resort pleased her. She told him of her long acquaintance with Dr. Seredinsky, whom she remembered from her school days, although Amelia was a few years ahead of her. Claire expressed concern that she had stayed longer than he had probably planned, but Thoene assured her that he enjoyed their conversation. He got up from his chair, when she was ready to leave, and came around the desk, to shake hands with her. She noticed that he had a slight limp and asked about it, concerned if he had injured himself.

"Yes," he said with a smile, "a long time ago, when I was a young boy and thought of myself as one of the flying trapeze artists at the circus. I broke my leg in several places and almost lost it in the fight with infections. The doctors put it nicely together again, however, a little shorter than God had created it. Well, it kept me out of the military, if that is something to be proud of or happy about?" Claire was embarrassed to have been too personal in her question, but Paul Thoene did not seem to mind. He shook her hand warmly, and now standing closer to him she saw a pair of lovely large brown eyes in that handsome face under a shock of dark, wavy hair. He said that he hoped to see her again, and to keep up her writing.

That was an unexpected lovely afternoon, Claire thought. Since feeling much stronger again, she had started to miss some of her former intellectual contacts. Amelia was a nice person to be with, but there were not that many occasions for longer conversations with that busy doctor.

At the end of July she received notice from her insurance that her stay at the resort in Velden was coming to an end. It had been extended twice upon the recommendations of her physician. She had expected that and had already looked for some place in town to rent. She would have liked to stay in the area which she found quite beneficial to her health. Why would it not be here? Velden with its warm baths from natural springs used to be a well known and preferred place "to take the waters." Even Napoleon had been enthusiastic about them here, before him Paracelsus, and earlier yet the Romans.

She talked to Dr. Seredinsky about her desire to stay on in the area, and Amelia said she might be able to help. At the place where she had her private apartment, was another, much smaller, but a really nice one. Her landlord had recently mentioned that he had been asked by the housing authorities to make it available to refugees, although he had hoped to keep it for his own family members as they came for occasional visits. The housing people had pressed him hard. Amelia would talk to him. He could not find a better tenant than Claire, she said. Mr. Morascher, the landlord, met with Claire, and agreed. She could move in immediately. Of course, he was aware that she would eventually have company, but a little baby did not worry him. Better than a bunch of growing boys, who could tear the place down, as some other homeowners experienced when they were forced to sublet.

Now Claire could bring some of her belongings out of storage to make herself at home in her own place. Modest, very modest, she thought, but comfortable with some furnishings borrowed from the landlord, and her own linens, dishes, etc. When Amelia had a free evening, the two spent time together. Claire found it nearly perfect.

During her time of recuperation, she had tried bravely to free herself from thinking of Peter, but with the little person in her belly kicking her daily as a reminder, it was useless. He had been on her mind since she was a young girl playing on the beaches of Kammerlake; the memories of ten years of her life could not just be put aside.

Just before moving into her new domicile, Claire had received a letter from Magda which was somewhat encouraging. The Brechts were informed by the Red Cross that their son was a prisoner of war somewhere in Russia, no details of course. The Red Cross would try to forward a letter, but could not verify if it would be received. Magda suggested that Claire add a little note for Stefan to their letter, and hopefully they would somehow get connected with their son. Claire wrote immediately short, as suggested, and with just a few words of love and hope for his healthy homecoming.

Nineteen-forty-three was a nice summer in Velden, and the good weather lasted into the fall. Claire took advantage of it with many strolls through the parks, and even ventured on longer walks outside town. It really was very beautiful here—she wished that she could perceive her time here as a true summer vacation as it had been in the old days, but wherever she looked, it reminded her that these were not normal times. So many refugees, mostly women and children from the bombed areas of western Germany, trying to survive here, where the bombs had not yet caused tragedies as in their homeland. The enemy flyers were sometimes observed flying over the area, but mostly on their way to more important destinations.

Other refugees came from the occupied and conquered areas of the Balkans. Some were Germans who had lived there for generations in pure ethnic German communities, from where they had been forced to flee by the native population in an ethnic cleansing process. Others were political fugitives, escaping from communist tyranny. They were of different backgrounds, education, and lifestyles, but had one thing in common: no matter what they had been able to save from their former life, they were all poor now.

It occurred to Claire that in some way this applied to her also, although a little differently. She had not lost her home in Vienna, her family had not suffered personal losses, except those of compassion for others who had. But she had lost much also. She had lost Peter—possibly also Stefan—and her innocence too. Not in the way one normally thinks of a girl losing such, but in the way she had lived her life "before"; before war had changed all of their thinking and planning. Before when she was young—she was now twenty-seven years old and felt she was getting "old"—and carefree, full of hopes and fantasies about her great and happy future. For some reasons, her hopes were becoming more oriented to the imminent. An end to the war was still her biggest hope, but she did not argue with God about that anymore, though prayed fervently for the well being of her child and a better future for it. Its coming filled her with joy and happiness, tinged with a little sadness and uncertainty about explaining its existence to her parents and her friends. When she wrote to her parents that she intended to stay longer than the medically prescribed time, her reasons always had to include a lie, and she was anguished by it. Could she have acted differently right from the beginning? There was no answer to her dilemma.

Claire had been raised in the catholic religion, although at her home there had never been a strict adherence to its dogma. Her father ignored pretty much all references to it. Her mother went to church often enough, but mainly to enjoy the music and the rituals, without any close affiliation to the church as an association. Claire had regular classes in Religion in school and was comfortable with its teaching of history and morality. When very young, she had been regularly to confession and communion with her classmates, and took that quite seriously. As an adult, she chose a different way of communication with the God she believed in with all her heart. It became personal. Therefore, when the thought crossed her mind that she could find advice about the matter that plagued her conscience, the lie, from a priest at confession in church, she rejected that quickly as an unworthy way to deal with her problem. She prayed for guidance.

Walking one day along a narrow path which had led from the park to the shore of the lake, she was faced by a man in swimming trunks, dripping wet, who apparently had just stepped out of the water. Claire was startled when he said:

"You are trespassing on my property, Fräulein," and then she recognized the smiling face of Paul Thoene.

"I am so sorry, I did not know, I was just following the path, not knowing where it would lead me."

"Fortunately, it led you in the right direction—this is my home," and he pointed to a substantial villa across the lawn, situated on a terraced ledge. Claire found the situation somewhat embarrassing, but Paul Thoene just laughed and apologized on his part for his unconventional attire for encountering a lady.

"I would like to invite you to my house, but maybe some other time, when I am dry and dressed. Will you come?" Claire just nodded, and he ran towards his house, limping somewhat, but not too much impaired, it seemed.

Several days later, Amelia Seredinsky came home at night and said Paul Thoene had called her at her office and asked her and Claire to tea the coming Sunday afternoon, if Amelia could make herself free. It happened that she was free, and she had accepted also for Claire.

Claire was actually looking forward to that day, thinking how few diversions she had really had lately. She had no complaints about it, but it was nice to think of an afternoon in pleasant company. Unfortunately, she could not plan to wear something nice, as she would have in her "former life," because her old dresses had already become much too tight. She managed to wear the light blue one—blue was her color, everybody always had said—but just did not use the belt with it. Looking into the mirror, she did not feel too bad. Amelia looked at her and said

"You look absolutely beautiful, Claire," who accepted the compliment with a doubting smile. Amelia never cared much for her own appearance, her white physician's coat covered any old skirt and sweater, and she had no time to be vain.

Paul Thoene awaited them in front of his house where he tended to some of the roses that were now in full bloom. He cut a lovely fragrant pink one and handed it with a bow to Amelia, and a deep red one to Claire. After they admired his garden, he took them inside the house. A wide, marble floored entry hall and a staircase of exquisitely forged wrought iron greeted the visitors. On the wall were old prints and etchings and a large set of antlers above one door, through which Paul led his guests into his study. It was a large room, with book cases on the walls stacked to the brim with books, a monstrous desk and a couple of worn armchairs around the fireplace. A Persian rug, also showing usage through the years, partly covered a dark parquet floor. There was not exactly neatness in that room, but it felt warm and comfortable, and happy, was Claire's observation. Paul explained that the room was really the library, which he had converted to his living room at present. His bedroom was across the hall and was formerly the maid's quarters. A large old fashioned bathroom was for his personal use only, but he shared the kitchen further down the hall with his refugee tenants. They were two families, that meant two mothers and their five children, who had their quarters upstairs. One could hear some commotion coming from there, and Claire asked Paul if this did not disturb him. Paul said that he did not mind at all—it was little enough that he had to contribute to his fellow men during these trying times. She really liked that kind and charming man, and he was well practiced being a host, serving tea and cake on the terrace outside his study. Claire was wondering how much he had to sacrifice from his ration cards for such a splendid offering, and in a joking tone she asked, if he, by any chance, had baked the cake himself.

"No," he replied with a smile, "I am not really an accomplished cook, and except for breakfast I eat all my meals at the restaurant."

They talked about this and that, but had no earthshaking discussions. Paul showed great interest in Amelia's work at the convalescent center, and she responded with some stories about her patients. He never asked Claire anything too personal, and she was grateful that she was spared from lying again. It was a pleasant afternoon, and when leaving, Amelia asked Paul to come and visit them any time he felt like it. Paul said he would like that very much.

Indeed, Paul came quite often for a chat with the ladies, sometimes just for a few minutes, bringing some flowers from his garden, or a book for Claire; other times he spent the whole evening there, especially when Amelia was not at home and Claire was alone. She enjoyed that very much, it was so easy to be with Paul, and soon she really considered him a friend. She could not help but mention that her fiancée was a prisoner of war in Russia, and she had not heard from him for a very long time. She almost caught herself saying how long, but then she would have revealed more of her past than Paul could figure out for himself. She began to wish that she could tell him everything, which was different from her relationship with Amelia. She never felt like sharing the truth with her.

When fall was finally upon them and the weather had become nasty, Claire had to curtail her long walks. Upon Paul's urging she took up writing again and it was comforting, like talking to a friend. She attempted to start a novel. Maybe there she could incorporate her own experiences, letting her fantasies take over as to how she would like her own life to go on.

She had a pretty good start at that, when real life once again told a story she had not created out of her own imagination. She received a long letter from Magda von Brecht. Against their expectations, their son Stefan had been released from a Russian prison camp in an exchange for Russian prisoners in Germany. How, and why, she did not explain. They were told that their son was very ill, and was presently at a military hospital in Danzig, East Prussia. Immediately after getting this news, the Brechts went to Danzig to visit their son, and to find out the details of his illness. Sad to say, they could not in their wildest dreams have imagined what they were confronted with. He had been wounded, and although they had not been life threatening but only flesh wounds, they had become infected because of neglected treatment. He had lost weight to such an extent, that he appeared to be just a skeleton covered by his hospital gown. They had a difficult time in recognizing him among the group of other patients. Bearded, a listless expression in his eyes, there seemed to be no life left in him. He did not show any emotion on seeing his parents, and the doctor told them that he hardly ever spoke a word. The medical team which was taking care of his case, had concluded that they might be able to restore his physical health, but his mind would need more treatment than the hospital could provide. After consulting with the military authorities and with the help of government interventions through the connections the Brechts had, they were given hope that Stefan could be released into their care; at this time they were awaiting that decision.

Magda said that she could understand this news would be very painful to Claire also, but if she had any plans to visit Stefan they strongly advised against it. The doctor's orders were that Stefan had to be protected from any disturbance of his equilibrium, if it was to be hoped that his mind would heal again.

Of course, Claire was very perturbed. She could not imagine seeing Stefan other than in his self assured stance, a proud officer, confident in all his ways. To see him in her mind as his parents described him, was nearly impossible for her. She was devastated. She could hardly talk to Amelia about it, and preferred to let her read the letter herself. Paul Thoene heard it also. He and Amelia did not know how to comfort Claire other than just let her know that they were her friends who loved her.

In her position as a doctor to convalescent military patients Amelia had some experience with cases similar to the description of Stefan, but never so serious a case. She said to Paul, but not to Claire, that she feared there was not a good prognosis of recovery for Stefan, but she added, that it was clearly not for her to speculate without having seen the patient herself, or at least a detailed doctor's report.

Claire wrote immediately to the Brechts, thanking them for their frankness, sharing their pain, and begging to be kept informed about Stefan's condition in every detail. She would like Stefan to know—if he cared—that her thoughts and prayers were with him, and also her love.

Close to Christmas another letter from the Brechts told her they had been able to take Stefan to Switzerland, to one of the foremost sanitariums in that country, known to deal with such illnesses. They added that Stefan had not said one word since they brought him home, he was turning away from everybody who came near him, including his parents. They returned home with the very painful knowledge that only hope and prayers were left for them.

Amelia admonished Claire to think of her unborn child. All her emotions were transferred to the fetus. She had to let go of her depression, even if it was difficult.

"Think of Christmas, remember happy times, let joy fill your heart. You can't help Stefan by grieving. There is so much unhappiness all around us because of the war. If we succumb to so much brooding, there will not be much strength left in us for a renewal, when normal times come again."

Claire tried to concentrate on the upcoming holidays. Her parents had urged her to come home and spend a few days with them. She was wondering for a while which excuse she would have to invent, as to why she would not be able to come. As much as she hated to be deceitful, she decided to send them a copy of the Brecht's letter and explained she did not feel well enough to celebrate Christmas at this time. They were more than understanding and could imagine Claire's sorrow. They also told her that they had had to accept a boarder for the bedroom that used to be Claire's, which the housing authorities had declared surplus and available for refugees. It was difficult for her father, whose privacy had been so important to him all his life. Fortunately it had happened that they heard from cousin Catherine from Silesia at about the same time. She had had to leave her home in Breslau and desperately needed to find a place to live, so father consented to take her in, rather than a stranger. Their quarters were now a little congested, but it wouldn't be forever. As soon as the war was over...*Yes*, Claire thought, *here we go again*. Will that war be ever over? History tells about the thirty year war, does it not? In a happy note her mother included in that letter, she wanted Claire to know that Mucki was doing well, her favorite napping time was with father on the sofa, and he was even looking for her to join him. He probably did not remember that only a few months ago he had resented to having a pet around.

Claire looked in the stores for possible Christmas gifts and decorations, but there was hardly anything to be found except here and there some simple toys for children. She decided to skimp a little now on redeeming all of her ration slips, and to save it for the holidays, so they could splurge in an imitation of past Christmas celebrations. It helped that Amelia had most of her meals at the center, although she had to leave some of her ration coupons there, however, every little bit helped. Claire's small apartment was separated from Amelia's by a hallway, but the two women spent most of their time together in Amelia's living room when the doctor was at home, and most of the cooking was also done in Amelia's much better equipped and larger kitchen. As a matter of fact, Amelia suggested that they combine their households, to which Claire showed some resistance. She saw advantages in it, but could not make herself give up the independence to which she had been accustomed since moving from her parents' home. Of course, Amelia's place was much more comfortable, nicely furnished and equipped, while Claire's lacked all that; her crates, filled with things she had brought along from Vienna, were now covered with various blankets, table clothes and pillows, and stood in for chairs and tables.

Claire was baking the traditional Christmas cookies, as best as she could afford. She had to admit that it became increasingly difficult for her to keep up with all her activities when the time was closing in for her day of delivery. She tried to prepare for the arrival of the baby, who would share Claire's bedroom, but needed a corner of it to be devoted just to the child's care. A crib was found by Amelia in the Center's storage, for which there was no need anymore, since only adult patients were residing there these days. Baby clothing etc. came in a large package from Bruck, including Heidi's letter expressing disappointment that Claire did not move in with her, where she could be a much more effective godmother than from the distance. Claire was grateful to have such a good friend.

It was difficult to find gifts for her friends here. She could spare one of her silk scarves which Amelia had once admired. She wrapped it in tissue paper, tied with a gold ribbon, and it looked festive. For Paul who had already announced that he would like to be invited for Christmas Eve, she embroidered a silk ribbon with ornamental designs to be used as a bookmark. Amelia had some tree ornaments in her "treasure box," and Claire found a few old wooden figurines at an antique store, which she refreshed with a little paint; a few sparklers showed up at her grocery, of all places, where you never would have expected it. It seemed their little Christmas tree would look festive after all. War activities were reported to slow down a little also, but.....

"Peace on Earth?" Don't hold your breath," Claire said to her friends.

Christmas Eve came around, snow was on the mountains, as expected, but only a trace on the streets, so from the point of "looking a lot like Christmas" as one traditionally thinks of that season, there was not much.

"Christmas is in your heart," Paul had reminded his friends a couple of days ago.

As it turned out, Amelia could not join them on Christmas Eve, as she had to be on duty at the center. All unmarried and childless employees, including the medical staff, had to replace those with family obligations. Amelia was torn between disapproving Paul's visit in her absence and seeing Claire spending that most important feast day alone and depressed. Neither Claire nor Paul thought of changing their plans anyway, and Claire was nearly as excited about the evening as in the days of her childhood. She knew in her heart that she should really be mindful of all the sad things happening in her life, but she also longed to be happy for a few hours, to allow the Christmas spirit to enter her heart.

Paul came with an armful of precious firewood which would provide the living room with warmth for the evening. Claire put the last decorating touches to the tree, and Paul admired the results of her efforts. She brought from the kitchen her previously prepared tray with snacks of smoked trout, Liptauer cheese, even some slices of ham, and good dark freshly baked bread. On a silver tray were her delicious cookies, made from her old Christmas recipes, changed to use less sugar and less butter, just as published in Paul's newspaper, she told him laughingly. They had plenty of hot tea with rum for the festive occasion. The latter made her bubbly and loosened her tongue enough to tell about Christmas times when she was a child. They were happy times, but she always regretted that she was an only child since her little brother had died when he was very young; she always had hoped to have many children of her own.

Paul said he too was an only child, but there were always many cousins around, therefore he never felt lonely; as far as wanting to have children of his own, these thoughts had occurred to him only lately. He admitted to having been a rather wild youngster, not easily tamed, and often enough he got into trouble at school; but since he was a good student, his good grades provided him with more protection from serious reprimands and punishment. He was eleven when, wanting to show off, he had climbed a large old oak tree, trying to balance himself on a long branch. The branch broke, he fell to the ground and broke his leg in several places. It put him into a cast for half a year, and that is where the taming process finally succeeded, at least as far as physical prowess was concerned. When the breaks had healed, they found that his left leg was several centimeters shorter than his right one. That was about twenty-five years ago, and his doctors concluded that nothing could be done to remedy it. At first he was angry about it, but learned to accept it soon enough, thanks to the wise guidance of his parents. They had always indulged his friskiness and he was brought up with the idea that a child should not be restrained too much to express himself freely. He had to obey certain rules as to acceptable behavior, but if he chose to climb a tree again even after the accident, they did not prevent him. He had to learn to make his own decisions very early. His parents were of the opinion that a child would turn out healthier that way, than when facing restrictions all his life. Paul forgot the name of the child psychologist who was then the guru for many parents with his advise about child raising. Paul did not know if his methods were sound, but his relationship with his parents had always been a good and loving one, even now. Paul continued:

"After that accident, I could not run around as much anymore and I had to learn to face the teasing the kids heaped upon me because of my limp. Although I did not like it, it did not hurt my psyche very much. I turned to things I was good at, swimming for instance. Having lived on the lake all my life, water sports have been part of my life since I can remember. I was a very good swimmer and often won awards on the school's swim team. I became a sailor and competed in lots of boat races. I always loved to read, and my father gave me the job of editing some of the manuscripts that were sent to his publishing business. I may have been diagnosed as handicapped by the doctors, but never by myself. You must have noticed, Claire, that I am really quite sure of myself and often even brazen-did I not invite myself to spend this loveliest of all the nights of the year with the loveliest of all maidens?"

Claire laughed loud and said that she could hardly imagine him as a rambunctious youngster, but to fantasize about having a son like him instead of a namby pamby weakling would just thrill her. Paul looked pleased.

Then they lighted the tree, played some Christmas music on Amelia's record player, even sang "Silent Night" together. Paul had a lovely baritone voice that mingled well with Claire's alto to the joy of both of them.

Claire brought out her little present for Paul, and he too searched his coat pocket for something he had brought for her. Paul admired Claire's fine stitchery on the bookmark, and said that he was amazed to see so many talents combined in one young lady.

Paul's present took Claire's speech away for a moment. It was a small book, bound in fine burgundy leather with gold lettering, that said: "To Claire." It contained a number of very touching love poems. The first page was inscribed: "To Claire—my inspiration—with all my love—Paul Thoene."

Claire become emotional; her eyes filled with tears, and she embraced the man before her tenderly. He looked into her eyes and said only:

"Claire, marry me!"

Claire was shocked—She did—and did not—want to understand what Paul had just said. She loved Paul—as the best friend she ever had—as the brother she imagined would have grown up to be like him—she stammered:

"Paul—you do not know what you are saying. You know that I can't marry you. I am not thinking of marrying anyone, but I do love you dearly—my friend!"

Paul was not deterred by what was obviously a refusal. He patted Claire's hand and said in a soft voice.

"I know what you are going through; I should have been more thoughtful—my feelings overcame my sensibility, forgive me. But I will tell you this: it won't be the last time that I am going to ask you the same question."

The last piece of the firewood had burned to ashes in the little pot-bellied stove, and it was close to midnight. Paul asked:

"Should we go to Midnight Mass, St. Joseph's Church is not far away?

"Oh, I would love that" Claire said, but added haltingly:

"Paul, you would not want to be seen in your town with a woman in my condition, it could be embarrassing. Don't you think so?"

"I would be honored if people would think of me as the father in the coming event. Let's go and celebrate the birth of Baby Jesus." On the way to the church, Claire asked:

"Paul, do you believe in God?"

"With all my heart," was Paul's answer, "and you?"

"I talk to Him daily."

This was Claire's Christmas in the year of 1943. It had been a year of hardships and many sorrows, but of some happiness also. She thanked God for that.

Chapter 11

Claire started to be somewhat anxious during the coming weeks. She had visited the clinic where she was supposed to give birth. They checked and found that her insurance was still in force, since she became pregnant while she still worked at the Stehle Company. She was glad about that, although her funds were still holding up, despite the fact that she had to pay rent on two apartments. The one in Vienna was quite low because of the rent-control, and the one for the apartment she was living in now was also moderate. So were her living expenses. Few things were available at the stores besides the rationed items and prices were set by the government; therefore she did not have any financial worries now, but she was thinking of the future. She would not want to have to look for a job, while the child was still an infant. Dr. Seredinsky mentioned once again, that they could combine their households and raise the child together, like a family. Claire was uncomfortable with that thought and avoided talking about it.

Her child was born on January 23rd at the maternity ward of the county hospital. It was a healthy little girl, with wonderful blue eyes, not much hair, but it seemed to be blond. Claire was ecstatic, and could hardly wait to be allowed to take that precious little bundle home, where she could take care of it the way she had always dreamed about.

Paul came to visit, and Claire was moved to tears when she saw how tenderly he took the baby into his arms and how lovingly he looked in its face. She was thinking of the man who should have been there in that position instead of Paul, and could not help but feel some bitterness, however unjustified. Claire named her daughter Elizabeth—she never forgot the name she had pledged more than seven years ago; she had not forgotten one minute of that day.

Not having thought too much about a middle name for the child before—Claire did not have one herself—she all of a sudden decided on "Paula," honoring Paul, and as a second "Heidi" after the godmother. Now it was Paul's turn to be moved, and when the child was baptized in his presence, he whispered to Claire again, "Marry me," but she did not answer.

It became obvious, even a little embarrassing, that Amelia did not seem to care for Paul's frequent visits, however short he always tried to make them. Was Amelia jealous? Why? Neither Claire not Paul, could understand, but they did not talk about it. When the weather became friendlier, Claire took Elizabeth out in the baby carriage to the park where they sometimes met when Paul took a break. He was busy, more with the newspaper business than with book publishing, and both activities were fraught with constant annoyances about censors. It had driven his father out of the business and into partial retirement, Paul said. He could not take the government's interference. Paul was not as perturbed. He had decided to conform in order to survive. What to publish and what not to publish, was like walking on a tightrope, he told Claire. Where his father exploded in the face of such curtailment of open and free reporting, Paul was willing to bite his tongue and made his reporters bite theirs, in the hope that the political climate would change again in the future.

Paul was not only kind, but wise too, Claire thought. And very handsome also, she had to admit and she hardly ever noticed that he limped. Paul was her only intellectual contact these days. Of course, one could also have an intelligent conversation with Amelia, but she was so busy, tired, and stressed from her strenuous occupation, yet she was always kind and generous towards Claire, and they did get along very well.

Little Elizabeth thrived. Claire was convinced she was the most perfect baby. The child responded to all the loving care in kind. She did not cry too much and only at certain times, started to answer her mother's endearing noises with a smile and gurgling sounds. She was pure joy. Despite that the nurses at the clinic had said that every baby has blue eyes at birth which usually soon change, Elizabeth's deepened to the sapphire color Claire knew so well.

There was no news from the Brechts, but she had an urgent letter from her father to try to come to Vienna for a visit to look after her apartment. They had wondered for a while if the housing people had not been aware that she was not living there at the moment. Many people were homeless or living in substandard and congested situations. When Claire's father had checked on the apartment recently, as Claire had asked him to do, the manager brought to his attention that official inquiries had been made about Claire's absence. It was in her own interest to look after things. The letter was somewhat accusing, Claire felt, but she could not blame her father. It was nearly a year since she had left Vienna and she had not visited once. They understood, her parents said, that with the increased insecurity in traveling, as well as the increase of bombing in the city, it was wise of her to stay away if she could, but it would be prudent to make a decision about her apartment. Was she planning to stay indefinitely in the province?

Claire knew that she could no longer postpone a visit back home. Of course, she could not take the baby along at this time, and so she asked Heidi if she could bring her there to take care of her for a couple of days. Heidi was delighted. Paul was concerned and offered to accompany Claire. She thanked him, but declined. She had to make her decisions by herself.

She took the train to Bruck, staying there for a few days, and with a heavy heart she left her little one and went alone to Vienna, where her first stop was at her apartment. Everything was in order there, except for the dust on the furniture and a musty odor from the unheated and unaired condition during such a long period. She talked to the manager who told her the same as her father had written about, namely that she had to make a decision to give up, or to sublet her place. The latter appealed to her more, because she really wanted to return to Vienna one of these days after she had found enough courage to face the consequences and explain her situation.

The manager told her of one of the tenants who had already taken in a family. They were looking for a room for their niece, who was a student at the University and had no place to stay other than on a sofa in a friend's living room. That was perfect for Claire. She met the girl the same evening, everything was arranged, and a stone fell from Claire's heart.

The next day would be devoted to her parents. On the way to their place she saw with sadness some bombed-out buildings, and there was a certain dreariness in the city that she had not seen a year ago. The streetcars were as crowded as before, but the people did not take the pushing and shoving as good humoredly as they had once. Their clothing seemed to be shabbier, as if they did not care. Everybody and everything had a drab look, it seemed that even the once famous "Springtime in Vienna," which had inspired poets and music makers through the years, was dust colored this year. Songs that were heard now were often parodies of old ones, where the once sentimental words were substituted by commentaries on the present life, such as...*just be patient, maybe next December we may get again another egg on our ration card.* Some humor remained but it was grim humor.

Friedrich and Rosemarie Baumann were glad to see that their daughter had regained her health and even looked a little heavier than she used to be. The country had done her good. Claire could not see the same in her parents. They looked frail and so much older than she remembered them. Her mother was still only in her fifties, and her father should not look stooped and have shaking hands at sixty years of age. During her train ride to Vienna she had given some thoughts to possibly confronting her parents with her secret life, to finally tell them the truth and unburden herself from the lie that she carried on her conscience all that time. Now she could see that it would benefit only her, and put another load on them which they did not deserve to have to carry.

Rosemarie had scrimped on their own meals for days in anticipation of Claire's visit, in order to prepare a more festive meal. Claire was sorry she had not anticipated the situation and brought some things from home. There she had also no abundant food supplies, but with Amelia's taking many meals at the clinic, it was a little easier to manage. She decided to leave all her own unused ration coupons here when leaving the next day. By dinnertime, cousin Catherine had come home from work and joined them. Claire was glad to see that they all seemed to get along well and noticed that Catherine in some way had taken her place in caring for her parents. She was feeling a little envious, or was it guilt? Another thing surprised her. Her dear old Mucki, the cat, could care less about seeing her formerly beloved mistress. She gave her a look that could be interpreted as that of a lover who had found solace in a new and much better relationship, where she was not abandoned every morning for a whole day. She purred and snuggled up against Friederich's legs, and he patted her head. That man had once said that he hated pets, Claire thought in amusement, and was glad that it had turned out that way. Rosemarie said that he even took Mucki to the air-raid shelter with them, hidden in a bag, because he did not want to leave her alone.

That night there was an air raid, and Claire admired her parents, how matter of factly they reacted. Every action was planned, certain bags with important papers and valuables were always ready to be grabbed at a moments notice. They went down below into the cellar of their building, which appeared to be safe enough, at least no bomb had hit so far. Other tenants were there too; some tried to lean back in the chairs they had permanently set up and catch some sleep, some of the men even played cards. Here and there a little child was whining. There were not many people in that building, but others came from neighboring buildings also, because it was safer here. After a while they heard the sounds of airplanes above, then everybody started to listen, and when there was no immediate shaking nor the sound of a blast, they relaxed. As long as it was not in their neighborhood.

The Baumann's showed the strain of being interrupted many nights from their sleep in such a manner, and Claire felt sorry and helpless. She thought again how fortunate she was to have found a refuge in Carynthia. She had told her parents in her letters that she was working for a newspaper, and could therefore now explain that her schedule was very tight and she had to return as quickly as possible. Then she noticed that she did not need to worry that they would be disappointed about her rushed departure. Life was difficult these days and even the visit of a beloved daughter could be stressful. There was enough sadness between them that she could not add to it by telling them about her own situation. Mother had asked about Stefan and Claire had told what she knew. They felt that Claire was holding something back, but believed it had to do with Stefan, and she was glad that they did not ask further. Lying was so distasteful to her, yet sometimes it could not be avoided.

Claire returned once more to her apartment before leaving for her return trip. She was going to arrange a few things for the young woman who was ready to move into the guestroom. Claire's own bedroom and the living room would be closed off, but she wanted to be sure it was in good order. She looked somewhat nostalgically around her belongings, comparing the comfort here with her modest situation in Velden, and hoped that one of these days she would return and take up life here again. It would be a changed life, that she knew, but she had confidence that she could handle it. Then she thought of Grandmother's silver tea service, which was stored in the bedroom closet. She decided to take it with her, it would bring some luxury into her humble abode in Velden. She also looked into the drawers of her dresser and found Stefan's photo, which at one time a jealous man had hidden there. She smiled, thinking about that, and wanted to take it back with her also. On second thought, however, she put it back on her nightstand, where it used to be. She took some of her old photos from her childhood and younger days along to share them with her friends. A few pieces of clothing which would now fit her again, also found space in the large suitcase, and that was all. The green silk robe remained behind. It belonged to a different Claire. She was quite anxious to return to her little daughter, every hour here away from her would be wasted time.

In Bruck she found everything in the best order, the baby had been well taken care of, Heidi's boys were crazy about her and could not understand why they could not keep her. Neither did Heidi—the room for Claire was as ready as ever. Indeed, it was larger and friendlier than the one in Velden, but Claire could not make a decision to change at this time, considering also that Bruck could be a more likely target in the ongoing and apparently intensified air war. Velden had no special interest for enemy air attacks; although airraids were not unknown, bombings had not occurred.

On their return to Velden, she and her daughter were welcomed back lovingly. As much as Claire missed some of the comforts of Vienna, she knew instantly that her home would be wherever she would be with her child, be it a castle, a cottage, a room anywhere—she would be happy.

On one of their strolls through the park with the baby, Paul mentioned again that his garden would be a great place for a child to play. He had already made plans for repairing and restoring the house as soon as the displaced people living in it now would go home again. It all sounded so wonderful, Claire had to admit. Paul was very special too. She truly loved him—in a way. His kind, brown eyes under the long lashes did warm her heart when he was looking at her with that devoted gaze of a faithful dog. It was a beautiful face—and yet—no spark, no magic occurred. Intellectually, she could rationalize her feelings, but emotionally, she knew that she could not accept the lack of that mystical power that had drawn her to Peter as long as she could remember even at the beach at Kammersee when she was only a teenager. Some people call it chemistry; this sounded too banal, too commonplace. No definition could explain it.

Here was Paul, sincere, a truly good man, offering her not only his heart, but a comfortable future for herself and the child. There was Peter, wherever, who could remain only a dream. Only once in the ten years since she knew him had he had said, "I love you," yet it was enough for her.

Paul did not know anything about her past. Could he accept the truth? He was a noble man and probably would, but would not she herself always be living a lie nevertheless? It was impossible for her to forget Peter. That would not be fair to Paul.

Again, things took an unexpected turn The weather during the summer months was very pleasant. Elizabeth grew into a delightful and contented baby, and Amelia showed quite a fondness for her. One mild summer evening they were sitting on the balcony outside Amelia's living room. The baby was asleep and Claire had stretched herself comfortably in the chaise lounge, thinking that on a day like this one could almost forget the war for a little while. Not that she really ever did. It was always in the back of her mind—how could it not be. The newspapers were full of horror stories, at least horror to Claire, because she read between the lines when the heroic deeds of our brave soldiers were detailed. She always thought of all the sacrifices that went along with it. Listings of the names of the killed in the daily newspaper perturbed her, and she asked Paul why the paper published them. He explained that even if the life of a son, a husband, a dear one, is gone forever, his loved ones want everybody to know about his dying a hero; it made them proud in a perverse sort of way. Amelia looked at Claire for a long time, and said suddenly, "You are beautiful, Claire." Claire smiled as if tolerating a little joke, but Amelia continued:

"What would you say, if I said that I loved you? Would that shock you?"

"Why should it," Claire said, only half listening." I love you too."

Amelia got up from her chair, bent down towards Claire, kissed her on her mouth and touched her body. Claire drew back, not understanding, or not wanting to understand. She did not say a word, trying to hide her displeasure and her vexation. She was baffled and angry, but it was not in her nature to make a scene. She sat still for a while, and then said "Good night" and left. She could not sleep for a long time. Now she put two and two together—Amelia's resentment of Paul, her constant reminding that she and Claire could combine households, could raise Elizabeth together, and so on. How could she not have noticed Amelia's feelings before? She had always accepted them as kindness and friendship.

Amelia was not much around during the next few days and barely spoke a word when she was. Claire knew that she could not remain, that she must leave as soon as possible. She did not want to involve Paul, yet she had to tell him that her stay with Amelia had come to an end. She tried to hint that there had been some disagreement, without having to tell him details. She did not have to, Paul was sensitive enough to guess, for he had once heard some rumor about Amelia. However, he had wanted to give her the benefit of the doubt and not to misinterpret her kindness towards Claire. It was a mistake, he should have told Claire. He wanted to help her find another place but this was quite difficult now, the area was choked with refugees, displaced persons, and others.

Chapter 12

Claire had already made up her mind what she had to do. She wrote to Heidi that she would now accept her offer to stay with her. Paul had to admit that this was a good solution for now. He was distraught about her leaving, but offered to help her move, for which she was grateful, promising always to stay in touch. She would miss him terribly, and he would be welcome in Bruck whenever he could get away. She would find a place for him to stay, Heidi would surely help there. Within one week everything was arranged. For Amelia's sake, who after all had been kind and helpful to her in many ways despite the last unfortunate incident, Claire declared that she had finally given in to her friend's urging to come and stay with her. Amelia knew better, but nothing was said and the parting was cool. Paul took all the responsibilities connected with the move upon himself, so that Claire had just to take care of Elizabeth. When they arrived in Bruck, they were greeted with a heartwarming welcome. Heidi had heard about Paul before and was now impressed by his charming and thoughtful ways. How could Claire resist him and his generosity for so long? Did she not know that men like that were hard to find—if ever? Paul left with the promise to come often, maybe every other weekend if that was all right? Heidi said that she could still furnish a small attic room in her house with necessities for overnight stays.

Heidi had a surprise for Claire. At the nearby high school, where her husband Edi used to teach before entering the military, there was a part-time opening for a teacher of English and History. She was sure that Claire would qualify, and since Heidi was a good friend of the principal, Dr Grete Rosegger, she could speak for her. She would be glad to take care of the baby for the few morning hours every day. Claire was hesitant at first, but then realized it would be a good solution in many ways. Her first thought went of course to Elizabeth, but she knew that Heidi would be an excellent substitute mother. Since her own boys were already in Kindergarten and Nursery school, her mornings had been almost lonely. She ached to take care of a little one again. Besides, Claire needed both an addition to her funds and also some intellectual stimulation; teaching had never been too far off her mind.

Things seemed to fall into place. She did get the job. Approaching nasty fall weather reminded her of the coming winter. Wood and coal had to be purchased for that time, but were more and more difficult to find, even in areas that were surrounded by forests like here in Bruck. Forest management had to preserve them for the future and protect them from uncontrolled cutting. Lack of fuel was not people's worst concern, however. The reports from the fronts were now changing: previously, there were always announcements of great victories but now one could also hear admissions of great losses and retreats. The newspaper columns carrying the names of men who had fallen on the battlefield grew longer and longer. The Russian army was approaching Vienna from the Hungarian border, and reports of more and more bombings in that city itself came through. Finally, at the end of November, Claire was informed that the building where her apartment had been located, had received a direct hit, and had been destroyed. She was surprised that she did not even feel agonized about such news. So many people were losing their possessions and more, the lives of loved ones; who should care about mere material losses? She was very concerned about her parents though, but they assured her in letters that they had been spared so far.

Paul came and suggested he accompany her to Vienna, if she felt like looking at her place to find out if anything could be salvaged. This time she accepted his offer gratefully. They thought that they might need a couple of days to do that and arranged it for the next weekend. A safe train ride was an additional concern, but so far the train route to Vienna had not been bombed.

After their arrival in Vienna they went immediately from the train station to her place, observing much devastation in the streets on their way. The three upper stories of the building in which her apartment used to be were in ruins, but a few of the tenants were crawling through the debris to find what might have survived of their former belongings. Claire looked from the street, which was also covered with rubble, and could not see anything which could be identified. Her "Biedermeier" chest was on her mind—she mourned its loss when she did not see even a trace of it, but caught herself quickly and was ashamed to be looking for things even before asking if people had been hurt. She saw a light through the window of the still standing first floor, where the manager used to live, and, indeed, she found the woman and her place in general good condition, aside from cracked walls and much dust. Frau Lucich said she was glad to see Claire, although Claire did not feel her friendliness was genuine. To her anxious inquiries if anyone had been hurt, the manager assured her that everybody in the building's shelter had escaped, dusty but with only a little discomfort, however, all their belongings were destroyed. Some of the tenants had found remnants here and there, but not much. While she was talking, she tried to cover her dining room table with her large body, and when Claire looked closer it appeared to her that she saw a few porcelain pieces looking like the *Meissen* she had owned. For a moment she felt anger, but then reason replaced it. What if the woman had retrieved more than was her own? Claire had left it, knowing very well that one day it could be lost like that. She had preserved her life, her baby's—what value could trinkets have now for her?

Paul had also observed and said nothing. Claire could not avoid tears and feelings of anguish despite her resolve not to mourn material losses. Paul tried to comfort her, leading her gently through the rubble back into the street. They went to Claire's parent's house. It was undamaged, and the old and architecturally significant building in neo-baroque style looked as prosperous as before. Inside, it was not the same. Neglect in upkeep, painting, etc., for several years now, showed itself very clearly.

Rosemarie was at home, Friederich had gone to see if the grocer had finally received a few food items for distribution. Rosemarie had not expected Paul, and was somewhat surprised. Well mannered as always, she refrained from asking the probing questions which were on her mind. Claire had just introduced Paul as a friend from Carynthia, who was trying to help her assess the damage to her place. There was nothing to be found, she said. Rosemarie nodded, they had been there also, and when they saw the damage they could not fathom that there could have been anything left. Rosemarie expressed great sadness over all that was lost, and remembered many things that had not only been valuable, but also a precious memory to her; she started to cry bitterly, but dried her tears quickly when she heard Friederich open the door. He did bring home some bread, a little bit of sugar, and also some dried beans. He said it was remarkable that despite all the bombings and the interrupted transportation routes, food distribution remained well organized. Even if people sometimes had to wait a little longer for its arrival, the terms on the ration coupons were always a promise kept. He accepted Paul's presence without question, but asked a little testily, how the conditions in the province were. They probably had a better chance to procure additional food from the farmers, and how about cigarettes? Claire felt that she should have made some effort to bring a food package or at least some cigarettes with them, although despite the city people's wrong assumptions, there was no more available in the country either. The visit was not as happy as she had wished for. Everybody seemed to be on edge these days, and who could blame them? Claire said they had to leave to catch their train. Her parents expressed the hope that they had a safe ride home, and did not urge a longer visit.

On the train ride back to Bruck, Claire tried to find an explanation why her parents did not seem the way she had previously described them to Paul when talking about her happy childhood. She was depressed about it, but Paul assured her that he understood completely. Vienna was no longer the old city of song and dance; it was suffering now. How could she think that everything would have remained the way she would like to remember it? More than ever, Claire was grateful for Paul's presence, and she snuggled against him on the wooden bench in the crowded and unheated train compartment. He put his arms around her to keep her warm and thought: *One of these days she will say yes.* Claire thought at the exact same time: *One of these days I may love him the way he deserves to be loved, but I still cannot.*

Another Christmas ahead and it was a happy day only in the eyes of the little children around who did not comprehend. A few cookies, candles on the tree, an old doll that had been restored, a wooden soldier repainted— they could still be pleased with small presents, but for the adults it was even sadder than last year's. People no longer hoped for a good outcome to the war. They had stopped believing in the "Wunderwaffe," that was supposed to bring an end to it. What had happened? One had still to be careful not to express doubts in public. Such would be reason enough to land you in jail for a while. Some of the older boys in Claire's school were inducted into military service, and when she saw the sixteen-year-olds in uniform, her heart felt like crumbling. She was also terribly concerned about the rumors that the Russians were close enough to invade any day now. Everybody surmised they would be cruel, would rape the women, and kidnap all the children, who would then be shipped back to Russia and raised to become good and loyal Communists, and no one would hear from them again. Paul warned against believing such nonsense, stories that were told about any invading enemy force throughout history, but he was really not so sure himself what to expect. Claire hoped that the Americans and their other allies who were slowly approaching from the West would come first. If not, she would take the baby in the carriage and walk westwards to meet them. She thought they were civilized nations, and whatever might happen otherwise, her child could not be taken away from her. The baby carriage had a deep bottom, where she could store enough food for the child, and she herself would survive on whatever could be found. Claire, the intelligent, accomplished business woman, school teacher, sound of mind in all ways, found herself thinking and feeling like any ignorant peasant mother when confronted with a big threat to her child, true or imagined. Heidi was not as pessimistic as Claire, but she would take her boys and join Claire in her wandering westward also. Paul came for Christmas, but had no good news either. The stories that came his way officially, were as distorted as any rumors from the street, therefore he did not want to pass them on to his friends but he tried to calm Claire's anxieties.

A loyal few kept on with the old party line, that the Fuehrer would save them all. Not many believers were still left, many had paid for their convictions with their lives on the battle field. Bruck, with its iron ore mining, was an industrial center and many of its working class people privately considered themselves communist sympathizers, wherefore they hoped for better treatment from a possible Russian occupation. Even though people worried, there was no noticeable panic, rather a stoic acceptance of the inevitable. Friends of Heidi packed their valuables into crates and buried them in hidden places in the forest. Claire and Heidi decided against that, their concern was not for material losses. Claire had hardly anything left, except for a few pieces of jewelry and her grandmother's silver.

Train travel was severely curtailed, but Paul still made it occasionally, a bright light for the women in the house, as well as the one year old Elizabeth who reacted with special pleasure when seeing her "Uncle Paul," as she called him, the words not very clearly pronounced but still distinguishable by those concerned.

Claire's part-time teaching job worked out fine for her. She liked the variety it brought into her life, and since the school was close by, she never felt too much away from the child. The school holidays were often extended because of lack of heating fuel, and she could spent much time with Elizabeth. She tried to make up for the student's lost school time by being extra careful that the given time was fully utilized. She herself studied the subjects carefully and prepared her lessons and tests so that no valuable time was wasted. She was happy too that the children responded well, although in the beginning they had missed the fooling around, which previous teachers had tolerated. The contact with the students was very beneficial to Claire. Not only did she like her pupils, but the job occupied her mind enough not to let it go astray with unnecessary brooding about her precarious future.

Sitting at the kitchen table one evening, bundled up warm because there was no heat from the stove, Claire was correcting test papers, while Heidi tended to mending her boys' clothes, when a knock on the front door startled them. Heidi went to see who would come to visit that late at night, and encountered a tall man in a heavy coat, a scarf around his neck and his hat low on his forehead, so she could not see his face very well. He lifted his hat and inquired politely:

"Good evening. Is this the residence of the Karner family?"

Heidi's heart skipped a beat. She hoped that the stranger did not bring bad news about her husband, which could happen these days. She just nodded her head, when the man said:

"I apologize for the late intrusion. I understand that Miss Baumann resides here also. I just arrived on the train from Vienna, and would like to bring greetings to her from her parents." Relieved and almost jolly, Heidi said:

"Yes, yes, she is here, come in." The stranger followed her to the kitchen. Claire looked up and their eyes met.

"Peter..." she stammered, and felt so weak that she could barely rise from her chair. Peter drew nearer and caught her in his arms before her knees gave away under her. When she recovered, she still held on with the feeling that she never would let go—never again. Peter himself was overwhelmed with emotions which he hardly dared admit to himself.

Heidi, who was observing the drama playing out in front of her in the meantime said, as if it were just a casual reunion, "Why don't you go into the living room, I'll make some hot tea to warm us up."

Claire and Peter followed her suggestion, and sat down on the sofa in the living room. Soon Heidi brought the tea and a couple of blankets, apologizing that the room was unheated but unfortunately it could not be helped. Then she left them alone.

Claire was still speechless—she wondered if it was a dream, did she fall asleep? *If so, I don't want to wake up for a while, I want to dream for a long time.*

Well, it was not a dream. Peter held her tightly in his arms, stroked her hair gently and, as was his way, did not say a word. His heart was pounding just the same, and happiness, not felt for a long, long time, overcame him also. Then Claire said—and felt it was a dumb question:

"What are you doing here, Peter?"

"Finding you, dearest Claire." Claire poured the tea:

"How did you find me? Only my parents know my whereabouts, and I asked them not to tell."

"That is exactly what your father told me, but your mother gave me your address secretly, when I was leaving and she saw my distress. Are you angry, Claire?"

"No—no and no again" She looked into those sapphire blue eyes which she loved since she could remember, and when he embraced her again, she felt the same magic power that always had overcome her in his presence. There was no explanation for it, she had no thoughts, only feelings as if she were melting into his embrace, becoming just a part of him. Some time passed in silence, but then there was need for explanations from both sides.

"Peter, first tell me, so I can prepare myself—when are you leaving?"

"I will not leave you ever again."

"How can that be, Peter? I have tried so hard to accept that it is not possible and—as happy as I am at this moment, it probably is not good to open old wounds again."

Peter then began to tell his story, hesitantly at first, because it contained much pain and anguish, but ending with great expectations for their future:

When he had left Claire on that fateful April day in 1943 in Vienna, he did so with a heavy heart. Happiness and despair were constantly changing in his soul. The usual situation awaited him on his arrival at home. After telling Marlena that he had definitely decided not to take up a practice in Vienna—the meeting he had in Vienna was with a former colleague who had offered him a partnership in his clinic was for the purpose of seeing how something like that might work out—Marlena declared that the prospect of living in Vienna had been her last hope of ever being happy again. Peter was not surprised at her reaction; he had heard the same comments many times before. He also knew her constantly changing moods. He told her that his decision was final; he simply was not suited to serve the wealthy sick, he remained a country boy and that's where they were going to stay. Marlena countered that she would leave him, she had enough of the smelly country air, the simplicity of the provincial people. It would be better if he granted her a divorce, which she wanted now more than ever.

At that moment, Peter was thinking the same. Would it not be easy to throw the whole bundle of discontent on both sides overboard, let her have her way, and find a new life for himself and the love he had had to deny. He could not do that. Marlena did not know it herself, but she was not capable of taking care of herself, as much as she thought so. She was intelligent, and her accomplished academic studies gave credit to her abilities, but they did not extend to her emotional life; she was confused. Peter had suggested again and again that she consult a psychiatrist, but, of course, she found the suggestion insulting and refused.

Peter's further consideration was also in regard to his family and his practice. Divorce in that part of the country was not as accepted as in the metropolitan city of Vienna. He also had to admit that he himself shunned the idea of being divorced. He was not a religious man in the "church-going" sense, but was nevertheless conservative enough in his thinking that a moral person could not break a commitment made before God and the world. That was how his life continued during the months of 1943. Peter had submerged himself in his work, where he found much solace.

The year 1944 started out to be mostly the same. Much of his practice included many of the now returning servicemen, who had many ailments, and though they were often taken care of in military hospitals, some of their needs spilled over into his practice. Peter liked to be busy, and his patients provided distraction from his wandering thoughts of Claire and his regrets for having made the wrong choices in his life.

Shortly before the end of January, the message came to the Burghoffs which every family with a loved one serving in the military dreaded : their son Hans had died *a hero's death in the service for the Fuehrer and his country*. That is how the official notices always said it. Even knowing that a such a fate can befall ones own family, when the reality hits, it seems so unexpected. Hans, the beloved son and brother, was no more? As a doctor, Peter was often confronted with having to bring such news to despairing loved ones and he felt compassion for their sorrow, but when it came to his own person, he was greatly affected. He had loved his brother dearly and his loss caused much pain and anguish.

At that point in Peter's story, Claire felt great empathy for his sorrow. She knew what that brother meant to him and how close they had been since childhood, despite their differences in character and life style.

After a few moments Peter continued to tell how the family had tried to cope. Mother showed remarkable strength, and despite her grief, she kept the household running the same as before the tragedy had struck. Peter's father, on the other hand, was a broken man. Hans had always been his favorite son, he was the one who would continue to keep the Burghoff farm alive for generations to come, just as he himself had. The future of the estate was utmost on his mind. Would Peter be willing to give up his chosen career to become a farmer? Father and son were both struggling with that question. Peter was torn between haunting feelings of obligations and the knowledge that he could not give up his life in the medical world, but what about his father's plight?

Peter was concerned about his father's mental and physical health. One day around that time, Father Grumbacher stopped by at the Burghoffs to ask Anton for his ideas as to how to help a refugee family from Hungary, whose care had been entrusted to him by the bishop. The man in that family, in his early fifties, had been the manager of a large estate in Hungary, was versed in raising livestock: cattle and sheep. That was why Father Grumbacher thought of seeking Anton's advice first. He said that he thought Janosh Szolti was an honest man. His wife had done most of the cooking on the now defunct Hungarian estate, was therefore used to serving in some household capacity also. She was a little whiny and homesick, but Janosh seemed to be in control and of their two teenage sons also. Father Grumbacher said that according to his own investigation of the family, they could be very useful help on a farm. Of course, he did not say that he had come to Anton with the idea to place the Szoltis on the Burghoff farm, but in his judgment it was a good possibility. Anton did not say much at first, but then talked it over with Peter, who interviewed the Szolti family. He did not care much for the two boys, but found the father solid and knowledgeable. Financially it would be a burden on the Burghoffs to hire a manager, but with Anton getting older, and Hans now gone, some plans for the future had to be made. Once normal times returned, the farm would also become more profitable again when the government restrictions were removed.

The labor exchange approved the hiring of the Hungarians, and Peter was also relieved of some of his obligations on the farm. Hanna was only partially satisfied; she had no intention of giving up even part of her responsibilities, no matter how good a cook Annushka, the Hungarian wife, might be. At least that was so at first. Soon she became so busy with bookkeeping and organizing her part that she found enough work for Annushka also.

It was getting close to midnight, and Claire began to wonder, if she should offer Peter the room in the attic which Paul used on his visits. She said she would make another pot of tea—sorry, no coffee in the house for a long time—on the little gasoline burner they used when the gas was cut off to the stove at this time of night. When she came back with the tea, Peter said, that he was aware it was getting late, but if she could bear with him a little longer, he would like to tell all before he had to leave on the first morning train. Peter continued:

"Just when I thought that our life would somehow find some normalcy, another tragedy came our way. Marlena—did I say, that we had not had any marital relations for a long time?—not months, but years…Well, Marlena wanted to drive to Salzburg to go shopping, well knowing that I could not let her have the car. With the stringent control of gasoline, I can use the car only for visits to patients and for similar professional needs. It is out of the question to ever use it for private business. At present, I don't even have the use of the car anymore because of lack of fuel. I did not know what was on her mind that time. I was abrupt with her and she was angry. Shortly thereafter, I heard the front door slam and the car starting. I was annoyed, but she was already gone, and I could not do anything about it. I only hoped that she would not be seen using the car by people in town; it would give reason for reprimands from the authorities.

"It was not more then half an hour later, when the town's gendarme appeared at my door and told me that there had been an accident on the road to Salzburg and my wife was involved. We rushed to the scene. I will spare you the details. The front end of the car was pushed in like an accordion. A mechanic tried to extricate Marlena and had to cut metal parts away from her. The ambulance was waiting but it was too late, she was dead. She had collided head-on with a heavy truck. Luckily, the truck driver was only slightly injured. He stammered in shock that he had no way to avoid her, she was coming very fast straight at him."

Claire had cried out at Peter's words. Peter continued after a few moments, trying to collect himself also.

"I don't need to describe the state of my mind at that moment. I was distraught, and felt tremendous guilt, thinking how Marlena must have been upset when she left home after our quarrel. It came to my mind that she might have acted on purpose, that she had wanted to die, but I abandoned that thought, because Marlena was too selfish to think of ending her life. If I had been more understanding, kinder, more tolerant, she might not have been so angry when leaving the house. It was all my fault. The next few days

I was hardly able to think rationally, and was only too grateful when Dr. Krieger took over my patients' care.

"I finally received the autopsy report. It was unbelievable, but Marlena had not died in the accident, she had had a stroke, a brain embolism, caused by a tumor that had been growing for years and must have caused her often inexplicable outbursts and mood changes. Poor Marlena! If she just had submitted to medical examination, maybe she could have been helped. The neurologists at the hospital had their doubts. The tumor was situated such that a safe operation would not have been possible.

"I had always had my suspicions that Marlena's character was based on a medical problem, but was thinking more of a psychological than a physical one. I had little training in either of the medical fields that affected her. The findings were, of course, a great relief for me, especially with regards to Eva who had shown a temper very similar to her mother's. But I did not have to fear a genetic disorder; when she was evaluated by experts I was assured that she was completely healthy. Love and attention may cure her hostile behavior.

"Eva did not seem to miss her mother. She had had very little attention from her before, and not much had changed, except that my mother decided Eva should live with her on the farm for a while. The nursemaid was to come along also. I was so sad to see that nobody really liked the child—and accused myself for not showing enough love either—because of her refusal to bond with anybody. My nurse at the clinic suggested giving Eva a little dog to keep her company. I was not sure that she would not be cruel to the animal, but I relented. We found a young black and white spaniel, and told Eva that not only was he hers alone, but she had to take care of him in every way. She was pensive at first, but then, to everybody's surprise, took to the animal with a devotion and love one would never have suspected in her. The dog responded in kind and the two are now inseparable. A little nurse in my office knew more about treating a dysfunctional child than all the medical experts I had consulted.

"Weeks had gone by since the accident. I would be a liar not to admit that my thoughts of you were now on a different plane. You had never been out of my mind even for a day, but Marlena's death brought a different situation into light. I was ashamed to think of Marlena's death as the opportunity to be able to start a new life with you. I turned my full attention to my patients, and tried not to let my personal feelings come to the forefront, but finally decided to seek advice.

"It came by accident when I met one of my old classmates from the boarding school. We had been best friends there, but had lost track when our professional lives went in different directions. He went into the theological field, which surprised me because in our school days discussions both of us were critical of our religious indoctrinations, disliked some of the fanatics in the rank of the teachers, etc. I did not hear from him for years, and heard only later that he had become a priest, was successful and on a ladder to achieve rank in the church's hierarchy, and is now a bishop. I saw Franz Hinterberger when he visited a patient at the hospital. Consequently we had dinner together a few times, and renewed our old friendship. There was no one I could more easily turn to in my confused state of mind. My mother had always been my best friend, but I could not share this with her.

"I told Franz everything. It was almost like a confession to a priest in church, for which I never had a taste before, because I did not believe that one's sins could be forgiven just by paying the penalty of saying a few *Ave Maria's*.

"Well, I found out that confessions are beneficial. Franz was not only a priest but the friend I needed. He acted with understanding and sympathy, and let me see things clearly. He encouraged me to follow my heart. Guilt feelings had no place in my life, they are destroyers and not worthy of my soul. Of course, that was just the gist of what was said, we had many conversations, and I soon began to feel better and free of my previous inhibitions.

"I tried to phone you, but was told the telephone had been disconnected. The same with your parent's phone. That did not surprise me, because civilian telephone service was curtailed all over. I sent a letter, which was returned to me as 'non deliverable.' That disturbed me more. As soon as I could get away, I planned to take the train for a day to Vienna to see you. When I finally managed that, I found no response at your apartment. The manager was not helpful, she said only that you were out of town, and she did not know more. I went to your parents' home. No one at home there. I was in some ways relieved that you had left Vienna, because bombing made life there difficult, but wished to find you somehow. Several weeks passed again with so much work in my practice, the hospital filled with patients who needed my immediate attention. Whenever I could, I also spent time at the farm. They needed my help in many ways. Father retreated more to his forest lab and concentrates now more than ever on experimenting and growing trees from seeds. The Hungarian manager is a God-send—he does a good job. My mother copes in her natural way as the strong survivor of calamities.

"After Christmas—sadder this year because of the losses that occurred in the family and in the country—I decided I could not bear to wait any longer. I went to Vienna again, and to your apartment, and saw to my horror that it was no more, the rubble heaped upon buried treasures, but not my memory of the room on the once third floor. I immediately went to your parents' home and found it to my relief intact. My hope to find you there, and the fear that I would not, almost strangled my words when your father opened the door. He did not know who I was, but your mother came to my rescue and asked me to come in.

"I said that I had to get in touch with you urgently, and hoped to find you with them. Your father was very curt with me and said that you had left Vienna more than a year ago and did not want your whereabouts known to anyone. As far as they knew, you were well. I pleaded with him for your address, but he was adamant. I left shortly, greatly disappointed. On my way out, I found your mother putting a slip of paper into my pocket. It was your address—too bad I could not thank her openly, but in my heart I gave her thousand thanks. And here I am, Claire, overjoyed to have found you at last. Why did you keep your address a secret?"

While Peter was talking they had sat together on the sofa, wrapped in the blankets which Heidi had provided. It was cold in the room, but they did not notice. Up to now, Claire had not even been aware that she must be quite a sight, bundled up in that quilted flannel house coat and the old woolen sweater. Claire's face reddened with embarrassment about her appearance but also with excitement. If Peter noticed her outfit, he did not say. He seemed to be tired and emotionally drained. He had not talked that much and that long ever before.

"Forgive me for having taken all that time to tell about myself, but I was going to make sure you knew everything. It was important to me. But now, you have to tell me about yourself."

"There is not so much to tell. Did you know that the Stehle company closed the Vienna office? I got the news about their intent to do so the same day you left. They did give me time to find myself another position. The parting was not easy for me, and even less, of course, was the knowledge that I would not see you ever again. The time we spent together on your visit, and the knowledge of our love, would be forever in my heart, therefore happiness and sadness at the same time filled my days. The job termination left me with a long list of duties still to be performed, which was beneficial to my state of mind. I had to think about so many other things and people, and could not dwell on my personal problems. I decided to take a break, and visit my friend Heidi in Bruck before looking for another position. When I finally closed the door to my office I felt so drained and unusually weak, that I went to see our family doctor upon my friends' suggestions. He told me that I was severely anemic, and suggested a few weeks of recuperation at a clinic in Velden. And that is what I did." Claire stopped...how to go on now? Peter asked:

"Can I ask about your fiancée—you know, the photo on your nightstand, the dashing soldier?"

Claire took the interruption as an excuse to go into her room at the end of the hallway, where Elizabeth was slumbering sweetly in her crib. She covered her with another warm blanket, took Magda von Brecht's letter from her desk drawer and went back into the living room. She handed the letter to Peter and asked him to read it himself. When he had finished, he returned it to Claire, and said:

"Poor devil, I am so sorry—it must have been a terrible shock for you also." Claire did not answer, but after a few moments she took a deep breath and said:

"Peter, I have to show you something, please come with me. "Quietly, so as not to disturb Heidi and her children upstairs, she led him into her bedroom. Peter saw the sleeping child in her crib, and did not understand.

"This is Elizabeth, our daughter, Peter."

Peter's face reddened, his voice did not seem to function, until he finally burst out:

"Claire, how could you have kept that from me?" He seemed to be angry, confused—different than Claire had imagined and hoped that he would react. At first, she did not say anything, then asked quietly:

"Peter, what should I have done? Burden your life with that knowledge?"

"Yes," he said, "did I not have a right to know?"

"I did not think of your rights, Peter, but of what would be best for all of us. To my great distress, it involved getting used to live a life of lying. I did not want to burden you with the knowledge of my condition, for which even you could not have had a solution."

Peter interrupted, still angry, it seemed:

"You thought I would not help you, be with you?"

"Yes, Peter, I know that you would have—you would have come to see me, guilt-ridden to do so. I would have accepted you with open arms and be filled with happiness. Then you would have left after a day or two, more guilt in your heart, and I would be left alone again, sad and miserable. Should that be our future? I could not accept that. I did not tell my parents either. At first I had the intention to do so, but when I saw them suffering under all the distress of their daily life, I could and would not add to it. They would not only worry about me, but even more, their disappointment in their daughter would have been too much for them to bear. My doctor's advice to find renewed health in good country air, came so opportunely for me to explain my leaving Vienna.

"I saw my parents the next time only after Elizabeth was born, and if I had dared to tell them about it then, I found again, that the time was not right. By then it was probably not more only my concern for them which did not let me speak, but also cowardliness. The longer one lies, the harder it becomes to tell the truth, is that not so?"

"And your friends, and Stefan?"

"Of course, I felt very guilty towards Stefan. I had to tell him the truth. But when? I had not heard from him for weeks, so I assumed that he was involved in serious battles. Should I send the proverbial 'Dear John' letter at such a time? It had to wait until he came back. I had no illusion that Stefan's strict sense of honor would not be able to forgive me, but at least I wanted to tell him in person. You know now what happened since. And my friends? Only Heidi knew the truth from the beginning, and remained my moral support throughout. In Velden I found good friends again, for which I am grateful. I will tell you about them at a later time."

Peter had listened intently—his initial anger subdued, but he was still uncomfortable with the new situation, he felt he should have been told long before. Claire had spoken very softly while standing beside the crib, looking lovingly at the sleeping child, who started to become restless and woke. When she saw her mother, she smiled, reassured by her presence, stretched her little arms towards her, and called "Mommy" Claire picked her up, and keeping her in her arms, sat down on the chair next to the bed. When Elizabeth noticed the strange man standing close by, she turned to her mother and asked:

"Uncle?"

"No, Elizabeth, this is your Papa—can you say 'Papa'?"

The child looked up shyly at Peter, not saying anything at first, but leaning her head against her mother's shoulder, she finally said "Papa."

Peter watched the scene before him with great emotion. He saw an angelic looking baby with blond curls and deep blue eyes, just like his mother's, nestled in its mother's arms. It reminded him for an instant of the painting of Raphael's, *Madonna and Child*. Despite his denying it often, his religious background remained a part of him. He kneeled down and embraced the woman and her child, hiding his tears by turning his head. He did not say a word, but Claire understood it all and was filled with happiness. He had accepted it all.

Elizabeth became restless and rubbed her eyes, a sure sign that the child was still sleepy. Claire put her back into the crib, and Peter and she quietly left the bedroom. It was nearly five in the morning and outside the winter sky was still pitch black. Claire suggested that Peter should catch some sleep himself before he had to leave, and forced him to lie down on the sofa, took his shoes off and covered him with the blankets. He let her take care of him with a grateful smile and fell asleep immediately.

Claire returned to her bedroom, to prepare for the coming day. Heidi would take care of Elizabeth, but she wanted to be sure everything needed was ready. Then she turned to her own needs, freshening up, changing clothes and so on. She was wide-awake despite the sleepless night, but she somehow felt as if wandering in a dream—a happy dream at that, but she worried about wakening up to reality. They had talked about so many things, cleared up the past, yet so much remained unsaid.

In the meantime, Heidi had come downstairs. She was full of questions, but Claire withheld the answers until later that day. However, Heidi could see happiness in her eyes, and was satisfied. The two women prepared break-fast and soon Elizabeth and Heidi's boys were at the kitchen table, noisily making their presence known to Peter, who had joined them. He observed the children's antics with amusement, Elizabeth in her high chair pounding on the table with her spoon, and having some gurgling conversation with the boys which only the three of them could understand. They were laughing and teasing each other and had to be reminded by their mothers to quiet down, which they did for about two seconds. It was a happy family scene. Elizabeth would look occasionally at the strange man across the table, with-out being intimidated. The "strange man" on the other hand, was a little shy, especially in the presence of Heidi, whom he barely knew, and whose prob-ing looks he felt. His eyes mostly followed Claire. She wore a light blue pullover and a dark skirt, her school outfit, and looked lovely to Peter. As once before, he admired her graceful moves and quiet demeanor, even under the circumstances of the present situation. He could not take his eyes off her, and his heart ached when he thought of all the hardships she had endured, many caused by him, yet he was not being reproached for them. He knew that he loved and admired her with a fervor which he never thought that he was capable of. He pledged that he would make up for all the wrong, for all the pain he had caused her. He thought of Elizabeth as a part of her—more than as a part of himself. That idea was to grow slowly, but he was happy to see a future that included all of them.

It was seven-thirty and time for Peter and Claire to leave. She wore her old winter coat that had seen better days, but the nice fur collar framed her lovely face. She looked ravishing to Peter, and when Claire opened the front door, Peter closed it for another moment. He just had to embrace and kiss her once more. When Claire could catch her breath, she asked:

"Peter, do you love me?"

"You know that I do."

"Yes, but I want you to tell me."

"I do, I do…."

"Peter, say it, please."

"Say what?"

"Oh, Peter—don't you understand? I want to hear it from your own lips."

Peter finally understood—or rather did not. How could she not know how much he loved her, did he not show it constantly?

"Claire, I love you more than you know—more than I ever thought that I could love…."

Claire kissed him again:

"Thank you, Peter, you told me only once before, and I had to hear it again. Can't you understand that?"

Peter tried and probably did. They left the house and walked part of the way together before Claire had to take the turn to her school. Peter became very serious and all business. He explained he would go back and prepare for her homecoming. There would be some necessary explanations to his family, some changes in his own house, because he wanted Claire to be able to establish their future home without reminders of the past. He was also determined, that they should marry before her arrival there, and asked her if she had any preference as to the place, and where and how they should proceed with that. Whatever pleased Peter, would please her also. He said he would carefully weigh their options, and write to her about it in his next letter. He did not know how soon he could come again, not only because of his schedule, but also if he could obtain train tickets.

Everything was acceptable to Claire, but she had to tell him about her fears of a coming invasion by the Russians. They had not talked about the political situation at all during the night, although it should have been on their minds, considering the state of the war, when losing it was nearer than any hope of the *Wunderwaffe* promised by Hitler.

Peter said that they would probably have a difficult time ahead of them, but not to worry about the Russians and not to listen to all the gossip. He admitted to sometimes secretly listening to the broadcasts, which the allied forces directed to the Ostmark, or Austria. This was strictly forbidden. They assured the Austrians that they would be liberated as a result of Germany losing the war. Peter was therefore convinced no occupation would occur, the Russians would be kept at the border with Hungary, where they were right now, and the other Allies would not enter Austrian territory from the West either. Claire was not so convinced, because in the Bruck area the small underground of communist sympathizers were spreading different views. Whatever might come now, she and her child would be safe under Peter's protection.

Chapter 13

During the following weeks Claire was happier than she could remember ever having been. The man she had dreamed about for more than twelve years, counting the time in Kammerbach as a teenager, had returned to her with as much love as she could only imagine. Heidi was happy for her too, and together they started to think about the preparations that had now to be made for Claire's final move to be with Peter. As far as the wedding was concerned, Claire wrote to Peter, that she would leave the planning up to him, but her inclination was to have a very private ceremony, and if possible attended only by the necessary witnesses. Peter agreed heartily, this was to his taste also, but would she mind if he asked his friend Dr. Franz Hinterberger, the bishop, to perform it? How about her parents? Should they not meet with them before, so he could properly ask her father for her hand. Claire had to laugh when she read that, it was so much like Peter. Doing it properly? By telling her parents also that they already had a child, which she had kept secret from them? She still did not know how to confess to that.

She had not yet told Paul what happened either. He came by just once for a short visit, interrupting his trip to Vienna. He was distraught about the war situation at the time and he had information through his business, which had made him very concerned about the future of them all. Claire was glad that his visit was not conducive for her to confront him with her own affairs, which had taken recently such a dramatic turn. She was again keenly aware that she was a great coward also. She had tried to spare the feelings of everybody she loved, and he had become a liar whom nobody would ever trust again. All the people who had considered her upstanding, trustworthy, reliable, and truthful—she could hardly recall all the glowing adjectives her former employers and friends had used in their testimonials. She confided her conflicts to Heidi, who did not agree with her self-deprecation. She had always admired Claire and found that her friend had lost nothing of her reputation by just always doing the best she could under the most difficult circumstances. Heidi's opinion gave her a boost to regain a little self-esteem, but it did not provide a solution to the underlying problem.

Peter suggested they confront her parents together, and let the chips fall as they might. He had in the meantime talked to his parents, who took his news of bringing a new wife into his life with some reservations, especially his mother, but they accepted it as their grown and accomplished son's right to conduct his life in a way he found to his liking. He told them about his love for Claire ever since he could remember, but he did not use too many words to explain why he had failed with his first choice. Peter never used too many words—it was not his nature, and they did not ask him for more. His mother could remember Claire vaguely, but had no opinion of her. She was cautiously happy for Peter.

Claire had tried to keep up some correspondence with her old friends, mainly through good wishes at holidays, when one could just express simple hopes and did not have to be detailed. One time she had received at a short note from Lieschen Woerner, to say that her husband had suggested for her to leave Vienna temporarily—at least until he came back from the war—and stay with her mother in a little town in Germany, where up to now not many casualties had occurred. Her old friends—some in the military—sent occasional greetings, and she still remembered them with saved cigarette rations, but intimate contact had almost been lost.

When a newscast reported a devastating bombing of Dresden—the true casualties of the killing of one hundred fifty thousand people in a single night became known much later—Claire was shocked. She had once been to that beautiful city, known for its art treasures as well as its architectural beauty which enchanted every visitor. The destruction there meant a loss not only for their people but for the world as a whole. Why...why...and so close to the end of the war with its outcome not depending on destroying things of absolutely no military value? It hurt to think about, and raised her concern about the Brechts also.

Claire wrote immediately, but did not hear from them in return. After a while she contacted Lieschen, maybe she could find out if they were all right via the Stehle Company. Lieschen's answer arrived in shaky handwriting. She first apologized that it had taken so long, but she had written to her husband first, to find out if he had heard anything through his contact with the company. Georg was in an outfit that was steadily retreating from the western front. He was depressed, even without the report about Dresden. When it came with the news that the Brechts had also been victims of the carnage on that fateful night, he nearly had a nervous breakdown. He was well now, but still very shaken. Lieschen added that was also true about herself. She barely managed to express her hopes for Claire's well-being, and that she wished to be back in Vienna. Germany was in a sorry state of ruin. How terribly sad. Who would now take care of Stefan? Claire had to find out about him.

Vienna also took now a terrible beating, with bombs falling not only on military objectives like industrial areas and train stations, but also destroying the world famous Opera House, the Burg theater, the largest and most monumental stage for dramatic productions in the German speaking world, and many of her famous relics. Even the Central Cemetery got hit by five hundred bombs, which caused great damage (to the already dead?) The Viennese were shocked and scared. Mail service was erratic, and Claire had not received any communication from her parents for a long time, nor did she know if her letters had been delivered to them.

One evening in the first days of May, Peter arrived unannounced with an old truck and urged that they leave immediately. The roads could be blocked at any time now, and it was already dangerous to travel during the day as he had found out. Claire packed in a hurry. Her main concern was, of course, Elizabeth, who had already been asleep when Peter arrived. Heidi cried over the abrupt parting, but was helpful in loading Claire's belongings. Peter rushed them. Claire and the baby had to stay in the back of the truck and pretend to be sick patients if they should be confronted on the road about their civilian transport. At least he could identify himself as a physician. There was no pretense anyway. Claire was worried, the baby restless and crying. The weather was nice and the skies clear, which meant air attacks were possible, but on the other hand it made the roads easier to travel. It would take them the rest of the night to get to St. Johann.

Despite their concerns everything went smoothly; they were only stopped once by a gendarme who needed to know who the travelers were, but Peter's identification cleared them. St. Johann was still asleep, and only a few people noticed their arrival. The housekeeper who had been informed by Peter at the last minute about Claire's coming, took charge She was curious, but refrained from questions. She was a kindly older woman; she suspected some tragic situation, as was the order of the day, and trusted Dr. Burghoff completely. Peter took the truck back to the farm, where he had stored his motorcycle in the meantime. He was relieved that everything had worked out well, and his loved ones were well and safe in his home. He had not forgotten his previous plans, which had included a more formal entry for Claire into her new home. Their first concern was their survival in the days to come, which were not going to be played out as he had been made to believe by listening to those secret broadcasts.

While Claire and the baby finally found some sleep, Peter went to the hospital to make his rounds as usual. Pretending to be calm, he reassured his patients' anxious questions about coming events. He was nervous too. He noticed crowds gathering in the streets, some known political people trying to act with authority, some hoping for a new importance in their lives, others just hoping to survive. It was rumored that Allied troops were on their way and the province of Salzburg would be occupied either by the by English or the Americans. The Russians had already entered Vienna two weeks earlier, making sure that their control of that area was an accomplished fact. People who had fled from there, reported that the population was mostly hiding in the air raid shelters after experiencing heavy bombing, severely curtailed utilities, even the water faucets were running slow.

When Peter returned to his home at noon, he told the nurse at his office to cancel all afternoon appointments, because he had to attend to business in Salzburg. Then he went to see Claire in the bedroom where she was still sleeping, though restlessly. He woke her and told her he had a surprise for her. When she, still a little confused, realized where she was, she wanted to know about the surprise. Peter said:

"I know, that you like formality, so there it is," and he knelt before her and said:

"Claire, I love you, will you be my wife?" Claire laughed happily, and answered:

"I will consider it, but please, keep on asking me."

Then she saw that Peter had a very serious expression on his face.

"Claire, we have to hurry, please put on your light blue dress. Do you still have it?"

Claire was bewildered:

"Yes, but somewhere in the big trunk that is still unpacked."

"Well, never mind then, find something that you like, we have to make a quick trip to Salzburg."

"Is that the surprise?"

"Yes—please hurry. I already asked Frau Maier to take care of Elizabeth for the afternoon."

Claire was a little unsure, but Peter was in charge, she noticed with some surprise. What was going on in Salzburg—was it safe to go there—and why? When they left, Peter said to Frau Maier:

"My wife and I will be back before dark, if you could prepare a nice supper for us by then, we would appreciate it. You know how to take care of the baby, don't you?"

Claire winced when Peter said "my wife." Here we go again with our next lie, she thought. Frau Maier had heard the "my wife" also, and was more than surprised about it, but it was not her place to question the doctor.

Another surprise was that Peter asked Claire to hop on the motorcycle with him.

"I am sorry not to have more appropriate transportation, but it is safe."

Finally, Claire insisted on some explanation, and as they drove out into the highway Peter screamed against the wind:

"We are going to get married."

Claire was speechless. She was holding on to the man in front of her and found some symbolism in that. She was holding on to him for dear life—for all her life—and she leaned her head against his broad back, and relaxed. "Let him take care of me from now on." She was extremely happy.

Somewhere near the city of Salzburg, they took a side road and approached a charming old church, where Dr. Franz Hinterberger was already waiting for them, dressed for the occasion. Peter had made the arrangement with his friend a few days ago. The bishop greeted them very cordially and had a few pleasant words for Claire, who was almost unable to comprehend what was going on. Peter tried to calm her. He said that they had to make these hurried plans because of the approaching invasion, and he had been determined to bring her home as his wife. His friend, the bishop, had agreed, and together they had proceeded with the plan.

Two elderly church people, dressed in their Sunday best, were present as witnesses. Although it seemed to be such an unseemly rush for a wedding, the bishop took the ceremony very seriously, had kind and encouraging words for them, and even tolerated Claire's tearful participation with an understanding smile. It was not the church where he usually officiated, but he had chosen the charming little chapel with care, to add at least some decor to the unusual situation. Claire was vain enough to have wished that she had worn a nicer dress for the occasion, but nothing could be done about that now. Peter did not mind. He saw only her beloved, tearful face, and almost said "I do" twice, because he could not concentrate. The bishop smiled. He had someone prepare a little refreshment in the vestry, so he could toast the couple as a friend also, and with his promise to visit St. Johann soon, they went back on the motorcycle, Mr. and Mrs. Peter Burghoff.

Frau Maier had taken good care of Elizabeth. Since the child was used to having someone else other than her mother around, as it had been at Heidi's house, she did not mind her mother's absence, but showed a loving welcome on her return. Frau Maier had also managed to prepare a modest meal of delicious soup, liver dumplings, and a festive *Salzburger Nockerl* for dessert.

Their wedding night, the second night they had ever spent together, had the same romance in Peter's rickety old bed, as the one in Claire's apartment in Vienna, but with a happier awakening for the lovers. "No parting from now on ever again," Peter promised.

Just a few days later, on May 15, 1945, the loudspeakers everywhere pronounced Hitler's death and the capitulation of Germany. It had been expected for months. Not openly, because it was still dangerous to express doubt, but everybody knew. There was rejoicing in some political quarters, fear in others, but altogether everybody breathed a sigh of relief. In her nightly prayers Claire had never missed asking for the blessings of peace.

Of course, peace after victory is different, than peace in defeat. Claire, in her belief that all would be well if only the killing would stop, had to admit that it did not quite happen that way. A defeated nation—and there was no sign that Austria had been "liberated" rather than conquered—experiences much misery as the consequences of its downfall. Even those people who were triumphantly jubilant and hoping for a return to political life as it had been before the *Anschluss* to Germany, had to endure much hardship. Claire found that the most disturbing aspect was the hate and intolerance between them and the desire for revenge. This made life just as difficult as the continued and even intensified material deprivation. The Western Allies tried to reestablish a normal environment in the zones the four powers had established under an agreement between them, but the Russians dismantled all industrial equipment which the bombing had not destroyed in their zone (the area of the province of Lower Austria, surrounding Vienna and all of Vienna), transporting it to Russia as part of reparations. Whole factories were dismantled and taken away, as were all transportation vehicles, locomotives, and passenger carriages, and the oil pumped from the few oil wells Austria held in Lower Austria. This took away the essential life support for the starving and deprived population, and made their "rise from the ashes"— in the truest sense—a major challenge.

Claire had great concern about the well-being of her parents. Finally, a letter came from Claire's father. It read as follows:

> June 21, 1945—
> Dear Claire,
>
> *Yesterday evening around eight o'clock, your friend Heidi came for a visit unexpectedly and told us that you complained in a letter to her about not having any news from us for quite some time. Well, we are no better off.*
>
> *Heidi has some business here in Vienna and will take my letter with her and mail it from Bruck where, it is rumored the English have arrived.*
>
> *To make it short: We are well, although our nerves are very frazzled because of all the excitement we had.*
>
> *I don't know where to begin my story. The Red Army has been in Vienna since the 4th of June. On that date A TR34 tank stood in front of our house. We all remained in the basement for twelve days. I suffered at the time from high fever and pleurisy, remained without medical attention, medicine, or food. On the*

19th, I finally dragged myself to the doctor. It makes no sense to describe all the misery and despair we are going through. Vienna is no more, it is a heap of rubble. One has to wonder how one can survive all this.

Best greetings, your parents.

Relieved to hear that her parents had survived, she was nevertheless shocked by the tone of her father's letter. She could understand the terrible circumstances they found themselves in with the rest of Vienna's population, but the letter was so cold—not one word asking how she had fared. Of course, it has always been thought, that the people in the provinces had no idea about the hardships people had to endure in the metropolis. They—even her parents—thought that they were suffering, while she lived a comfortable life in the country without bombing, and with good food and good air. Claire felt a little resentment, but swallowed any bitter words when showing the letter to Peter. He read it and said only: "Poor folk! it is unfortunate that we are unable to help!"

It had been two months since the American occupying troops had settled in the area. While the general population was exposed to severe regulations, Peter had the advantage that the American Commander respected and used his professional services, even supplied him with a little more gasoline so he could carry out his visits to the hospital and his patients with more ease. For a time he had done it all on foot, which took much of his time and energy. It now made visits to the farm—a one hour drive—possible also, where he could get at least a few additions to their meager food supply. The rations had been cut even more since the American army took some supplies from the civilian allotment for their own needs. Although restricted by stringent rules about delivery of all goods produced on farms, the farmers were always able to keep a little more for themselves. One cannot measure exactly how much milk the cows gave on a given day, or how many eggs the hens had laid. In the past the Burghoffs had raised their livestock only for the purpose of trading, but since food rationing had come in they tried to raise their own supplies to the extent they were permitted to do.

It was a few weeks before Peter and Claire had a chance to visit his parents. Folks there were affected comparatively little by the cessation of the war and the American occupation, except for a new set of rules and regulations, and they were used to that for years. Little changed, there was just more of it, and they took it with the usual sighing and grumbling, depending on who had to deal with it. Father just grunted, and Hanna accepted the unavoidable with a resigned sigh.

They had been anxious to meet their new daughter-in-law and grandchild, and were willing to give them a warm welcome. Little Elizabeth immediately opened their hearts. The child was not shy, and accepted the strangers who were supposed to be her grandparents without reluctance, but she was drawn immediately to the dark haired little girl standing beside grandmother. Everybody was astounded, when Eva, the unapproachable, took her little sister by the hand and guided her into the house, talking to her sweetly, just as she did to her little dog. The adults had tears in their eyes. Claire, who had not met Eva before, gave her immediately a place in her heart. That little girl must have been hurt much to have acted so hostile towards everybody for so long.

When Peter told his parents that Franz Hinterberger, the bishop, had performed their marriage ceremony, they seemed to be surprised and pleased. Anton Burghoff embraced Claire and welcomed her into the family. Hanna was friendly and courteous, but Claire could feel that she did not trust her completely. Who could blame her, Claire thought. Hanna's moral values were no different than Claire's. She knew and acknowledged her transgressing, but felt no remorse either. She and Peter had been destined for each other by whatever fate had it in mind for them. She felt daily the magnetic force that drew them together. Peter also noticed his mother's reserved welcome for Claire, but was unconcerned. As soon as she got to know Claire, she would love her also.

Well, in later years Hanna would willingly admit that she appreciated all of Claire's virtues, but loving her? She could never come close to that. It may not have been Claire's past transgression that she blamed her, for her own son had been a part of that, she told herself, but maybe it was a little jealousy of Peter's complete devotion to his wife. Mother had lost the first position, but she contented herself with the words in the Bible, which say that it must be so.

The family agreed that it might be a good thing if Eva were to come back with them to live in her father's house. Eva resisted at first, but since she was allowed to bring the dog she relented, still holding on to Elizabeth's hand. From that time on, these two so different children in looks as well as in character, remained attached to each other throughout their childhood, and as best friends in their later lives: Elizabeth, the happy, outgoing one, who caught everybody's heart with her smile and golden looks, and Eva, dark, somber, and aloof.

Claire hoped that Eva would fit in well and not have a negative influence on her sunny Elizabeth, but she kept her concerns to herself in order not to hurt Peter, who was openly pleased about the arrangement. Her concerns were soon relieved. Eva was just as intent to take care of her little sister as she was at their first meeting. Being four years older, she could already teach her much of the ways of the world, and she protected the little one from any harm. It was moving to watch the two children together. Eva did not change too quickly in her distrust of adults, but made an exception with Claire. She did not throw her little arms around Claire's neck, as Elizabeth did, but she accepted her, and started to call her "Mommy," just as Elizabeth did. She shortened her sister's name to Lisa, and soon everybody followed. It was not too much to their mother's liking who had picked the name for a reason, in memory of that special night with Peter in the Volksgarten in front of the statue of the Empress Elizabeth. However, even the Empress had a nickname, was she not called Sissy? Claire relented and got used to "Lisa" also.

Claire soon found that her second night with Peter—or was it the third, or fourth, but not too many later—had the same consequences as their first night. She was pregnant again. Both were happy about it, and only a little concerned about the situation in the country which made life so difficult and still full of dangers. They had survived the war, surely they would survive the so called peace also.

Peter was very busy and was away from home a lot, but since his private practice was set up in their own house, she could at least get a glance of him occasionally. Dr. Krieger still occupied the cottage at the end of the garden, where he had moved to get away from Marlena, whom he had despised. He was retired now, but could pitch in when Peter needed him. He took a great liking to Claire, and the two had often exchanged words when she was in the garden with the children or tending to her crops. She had learned from Heidi how to grow vegetables, which was truly a welcome addition to their restricted diet. Dr. Krieger, a country doctor for decades, had also much good advice for her, and not only in respect to gardening. He was a wise old man, but had never been married, because, he said, he never had the time to look for the right woman. He was one of the few people Peter had confided in and therefore he knew their life's story. He had encouraged Peter, to go and find Claire again after the accident. Dr. Krieger knew the rest of the story, and was never shocked or found it disgraceful. In fact, he admired Claire and thought Peter, whom he respected, to be a very lucky man. He told him that often enough, which was really unnecessary as Peter said he was keenly aware of that on his own.

Dr. Krieger was Claire's only friend in her new surrounding for a long time. While Peter's reputation as a physician grew throughout the countryside and he was sought out by all the "important" townspeople who wanted him to take care of whatever ailed them, Claire was pretty much ignored. She had hoped to make friends in town, but was received rather coolly. She realized that in their eyes she must have a "past" which she did not seem willing to share. When people casually asked her whose child Elisabeth was, she always said "Ours," and left it at that. Of course the ladies gossiped, and did not take kindly to the fact that Claire did not. She had not counted on the possibility of having offended the town's high moral standards. She did not judge them on theirs ,when it was well known how political intrigues and jealousies were ruining good people's lives. Homecoming veterans often did not recognize the changes the war had made to the home front also. Every Sunday the priest of their church admonished his flock to return to the old ways, where neighbor used to help neighbor, and when they did not turn against each other, as many did now. Since fewer and fewer people went to church, his sermons were not heard too widely. Peter was not a steady churchgoer either and used his occupation as an excuse, which often enough kept him too busy, even on Sundays, when the people from out of town looked for the "medicine man."

Claire would have liked to give their home a little uplift by getting some badly needed furnishings. After Marlena's death, Peter had returned all that she had brought into their marriage to her family. This had been quite substantial, and he had replaced only the most necessary items with things he found as surplus on the farm at Waldegg. It did not matter much to him, and he had not given thought to Claire's needs for more comfort. He remembered now that on his visit to Claire's apartment in Vienna, he had appreciated the ambience of her surrounding. Claire admitted that for the first time she missed some of her former belongings, the Biedermeier chest, her desk, the paintings, the piano, the Persian rugs, and her brass bed with the good linens. She did not have a dowry either, she said, but Peter dismissed that with the remark that to him she herself was worth more than millions in gold. She smiled at that but was not completely satisfied. She still had some money in the bank, but all accounts were presently frozen by the government and only small monthly amounts were released for the most basic needs. That was not the real problem, because there was no merchandise available to buy anyway.

Many of Peter's patients could not pay for medical services either, but often offered goods in trade. He received a custom-made pair of shoes from one of the tradesmen in payment for his son's tonsillectomy, for instance. When a cabinetmaker brought a fine mahogany chest in grateful recognition for an emergency appendectomy, it was welcomed although never asked for. This way their home received some improvements. Claire had never done much sewing since her home economics class in school, but soon learned to make new from old, especially for the children. Her own wardrobe needs were again covered by the old maternity dress. She feared that Peter must be leery of seeing her in such unbecoming shape and clothing, but he insisted that he never found her lovelier. They were very happy and even the sorry state of the country did not diminish their joy in each other.

Their social life was as curtailed as it was for most people. There were some social gatherings, mostly political, where it was wise to appear, and Claire did her part alone when Peter used medical calls as an excuse for not participating. He did not really care for parties, and they themselves entertained only a few selected friends. One who came on a regular basis was the bishop, who loved both Peter and Claire. When his frequent visits became known to the townspeople through the housemaid's gossip, the Burghoffs rose in their estimation, even Claire. The doctor had always been honored, because they depended on him. Claire noticed that the ladies found him especially attractive, although he was only moderately affable. Some people found the reserved man arrogant, stern, and cold except those patients of his who had been severely ill and had seen his very compassionate side. He would agonize deeply when he had to recognize that all his medical knowledge was in vain and he had to watch some individual succumb in pain and misery. He challenged God's mercy when a young father of five died of an infection and he had to watch helplessly when the medications they had at the time did not work. Penicillin, the wonder-drug was known to be available already in the U.S.A., but the best they had here were some sulfa drugs and they were often not enough. Peter discussed God's apparent lack of compassion with the bishop who tried his best to straighten his friend out. Few people knew about his inner struggles; to the world, Peter was a cool and reserved man, the physician whose judgment many sought and whom they trusted almost to the point of thinking of him as infallible. His reputation grew nearly as fast as his belief in his own medical profession dwindled. He had to accept his patient's unquestioned faith in his power of healing, and often felt like a charlatan, because he knew how limited those powers were. He believed that a person could often better heal himself, and that his or her genetic make-up was a greater deciding factor in their recovery from illness than medical intervention. Nevertheless, Peter still performed gall bladder surgery, appendectomies, and other operations to save peoples lives, and he did prescribe medicines to soothe pain, but he struggled with the knowledge of the limitations of his profession, and of God's unwillingness to cooperate when compassion would demand it.

Because of Peter's busy schedule day in and day out, with free time spent at the farm, where his advice—medical and personal—was also always sought and where, according to his parent's thinking, he did not come close to fulfilling their expectations. Claire did not want to add to his burdens, and handled her problems bravely by herself. Not that they were many and difficult ones, but she missed her friends with whom she could share these little concerns of everyday life.

So far she had not told Peter much about Velden. He was satisfied when her medical report cleared her from her previous diagnose of anemia. She had to tell him about Paul and Amelia, both delicate subjects, the former because of Peter's jealous nature, the other because it made Claire feel uncomfortable to talk about it. On one early evening, the children were already asleep when Peter had come back from a house call earlier than expected, they decided to take a stroll to the edge of town, where civilization abruptly stopped, and nature loomed before them. The meadows had lost their last flowers, but the deciduous trees were still displaying a palette of golden hues against the dark evergreens of the dense forest beyond. They walked hand in hand, enjoying the peaceful surroundings, when Peter asked with thoughtfulness in his voice:

"Claire, are you happy—really happy?"

"Peter, with you at my side I don't know that I could wish for more. You, the children—including the one yet to be born—I have everything I have ever dreamed of in my life, Yes, Peter, I am happy, happy, happy." She squeezed his hand, the last rays of sun gave his so handsomely chiseled face a wonderful glow, but that did not come from the sun alone, Peter felt so warm and content, that he could forget all his daily doubts. Life was wonderful, he was truly blessed, that lovely woman at his side had taught him what love really was, above and beyond the passions of the night.

Claire had intended to use that time to tell Peter about Carynthia, but then felt that the spell of the moment could not be broken. Another time would come. And so it was nearly Christmas, and she had not said anything. She was getting uncomfortably heavier and had to slow down. This would be another Christmas to remember, but more joyful, at least in their hearts. The world outside was still in turmoil, the country barely able to provide its citizens any comfort or a decent living standard. The past had not taught people tolerance and understanding, political strife and quarrels continued. Some soldiers coming home from war prisons, had to face new persecution by their own people for sins they may have never committed themselves, but a flag or a campaign button may have identified them at one time as sympathizers of a now hateful regime. It should be said, that in some instances it was justified to expect reprimands or repercussions for actions that had been shameful. Claire was thinking of Fritz Engebrecht, the old "heartthrob of Kammerlake," as they had called him. She had not seen him, nor his wife, Gerda, also remembered from the beach at the lake, but their story had become known. Fritz had been a teacher at one of the country schools, and was apparently as popular as in the heyday of his youth as the athlete who had brought a number of medals home to his village. He had openly professed that he had great hopes that Austria's future would be a better one as part of Germany, he saluted the flag when receiving his medal at the Olympic games in 1936 in Berlin. He married Gerda just before the war started, and as most eligible material for soldiering, was inducted into the military service right at the beginning of the war. He had served in the military for six years on all fronts, not with enthusiasm for the war or the killings, but in fulfilling his duty with honor. He again received citations for bravery, occasionally came home on furlough, and fathered two children, a boy and a girl. When he came back at the end of the war, his intention was to resume his life as a civilian, continue teaching and his life with the growing family. Gerda had struggled in the meantime, to keep the family intact as did many other young women at the time. However, their simple plans for the future were not at all that simple to fulfill.

It was probably by animosity of an unknown old rival that Fritz was challenged to prove that he was not, nor had ever been, a Nazi, since everybody seemed to know that he had at least sympathized. In the meantime, he could not have his old job back as a teacher. He and his family had to move from the house they had occupied all that time, and which was the property of the local community, leaving all their possessions behind. Fritz had come back from Europe's battlefields with only minor scratches, but the home front did him in. He could not believe what was happening, he became a broken man, not even able to fight anymore. It became mostly Gerda's job to rehabilitate them. She was said to be a true fighter. She found a small, rat-infested bungalow, cleaned it out and moved her family in. She worked hard to establish a home, while Fritz hardly participated. He tried finding jobs as a laborer, at which he was not very good. They said he spent most of his time in the woods hunting, and supplying his family with some of his efforts from that, so they could at least eat. He used to love hunting as a young fellow, but had rarely done any killing, which he still abhorred. Gerda did all the manual work in fixing up the house. People in the village once had made fun of her as a spoiled city girl, who did not know enough to darn a sock! His aunt, the now retired school principal of Kammerbach, who had taken Fritz in when he was orphaned, was also helping to take care of his children now.

Claire was very moved by the Engebrecht's story when she heard about it. Peter did not comment. He still did not like Fritz. Claire loved Peter unconditionally, but sometimes she could not understand him. Still jealous? She asked:

"Don't you think the Engebrechts are getting rough and undeserved treatment?"

"Didn't the Jews get that also?"

"Yes, but what has that to do with Fritz?" Peter avoided the argument.

There was much snow that Christmas, which the children everywhere enjoyed, more so than their parents, but there were horse-drawn sleighs all over town, not only providing some exciting fun rides but also used as transportation, since gas rationing continued to hinder civilian movement. Peter was provided with a higher gas ration now, and he used his car again, but still only for his professional needs.

The Burghoffs had hoped that the family would spend Christmas together at the farm, but Peter did not want to expose Claire to the hazards of an extended sleigh ride in her present condition. Therefore they had their own little Christmas celebration without extended family or friends, and they found their intimate privacy very delightful.

The two little girls were excited with their presents: a doll for Eva, a stuffed Teddy bear for Lisa, a few picture books, and, of course, the Christmas tree, lighted by real candles, and even hung with some newly arrived chocolates from the grocery store. Slowly, very slowly, some food items appeared in the stores without requiring coupons from the ration card—expensive, of course—"Cadbury" chocolates, for instance.

When the children were finally in bed, together with their new toys and Eva's dog, who was always their escort, Claire and Peter could relax by themselves. Peter had found a bottle of wine somewhere, he did not want to give away his source, which may also have been where he got the doll, Claire assumed. He was mysterious that night, appropriately for the season of surprises. Claire played his little game by saying that he probably had to charm one of his lady patients who often sent him little gifts. While the females in town had their eyes on their handsome doctor, Claire knew very well, that he did not share their interest in flirting. Peter had, in Claire's opinion, many values, but charm—especially using it on the ladies—was not one of them, but she pretended to be jealous because it seemed to flatter him. She was willing to let the ladies admire him for his looks and his medical skills, but one attribute she kept strictly as her own secret, namely that he was also the world's greatest lover.

By the way, it had been a former patient of Peter's, an elderly man and not one of his female patients, who was eternally grateful for Peter's dedication when he was severely ill, who had brought him the doll, saying, his own daughter had outgrown it, but the doctor had two little girls, who might still enjoy it. His wife had made a new dress for the doll, and he had added a bottle of wine for Peter.

Relaxing, snuggled together on the old sofa with a glass of wine, the Christmas lights casting a soft glow around the room, they felt comfortable and sentimental and not too much was said. Claire remembered another Christmas, two years ago, when she was also close to giving birth, and when she had celebrated Christmas Eve in such different circumstances. Looking back, she could hardly remember that she could have been content and happy then without Peter. She said it out loud, and Peter wanted her to tell him more about her life then. It was finally the occasion to mention Paul. She had talked about him previously as her publisher and friend, but Peter had not paid much attention. When Claire said, that Paul had spent Christmas Eve with her—and alone too—his curiosity was aroused.

"You never told me about that!"

"I told you about Paul Thoene—he visited me and Amelia often, and became a really good friend, who helped me in many ways during a very difficult time."

"On Christmas Eve?"

"Amelia had to work, and we were both glad, that I did not have to spend the evening alone when Paul announced his visit since he would have been alone also. He was thoughtful, we played Christmas music on Amelia's recorder, even sang a few of the old familiar Christmas songs together, and then went to church for midnight mass."

Peter could not help but feel uncomfortable with the idea of seeing Claire in the company of another man at such a special time.

"Peter, would you rather that I had been alone, sad, lonely, thinking about you and a future that would never be? I owed not only myself, but my unborn child a happier disposition. Paul helped me to achieve that, and I am still grateful to him for it."

"And he was completely unselfish?"

"I think so—he never asked about my past, never asked whose child I am carrying—yet he asked me to marry him at Christmas Eve, the way I looked, and in all my wretchedness."

Peter stiffened:

"You did not tell me that before?"

"I should have, I am sorry, but it was never the right time. Maybe I was also trying to forget that very difficult time of my life…." Claire's eyes moistened, and Peter put his arms around her.

"What happened then? Did you make any promises to Thoene?"

"You should not have to ask. You know that I could not do that. I told him truthfully that I would not marry him, that I loved and regarded him more than as a friend, indeed as a brother, the one I might have had, had he not died as a child. To Paul's great credit he accepted that, and kept on being a dear friend. I really wish that you would meet him some day, I am certain that you would like him also."

Peter was not sure of that. He still felt some resentment, but at the same time recognized that he was more than unfair to Claire. She had had the right to lead a life of her own after he abandoned her. That is how he saw it now. It was all his fault, it was he who had made her life so difficult, he was guilty of hurting the woman who had remained true to him nevertheless. Guilt and shame overcame him, seeing himself as selfish and hard. He again promised in his heart to make up for all the pain he ever caused her; he would cherish her like no man had ever cherished a woman. The thought that he could have lost her had not occurred to him before, but now it filled him with fear. If that would have happened, his life would have been miserable forever. Why did he not think of that before?

This unplanned conversation did not exactly create a festive Christmas mood, but at the same time it brought both of them closer than ever. Claire felt free after having shared the story of her days in Velden, and Peter loved her gentle soul more than ever. They had not a "jolly," but a very meaningful Christmas this year.

Early in February of 1947, snow still covered the streets. Claire gave birth to a son, a healthy and strong baby with steel grey eyes, wisps of blond hair, and his father's deeply dimpled chin. He was more demanding than Elizabeth had been, and his voice was forceful in requesting attention. His parents took him to Kammerbach for baptism, since he was the "heir apparent" of the Burghoffs, who for several generations had been baptized in the village church of Kammerbach. He was named Anton after his grandfather, who was so proud of his new heir that for a little while he could forget the loss of his son Hans. Just temporarily, because one could never forget the loss of a child he said and Hanna agreed. She had prepared a meal for the guests, which, of course, included Father Grumberger, who had baptized the child, and the mayor, and all the farm hands. It was a country-style affair with music and celebrations the way Claire had not known from her life in Vienna. She found it heartwarming, but was also a little concerned and asked Peter:

"What if Tony"—that's what they called him—"does not want to become a farmer?" Peter said convincingly:

"Oh, he will—the firstborn of the Burghoffs knows that from the beginning of his life."

"You were the firstborn of Anton and Hanna—and you became a physician!"

"Well, that was a little different. When I turned out to be a very good student, it meant that I was to become a priest, a scholar of the church, and they sent me to the boarding school of the Jesuits. Only the priesthood was more important than farming. By then, Hans was old enough and interested in the land to make him the heir of the estate, and let me off the hook of becoming either a priest or a farmer. Not that my parents would have insisted after I had declared that I would rather become a Doctor of Medicine than study Theology. They always followed traditional ways and taught them to the children early on, but they would never have forced us to go against our own calling. I would probably have stayed on the farm if Hans had declined it. You know, that I am still devoted to it, that I am still a 'country boy.'"

Claire was satisfied. If Tony became a farmer, it would suit her also, but she did not want him to grow up with no other choice. She had heard from Paul only sparingly lately. He was so busy, not only in his publishing work, but also in politics. The new provincial government had asked him to serve in a leading position, and Claire learned for the first time, that Paul Thoene had been involved in some kind of underground political activity even during the war. So, he had also kept a secret from her? She was surprised; it did not seem like Paul. Maybe she did not know him as well as she thought.

Chapter 14

When Tony was born, she sent an announcement to Paul, and received in return another surprise, namely Paul's announcement of his marriage in Vienna to a Miss Melinda Moell. She could not believe it. For a moment she was almost hurt, that he could have forgotten her so quickly, but she recovered soon to recognize her foolishness. No, she was happy for Paul. She only hoped that the woman was worthy of him—she cared about that as a sister would about her brother's choice.

Peter had started to like Paul Thoene much better, and had no objection to meeting and getting to know him, which was Claire's fervent wish. That however, was still a while off, but they started a much more regular exchange of letters with reports of their mutual lives. Claire wondered about Melinda Moell. That name sounded somehow familiar, but she could not place it. Paul explained: Did she remember a short novel he had once brought her to read, the author being Melinda Moell? Yes, of course, that was the splendid suspense and romance combination she had enjoyed. Paul explained further, that he had met Melinda a few years ago at a social gathering in Vienna with people of various artistic backgrounds, writers, musicians and others. Melinda was the daughter of the well-known playwright Moell, her mother the acclaimed pianist Anita Carlotti-Moell. The close-knit Moell family had produced a number of members of the artistic community of Vienna, especially the noted theater actor Arthur Moell, Melinda's uncle. Melinda could not help being influenced by her environment and turned out to be quite a clever and accomplished writer, when Paul met her again at a writers' convention in Vienna. She consequently introduced him to writers who had recently returned from their exile—mostly in Switzerland—where they had transplanted themselves just in time before the National Socialists with their censoring attacks had taken hold in Austria. Paul said that he had been very impressed by Melinda, and proposed on impulse; he was almost surprised by her acceptance, but he was very happy that she did. They planned to live in Velden, in his home that Claire knew. Claire congratulated the couple warmly and hoped for a visit soon.

Travel restrictions were still in force, that meant a permit had to be obtained from the occupying forces for traveling between the zones. It was usually not difficult to get that permit from the English or the Americans, but the Russians often made entering and leaving of their territory cumbersome, even if the necessary papers were obtained. Traveling from Salzburg to Vienna on the restored rail lines would normally take three to four hours, but delays of many hours at the Demarcation Line were common. That is why Claire had not yet been to visit her parents and their contact had been only by letter, all mail was still being censored. Most people therefore felt intimidated enough not to want to express any criticism of living conditions etc. Claire thought it would be easier for her parents to come to Salzburg, than for her—who was again with child—to travel to Vienna, but her father said such a trip would be too strenuous for them.

Yes, Claire was pregnant again, and the baby was due not much more than a year after Tony's birth. Although Peter and Claire rejoiced in the growth of their family, Claire did not feel that such proliferation was a good thing in a poor little country like Austria and Peter agreed; also on practical financial grounds since he did not want to see the Burghoff Estate diminished by divisions.

A journey to Vienna to see the Baumanns was finally undertaken, difficult or not, Claire felt so much accrued guilt for not having done so earlier, that she could not postpone it any longer. Her parents knew by now about Claire's new life, but details were never discussed in their letters. She wanted to do it in person. Peter was somewhat hesitant, but planned to come along to face her parents together. She figured it might be a little difficult—like going to confession—but the sooner it was over, the better for her conscience.

Claire did not foresee, however, how difficult it was going to be. During the long and strenuous train ride on a steaming hot August day, she remembered with nostalgia the summer vacations with her parents during her childhood. In August the whole population of Vienna seemed to have left town—at least those who could afford it. The heat in the city radiated from the stone buildings, the air was stifling—Claire still suffered from morning sickness—when they knocked on her parent's apartment door. Claire had expected the welcome would be emotional, teary, warm, and loving, but it was almost awkward. None of them could seem to find the right words. Father retreated to his easy chair, and invited them to sit down with a gesture. Mother busily acted as if she needed to make preparations for setting the table; Mucki, an old cat by now, did not move from the corner of the sofa, but just stared at the intruders. Claire was ready to burst into tears—it was not the homecoming she had hoped for, but probably she did not deserve it. She had not been a model daughter to these dear old people. Peter, never talkative anyway, was no help in the situation. Finally, Claire having made herself a little comfortable in a chair around the old dining table, asked about her parents' well being, and was assured in a halting way that they were doing well, under all the circumstances and limitations. They could have said that they were not doing well—it sounded the same. Claire ignored it for the moment, determined to find out later if they were ailing or had any problems of other kinds.

She talked about the children, Elizabeth and Tony, and included also Eva, at which Rosemarie pressed her lips together, and made a sour face. *So that's it* Claire deducted immediately—nothing was forgotten, forgiven, or understood—the experiences of the war had hardened their souls also. Actually, it made it easier now to talk unemotionally, and retell just the facts. Yes, they lived very comfortably in the country, Peter's practice was doing very well, the family, his parents, were also doing relatively well. Of course, they were still mourning the death of their son Hans, but life goes on.

"Yes, it does, does it not?" her mother interjected in a lamenting voice. "I wish you would come for a visit to see the children. It would do you good to get out of the city also, especially right now, it is quite hot here. You could live in Kammersee, if you'd prefer; you know the place from long ago."

"It is out of the question; travel under today's conditions is not for people of our age. We are also dependent on the comfort of our own home, of the closeness to the medical care we are used to, as well as many other reasons," said Friederich Baumann sternly.

Up to now, Peter had not said a word, but he could feel the tension in the air and Claire's desperate attempt to establish a meaningful conversation. Her parents seemed to have created a wall around themselves which not even Claire was able to bridge. Now he spoke out:

"Forgive me if I interrupt here. You may have your reasons why you do not want to travel, but I feel there is more than that in your refusal to visit your grandchildren. I think there is some resentment here which needs to be aired. Claire is hurt—I am concerned."

"What about us?" said Rosemarie all of a sudden "Have we not been hurt for a long time, shut out of your lives, out of everything?" And she began to cry, and Friederich was agitated:

"Mother has suffered so much by your behavior, and now you appear and suddenly everything should be forgiven and forgotten. No, my daughter, it is not that simple."

Claire was pale and shaking, and Peter put his arms around her to comfort her. He said quietly:

"We are truly sorry you feel that way, but we understand, Do you want us to leave?"

"No, no, of course not, I have prepared a meal, it will be ready in minutes. We were looking forward to your coming." Rosemarie muttered and disappeared into the kitchen. Claire pressed Peter's hand thankfully for his support, and got up to help her mother in the kitchen. From then on the conversation became a little less stiff, but even more meaningless. Friederich inquired about the journey. Any problems at the Demarcation Line? No, just a little delay. Yes, the weather was hot. Yes, in the mountains of Salzburg, especially in St. Johann, where they lived, it was cooler. Yes, it was a lovely summer this year. No, Peter had not had much time for hiking. No, he never went hunting. Yes, there is much work on the farm. Do they still call the farm "the castle"? He did not know, he never paid attention to that; and so on.

In the kitchen the conversation was not more meaningful. Was the train ride strenuous? Yes, it was hot. Yes, the city air was different from that in St. Johann. Yes, the children were well taken care of. Would they like to stay here overnight? Rosemarie could fix the old room…Claire had automatically assumed that they would stay, but could see they were not really expected to. It hurt, it hurt deeply—she had become a stranger in her old home.

She was always trying to understand others and was willing to see her own faults before those of others, but sometimes it was very difficult. Without a doubt, she was guilty of not having confided in her parents, but had she not done so to spare them pain, disappointment, and worry? In hindsight, would she act differently now ? Probably not. If they interpreted her actions wrongly, she was sorry for them as well as for herself.

During the meal, the conversation went to Friederich's early retirement. It was evident that he was bitter about it. It was forced upon him for political reasons, he said. Claire was surprised:

"Papa, you were never a Nazi or even a sympathizer in all your life, on the contrary."

"Oh, if people want to get you, they invent a way. I was told that I had once written a paper in which I criticized a colleague, and since he was Jewish, it was deduced that I was anti-Semitic. Me—anti-Semitic? Had I not helped some of my Jewish friends many times—of course they are all gone now, and I don't have witnesses. Just this one, who has returned from exile in Shanghai, has it in for me. It could not be proven that I had ever done anything politically questionable, however, retirement was forced upon me."

Claire was really sorry for her father and expressed it. It did not seem to make him less cantankerous, and everything her mother contributed to their conversations was in a whining, suffering voice. She told them about the fate of some of her old friends and neighbors—this one having lost her husband through illness, others lost their sons in the war, and so it went. Some of the people mentioned Claire used to know, others she did not. She tried hard to feign interest, but felt that she too had lost her parents. This was no homecoming for her. How lucky for her to have Peter—nothing else really mattered anyway.

When her mother asked, where they had planned to stay, she quickly said they had reservations at the Hotel Regina, because they wanted to return very early in the morning, and would not want to disturb them by their departure. Peter looked a little surprised, but quickly understood, just hoping that they would really find accommodations somewhere.

Claire left in tears. She was overly sensitive because of her condition, Peter surmised, but on the other hand she had been hurt beyond her expectations. In order to make good Claire's fib about the hotel reservation at the Hotel Regina, which was close to Claire's former apartment, they called there first, and were unexpectedly lucky to find accommodations. A short walk to her former apartment building showed that the ruins were by now completely razed and the rubble removed, but there were no signs of rebuilding yet.

Claire was too exhausted for more excursions through her old city as they had originally planned and asked Peter to take her home as soon as possible. Indeed, it was early the next morning that they made it back. There she embraced her children passionately and tried to forget the painful experience of the previous day.

Chapter 15

At the end of March in 1948 Claire gave birth to another son At least at the time of his birth he seemed to be almost a copy of his brother Tony—same eye color, hair, dimpled chin, strong, and of loud voice. Claire was overcome with joy when she had the newborn in her arms for the first time. With the birthing pains quickly forgotten, she was almost sorry to have told Peter that this should be their last offspring in consideration of not wanting to contribute any further to the worldwide population explosion. Actually they did not think about the world as a whole, more about their own little world, including their own small country with its limited resources. Most people had to be satisfied with two or three children, and even the country folks who in the olden days produced large families, now preferred smaller ones.

Peter was as proud of the "next in line to the throne," as if he had given birth himself. He showered Claire with tender affection, and even held the newborn for a while in his arms, as he heard Paul had done when Elizabeth was born. Normally, the Burghoff men did not show such tenderness, even if it was felt. Peter was in many ways the old fashioned sort Claire thought, and admitted at the same time that she liked him that way. She had proved to herself in school and in her career, that she could handle a job as well as her male counterparts, but she was just as happy to feel taken care of by the big, strong man of few words and she loved every inch of him, body and soul.

The child was named Christopher, another name chosen from the Burghoff's family tree, and he was also baptized in the village church of Kammersee. The bishop, who had asked to be Christopher's godfather, came to the celebration which made the village quite proud of such attention to one of their own. Christopher's middle name was, of course, Franz, the name of the bishop.

When Paul was informed of the new family addition he wrote in his congratulation letter that he rejoiced in their good fortune, and added a little poem he had written for Christopher. Claire felt very moved by it.

The girls, Eva and Elizabeth, were loving sisters, but did not overreact to the new addition since they still had baby brother Tony to play with, who was much more likely to return their affectionate attention than this newborn baby, who seemed to them to be so useless. With time he became more like Tony, however, and was included in their foursome. Eva, now eight years old, was very capable of looking out after the babies when needed, but her affection was still oriented towards sweet little Elizabeth, now already a big sister herself at four. Elizabeth remained her father's very special girl. He could never look at the beautiful child with her blond curls and deep blue eyes without feeling his heart bursting with love and tenderness. What was it about that child that made him feel that way, he often wondered. He loved all his children, but this one was special.

Claire knew why Elizabeth was special to her also, but she explained it to herself more intellectually. She was her first child, conceived and born under special circumstances, the memories of which would never fade. However, she loved the boys passionately; they were so much the image of their father, they made her truly happy and proud. She also loved Eva, and never once considered her any different from the rest. The four of them kept her pretty breathless all day long, despite the help she had found from another elderly woman after Peter's original housekeeper had retired. Dr. Krieger, still living in the cottage at the end of the garden, needed looking after also, since he had become ridden with arthritis. The house, which originally also housed the offices for Peter's private practice, had become a little too small for them, so Peter moved his office into a another building, closer to the hospital. He was already thinking about taking on an assistant in order to get some free time to spend with his family, and not to forget the farm, where his father always relied on his help. How fortunate it was that they had hired Szolti, the Hungarian, as a manager. He could not have come to them at a better time.

A letter from Paul in August of 1948 announced, that he would be at a publisher's conference in Salzburg with his wife, and hoped that they could finally see each other again. It had been nearly three years since Claire had left and she was looking forward to seeing Paul and also to meeting his wife, Melinda. Paul wrote that they would have two very busy days with meetings, but would love to see Claire and Peter, if at all possible, one evening for dinner. They were going to stay at the hotel Goldener Hirsch. There had been little in the way of social events in the Burghoff's life these last few years, if one does not count the yearly harvest festivals and weddings which the country people celebrated with dances and hoopla. Peter only attended with reserve, and never danced.

Claire was longing for a good time and good conversation with dear friends, and Peter missed the concerts from years past. Salzburg was slowly regaining some of its renowned character as the city of music and arts and a few very good productions were starting up. Claire and Peter had not had much time to consider such entertainment, had not actually been in Salzburg other than for their marriage, although it was barely a one hour train ride away from St. Johann. Claire was very excited. She looked over her wardrobe, which was still unchanged from her former life in Vienna and little new was available. To be able to wear something beside her maternity wardrobe, that would already make her feel great. With great satisfaction she found she could fit into nearly all of her old things again and that her figure barely changed. Peter had told her many times that she looked like the beautiful young maiden he always remembered, but she had taken it just as flattery. He had even liked her body when she was pregnant, therefore his taste could not be relied upon, she said. Peter took the car to drive them to Salzburg. By now he had a little more gasoline for his personal use, and he wanted to make it as pleasant for Claire as possible.

Paul was in the lobby of the hotel when they arrived and greeted Claire with his usual warmth and kissed her hand tenderly. Then he turned to Peter with a charming smile:

"I have long wanted to meet you," he said, with no exaggerated speech, which Peter liked, and he shook hands with the legendary friend of his wife. They went into the dining room and Paul explained that his wife would join them shortly, she had been held up by a telephone call. Before they even sat down, Melinda entered the room. Her appearance turned the heads of other diners too; she looked strikingly attractive, although modestly dressed in a beige dinner suit. She had black heir, pulled straight back into a tight bun, dark, wide set eyes sparkling with intelligence, a prominent Roman nose, somewhat large, as was also her mouth, which showed a perfect set of gleaming white teeth in a smile. Her slim figure with its smooth movements reminded one of an exotic animal. Claire felt like crawling into her shell—she felt so insignificant in comparison with that stunning woman. After the usual introductions they all sat down and Paul broke the ice by starting an easy conversation. He wanted to know all about the children and their life in St. Johann. Claire had brought some snapshots of the children, which were admired with appropriate comments.

"St. Johann is a picture-perfect town surrounded by magnificent mountain ranges—you must have seen it from the train on your way from Carynthia. It is provincial, unsophisticated, and I love it!" said Claire with emphasis on the latter. Paul smiled:

"You do not miss Vienna and its glamor at all?"

"You forget, Paul, that most of my memories of Vienna are from the days—no, the years—of political upheaval and persecution, of war and deprivation. I loved the city for all its history, its monuments to people and events, its cultural ambiance, but I experienced only a little glamor—maybe a ball or two at the Burg and the opera house—I feel definitely more at home in the mountains of our province."

Melinda had listened with a smile, and said, "I tell Paul the same thing. I prefer to live in Carynthia rather than in the long lost glamor of Vienna—but most of all, I love living with Paul."

It was obvious, that she was very much in love with her husband. Claire found her charming, openhearted, simple, in contrast to her sophisticated appearance. They enjoyed good conversation during the meal. Peter was delighted and impressed with Paul, whom he still had secretly considered a former rival, but could now understand much better how Claire must have appreciated that gentle man during the difficult time in her life. He wished he knew what Paul thought of him, though. Peter was a proud man and to have an honorable reputation was important to him. Could Paul consider him as such? The guilt about his past actions had never completely left him. He should not have worried about Paul's opinion. When he saw Claire was happy, that made Peter all right with him. Paul was always a generous soul.

The food was good, the wine even better, and it flowed freely that night. The hours passed quickly. Most guests had left but they were still in animated conversation, even Peter was talkative. He said that he missed Vienna more than his wife did, because during his time as a student there he had gone to the opera as often as he could. He knew all the singers and conductors of that period, he remembered the best productions in detail and Melinda responded enthusiastically; the two had found common ground for a lively exchange on that subject. The piano player, who had played soft and lovely background music all evening, turned to more serious pieces and caught Melinda and Peter's attention.

"He is good," Melinda said, and Peter agreed. Paul said to his wife:

"You know what would be really nice? Sing for us—anything, one of your favorites, the piano player would surely accompany you. Is it all right if I talk to him?"

Without false modesty, Melinda nodded and Paul talked to the musician, who readily agreed, probably prompted by a hefty tip. Paul wanted to make that evening special for them all.

Melinda went over to the piano, had a little chat with the pianist, and started to sing. Her voice was as wonderful as her whole appearance. She had an alto range, rich and mellow, which went right to your heart. When she ended with a couple of Schubert-Lieder, Peter was ecstatic.

"What a wonderful voice. She could sing professionally!" he exclaimed.

Paul said, "Yes, she had musical training of her voice and had a choice to perform in public, but she chose to be a writer instead, and only pleases me and her friends with her other talent. It is not easy to say which one is greater—her singing or her writing. Melinda is a true artist." Melinda had heard part of Paul's praise, accepting it with a smile.

"I am glad that Paul found me as a writer—we probably would never have met if I had chosen singing as my career."

With that, even Peter became melodramatic, and inspired by both, his admiration for Melinda's singing as well as the superb wine, he talked about how fate can shape our lives in mysterious and unexpected ways, and how thankful he would be to the end of his days that it brought Claire back to him, when he in his blindness had almost lost her. Claire had never heard him say so much all at once in public, and with such emotion. She blushed easily and especially so right now.

Because of the late—or better, early morning hour—when they finally said goodbye with the hope of seeing each other more often from now on, Peter and Claire stayed on in the city. It had been a memorable evening. Claire was happy that Peter's apprehensions regarding Paul had vanished, but she jokingly asked if it were she who now needed to be worried about Peter's admiration of Melinda. He admitted he found her fascinating, and her singing talent truly enjoyable, but no thanks—he was quite willing to accept Claire's lack of that talent, since it was compensated by so many others which made him happy enough. Other women did not interest him in the slightest, but he would enjoy a closer contact with the Thoenes. They would indeed be desirable friends.

With travel restrictions becoming less stringent, the visits from the Thoenes became more frequent. They enjoyed the children, especially Paul, and he was becoming their favorite uncle. Claire and Melinda hit it off well also, despite their different lifestyles and interests. Claire wondered why she and Paul had no children. She knew Paul loved children, but she was to shy to ask, and Melinda did not volunteer.

Chapter 16

The next year went by without major event; the children were growing up. Eva did very well in school, but remained not very outgoing, had few friends in school, but always doted on Elizabeth, who was everybody's darling. Claire's parents still had not come for a visit. Not really eager to take the children to Vienna herself, she felt it her duty to give grandparents the opportunity to meet the children nevertheless. When, Eva was eleven, Elizabeth seven, Tony five, and Christopher four years old, they undertook the journey to the big city. The children were very excited about the train ride, although it was anything but comfortable for Claire and Peter. He did not want to go in the first place, but since Claire insisted she had to do it, he went along to be helpful with the children. The girls were no problem, but the little boys were quite lively and adventurous and needed constant supervision.

They planned to stay only two days in Vienna so as not to tire everybody out. The grandparents were friendly and tried to show interest and love, but Claire knew that both could not be created in a day or two. Her father appeared awkward, and did not know how to talk to the children; her mother, a little fuzzy, could get their interest with the cookies she had baked for them. After stuffing himself with as many as he could, Tony asked:

"Can we go now?" and Chris immediately chimed in. He too was ready to go. The girls had already learned to be polite and refrained from complaining, but Claire knew by their manner that leaving was on their mind also. In the meantime; Peter had taken up a conversation with Friederich about politics, which stimulated the old man more than the baby talk with the children, in which he had never been very well versed, even when Claire was a child. They had hotel reservations for the night, and said that next morning they would either go to the Zoo or to the Prater, Vienna's great amusement park, whichever was likely to be open to the public again. The Baumanns did not know, but guessed that probably both would be. Before they left on the afternoon train they would come by again and say goodbye to the grandparents. Claire saw nothing had changed, even her steady letter writing had not found any appreciation. She remained the estranged daughter.

In 1953 Friederich Baumann died suddenly. Claire went to the funeral without the children and without Peter, who had some emergency operations scheduled which he could not avoid. She thought her mother would be distraught and helpless and would need her assistance for a few days, but that was not so. Rosemarie was grieved, but not desolate. She was grateful for Claire's help in finding a mourning dress, but seemed to be otherwise prepared. She said she and Friederich had it all planned in case it should happen, so she knew what to do. Claire was glad to see that her parents had grown closer to each other in their old age than they had been in their younger years. Her father, orderly as he always had been, had put all his affairs in order and left instructions for everything. Rosemarie was intent on following all his admonitions, which included her future life. Claire suggested she come to live with them in St. Johann, but she declined. The Baumanns had employed a good woman for years to help with the household chores, and that woman was willing to move in completely. Rosemarie could well afford it on the pension she received and the investments that had become fruitful with time.

The funeral went also in prepared orderly fashion. Many former colleagues and friends came to show their respects, and Claire had a chance to talk to some of them. To her surprise, she heard that her father had not been sent into early retirement because of any personal vendetta—the colleague in question was even attending the funeral—but because of a reorganization at the University, where some of the older professors had to make room for the younger. Rosemarie had told Claire, that her father had died of a broken heart, hinting that Claire was partly to blame. Dr. Novak, now retired too, who had still taken care of the Baumanns just for old friendships' sake, told her that Friederich died of pneumonia, following a serious bout of influenza.

With her mother's assurance that she needed no further assistance, Claire went back home, sad about her father's passing but also about their relationship which had taken such a strange turn. Father had always been distant; she thought her mother had been lonely, a gentle, kind, but a weak woman, completely subdued by her strong-willed husband. Now she saw her mother being strong and determined herself and she wondered what the relationship between her parents had really been. Were there family secrets she had not been aware of? She would never know, and that was probably good. The memories of her growing-up years were still pleasant ones, why would she want to unearth possible conflicts? As she so often did, she thanked God for all the blessings he had bestowed upon her: Peter, children, and friends. How lucky she was. At home she shared her experiences in Vienna with Peter, whose supportive understanding was all she needed to overcome the sad event.

Chapter 17

One thing remained as unfinished business in the back of Claire's mind: Stefan von Brecht. She felt she had to know how he was doing; was he regaining his health or was there truly no hope? She contacted the Woerners, now in Nuremberg, where Stehle had opened one of its postwar branch offices and Georg Woerner was again a branch manager. Lieschen wrote that she had little information about the situation, but would inquire at Stehle headquarters, as she was once told that Stefan's aunt, also a daughter of the old founder like her sister Magda, had taken over the responsibility of Stefan's care after his parents death. Soon her report came saying that Stefan had been transferred from the sanatorium in Switzerland to one in Germany, near Munich, where he apparently continued to live without hope for a recovery. Claire was determined to visit Stefan. Peter was not convinced that it was a good idea, but since such a visit would be beneficial to Claire's conscience, he agreed to accompany her. Claire thought it would be better, if she went by herself, maybe accompanied by Lieschen Woerner, who had also been a friend of Stefan. Lieschen agreed and they set a date when they would meet in Munich.

This was the first time in ten years that these two women would see each other again, and they both looked forward to it. It was a very joyous reunion. Although they had kept up a correspondence through the years, it was never detailed enough. There was so much to tell about how each of them had survived the dreadful war years. They shed a few tears but also recalled happy memories. This alone would have been worth the trip for Claire.

The next morning they drove to Stefan's sanatorium. They had announced their arrival in advance; the physician, in whose care Stefan was, had requested they confer with him before seeing his patient. During that meeting Dr. Freund, a psychiatrist, tried to tell them how patients in that category were likely to react. He wanted to be sure that they would not expect too much of Stefan, who had remained uncommunicative up to now. Then they were led into the garden, where Stefan took his usual afternoon walk. A nurse pointed him out. It was agreed that Claire at first approach him alone.

A shiver went through Claire, when she went towards the figure pointed out to her as being Stefan Brecht. He was not recognizable as the man of her memory. Tall—he looked even taller now since he was so thin and it appeared as if there was no flesh on his bones, just parchment-like skin. He walked slowly, a book in his hands, but he did not read. Claire called out his name, and made sure his eyes were in her direction. There was no reaction; those once wonderful gray eyes were set deep in their sockets and looked at her completely blank, without any glimmer of seeing her. Claire came close and touched his arm, calling him again softly by name, telling him it was she, Claire, who had come to visit. No reaction—he kept on walking past her as if she were invisible. Lieschen joined her then, but another attempt to get Stefan's attention was without result.

Both women were shaken to the depths of their souls. It was as if they had seen a ghost of Stefan, not a living being. When they returned to the building, the doctor was still there. Since he had been told that Claire had once been engaged to Stefan, he had watched, with no expectation, however, that Stefan would react in any way. Nothing. He might just as well be dead; the man, Stefan von Brecht, did not exist anymore. Claire and Lieschen left in a somber mood, as if they had been at a funeral of a dear friend, only worse. They had just enough time for a cup of tea at the train station, where they parted in opposite directions, promising to visit each other again soon.

Arriving home exhausted, Claire told Peter he had probably been right in questioning the wisdom of a visit to Stefan. It was a very depressing experience, but she had had to do it in order to close a chapter in her life that had plagued her for a long time. Poor, dear Stefan.

Chapter 18

The next few years passed in the manner usual for a young family: Father works diligently to establish himself in his profession, seeking to provide a reasonably comfortable existence for the growing family, mother taking care of the everyday duties of running the household and tending to all of her children's needs and wants. That also applied to Peter and Claire.

Living conditions in the country were improving markedly; goods became available again, although prices were high. Occupation of the country by the four powers continued, and the lifestyles of these foreigners were often copied, or adopted. The greatest influence was that of America, which had always been the dream of many for whom the lure of all the golden opportunities was like a fairy tale, fanned by the stories told by past emigrants in their letters home. During the war there was, of course, some change in the fascination about everything American, since they had to be considered the "enemy." American politics at the time did not make it easy to continue the previous admiration either, but when the war was over and the wounds were licked, the old sentiments returned, especially when the "Marshall Plan" was introduced, a recovery plan for the devastated countries of Europe, developed, financed, and executed by the United States. Without doubt, this saved Europe from a take-over by the communists.

In Vienna, as in other areas where the war had left devastation, new construction was everywhere. The streets had been cleared from the ruins. The roof of the beloved St. Stefan's Cathedral, burned during the bombing, was beginning to be carefully rebuilt with mosaic tile in the exact same pattern. New life was blossoming among the ruins. Vienna was proud of the new construction of the Westbahnhof, completely modern and on a grand scale, the square in front beautified with gardens and underground passageways for foot traffic. Other destroyed train stations were similarly rebuilt, high speed subways were constructed, as well as skyscrapers, and the Schwedenbruecke, the very important bridge over the arm of the Danube, where the fighting against the invading Russian army had been the heaviest. A new sports stadium, the largest in all of Europe, was planned, a new hospital and a museum, but most important for many Viennese after restoring St. Stefan, was the rebuilding of the Opera and the Burgtheater. The opening of these two was hailed with much fanfare and people from all over the world were expected to attend the ceremonies.

No less important for Vienna than the reopening of the cultural world, was the treaty Austria finally received to establish its old independence. This was in 1955, and Peter and Claire found it significant enough to take their children to Vienna to participate in the celebration of that event. They went to the Belvedere Garden with thousands of others, where the Austrian Chancellor Figl appeared on the balcony of Prince Eugen of Savoy's famous castle, holding up the signed agreement and showing it to the people below, who cried, and laughed, and embraced each other in joy. It was ten years since the war had ended. It had taken that long for the Allies to recognize Austria's right to be its own country again. There had been bitterness over the delayed recognition, but on that day everything was well and happy people celebrated with music and dances in all public squares throughout the night. The Burghoff family celebrated long into the evening until the children, who had been begging for more and more, were exhausted themselves and ready to sleep off all the excitement. Next morning they paid a visit to Grandmother Rosemarie, and got on the train to take them home, enriched by an experience they would never forget.

On their return, Peter had a surprise for Claire. He had been offered the position of the Chief of Staff at the most prestigious hospital in the city of Salzburg, which included an elegant residence in a fine area of distinguished homes. He had not yet accepted, and asked Claire's opinion. He had assumed that she would be more than pleased to change from the simple life of a small town to the sophisticated atmosphere of Salzburg, but Claire was more concerned about the change than he expected. She was in full support of whatever Peter decided. This offer had to be recognized as a great opportunity for Peter and an honor and had to be considered carefully. As far as she was concerned, she was happy in the present situation.

Peter had to wrestle with the dilemma himself. He had always maintained that all he was meant to be was a simple country doctor, bound by his roots; yet suddenly he recognized his ambitions went beyond that. He realized he had not only to think about Claire's needs and desires, but professional recognition was also important to him. Since Claire would not help him decide, he talked to Hanna, but here too, he got no more advice than he had from Claire:

"You must decide that for yourself."

His friend, the bishop, could not see why there was a conflict in the first place. The new position, although more prestigious, did not have to change Peter's values at all. The class of patients at St. Markus consisted mostly of the well to do, the so called cream of society, often including visitors from foreign countries who were lured to the city of Salzburg every year for its renowned music festivals, as well as the many tourists who came for a variety of reasons. Peter told the bishop that he did not have the stomach to cater to the imagined ills of the spoiled and idle.

"Do the privileged of our society not deserve the same medical attention as the simpler country folks?" his friend asked; and added that Peter's hang-ups were misplaced.

"As far as I know, the job description does not regulate any distinction between wealthy and poor patients," said the bishop, and continued:

"You have succeeded and received recognition by being a dedicated doctor, accomplished in your profession, and not because you kowtowed to any special group of patients. All that is expected from you is a continuation of your work with the integrity for which you are known and in pursuit of better and newer medical treatments."

What Peter did not know was that the words of the bishop were the same, with some additions, as they were in his recommendations to the hospital board when he had been asked about Peter's qualifications for the position. Franz did not want Peter to think he had anything to do with the appointment. Peter was always so proud and sensitive, but Franz was sincere in his recommendations, not because of their friendship, but because Peter was truly the best choice.

Claire, at first a little sentimental about having to break the ties that bound her to the home where she had tended to her little family, soon found some benefits in the change. Some time ago she and Peter had discussed the schooling for the children beyond the elementary grades and had been concerned because the local schools in St. Johann did not offer the type of education that they wanted for them. Peter was determined that the boys would go the same boarding school he had attended; she had dreaded the prospect of parting with the children.

"You loathed it," Claire tried to remind him.

"Times have changed, and so have their teaching and educational methods. You know only too well that the boys need a little more restraint; they are moderately spoiled, and a greater discipline will be good for them."

Claire laughed, and admitted that their sons' temperament was in need of some taming at times. The boys, so close in their ages, were always paired off in their activities and, although they were never in real trouble, were sometimes admonished by their teachers. Claire could not resist the charm of their youthful spirits, and was seldom angry with them. Peter, on the other hand, put up a stern facade, and did not easily tolerate mischief. Since he was so busy in his job, he felt that stronger supervision was necessary. The boys, who resisted going to the Jesuits' boarding school, had two strong advocates in their corner: Paul Thoene, who loved roughhousing with them on the farm, taught them swimming and diving, and acrobatics which he remembered from his own youth as the untamed offspring of very tolerant parents. The boys in return adored uncle Paul. Peter said Paul should have sons himself to challenge his tolerance, but even though not admitting it openly, he was very proud of having sons who were "rough and tough" rather than weaklings. The other support for the boys came from their grandfather, Anton. He had introduced them to horses when they were quite young, and at eight each had his own to ride. Anton Burghoff was proud of the strapping youngsters, true descendants of the Burghoff dynasty.

Respected as both men were by Peter, he did not change his mind regarding the boys' educational needs. The move to the city of Salzburg made it possible, however, for the boys not have to board at the strict institution full time but instead to attend their day school, from their tenth to their eighteenth year. Claire was so relieved, and so were Tony and Chris, who wrangled permission from their father to spend as many weekends at the farm as they possibly could. How could Peter refuse; remembering his own youth, when he and his best friend Franz Hinterberger, used to groan about their "incarceration," as they called it, when their freedom was so curtailed that even weekend visits to their homes were only allowed occasionally? Claire was happy, Anton Burghoff was pleased, and Peter was finally satisfied with the arrangements.

Weather and Peter's time permitting, he and Claire loved to take day-long hikes into the surrounding mountains, biking or wandering through the forests of Kammerbach, such as this outing on a very warm summer day during a weekend visit to the farm. They took a rowboat to cross Kammerlake, climbed up an incline to the forest along a narrow, seldom used path, very familiar to Peter. He had not been here for ages, but asked Claire if she remembered. She did not until they heard the roar of rushing waters somewhere nearby.

"Is it the waterfall?" she asked with surprised joy in her voice.

"Now you remember! It is one of my favorite places where I used to wander when I was a young boy. This part of the forest belongs to Waldegg and few people wander this way. A little further up is a clearing, from where we can look down to the lake and Waldegg on the other side."

It was a sunny day, the air still and hot, and they rested at the clearing, a grassy area covered with the season's blooms of white margarites, blue gentian, red clover and so many others. Claire lay down in the grass with Peter next to her, she enjoyed a moment of complete bliss. No disturbing sounds of civilization, but the humming of insects over her head, flying from flower to flower, sipping from the nectar. The sky was deep blue, only tiny clouds passing by. This was the peace she had dreamed of so often in the dark days of the past. Had it truly become reality? She quickly stretched out her arm to touch Peter's—he was there! Even such a golden day can eventually become too hot, and Peter suggested they find respite at the waterfall. A misty spray greeted them as they came near. True, it was not one of the most spectacular waterfalls, but was respectable nevertheless. Peter recounted the days when he took off his clothes and let the cool water run in sheets over his body—a different experience than just to get into a prickling shower, he said.

"Did you have that in mind when you took me up here a long time ago?" Claire asked.

"You know me better than that," Peter protested. She did indeed, and was glad about it. She recalled that day. She was only seventeen then, and would have been turned off forever if he had suggested such a thing. Peter continued:

"But how about trying it now? It really is a wonderful feeling, kind of a Kneipp Water cure—you heard of that? And no one ever comes this way, we are completely safe."

Claire did not need any prodding, she shed her clothes, and so did Peter.

"Just remain to the side, the fall is too powerful in the center," Peter said.

Claire was already enjoying the cooling waters splashing over her body, but took an unexpected step forward, slipped on a wet boulder, and slid into the cascading throw of the water. Peter, frantic, jumped after her, but the swirls had grabbed her and thrown her into the rushing stream. Peter saw her head bobbing up and down at some distance. He tried to scream to her to keep to her right, where she could grab on at brushes leaning over the water at a bend in the river; of course, she could not hear him over the noise of the gushing water. But when Peter reached that area he saw Claire holding on to a branch, as he had hoped she would. She did not have enough strength to lift herself to shore, but Peter pushed her and himself up the embankment. At this stage, the real danger of being caught up in another whirl had not been great, but both felt relieved to have escaped a nasty experience. Except for bruises and scratches, they were not injured, but they were anxious to make their way back up the stream to the waterfall where they had left their clothes. It was awkward, to say the least, to find themselves naked in the wilderness. There was no great danger of being seen, Peter assured his wife; however, even a slight possibility would be embarrassing, therefore they made their way back hurriedly through the underbrush near the river bank. It was probably not much more than a quarter of a mile, but running through the thickets was very uncomfortable. They had to go a little distance above the waterfall, where the river was slow and easy to cross, to reach the place where they had deposited their clothes. They made it without incident and rushed to get dressed. Then they finally relaxed, leaned back against a big boulder by the riverside and tried to remember how the accident could have happened They were both tired and quiet for a while, when all of a sudden Claire started to giggle. Peter turned towards her, smiling at first, but being soon infected by her continued laughter, he joined in. Soon they both shook with laughter until the tears rolled down their cheeks. When they got hold of themselves again, they recounted their adventure as such a ridiculous event, especially running through the forest naked, not even having had the grace of the fig leaves as Adam and Eve had worn. They chuckled all the way home, but did not tell anyone the reason, when asked about it. Never! It was funny, but embarrassing nevertheless, Peter thought.

The schooling for the girls had been decided a while ago. They were quite excited about the prospect of spending a few years in Vienna at the boarding school for girls at the Sacre-Soeur. Claire was not very happy about it, she wished the girls could have had the same opportunity she had at the co-educational Gymnasium, but she conceded they would receive a good education at the Convent of the Sisters of the Sacre Coeur. The whole question of the girls studying in Vienna came only after the maternal grandparents of Eva, who had not shown much interest in her when she was growing up, started to complain, that they were being deprived of knowing their granddaughter because she lived so far away.

Chapter 19

The year of 1956 brought many changes in Claire's life and Peter became aware with some concern that she was often in a melancholy mood. It had always been upmost in his mind to make her happy; she still filled his heart with gratitude, but most of all with love and passion. At least, they were now settled in a comfortable home, furnished by Claire with care and in an appropriate manner to her husband's position. Despite Peter's continued resistance to social functions, entertaining had become a necessary part of their life in that sophisticated city. Even though Claire's heart was not fully content with it, she was a gracious hostess, most likely a trait inherited from her mother.

She admired the city of Salzburg, especially the old town with its historic buildings and monuments, the remarkable baroque churches, palaces, and spacious squares; memories of Mozart everywhere, quaint shops, the outdoor market, the old book store, the fortress of Hohensalzburg, dating from the eleventh century. She loved to stroll through the lovely Mirabell Garden, next to Schloss Mirabell, reconstructed after a fire, but originally built for the mistress of the Bishop Wolf Dietrich in the early sixteen hundred. She and Peter enjoyed the many musical and cultural events; there were the Salzburger Festspiele, the Schlosskonzerte, concerts also at the Hohenfestung. All this had never been far from the farm in kilometers, but a world away in its atmosphere, and now they lived in its midst. Not that Claire preferred city living over the country, but it was an exciting change. However, she knew in her heart that she most likely would have prefered to live on the farm instead.

The villa which the Burghoffs occupied was surrounded by a lovely garden of its own, which was tended by the gardeners of the hospital grounds. Claire missed her vegetable garden from St. Johann, which she no longer needed to supplement their food rations. That sorry time had passed, but with it also the feelings of satisfaction in the struggle to provide and survive, which had once been connected with her gardening chores. As always, Claire enjoyed the visits to the farm, and the boys never failed to remind their parents of their promise to go often. Actually, the farm was no further away from the big city than it had been from St. Johann, so visits there had not been complicated by the Burghoff's move.

Claire's fortieth birthday was to be celebrated at Waldegg in August. Hanna had insisted and made all the preparations. Peter had grander ideas, but was content with postponing his until after all the children were at school in the fall, and he and Claire would have more time for themselves. Claire accepted it all with a grateful smile. Forty years was indeed a milestone, and she looked more carefully in the mirror for unwelcome signs of aging. She had never been vain, but seeing her handsome husband grow even more handsome with advancing age, she did not want to fail him with declining looks. She discovered a single gray hair here and there, which could still be easily removed, but she decided to keep them. Her skin had always been clear and nearly perfect, although with a tendency to look a little pale. This whiteness would have been lauded in past generations, but now the fashion was a healthy tan. She achieved that easily during the summer months. Her figure was nearly unchanged since her youth—a little wider in the hips perhaps and fuller around the bust, but graceful as ever and still turning men's heads when she walked through town.

The Thoene's came to the birthday party, and so did Heidi with her family from Bruck, who came every summer for a few days. The tables for coffee and cake were set festively in the garden, and garlands and lanterns were strung between the trees. Hanna's older brother, Karl, just happened to be in town also with two of his grandchildren: Martin, who had just graduated and was on his way to the University in Innsbruck to study veterinary medicine, and his younger sister Annie.

Claire's children were more excited than the birthday girl herself. They felt that it must be a dramatic time for their mother to be "that old" now, as Tony mentioned several times. They felt they must be especially nice to their aging mother. They did not think of Grandmother Hanna as "that old," because she had always been that way in their eyes, and besides, she was a grandmother! That is how children see the world around them.

Before the cake was cut, they were ready with their presents for their mother. Eva and Elizabeth had labored for weeks under the guidance of Hanna to embroider a dainty cloth for Claire's new tea table, and it was lovely. Each boy recited a lengthy poem, composed by Paul for that occasion, which consisted of a very moving homage to their mother. It was a real surprise to Claire, as well as to Peter, and they could not believe that the boys could have kept it a secret for what must have been quite a while. Claire had tears in her eyes. She was leaning against a nearby tree trunk while listening; sunshine filtering through the leaves created changing highlights in her chestnut hair, her cheeks were flushed in excitement; she wore one of Peter's favorite *dirndl* dresses, an original costume of the region of Pongau. She looked absolutely enchanting, and not only Peter felt that way. He had listened to the boys' recital and observed Paul looking at Claire. Peter felt with a twinge in his heart that the poem expressed what was in Paul's heart, although it spoke through the children's voices. They certainly expressed a continuing admiration of Claire. Who could blame him? Peter felt generous; jealousy had no place here.

Tony and Christopher were duly praised for their performance, their mother embraced them with much emotion. They were proud of themselves and felt a reward was due to them soon: Hanna's lavish cake was enjoyed by everybody. Some of the farm help came by and took part in the festivities. Later in the evening, they were also joined by a few close friends from the village, including Burgl who had been at home with her parents, the Maiers, for a visit. Claire had not seen her since the "days on the beach." Both women enjoyed their reunion very much after all these years, telling each other, how little they had changed, and how happy they were about the turn of their lives. Since it was not a good time then to chat about the past, they promised each other another visit, possibly at the new and more grandiose tourist hotel in Tyrol that Burgl and her husband had just opened. A few musicians were also on the list of invited guests, and zither-playing and singing continued until late at night. The boys had to leave the party at the proper bedtime, but the girls were allowed to remain, so they could entertain the visitors, Martin and Annie from Tyrol and Heidi's two sons, also teenagers by now. Sunny Elizabeth was, as always, the center of attention, while Eva acted as observer, quiet, and on the side lines, but when decisions were to be made, Elizabeth turned automatically towards her older sister— as it had always been.

Claire's fortieth birthday party was a success, everybody had a good time. However, later that night, Peter mentioned to his wife that he had another surprise in mind for her; next month, when the children were off at school, they would take a few days off by themselves.

With a heavy heart Claire accompanied her daughters to Vienna to their new school. The girls had been excited about the adventure at first, but when reality set in, a sense of being deserted overcame them, and there were even tears the first week. It affected Eva more than her younger sister. Throughout the years, since she had been a very small child with big problems, she had flung herself at Claire, which had surprised everybody familiar with the situation, especially Grandmother Hanna, who had herself tried without success to make friends with that belligerent little child who resented all advances.

The dog had helped to open the heart of the child, and soon after that she had included Elizabeth. However, from the day when Claire took her warmly into her arms, the child had never wanted to let go. Growing a little older, she often challenged Claire into admissions that she loved her too, although always maintaining that Claire could not possibly love her as much as she loved her own children. When Claire asked, why she would feel that way— did Eva not love her as a mother also?

"Yes," Eva said, "you are the only mother I have, but you have other children, and I am not one of them."

In the mind of the child it was a logical explanation. That conversation was repeated often, but as Eva grew older she seemed to understand better. Her intensive show of love towards Claire continued, and Claire was glad that the other children did not show any jealousy. All of them argued sometimes and had disagreements with each other as all children do, but nothing of permanence or importance. The boys were not much affected at all by their older sister's behavior. Elizabeth accepted Eva's mothering style freely and often even took advantage of it. Eva had to smooth things out, when Elizabeth had misbehaved. Actually, that was not too often, because Elizabeth was never confrontational, she tried to please, and apparently enjoyed being lovable. She also knew how to wrap her father around her little finger. Peter maintained, especially to himself, that he loved his children equally, but when thinking of Elizabeth, there was an additional warm feeling within him which was difficult to define. He had tried hard to overcome the past of Eva's existence, but a little nag remained, especially since Eva herself never seemed to be able to show affection towards him. He played with her, cuddled up with her, but she always tried to pull away. Peter felt it; it hurt, but he also understood. Her mother's legacy was in some way still with them both.

In Vienna, Claire arranged that the girls would visit their respective grandmothers regularly, that is, to spend at least one weekend each month with them. Rosemarie said that she was looking forward to having Elizabeth with her, and Marlena's family welcomed Eva's visits also. Claire did not meet Marlena's parents though, because they clearly declined her visit. It was awkward, but Claire respected their wishes, only hoping it would turn out well for Eva, and not cause any emotional problems.

As Peter had hinted, his birthday celebration for Claire was in the planning stage. First, he wanted Claire to find a formal evening dress. Since her "ball-days" in Vienna before the war, Claire had not owned one, nor missed such luxury, but the thought of purchasing one now was not unpleasant. Peter said to find the best, and not to look at the price tag. He, usually rather frugal, was in a spending mood. Salzburg has plenty of establishments where one could find fine clothing, and in 1956 it became possible to purchase quality items again. Imported silks from Italy in all colors, weaves and designs, were available, and made the choice difficult. Claire chose finally a simple but elegant cut for the made to order gown and was satisfied with the result, but kept the details from Peter. Since he wanted to surprise her, she would do the same.

Peter finally managed to coordinate the dates for the "Big Party," as he called it, and Claire now became curious. Peter had to arrange for a few days absence from the hospital and for tickets to the events he wanted to attend. He wished to go to the opera, hopefully a Wagner presentation, as well as to the Burgtheater, which Claire would love even more, and, if possible, to a performance at the Theater an der Wien also. The reconstruction of these elegant buildings was now completed, and, as in the past, they presented first class productions. The Viennese, as well as many visitors from foreign countries, mostly Americans—snapped up all the good tickets, so they became hard to get. Peter called the Thoene's, not only inviting them to join in the Vienna party, but also asking for help in obtaining tickets. That became Melinda's job, as she had some clout through her family connections. She and Paul had attended the first day openings at the opera, as well as at the Burgtheater, about a year ago, and had been full of praise and pride for the cultural atmosphere that seemed to have risen again in Vienna

Melinda was able to oblige and procured five tickets for both events. At the opera it would not be Wagner, but Richard Strauss's "Rosenkavalier," and at the Burgtheater Goethe's "Faust," both performances with an exceptional cast. The fifth ticket was for Bishop Hinterberger, who was also invited in order to give—as Peter saw it—the whole affair the importance and dignity it deserved. Peter was elated about his plans, feeling like a little boy, and not the dignified head of a medical establishment. He was indeed regarded as such by his staff and subordinates, although it was not haughty behavior that made him appear so dignified, but his reserved ways—a trait that had been with him forever. Only Claire, and Franz Hinterberger knew the other Peter, the warm, sympathetic, somewhat shy man, hiding behind a forceful demeanor to which his tall stature, the finely chiseled features of a masculine face, deep blue eyes, and a strong chin, softened by a dimple, contributed. Already a slight graying at the temples added to the imposing handsome appearance, which may have also played a part in his selection as the medical director, because the hospital board was quite unanimous in their opinion that appearances also count in the public eye.

Peter finally had to tell Claire about the Vienna holiday, because she had to make proper preparations for the affair, but she was not told about their friends' participation. One surprise at least could be postponed. Claire was looking forward very much to the holiday, hoping especially to see the girls at the boarding school. The letters from them had not been too happy lately, not about the school, but about their classmates, who came from different back-grounds, mostly metropolitan, and looked down upon the "country girls." Elizabeth also said, that a weekend with Grandmother Rosemarie was as bor-ing as one could imagine. Eva was not bored, but called her maternal grand-parents and the aunt living with them "really weird," and said that she did not ever want to become a part of that family. Both letters contained youth-ful exaggerations of course, but Claire wanted to see for herself if they were really unhappy. She packed usual weekend clothes and carefully wrapped her new evening gown and the accessories: long white gloves, silver slippers, etc. She wanted to make a good appearance for Peter's sake, since all of this meant so much to him.

A taxi brought them from the Westbahnhof to the Hotel Imperial on the Kaerntner Ring, probably the most elegant of all the expensive hotels in Vienna. Claire just gushed; she was not sure she approved of Peter's extrava-gance, but he told her firmly that he did not want to hear any disapproval—this birthday party was a present to her, and she knew better than to criticize a gift from the heart. *Oh Peter—dear, dear Peter*, she thought and smiled. He should have told her, however, because the clothes she was wearing did not do justice to the elegance of the place. Peter assured her that she looked per-fectly appropriate.

They had dinner reservations at the Augustinerkeller, a nice old estab-lishment within walking distance. Claire felt elated walking through the ele-gant streets of that part of Vienna on the arm of her husband. It was only twenty years ago that they had spend a wonderful romantic night in the Volksgarten, young lovers, with hopes and expectations for a future togeth-er. Then came the waiting to hear from him, the longing—and the realiza-tion that it had been just a youthful encounter, a dream, never to come true. The long and cruel years of the war that followed overshadowed even the memory of those happy hours. Peter had become just a romantic figure of her silly girlish fantasies. She had tried hard to forget—and almost had. Then the fateful encounter seven years later—and again she had to stand back and try to forget once more.

Now, here they were—had not all her prayers come true? She was so grateful for everything—for Peter, for her children, for the moment—she wished she could cry a little, but what would Peter think about that! So she just pressed his arm firmly and smiled up at him. He was so glad that she finally seemed to relax and enjoy his birthday present, more of which was still to come. He did not think of the past like she did. Peter could be so loving and thoughtful—but he was not melodramatic in his emotions, Claire thought. In the best of moods, they entered the dimly lit restaurant and were shown to a table occupied by two other people. Claire could not suppress a small cry of joy when she recognized Paul and Melinda.

"What a coincidence to see you here?"

"Coincidence?" Paul said. "Did Peter really manage to surprise you?"

An evening full of warmth and friendship followed, and Claire was in great spirits. When the disclosure of the next two gala evenings which they were going to spend together followed, she was truly overwhelmed. The Thoene's also stayed the Hotel Imperial.

On the next day each couple went their own ways. Claire and Peter went to see their daughters at the boarding school to find out as soon as possible if they had adjusted by now. Their letters still showed unhappiness. Was it just homesickness or was it more serious? Claire was ready to take them home with her, but Peter admonished caution. They had not announced their visit, and no special time has been set aside for a meeting, which met with some disapproval from the headmistress, a severe looking, no-nonsense nun. Peter apologized, saying that they had come to Vienna for other reasons than visiting the school, but since they were in town, they would like to have the opportunity to see their daughters. The nun made arrangements for half an hour at noon and invited them to take lunch with the girls. In the meantime, they could watch the children at their recess-games on the play field from a window in the dining hall. Since all the girls wore the same outfits, Claire and Peter had some difficulties in finding their own, but eventually recognized them within the screaming and exuberant bunch playing a lively game. If the girls' letters had told of loneliness, discrimination, boredom, etc. Peter and Claire did not see anything of that kind in the rosy cheeks of the breathless youngsters, when they saw them returning to the building. Eva, who normally was in a different group of students from Elizabeth, had permission to take her meal with her sister and her parents at a specially set table. The girls were excited to see their parents and wanted to know why they were to here. Peter explained the birthday extension, and he and Claire observed with some wonder that the girls almost seemed to be relieved when it was clear that they had not come to take them back.

"Should we take you back home with us?" Claire asked, and Elizabeth answered quickly:

"Well, not yet. Right now we are preparing a musical play for Christmas. I will have a special role, and it should be much fun. I would not want to miss it."

"And you, Eva?"

"I miss you very much, but I have interesting classes and a chance to learn things they did not teach in St. Johann. Also, Christmas is not too far off, and we will be able to come home for vacation then, won't we?"

"You see" said Peter afterwards, "they are not as unhappy as you thought," although the three females had shed a few tears at the parting. Peter wanted to call on a couple of his old friends from his student days, and Claire went to visit her mother.

Rosemarie looked her old self when entertaining her daughter at her lovely tea table, using her fine porcelain and silver service, offering delicate pastries, purchased from the finest of all *konditoreis* in Vienna, Demels' at the Kohlmarkt. Claire looked at her mother and thought of the times when she was a young girl. Her mother hardly looked any different today. Claire had always admired her dainty moves, her refined taste, her reserved manners, and her lovely appearance. She wondered that the years of struggle and hardships seemed to have disappeared, except that she had adopted a little tremor in her voice and a lament in her speech. Well, we all change with age, she told herself, and was glad that Rosemarie was doing so well. She told Claire about her bridge parties and visits with friends, and then, with some hesitation, that she had found a gentlemen who had become a dear friend to her. He had been one of Friederich's colleagues at the University, was now retired, and was recently also widowed. They had so much in common, Rosemarie said, and he was a great help to her. Claire was stunned. "Help" what help did her mother need? She did not say so, just asked about the housekeeper, did she not work out?

"Oh yes, I could not do without Agnes. She is an angel. Who do you think would be doing my shopping and cleaning, and all that?"

"I would like to meet your new friend," said Claire.

"One of these days we shall arrange for that," said Rosemarie, in a tone of voice that let Claire know the theme was closed for now.

"You spent a couple of weekends with Elizabeth. How did that go?"

"Ah well, today's youth—they are so demanding. Elizabeth is a lovely child, and I love her dearly, but I am an old lady, how can I entertain a twelve year old?"

"Are these visits a burden to you, Mother?"

"No, of course not, but we had a hard time getting to know each other, you know."

Yes, Claire thought, but it was not the distance of miles that had kept them apart so that they did not know each other. Her mother had never reconciled to Claire's past; she was the daughter that had strayed and Claire wondered if her mother had problems explaining this wayward daughter to her friends, and that was why she acted so distantly.

Rosemarie asked about Peter and the boys. Claire could not help saying that she and Peter were in town for her extended birthday celebration. Her mother had not even sent birthday greetings to her. Claire was not normally given to bragging, but all of a sudden she had to tell her mother about the new gown, the visits to the opera and the Burgtheater, and that they were staying at the Hotel Imperial. Not a bad come-back for the once unvirtuous daughter She also told her about the birthday celebration at the farm and her children's moving tributes. It was not lost on Rosemarie. She only said, that she was happy that Claire had a good life, and wished that Friederich had lived long enough to see that too. He had been greatly worried about her future.

Claire felt sick. She had to accept the estrangement. It was not a surprise, she had known it for a long time, but it was painful nevertheless. She felt sorry also that she had behaved badly by trying to impress her mother with her life in revenge for her mother's diminished opinion of her. When she came back to the hotel, Peter was already there and she threw herself into his arms where she always found comfort and peace. He guessed what might have caused her distress, but they did not talk about it. They looked forward to the evening.

Peter and Paul waited in the lobby of the hotel for the ladies, who took a little longer with their toilet. When Claire and Melinda descended the stairs, their husbands looked with pride at these two beautiful women.

Melinda was dressed in a crimson sheath with a low neckline, showing off her splendid white skin, which contrasted deliciously with her black hair, pulled back in a chignon and adorned with a diamond spangle. Melinda's features were not exactly beautiful in the classic sense, yet she always attracted people's admiring looks. One would call her appearance striking.

Claire had chosen a pale green color for her gown, whose soft folds fell gently from her bust, revealing her superb figure with every move: long legs, small waist, well formed bust. The décolleté would have been too revealing were it not for the shawl of the same material draped around her shoulders and held by an ornate clasp. The dress was a copy of a French contemporary design, yet reminded of the "days of wine and roses in old Vienna." Claire looked like an artist's portrait of a lady from a bygone era.

Both men were very delighted with their ladies' appearance, and when the four of them entered the Loge at the Opera House, many opera glasses were turned towards them. Melinda and Paul were known to many in the audience, Melinda in her own right, having been to many social affairs as a member of her family; Paul because of his profession as publisher, as well as for his involvement in politics and the rebuilding of the country after the war. Peter and Claire were strangers to the "in-crowd" and the guessing began: "elegant-expensive, probably *nouveau riche*, most likely war profiteers "—so the speculation went from the rows of the expensive seats, but in one of the back rows two women also noticed them, when one of them said:

"Hilda, look, is that not Claire Baumann from our school?" Hilda said:

"I don't remember her much, is she the one of whom it was said, that she was bombed out during the war?"

"Apparently she survived. Let's find out all about her during intermission."

Just before the overture started, another gentlemen entered the Loge and occupied the fifth seat. Claire had just looked a little from the side, when she recognized the bishop. She had to hold unto herself, not to jump up and embrace him. She was overjoyed, while Peter and her friends smiled with delight. Another surprise for Claire had worked out well. Franz put his finger to his lips—the music had begun. Claire was full of emotion and, as often when she felt sentimental, would have loved to cry a little, but she could not afford that luxury right now.

During the overture her eyes turned towards the auditorium, whose magnificence she had not immediately taken in with all the excitement. Out of the rubble of the old beloved musical institution, destroyed in a savage war, a new one had arisen, or was the old one miraculously resurrected? Claire had heard about the sacrifices the Viennese had made to recreate the Opera in the old style as a symbol of the musical spirit of that city, but also that large amounts of money had came from music lovers all over, especially from the United States—some also from Dr. Peter Burghoff.

The curtain rose and the play began. The singers were superb, the music enchanting, and when Claire looked at Peter, she saw him completely enrapt. During intermission he told of a time during his student's days when he had been to hear the Rosenkavalier, and then, walking the long way home at night, he could still hear in his head every aria, every movement of the music which filled his soul. Claire enjoyed the presentation also, she loved the singing, it was all very wonderful, but she did not feel that deep emotion that Peter expressed. She would ask him later, if today's experience lingered like the one from long ago.

On their way to the foyer, where people mingled, they had a chance to admire the grandiose architecture and superb decor. The walls were of marble high up to the galleries—others were mirrored walls—and crystal chandeliers glittered and reflected in them. The color scheme was kept in gold and creme. Claire felt as if caught in a fairy tale. They walked through the Goblin Hall, where the walls and doors are encased in tapestries with motives from the Magic Flute: Papageno and Papagena in the Magic Forest. Most people were dressed elegantly, and much beautiful jewelry was displayed.

While Claire was slowly walking behind her friends, admiring her surrounding, Hilda Kohler and Gertrude Hammer approached her to greet Claire, who did not immediately recognize them; but Hilda introduced herself and Gertrude reminded her that they had been schoolmates at the Gymnasium.

"Of course," Claire said, "how are you?"

"Would you believe that we are now teaching at our old school?"

"Congratulations," Claire said.

"How about you, we had heard at one of our school reunions that you had worked for the Germans." Hilda said it, as if catching Claire on something rather embarrassing.

In 1938, when the *Anschluss* to Germany had brought much needed employment opportunities to Austria, everybody had clamored for it. When that whole political period ended in a destructive war and bitter disappointments, these same people chose to forget their welcoming of the Germans then. This was not new to Claire, but she said only, without feeling the need of an excuse:

"Yes, I had the good fortune to manage an office for the Stehle company—you do remember the name?"

"We also heard that your boyfriend Lixel was killed in the war, and nobody knew what had happened to you afterwards. Apparently you did well, your dress is gorgeous."

Claire had enough by now—she had no intention of satisfying the gossipy curiosity of two women she barely remembered.

"You have to excuse me, my party is waiting for me."

And indeed, Peter and Franz were standing at the bottom of the wide staircase, chatting, while Paul and Melinda were in conversation with another couple a few steps away. Claire descended slowly, looking for them. She was truly beautiful, both men thought so at the same time, and the bishop said:

"You are a lucky man, Peter."

"I know," Peter said, and then, with some pity in his voice:

"I am so sorry that your vows don't allow you to experience a relationship like Claire and I have, namely to love and be loved in return." Franz turned towards Peter and said smiling:

"Ah, Peter, I have loved also, I do know what it means," and added to Peter's surprised look, "But do not worry, I kept my vows—I did not sin!"

Then both men smiled but Peter was somewhat speechless. He had always confided in his friend, but it seemed Franz had not returned this confidence in the same way. Maybe it was better so, he did not need to know. He loved his friend now even more. Since their school days together at the Jesuit's boarding school, he had hoped that a priest could also be human.

The Opera ended with great applause, and the friends parted from the bishop with reminders to meet the next evening at the Theater. During the day all of them had different plans and obligations, but the evening would again be devoted to their common enjoyment.

Before retiring, the two couples had a nightcap together at the hotel bar, with soft music and schmaltzy songs, not to Peter's taste after having had the experience of "real music" he said. Melinda told him not to be a critic of a genre he did not understand. Music has many facets and reaches people in different ways. Peter laughed, saying if Melinda could appreciate it, he might just as well learn it too. Claire was happy about Melinda's friendly advice, it supported her own musical taste for some popular tunes, which Peter always found trite.

It was long past midnight when they parted. Claire had been in high spirits all evening, relishing the occasion, and Peter had his satisfaction in seeing her happiness. They both stayed at the window of their suite for a little while, watching the traffic along Ringstrasse, showing that this city was still awake even at this late hour. At least here, in the center, around the opera, where people are used to strolling from the opera to the restaurants or cafes, or bars, or even to the lovely parks nearby.

When Claire was in bed, and Peter had turned the lights down, she asked all of sudden:

"Peter, you did not say if you liked my dress."

"Of course, I liked it. It was very becoming, and you looked ravishingly beautiful."

"Do you like its color?"

"Yes, I do."

"Do you know why I chose it?"

"What?"

"The color?"

"Because it suits you."

"I thought you liked me in blue."

"Well…what do you call the color?"

"Reseda."

"As far as I know, Reseda is a plant, quite fragrant, I think we have it in our garden."

"Then you know the color of my dress!"

"Claire, I don't know what you are getting at, but I don't feel like guessing colors."

"Just one more thing, please. Do you remember the fateful night when you visited me at my apartment in Vienna?"

"How could I ever forget, darling?"

"Do you remember the color of my dressing gown?"

"Dressing gown? You must forgive me, I can not remember what you wore, though I remember clearly, when you did not wear it."

"Oh, Peter—its color was Reseda. I had a hard time finding that color, thinking it would remind you of that night." Peter laughed out loud.

"Dear, dear, sentimental Claire, You must forgive my lack of sophistication; do you still not know that you married a country boy? I could not distinguish between reseda and grass-green."

Now it was Claire who felt silly to have had such a sentimental idea that men could remember things like colors.

"One more thing about my dress tonight."

"Yes?"

"I did not wear anything underneath!"

"What, nothing?!"

"Well, almost nothing." Another laugh, but more subdued and he reached for his wife:

"You wicked, wicked woman!"

The next morning promised one of these balmy days of fall, a little fog in the morning, but the sun warming up later, and nature showing the finest color scheme in its last efforts of the year. Peter had another marvelous idea, he said. Claire told him that she had not seen such enterprise in him for a long time! He suggested they take a ride out into the Vienna Woods, maybe another sentimental repetition of the day before that fateful evening?

Then it had been springtime. She remembered the day as being full of bliss and happiness just to be near him, but also the painful awareness that it would be only short-lived. How could she have imagined in her wildest dream the ways their lives would eventually come together! She would not even have dared to pray to God to grant her such an enormous wish. With her lifelong belief in the power of prayer, she would never ask for the unattainable. She had a good relationship with God, but knew what he must deny her. For her, Peter was a dream come true. Or did God already then plan their future? Claire did not want to speculate, but would always remember to be grateful, and she continued to give thanks in her daily prayer.

The stroll through the meadows and forest was as joyful as the one in the spring of long ago. They held hands as before, but their walk was slower, and they looked at each other with contentment, and they kissed in the knowledge of belonging and not of parting ever again.

The views over the city were as breathtaking as ever, and the knowledge was to be treasured that it and they had survived the gruesome war, which had then began hanging over their heads with such dread. How lovely it was to be able to sit in the restored restaurant on top of the Kahlenberg and have a fine meal—no ration cards, no sloppy food made of imitation ingredients, or bread with the addition of sawdust and coffee made from chicory.

The evening presentation at the Burgtheater of Goethe's great drama "Faust"—again in the company of their friends—was a real treat for Claire. She followed every word in every scene, knowing it almost by heart, but delighting in the performance, the style, the speech of these actors who knew how to use the language to its perfect expression. It was called "Burgtheater Deutsch", meaning the style of the German language, which only the best actors who had studied hard and long learned to speak to perfection, just as only the best English actors can speak "Shakespearean English."

During intermission they had a chance, just as at the opera the day before, to admire the reconstruction of the Burgtheater, that venerable building which was so heavily bombed during the war and just as at the Opera House, they were full of praise and wonder how "poor old Vienna" could have afforded to replace the old with new, equally, luxurious elegance. They concluded that it had to be done for the self-respect of its people. Melinda mentioned a letter from one of her Viennese friends, who had told her proudly:

"We are still wearing our old shoes and can't afford to have them resoled, but we just subscribed to the first season's tickets to the Burgtheater. It makes us feel that we have survived a tragic past, and can look forward to living with dignity again."

After the theater they all went to the Cafe Landtman next door, where patrons and actors of the theater usually gathered after a performance. Melinda found her uncle Attila, who had played a leading role that evening, in the company of some friends, and he joined them for a drink. He complimented Melinda, and also bowed before Claire, saying that he had noticed their party in their loge from the stage, and that the ladies had given the theater a special aura with their lovely appearance. Kissing the two women's hand, he joined his party again. Claire had not had experienced such typical Viennese manners in a long time and much enjoyed it.

Next morning, Paul and Melinda took their train from the Suedbahnhof to Carynthia, and Peter and Claire went to the Westbahnhof for their trip home to Salzburg. What a beautiful birthday party it had been. Claire said that it was worth it to be forty years old for such an affair, and Peter was proud of himself for having had such a splendid idea.

Chapter 20

It was a very good Christmas that year. The whole family again was united. The girls found home more wonderful than ever, and said they could last in Vienna till the end of the school year at their boarding school, but no longer. The Christmas play at the school had been a great success, and Eva said that Elisabeth's acting and singing had contributed to it.

The boys were growing up also and not so intent to tease their sisters anymore. There was lots of snow, and in the village of Kammerbach and on the farm there were daily sleigh rides for visits from friend's or to friends' homes. Peter tried to join in as often as he could, but his duties at the hospital did not slacken for the season. Setting skier's broken bones were pretty routine, but when it involved the neck or the head, Peter was always consulted. He did not mind the medical calls, but his administrative duties as head of the hospital and the connected social obligations were not to his great liking. Claire stood by him, and gave him support, but would have preferred to be at Waldegg with the children at all times also.

A few days after the New Years celebration, Hanna asked Claire to join her for a gathering of the women of the village, celebrating one of their oldest members, ninety year old Farmer Lisl Wagrainer. There she met Gerda Engebrecht whom she had not seen for many, many years. One could still see that Gerda had been a very pretty girl when she was young, but now she looked a little worn out, tired, and older than her age. Claire was almost embarrassed—they were the same age—yet Claire had not felt herself to be old, despite her recent meaningful birthday. Gerda was cheerful, however, and seemed to join easily in the gaiety of the group. When they had a chance to exchange a few words, Claire asked about her family, and Gerda pointed to her daughter, who was in a group of young ones, including Elizabeth and

Eva, enjoying themselves in the snow outside. Her name was Ingrid, a lovely thing with light blond hair, kept in thick, long braids, like the oldest of the
women, Grandmother Hanna included, despite the modern fashion of short
hair for all females. She was very pretty, Claire thought, with no resemblance
to her father, the dark curly-haired "heartthrob" of long ago at the beach on
Kammersee. Ingrid was two years older than Elizabeth and her brother, who
was not present just then, was two years older than his sister.

"He probably resembles his father?" asked Claire, immediately thinking
that she was asking stupid questions, but Gerda did not mind.

"No, Helmut is just as blond as Ingrid, they apparently take after me.
They are good children, but Fritz thinks that Helmut is not serious enough.
You remember Fritz—he has not changed, is even more melancholic these
days. Of course, life has not treated him fairly. Orphaned by the shooting
accident, that left him blind in one eye; then the war, and worse when he
returned from that and was treated badly. But now it is all over. He has his
old teaching job back, he is even director at the school. He still roams the
forest whenever he can get away, and has never spent much time with the
children. He adores Ingrid, but is too strict with Helmut. I try to make up
for that, but a boy needs to be with his father. I don't know why I am telling
you all this, you probably think I am a gossip."

"On the contrary," said Claire, "I am very interested, I had not heard
from you since those ancient summer vacations."

"I know all about you though, "Gerda said." Everybody in the village
does. It seems you are happy, and I am glad. You deserve it; I remember well
that you were always nice. I hear that Peter Burghoff—forgive me, Doctor
Burghoff—is doing very well; people around here have great respect for him
and for the whole Burghoff family too. 'The people from the castle give the
village some importance. They say that the council has some ideas to get the
county to recognize the historical importance of the castle itself."

Claire was surprised; she had not heard anything—but leave it to village
gossip. Everybody usually knows more than the people involved. She was
going to ask Hanna about it. She enjoyed her conversation with Gerda and
told her so, which seemed to please her. At the end of the afternoon, when
everybody was about to leave. Hanna, Claire, and her girls were to be driv-
en home by one of the farm hands, she encountered Fritz Engebrecht at the
door. It was also the first time since they had seen each other after so many
years. Claire felt friendly and stretched her hand out, but he ignored it, only
made a short bow, saying "Good evening" and went inside. She was taken by
surprise—why did he not want to talk to her? She remembered the sentimental letters and poems he had written to her once upon a time. How had
she offended him? She was glad that she had had such a nice conversation
with Gerda just before that incident, and concluded that she could therefore

not have been guilty of something important. She decided to forget his rudeness. Looking for her daughters, she saw them with the others surrounding one tall handsome young fellow with very light, blond, curly hair, and she wondered if that was Helmut.

A few days later, all the children were back in school and the ball season had began in Salzburg as it had in Vienna. In economic terms, life was just beginning to be felt to be back to normal again and people wanted to be gay and happy once more. Peter and Claire attended one important function in the city of Salzburg, where Claire's evening gown was of good use again, but then participated only in the local Mardi Gras ball, which Peter hated, but could not refuse because it had been a yearly tradition forever, it seemed, and Hanna had always insisted that the family honored these local festivities. The masks were not of any specially clever disguise and were mostly the same year after year, worn by a family for generations. The gaiety on these occasions was enhanced by drinking and carousing. Peter enjoyed a glass or two of wine with his dinner, but had little taste for the local liquor, distilled from orchard fruits and with a high alcohol content. The music was always lively and much singing by the locals went with it. Claire enjoyed that part, but had to be careful to avoid being asked to dance, because Peter did not like it. He never danced himself. Old Anton was always granted the exception, and he took advantage of it. He was very fond of his daughter-in-law, and being a good dancer, he was proud to show off with her on the dance floor. Hanna liked to dance also—not modern steps, but the old traditional ones she knew from her youth.

When Claire told her daughters in a letter about the dances they had attended, the girls expressed a great desire to join them in the future. Elizabeth said that they had had one party at school and boys from another school were invited, but it had been a real bore. Claire looked forward to a time when she and Peter could take their daughters to a ball. Peter frowned a little when she mentioned it to him, but knew that it would probably happen.

The boys, Tony and Christopher, were so far only interested in sports, mostly soccer, and skiing in the winter. They still considered girls a nuisance if social occasions made them join them. Both were good students. Christopher excelled in many subjects, especially the sciences, and his father quietly made plans for him to succeed him in his career but he kept quiet about it, knowing well enough that young people hate to have their future planned for them. On the other hand, Tony had known all his life that one day he would take over the farm, and it did not displease him. He was proud to be the future "Squire of Waldegg," which was the official name for the farm in old documents, and sometimes he had to be reminded by his grandfather, that he still had to prove himself before becoming that. Tony liked to ride around the farm, inspecting all the activities, and even offering suggestions to the farm hands. When he was very young, they just laughed it off. Now he was a tall boy, and they did not always take well to his admonitions and complained to Anton, who, though proud of his grandson's managerial attempts, had to reprimand and remind him that he was still just an apprentice. First he had to learn to do the work himself before ordering others to do it. Tony always accepted his grandfather's admonitions and advice. He loved him and considered him a wise old man, and told him so. Anton laughed, and said he would accept "wise" but not "old."

Although nearing seventy, Anton was still strong and capable of running the estate. Lazlo, the Hungarian, was still at his side; this was the best decision both had made in those war years. Then there was Hanna! Anton was as deeply in love with his wife as when he first met her. She was a strong woman, and sometimes sparks flew between the two of them over one thing or another. They respected each other enough not to let anything interfere with their true feelings for each other. They each played their separate roles in that household. She also managed her own property. The inheritance which she had brought from her parental home in Tyrol when marrying Anton Burghoff, had remained in her name. The woman's dowry was often used to enlarge the bridegroom's property or was invested in it in some way, but Hanna and Anton had decided that she would keep it separate. Fortunately, she had not kept it as money in the bank, where devaluation would have ruined it after the financial breakdown in the country after the war. When a neighboring sawmill had come up for sale, Hanna had purchased it. She found a good manager for it and it turned into a profitable investment, enough so that in 1920 she had also bought a dairy, which in later years became a large operation as a Cooperative for a number of the neighboring farms, in which she owned a major partnership. Hanna was a wealthy woman in her own right.

Claire asked Hanna about the rumor that Waldegg was receiving attention as being of historical interest. Hanna said, Anton had been approached by a member of the town council to get permission to point its history out in the tourist pamphlets. Hanna and Anton did not want to refuse, but were concerned about the invasion of their privacy. They themselves did not know too much about the history of the place, except that it dated to the thirteenth century, and had undergone many changes in ownership and structures. The church of Kammerbach had celebrated its nine hundred year not long ago, and Father Grumbacher had thought of digging up some old church records where he had found Waldegg mentioned. Claire became very interested and asked if she could do some digging herself, and Anton and Hanna gave their approval. Peter also found the idea worthwhile and suggested she should ask Paul how to go about it. There must be more sources available for her genealogical searches, and on their next visit to Velden they had a chance to discuss it with Paul, who was indeed very helpful.

The Thoenes also had news for their friends: They were contemplating a move to Salzburg for several reasons, one being that Paul's publishing business required him to travel to Salzburg so often that it would be more practical to transfer their residence to that city. Melinda welcomed the opportunity not only because of her involvement as a writer, but also as a friend of many artists in the musical arena. Salzburg was definitely a center for culture and music. Paul also had another reason, as he confided. He had been politically active in an anti-Nazi movement during the war, with great hopes for the restoration of the old Austrian Republic. It was therefore no surprise that at the end of the war he was asked to continue in the new provincial government. Paul had always been a dreamer; but the reality was not exactly what he had envisioned. Jealousy, rancor, and revenge were the order of the day. Paul did not fit in. He looked for a way out, and his personal business obligations gave it to him. Claire was overjoyed by the prospect of having her friends also become neighbors, and future plans and ideas were hatched and gave their visit a special meaning.

Claire's search of the history of the "castle" of the Burghoffs, as the people in the village still referred to it, found old yellowed church registers with the family name mentioned as early as the sixteen hundreds; but these included no stories, just births, marriages, and deaths were recorded with the titles of counts and coronets; some of the pages were worm-eaten and could not be properly deciphered. She found more interesting items in the part of Waldegg which had remained little changed in its old condition at the corner of the main house, where the walls and an old tower appeared to be the remnants of a fortress. These parts had not undergone much change and were now a storage area for old, unused things. Claire found heavy wooden chests with rusted hinges, old weapons, farm tools, unrecognizable paintings in broken frames, everything covered with century-old dust. It was evident that nobody had shown any interest. When Claire brought some items out to show Anton, he remembered his grandfather telling him that Napoleon had passed by the castle and the farmers had resisted the French army with their farm tools, metal picks, and shovels, since they were lacking real weapons. The French destroyed what was in their way, and passed through the area on their way to conquer all the lands from here to Russia.

In the trunks Claire found old prayer books, falling apart at a touch, as were silken shawls and dresses, moth-eaten furs, prayer beads, trinkets, not of much value, as far as Claire knew, but she would bring Paul there to help her sort through it. While she was investigating that forgotten part of the house, she looked into other areas which were not as old, but had remained unused.

When Hanna had come here as a young bride she had started her own restoration of the southeast corner, which was in excellent condition but needed modernization. She loved the old kitchen with its vaulted ceiling.

The center was dominated by the big hearth dividing it into two areas, one used for preparing the food, the other for family gatherings and friends' visits. This part enjoyed the heat from the tiled oven walls, and was very cozy and warm in the winter. The walls of the house were several feet thick, with small, lead-glazed windows. Along the walls were wooden benches, and in one corner stood a massive table and several heavy chairs. In the corner, above the table, was a carved wooden crucifix, as was customary in every rural home. Except for renewing the old wooden floor with new strong pine boards, Hanna left that part of the house unchanged, but had electric lights installed, which were the newest things at that time. The entry hall was expansive and was also used as the dining area for the family and those farm hands, who had been at Waldegg for such a long time that they were included in all family gatherings. The other servants ate in a smaller room adjoining the kitchen. The wooden floor of the hall had been replaced with marble, as was the old wooden stairway at the end of the hall. Hanna had replaced the carved railing with one of hand-wrought iron, which was not only very decorative, but also gave the entry an impression of great craftsmanship. A carved door to the left led into a very large room, used only for special occasions and large gatherings. The heavy table was surrounded by fourteen chairs, but could seat more. Along the walls and in the window niches were carved, built-in benches, covered with thick upholstery; the walls were hung with old paintings, done by native painters and depicting mostly the local scenery of mountains, forests, lakes, and animals. Two enormous wooden carved chandeliers, formerly lighted with candles but now electrified also, hung from the arched ceiling and provided the lighting for the room. The old pine wood floors showed the use of years of dancing feet, but sparkled as if new from extra good care. The main attraction here was a massive fireplace in the corner, covered with ceramic tiles, each one of which was a masterpiece, handcrafted by skilled artisans and depicting rural activities. That fireplace was fed from an adjoining room; the heated tiles warmed the great hall and did it well. Claire loved that room, and could see in her mind's eye a wedding party in progress for her daughters.

On the second floor were a number of bedrooms for the family and guests. In 1909 Hanna had added one large bathroom with running water and even a shower fixture, not too common in rural areas at that time. Some remodeling with modernized plumbing had gone on throughout around here the years, but Claire felt it should be improved. However, she did not feel that it was up to her to criticize her in-laws' domain, and she did not make any suggestions. She complimented Hanna on the furbishing of her and Anton's quarters—a lovely, comfortable bedroom—sitting room, where Hanna practiced much of her handicrafts. It even had an old spinning wheel in a corner which was still being used. The room was very nicely furnished, showing the Tyrolean influence in the choice of furniture and patterns of materials. Here also was the *Kachelofen* (the tiled fireplace), that provided heat in the winter. Originally, this room had been heated only by an opening in the wooden floor which let warm air from the kitchen below rise up. Anton used an adjoining smaller room as a den, where he could take an afternoon nap in the big comfortable armchair which his father had used before him. A nice room, less orderly, beloved old jackets and coats hanging on wooden hooks on the wall, hunting rifles displayed behind the glass doors of an old chest, a few books—not too many—on a shelf, a bear skin rug on the floor.

The other bedrooms, including the children's rooms, contained the usual country style furnishings, bed, chest, table, commode with water pitcher and washbowl, etc., everything of solid quality and used for generations. Claire thought that if her own family were ever to move in here, the children would certainly not be satisfied with such Spartan equipment. That was futile thinking anyway. As much as she would always have liked to move to the farm, it would not happen in the foreseeable future. The children would be grown by then, as a matter of fact, Tony would probably already be the "Master of Waldegg!"

While she was exploring other areas of the "castle," Claire was becoming more and more interested in its past. It was obvious that a large part had not been used for many years. The upkeep had probably become too expensive and troublesome for the owners, and as time went on all interest had been lost. She saw a great potential for restoration, however, and decided to talk to the village fathers to see what they had in mind when they wanted to include Waldegg in their tourist attractions.

It turned out that one native son was a student of history at the University in Vienna, and all the ideas about the historic importance of the Waldegg property had come from him in the first place. He knew a lot more about the background of the original castle and said that it had been built in the twelfth century as a fortress by the Lords of Pongau who were subjects of the Prince Bishops of Salzburg. The still standing walls with the tower dated to about the middle of the thirteen hundreds. It later passed on to other gentry, under whose ownership artists had been employed to paint frescoes on wood, still recognizable in some of the deserted rooms and also on some carvings in the local church. That was around the sixteenth century. Young Kurt Boehmer, the history student, had not found much written history about later times, but Claire asked Anton if he would permit him access to the old trunks stored in some of the empty rooms. Kurt Boehmer could only work during his vacations, and since Anton knew his father and grandfather, who owned a respectable hotel-restaurant in Kammerbach, and considering young Kurt Boehmer's history studies, he had no objections.

Peter had only casual interest in Claire's searches of Waldegg's past. He was more concerned about giving public access to tourists, which could mean an invasion of the Burghoff's private life. He knew enough about their own family's genealogy through the written documents in their possession to pass on to his children a respect for the traditional values of a long line of forbears and the responsibility to them. As far as searching for aristocratic titles the Burghoffs might be entitled to, he had no desire to find out. In Peter's opinion there was no justification for such claims in today's society. Claire said teasingly:

"Peter—who would have suspected it—you talk like a hard core socialist?"

"Because I agree with some of their ideas? I believe every human being is worth the same at birth—how they conduct themselves for the rest of their lives should determine their value to themselves and to society. A 'noble' birth is in itself of no greater value, than a so called 'lowly birth.'"

Actually, Claire's opinion did not differ from Peter's, but she found her search into history—even their own family's—exciting.

Before continuing with her new hobby, Claire received a letter from her mother. She was surprised when she found it with her other mail, because lately they had communicated mostly by phone. Her surprise was even greater when she read the content. She had to sit down and start again, the shock was too great. It said

Dear Claire—

I know that my letter will come as a great surprise to you, since I have avoided discussing the subject with you up to now.

You remember that I told you at your last visit here that I was seeing an old friend whose company I greatly enjoyed? Well, maybe I did not say it exactly that way, because I did not want you to draw any conclusions. The fact is that Dr August Klemperer is indeed an old friend. We have known each other for about forty years. He was a fraternity brother of your father's and later his colleague at the University. Your father did not relish close friendships, therefore we did not see each other often but I enjoyed the occasions when we did.

It happened that August's wife and your father passed away at about the same time, and we met by coincidence at a lecture at the Museum. From then on we saw each other frequently, and being in the same boat, namely lonely, found our companionship pleasant.

About two months ago, at Christmas exactly, August asked me to marry him, and I said I would think it over. Not for long though. I am happy to tell you that we married a week ago at City Hall here in Vienna. The attendants were two of August's closest friends. We decided to keep it simple and private, and to invite our respective children upon our return from a vacation in France and Italy, beginning tomorrow.

I have given up my apartment. Agnes, my old housekeeper, is taking it over, and

will turn it into a Bed-and-Breakfast Pension. The location is good for the tourist business which is expected to return to Vienna, and she needs the income. I took my favorite furnishings along to August's villa in Doebling which is a nice place with a lovely garden. You may remember that I always longed to have a garden, but your father preferred the inner-city environment.

That is about all I have to say at this time. When we get back, we will all have the opportunity to get acquainted with each other. August has a son who lives with his family in Vienna, and a daughter who is married to a German businessman and lives in Bonn.

I hope that all of you are well—I will send postcards from our travels.
Your loving mother.

Claire was stunned—her mother married again? And without prior notice! The fleeting thought occurred to Claire, that her mother was trying to pay her back for when she had been secretive about her life. That was so different—she did it to spare her parents worry and embarrassment, but who knows how Rosemarie interpreted it. That was not the only thing that concerned Claire right now. Why would her mother want to remarry at her age and after a life so devoted to her husband Friederich?

Claire could hardly wait for Peter to come home. He immediately noticed that she was perturbed, and relieved when he read the letter.

"Well, well, that is good news!"

"How can you say that? We don't know anything about that man, his character, his life. Maybe he is a woman-chaser, or after mother's money. She does not have a fortune, but it still is substantial and enough to provide comfort for the rest of her life. Remember, she found travel to Salzburg too strenuous, and now she is going abroad and is looking forward to it! I am really worried!" Peter smiled.

"How old is your mother, Claire? Sixty-four? I think she is old enough to know what she is doing, and young enough to still enjoy life—a married life—being loved and cherished, and all that, you know, even sex."

"Oh, Peter...do you really think it is all right?"

"Indeed, I do—tell her as soon as possible that we are happy about the news, and we wish her the best."

Claire sighed, but was relieved by Peter's assurance. She could always count on him. He saw things in realistic terms, he was so good and strong, and she could always trust his judgment and feel secure. What would she do or be without him? An unthinkable thought and she quickly banished it from her mind.

She wrote the news to her daughters, who were also greatly surprised, but they found it comical rather than worrisome. Their grandmother got married? The only problem they saw was that they had not been invited to the wedding, but mother explained that they would make up for that when grandmother Rosemarie would return from her honeymoon.

"Honeymoon?" the girls giggled again.

Tony and Chris accepted the news about their grandmother with no more excitement than news about an earthquake in the Antarctic would have caused. They hardly knew Rosemarie in the first place, and getting a "step-grandfather" was not that important. Did he have horses? What were his hobbies? Did he attend the big soccer games at the stadium in Vienna? Did he have grandchildren? Hopefully, boys—how old? Claire was surprised when she had hardly any answers to all these questions.

Except for an occasional postcard, Claire did not hear from her mother for the next two months. Then one day a short letter arrived, inviting them to a family get-together in two weeks; she hoped the timing was acceptable? Of course, Peter had a conflict, but this time he had to work it out, so that he could join the family. They took the morning train from Salzburg and rented a limousine which could transport the six of them to Rosemarie's new home in the suburbs.

The white stucco house had a modest frontal appearance from the street, and was entered through a small iron-fenced garden. To each side of the centrally located front door was a window with a decorative, as well as protective, wrought iron cover. The plantings in the front garden consisted of evergreen shrubs and ornamental trees, but at the entry was a stone bowl filled with colorful seasonal plants.

Rosemarie greeted them at the door, and led them through the marble foyer into a charming living room. The furniture here consisted of a number of comfortable chairs, a sofa, and a tea table, all arranged to take advantage of the view to the outside through the windowed wall into a terraced garden and beyond. To the left of the living room through an arched doorless entry, was the music room with a grand piano. To the right was the dining room, where Claire saw, to her satisfaction, some of her mother's old, treasured, antique rosewood furnishings. From the dining room one entered a windowed sun room, comfortably furnished with white wicker furniture and upholstered window seats, covered in flowered chintz. They enjoyed having their breakfast and afternoon tea here, Rosemarie explained. The large kitchen, all in white with copper accents, was inspected later, as well as August's library, a den off the foyer, a room that showed that its occupant enjoyed relaxing in comfort, surrounded by books on shelves along the walls, reaching to the ceiling.

The Burghoffs soon met the other family members, August's daughter Annemarie and his son Walter with his young wife and two infant children.

Annemarie was rather cool and reserved, Walter was distracted by his whining youngsters, and his wife was frazzled by them. Dinner was served with the help of a maid, and Rosemarie performed her role as the hostess as graciously as she always had. The food was very good, not lavish, that again showed mother's consideration of the feelings of others, like August's children, who seemed to eye her as an intruder who had taken their mother's rightful place.

August was charming and cordial, and Peter liked him instantly. When they had a little talk after dinner on the terrace. August inquired about Peter's work with knowledgeable interest. He himself had taught philosophy at the university, but had always been interested in the sciences and had kept reading related materials.

Annemarie had come from Bonn alone, saying the children could not travel that far at this time, and her husband's business made it impossible to leave right now. She snooped around eagerly, and finally mentioned to Rosemarie that she wanted some mementos of her mother. Rosemarie immediately told her to take whatever she desired, but to tell her father about it. Walter seemed to be disinterested in his father's new family; his wife was preoccupied with her little ones. Eva and Elizabeth asked if they could take care of them for a while, which apparently pleased her and she relaxed somewhat, only to talk about how difficult life with children was. Rosemarie and Claire tried to smile at her, pretending understanding. Tony and Christopher were visibly bored and restless. When August asked about their schooling, they just gave polite, but short, answers. He inquired if they knew anything about postage stamps, and when they declared that each had a small collection, he led them into his den and produced his own extensive collection for their inspection. They were enthusiastic, and from then on they were quite satisfied with the visit. Eva and Elizabeth enjoyed playing with the two and three-year-old little girls, and Claire followed her mother into the kitchen. Rosemarie showed her the herb garden outside the kitchen, and later they joined August and Peter on the terrace. The view from here was lovely, over the bordering vineyards into the valley of Nussdorf and over parts of Vienna in the distance. It was clear to see that Rosemarie was very happy here. Claire could not remember ever having seen her like that. August was warm, attentive, and without a doubt, very fond of his wife. Claire could not help liking him and felt glad for her mother, but something was nagging her for which she had no explanation. Her mother had mentioned that she had known August Klemperer for a long time, but that there had been no special friendship between him and Friederich Baumann, or their respective wives. Yet here August and she acted as if they had been lifelong friends. Since Rosemarie did not volunteer anything, Claire did not want to ask indiscreet questions. On their way home, Peter said August had told him that he and Rosemarie had once dated seriously in their early youth, but each had been forced to make other choices by parental decree, with unhappy results for both of them. When they had found each other again after about forty years, it was as if fate had meant it to be. They were quite happy.

Claire would have never expected a romantic story in her mother's early life, but she had often wondered about her melancholy ways, never seeming to be really happy. She had attributed it to her father's reserved and cold nature and his devotion to his studies that left little time for family. As surprised as she was, she was also very happy for her mother.

Chapter 21

Nineteen-sixty was Peter's fiftieth year, and Claire asked the girls how they thought they should celebrate his birthday. It was not too easy, because the more elaborate their ideas became the more they knew their father would not like it. At last, Anton Burghoff interfered in their planning by asking for a strictly private family affair. He had his own plans. The dinner was, of course, carefully planned under Hanna's direction. Claire was a little disappointed that she did not have any input in this, but then Hanna was his mother; on this day she should have her own way.

This celebration was also to take place in the large dining hall, and the table was set with the finest of everything Hanna had kept for such occasions. Damask cloths, fine china, old silver, many candles, flowers in crystal bowls— but there were four more places set than Claire had expected. She soon found out that Anton had invited a personal friend, his longtime lawyer Thomas Knoebel, Hanna's oldest brother Karl Greiner and his wife Gundel, and the Hungarian manager, Szolti. The food and drink were well chosen and served in abundance, after prayers with remembrance of past years of deprivation and personal tragedies. A special prayer was said in memory of Hans, and it nearly became solemn, but that was not Anton's plan. Today was a celebration and thanksgiving for a son who had given his parents love and joy for fifty years—half a century. At these words, Peter interrupted with a sigh.

"Do you have to call it half a century, father? I still feel young and strong."

"That is a good thing, son, for what I have in mind for you will need you to be strong." With this he raised his glass and toasted his son, the new owner of Waldegg! It was a surprise to all, because Peter had always assumed that he had never been in line to inherit the estate, and that his son Tony would be the next owner. Anton agreed, but said he felt it should go to Peter in the interim, until Tony came of age, or be mature enough in his father's opinion. Peter had given so much support and advice throughout the years. Thomas Knoebel had been invited to the birthday party to present the legal papers and he did so at this time. It was an emotional moment. Peter was not even sure that he liked his new status, but the men discussed all the practical aspects. Anton suggested, and Peter fully agreed, that Laszlo Szolti would remain manager. Anton himself would not change his activities either, nor would Hanna give up her rule over the household, unless, or until, Peter and Claire would like to take over immediately. Peter felt relieved they did not expect him to do so at this time. He was very happy in the medical profession. To give it up for the sake of the farm would be a great sacrifice, which he would only consider if he had to. He hoped that father could continue to reign over the estate for many more years.

Everybody agreed Peter's birthday celebration had been a joyful event. As the evening wore on with everybody in good spirits, the people who were serving the estate in various capacities were invited to join in the festivities and were told what had transpired. All had known Peter for so long, it meant nothing new. As long as their jobs were safe, they were content. The party continued with the usual singing and merrymaking, music and dancing in the country manner.

Chapter 22

By 1962, Elizabeth had also returned from boarding school in Vienna. Eva had graduated two years earlier, and now attended a teacher's college in Salzburg. When her sister had left school, Elizabeth was unhappy to be on her own in Vienna, but Peter had insisted that she must stay for the rest of the time until graduation. Claire would have given in and let her attend a school in Salzburg, but Peter remained firm in his opinion that schooling with the nuns in Vienna would be very beneficial for his second daughter too, although he had found his own time at boarding school to be too strict. When Claire reminded him of the conflict, he quoted Bishop Franz's assurance that things were much better and easier now. She had to admit that the boys were content at the Jesuit's school, except for complaints about too much homework, but she was sure that would have been the same at a public school. They were doing well otherwise. The year-end reports from the nuns about the girls showed thoughtful observation and understanding of both of them.

Eva had had an excellent scholastic record. She was described as dependable, serious, quiet, appreciated by teachers and classmates who could always count on her cooperation.

Elizabeth was sweet, good-natured, loved by everybody, had many friends—the criticism reserved for her was her lack of ambition. She had many talents, the teachers said, yet she did not strive to excel in any. She had a lovely singing voice and her musical talent was envied by her classmates, but she lacked the will to add practice to her studies. She played the piano fairly well, but played only when and what she liked; no etudes and exercises for her! This attitude applied to almost all of her activities. Elizabeth graduated with average marks in all subjects, which would not have been too bad but it was not commensurate with her abilities. Her parents sighed when they read the reports, and then smiled: *Dear, dear Elizabeth—you rascal—but we could not love you more.*

By the time Elizabeth returned from Vienna, Eva had graduated from the teacher's college, but was still unsure if she was ready to take on a teaching job. She asked to stay with Grandmother Hanna at the farm for a while, if she would have her and if Claire and Peter agreed. They were all delighted; she was still so young, too young to be a schoolmarm. Some relaxation after all the years at school would do her good.

Elizabeth had the same idea, still trying to follow Eva's model. Peter insisted, however, that school had not ended for her as yet. One day when she came home from one of her strolls through the city she declared that she had found what she wanted to do. She had passed one of the better stores in the old city, where tourists massed to admire the old baroque buildings, the churches, Mozart's birthplace, and others, and were also purchasing local specialties. The store which Elizabeth described offered authentic arts and crafts of the region, museum copies of every genre. She had stepped in to admire some material for a new Dirndl dress in authentic Salzburger style, which she hoped her mother would let her purchase. Her lovely appearance and demeanor caught the attention of the manager who involved Elizabeth in conversation, at the end of which she asked if she would like to join the sales staff. Elizabeth was enthusiastic when she came home with the news. Peter did not want to hear about it, but consented that Claire investigate. Claire was not sure Elizabeth would stick it out anyway, knowing her fickle nature. However, her daughter was so insistent that her parents agreed to give her a trial period.

To their surprise, Elizabeth did well at her job. She was praised for her sales ability, the tourists liked her friendly manner and lovely appearance and used her again and again as a photographic model of an authentic Salzburger maiden. Claire reported this to Peter, who was still not convinced of the propriety of that kind of job for his young daughter, but his wife assured him that a talk with the manager had led her to believe that she held her employees to high standards and the environment of the establishment was conducive to Elizabeth's artistic bent. Indeed, after the summer tourism subsided and business slowed down, Elizabeth became inspired to take music lessons, learning to play the zither and the guitar.

Kammerbach had grown in the last few years, because former refugees had decided to stay on; repatriation efforts by the occupying powers had not been very successful. Also, new businesses opened to cater to the increased tourist trade and more jobs opened up for people. Kammerbach had slowly reached enough population that it could be called a town. Formerly small restaurants enlarged and became hotels, some of them even offering live entertainment, at least on weekends, another attraction for vacationers. While the local youth had become infected—as Peter put it—by modern sounds; the traditional folk music was still appreciated by the adults and especially by the foreigners, who enjoyed the mountain scenery together with the original sounds of the century-old tunes of the region. Those had always been a part of the culture of the country and were practiced in homes, promoted in school, and nearly everybody in the country with any singing voice or musical talent belonged to some kind of choir or band.

One of these singing-playing groups was led by Helmut Engebrecht. His band consisted mostly of local boys, picturesque in their native costumes; they were in demand at weddings as well as other festivities, even in the fancy hotels in the city of Salzburg. Despite their success, Helmut's father, Fritz Engebrecht, was not proud of his son. He had hoped Helmut would continue with his education and become a teacher, or at least find employment in a related field, but this was not Helmut's plan. He could see himself neither as a teacher nor as working behind a desk all day. During his summer vacations he had labored on the farm at the Burghoff's, and Anton liked him well enough to suggest that he work to become a foreman, but that was not Helmut's idea either. He said that he would not mind being a farmer, but only on his own farm. Anton said, smiling, that he should marry a farmer's daughter. Helmut also smiled:

"Maybe—but not just yet; I want to be a free bird for a long time."

He returned to his carefree life and his music. His father threatened to make him leave home but Gerda was too fond of her handsome and charming son to let that threat come true. She reminded her husband that it was she who had kept the family together for so many years in the first place, and Helmut could stay home as long as he wanted to. She gave Fritz credit for being a good and conscientious educator, but—as incongruous that may be—he was not an attentive father, having preferred to spend his free time by himself in the mountains and the forest. She had raised their children without his help, and she did not care for his criticism of them now. Helmut was a good and decent boy, a little wild in some respects, but he was well liked in town, and she had not heard any complaints about him ever. Fritz grumbled something to the effect that spoiling their son could only lead to a bad end, but Gerda did not relent and Helmut continued to enjoy his mother's cooking for some time.

Eva had seldom attended local dances after her return to Kammerbach. She was quite happy with her time at the farm and became Claire's companion in many ways. They worked together in the historical society which Kurt Boehmer had initiated with his interest in local history, and she accompanied Claire on shopping errands or social functions in town. Eva remained devoted to Claire, who was more than grateful for her stepdaughter's dedication, never feeling the "step" in stepdaughter.

Peter was happy about that relationship and gave all the credit to Claire for having been a very loving mother to the children. He had to admit to himself—although never letting it show—that his relationship with each of his children was a little different. Despite great efforts to show her his affection, there was always some resentment in Eva's attitude towards him and he could feel it. It had not changed through the years. Neither had his love for Elizabeth. She was so special, and Peter could forgive her almost anything, even her lack of serious pursuits which were so ingrained in him. He did not want to compare her to her mother, who in his mind was and would be always the best example of womanhood; nobody could take her place in his heart, but Elizabeth, being a part of her, came pretty close.

The boys, Tony and Chris, were Peter's pride and joy. As strict as he seemed to be with them, he saw in them all that he had wanted to be and he was going to see to it that they would have all the guidance and opportunity to achieve their goals. He had help with that. First, Claire, their mother. He always remembered how important his relationship to his own mother had been while he was growing up, and even now he still often had heart-to-heart talks with her. He felt with gratitude that Claire was an ideal mother to their sons also, although in a different way than his mother was to him. Peter believed the difference came from these two mothers' varied backgrounds. Hanna, the strong, earthy woman, simple, deeply religious, bound to the land, its traditions and values; Claire, city-bred, well educated, intelligent, honorable, passionate, sensitive, loving—Peter could not find enough adjectives to describe all of Claire's virtues—and if she had heard them she would have laughingly protested and said that he was very prejudiced in her favor; yes, she was also modest.

Claire watched their sons' development with great joy. They seemed to be an extension of their father in character as well as looks, but they were more outgoing than he, less restrained and reserved. They had been bundles of energy from the very beginning and always let it be known that they were around. At the same time, they were just as thoughtful and loving as their father. Since they were just about one year apart in age and of similar looks, they were often thought to be twins, and often even acted that way, although Tony made it quite clear that he had seniority. They got along with each other splendidly, except in competitive sports or wrestling matches, when each one wanted to prove superiority over his sibling.

The Thoenes had found a nice apartment in the city, not far from the Burghoff's home. It was to be their headquarter for business activities, but they hoped to find a place outside town, possibly at Kammerlake or on the lakes of the Salzkammergut for weekend retreats where they could entertain friends and business associates. Melinda consulted a realtor in the area and she and Claire scouted places of interest. On Fuschlsee they found a nearly perfect one. Once a baron's hunting lodge, later the summer residence of a Nazi official after whose departure it had been occupied by war refugees; it needed much repair and remodeling, but it had great possibilities for restoration of its previous charm. The location was perfect. Half an hour driving distance from the city, yet in a secluded country setting, the lawn in front reaching the water's edge, a fact which would especially please Paul, who had left that part of his former home in Velden with some regret. The property behind the house was bordered by a dense forest. It was not a large house, but would on occasion easily accommodate a couple of visitors. Melinda was very excited about it and when Paul saw it he approved completely. Claire was delighted to help Melinda with decorating choices, and they often took Eva along, who showed much interest and good judgment.

Elizabeth took her music studies more seriously than anybody had expected, but her weekends were given to singing and dancing at Kammerbach, and more and more in the company of Helmut Engebrecht. Eva frowned—she was concerned about that. Helmut was not a bad guy—but was not to be taken seriously. He was a great flirt, he attracted girls, he was what "fly paper is to flies" as one of the fellows had said jokingly, maybe a little jealous too. Eva did not want Elizabeth to be one of the "flies." That did not seem to happen—it was more the other way around: lovely Elizabeth was the center of attention herself.

Eva was torn between her love for Elizabeth and her loyalty to Claire—should she mention anything to her mother? In the meantime, she herself became somewhat distracted—not in the dance hall, but during her continuing studies of the history of Waldegg which had been taken up again by Kurt Boehmer upon his return from the University. The two young people spent many hours going through old trunks which contained a treasure of old writings, letters, documents of various descriptions, books, manuscripts, weapons, tools, clothing, etc. To sort it out, to trace its origin, was no mean undertaking, but both of them enjoyed the challenge, and apparently each enjoyed the other's company also. When both admitted their growing fondness for each other, they had long talks about what each would expect from a life's mate, and when they found that their expectations and hopes for their future, their likes and dislikes matched, they made it known to their respective parents. The Burghoffs were pleased; Kurt's father on the other hand, who owned the prosperous tourist hotel in Kammerbach, was less so, because he had not given up hope that his son would take over the Hotel Zur Post and marry a girl who was familiar with running such an establishments, as was the daughter of his competitor from the Hotel Schlosshof, "a lovely and available girl, by the way," he said. Kurt just smiled. What his father said was true. Annerl was a sweet girl, he told his father. However, he wanted to marry Eva Burghoff, and to teach history at a college or similar school. Brother

Heinz was more suited to become a hotelier, even if he first needed to grow up a little. Father Boehmer grumbled in his beard, and accepted his son's decision. He probably should not have sent his son to the University in the first place, he said to himself. That had spoiled his interest in becoming a wealthy restaurateur rather than a poorly paid college teacher! What can a father do about that, when his son has already decided? Then he considered the family ties with the Burghoffs. He and Anton Burghoff had been friends for more years than each could remember, the connection would be pleasant.

Anton Burghoff was of the same opinion. He liked Kurt, who was roaming through the old building with great zeal, which Anton at first just tolerated but later admired. In his opinion, Eva could have done better than marrying a "boy from the village," but that's what all prejudiced parents and grandparents think about their offspring. Eva's and Kurt's choice were favorably accepted by all concerned. They wanted to wait for marriage until Kurt was settled with a position, hoping they would be able to stay in the area they both loved. Besides being a serious student, Kurt was also a passionate mountain climber and belonged to the Salzburger club of Mountaineers.

Claire would have liked to have the wedding festivities at the farm, but Eva cautioned her to wait with such plans. All of the bigger weddings in the area were celebrated at the Hotel Zur Post. Father Boehmer counted on theirs to be there too. She and Kurt had already talked about something else also.

"Not eloping?" Claire warned, and Eva assured her that was not being considered, but rather something small, romantic, untraditional. There was still time to consider a few options, she said, and Claire consented to wait.

The restoration of the Thoene's new home in Fuschl progressed well, and Melinda already made plans for a party there for all their friends. It was supposed to be an important social event. Paul's business was doing so well—so many young writers were sprouting all over with uncensored material available again to the public, who were quite ready for it. The key word was "uncensored," not that the modern writings were of better quality, although the new generation thought of itself as being superior, but that had been always so. Melinda had not written much herself lately, having been too busy with promoting new and young talents. Her social life in musical circles also took up much of her time. Brought up in Vienna in such an artistic environment, she thrived in that genre also. Claire wondered if the more reserved Paul enjoyed their busy lifestyle, but he made no comments to the contrary.

Peter and Claire were frequently invited to Melinda's parties and marveled at the ease with which she would perform her role as hostess, be it at a formal soiree or with a group of beatnik youngsters. Peter could not always accompany Claire, especially to the latter, for some reason he seemed to be busier when such gatherings occurred. Claire teased him about it, but she herself often had difficulty participating when the so-called music was painful to her ears. She was astounded how Melinda, with her classical musical training and her sophisticated taste, could tolerate it. When she was accompanied by Eva and Elizabeth, she also wondered how her own daughters felt comfortable and concluded that she herself must be getting old. Not that Peter gave her reason to think so, which the following story will prove.

Peter used to meet with one or an other of his old friends from school, which included Franz Hinterberger, on a more or less regular basis in town for lunch. He felt it was good for him to leave the medical environment behind for an hour and enjoy old comradeship with men of different occupations and callings. Franz was the only clergyman and Peter was the only medical man in the group. On one such occasion they lunched at a local restaurant and in the banter of friendly conversation, one fellow, the only bachelor in the group, said to Peter:

"Peter, I have often wondered—how do you feel when you touch the body of a lovely female patient during an examination?"

Peter was used to getting medical questions from his friends and answered, without giving it much serious thought:

"It's no different than touching the flesh of a plucked chicken!" Everybody laughed at his remark.

Two young woman were eating their lunch at a nearby table, and heard that part of the conversation. One, Connie Springer, a nurse at the hospital, was angry to hear such talk, which she found demeaning to women in general. She said to her friend:

"That was the chief of staff at our hospital. What a male chauvinist he is!" One of these days she would get even with him.

When Peter was between operations, he often used to rest for a while in a small room next to his office. There was just a cot and an easy chair in it, and either was comfortable for an occasional nap. It was also used as a storeroom for medical files, etc. Sometimes other personnel had access to it, but most of the time he could find a few moments of undisturbed rest there. On one hot summer day he wanted to do just that. He left his jacket in the office, and entered the small room, which was windowless and lit only by a little bedside lamp. In that half darkness he noticed a young woman standing there stark naked. Peter was startled.

"What's going on here?" The first thing that came to his mind was that he had interrupted some hanky-panky by some hospital employees. The girl now stood right in front of him, grabbed the hand with which he had just begun to loosen his tie, and held it against her breast, saying:

"Touch my skin, doctor." By then Peter understood. He withdrew, and stepping back said coldly:

"Don't make a fool of yourself, get dressed and get out of here." He left the room, stormed through his office grabbing his jacket as he did so, and went outside. He was angry, despite admitting to himself that for a moment he might have had a manly reaction in there, but it did not affect his brain! He went home on foot, angry. What if someone had come to his office at that time and found him in such a compromising situation. How could he have explained that? What if it had been Claire? A dumb little girl's foolish action could have destroyed his career, and worse, his marriage.

He opened the front door and called for Claire.

"In the kitchen" was her reply. He went there. Claire was standing at the sink, scrubbing some carrots for dinner. The window was open, and the shutters provided a little sunshine to filter through, just enough to surround her figure with a halo, which touched Peter's heart. He was a sensuous man, although he would never have described himself as such. He would have accepted being called serious, decent, intelligent, reserved, and a simple country boy, but never a romantic. The sight of Claire at that moment filled him with joy. He noticed small pearls of perspiration on her upper lip and forehead which he found for some reason moving and delicious. It was a hot day, Claire wore a white sleeveless blouse and a pale blue short skirt, with sandals on bare feet. She looked ravishing to him. Her scent had had always magical powers over him—it was not perfume, she never wore any—this was Claire, pure and clean, as he knew her from the first days of their acquaintance on the beach at Kammerlake. Then he did not dare to take her in his arms, but what prevented him from doing so today? He kissed her gently, inhaling the tiny droplets from her forehead and her lips. She dropped the carrot and put her arms with hands still wet, around his neck, eagerly responding to his kisses. Peter unbuttoned the rest of her blouse and touched her bare breasts—the skin of which definitely did not remind him of chicken…the rest is marital history and does not need description.

Peter spent the next two hours resting in bed at home, until duty brought him back to the hospital. He had other matters on his mind than the silly incident with Nurse Connie; but the girl had not. She was nearly frantic. Humiliated at first, she realized how wrong she had been. She was not a wicked girl. As a war orphan she was sent to school at a convent on a scholarship, and had been a model student. The nuns were strict and made sure their girls were taught moral values along with academics. Connie never got into trouble. At nursing school she found friends from a more liberal background, who teased her naiveté and unwordliness and suggested some books for her to read; mostly trash literature, but Connie found it interesting. A few articles about the new women's movement provided additional education. That's where she learned that most men were chauvinists, a term she wanted to hang on Dr. Burghoff. She expected, as she had heard numerous times lately, that no man could resist a sexy overture from a pretty female. She was pretty, she thought, at least she had a perfect body. With no experience but much fantasy, she was going to teach Dr. Burghoff a lesson and maybe get something out of it for herself? She had read about pretty girls being discovered by important men and finding happiness and love. Poor Connie!

Now she was scared. Her plan had misfired, and she feared she would lose her job and, even worse, he would tell his friends at the restaurant; they would laugh and she would not be able to show her face around town anymore.

Dr. Burghoff, on the other hand, did nothing of the sort. He had nearly forgotten about the incident. Just once he had thought about his own daughters who were of the same age as that nurse, would they ever? No, certainly not.

Chapter 23

Tony graduated in 1964, and used his sisters' example to beg for a year of "experience" on the farm before leaving for his studies in Vienna. By then, Christopher would have finished his term and they could go together. His father was agreeable, especially since he had been searching for boarding possibilities in Vienna for his sons. He sought the advice of his former land-lady, and was more than pleased when she said that she would gladly take care of the young men as she had of Peter for six years, a long time ago. Peter had thought that she would be too old by now to take in boarders, but she said that her widowed daughter was now living with her and helping out. Claire was glad about the arrangement also, as she had been concerned about letting her "two little boys" loose in the dangerous environment of the big city of Vienna. Peter laughed about her motherly concerns and reminded her of her own youthful days in that big city. Was it a dangerous place? He never found it so. Claire had to remind him that he was one who was interested only in his studies, as he had said, but as he should know by now, their sons had inherited a more adventurous streak from somewhere.

Franz Hinterberger never forgot that he was Christopher's godfather, and promised the boys that he would reward them with a journey to Italy after their graduation. That plan was also in progress.

In the meantime, Claire and Peter were faced with an unexpected incident involving their special child, namely lovely, sweet Elizabeth. She had become a little more independent during the last year or so, studying music at the Salzburg conservatory, surrounded by friends on weekends in Kammerbach, singing and dancing through her carefree life. It seemed to be innocent enough. Eva, who knew these kids better because she had gone to school with most of them before leaving for boarding school at sixteen, even agreed that nearly all of them were nice local youngsters, but she had some reservations. Most were simple country youths without much education and not equal to Elizabeth's family background. Claire was concerned, but then Peter and she concluded that they did not have enough reason to forbid Elizabeth the company she enjoyed.

One Sunday evening, Elizabeth returned from the farm and found her parents together in the dining room finishing their supper.

"Would you like to join us?"

"No, thank you, I ate at grandmother's," she was unusually short on words. Normally she came in bubbling with news:

"I am glad that you are both here, I have to tell you something."

"Well," Peter said, and Claire looked startled. Elizabeth was never so formal.

"I am getting married."

"Of course you are," Peter said smiling.

"Soon," Elizabeth said with a sullen expression in her face. Claire still did not say a word, instinctively feeling a serious development. Peter was in a smiling mood, and said:

"And who, may I ask, is the lucky groom?"

Elizabeth's face grew angry and she said:

"You never take me seriously. You think of me as still being a little girl, always saying 'Yes, Papa, Yes, Mama.' I am fully grown and in control of my own life, and I am telling you again: I am getting married. That's it."

Claire stood up, but now her knees felt weak, and she sat down again. It was Peter who asked again:

"You have to be more clear in what you say. You are not serious? You are too young for such a far-reaching decision. Marriage is for grownups, not for adolescents."

"You see, you don't see me as a fully grown woman. I am in love with a wonderful man, and tonight he asked me to marry him."

Claire breathed a sigh of relief—her daughter was in love for the first time, she was overwhelmed by the sensation—it would pass.

Peter said quietly, but sternly:

"You tell the young man, whoever he is, that you will think it over for a while."

"No, I have made up my mind, you both just have to get used to the idea. If you don't like it, it is too bad."

Elizabeth had never talked to her parents that way; the situation became painfully serious. Peter tried to control his annoyance, and said calmly:

"Explain yourself. You cannot just burst in with such news and be taken seriously. We understand—you are in love with a wonderful young man. Now, who is he? When are we going to meet him and get acquainted with our prospective son-in-law and his family? Sit down here and tell us about it."

Elizabeth remained standing, defiant in her posture.

"There is no need to get acquainted, you know him already, it is Helmut Engebrecht."

With that, Peter turned pale. It could not be. The son of the man he had detested since he could remember. Claire was not quite sure of the reasons for it, but she remembered that Peter had so often said of Fritz Engebrecht that his father had been an alcoholic and had died as such. Claire had always believed Peter disliked Fritz for some other reason than that, and she had countered before that Fritz could hardly be blamed for his father's problem. He was just a child when his father died, and his upbringing by very upstanding relatives, may have been hard, but was not questionable. They also knew that Fritz as a young man never touched alcohol. Peter said that was because he knew the seed was in him and he could succumb to that illness just like his father. Now his beloved daughter wanted to marry one of the descendants of that family. Peter felt ill. Claire was only slightly less upset. She sympathized with her daughter for being in love, but hoped it would be a passing emotion. It had to be, Peter would never consent. She asked:

"What will you live on? Does Helmut have a job other than his band? You know that you could not live on such an income. You have never had to earn your upkeep, Do you know what it takes?"

Elizabeth said:

"Helmut will find a job, and in the meantime I thought Papa, and maybe Grandfather, could help out."

"Oh, that is it. The fellow is clever, is he not? He thinks if he marries you we will be so grateful as to support you both?" Peter asked sarcastically.

"You are terribly unfair—you don't know Helmut, nor me either. I love him and I am going to marry him."

Peter said gravely: "I forbid it."

"I don't need your permission—and you may just as well know it now: I am pregnant."

A thunderbolt could not have felt more devastating.

"Elizabeth," Claire cried out. "How could you?"

"Oh, Mother, don't be such a hypocrite—do you think that I don't know about your past? That you were not even married until I was already a year old? And who is my father anyway—did you lie to me about that too? I know that Papa was not where you were at the time but Uncle Paul was. Why is my middle name Paula? Everybody knows that Uncle Paul loves you. Why did he not marry you? Why did you trick Papa into marrying you instead? Do you think it is so easy to live with all these questions about your parents?"

On she went in an excited gush of words. Claire was dumbfounded, unable to say one word. She looked at Peter, his face was ashen, his hands turned into fists. For the first time ever, Claire was frightened by his look. She saw, that he could not take any more of this unbelievable outburst from his favorite child. She got up from her chair and went behind him, putting her hands on his shoulders and said:

"Peter, darling, let's go outside…" He did not let her finish:

"You ungrateful wretch…and I used to love you more than I could have expressed! Leave our house at once." And before Claire could prevent it, Elizabeth slammed the door and was gone.

Peter paced the floor in a rage. Did this scene really happen or was he dreaming? Although all of Elizabeth's scorn was directed towards her mother, it was Peter more than Claire who felt the pain of outrage. She was torn inside about Elizabeth's confusion, but somehow she also understood. What hurt more than her daughter's damaging outburst was to see Peter being so devastated by it. That night Peter cried in her arms and she had to be strong and comfort him, when in the past he had been always the stronger of the two and she had leaned on him for support.

Peter did not speak of Elizabeth anymore. He and Claire shared their pain in a quiet, unspoken manner. Claire was not too concerned at first, as to where Elizabeth might have gone after she left their home. She knew that she would take care of herself and had many places where she would find shelter, but she called Eva to come to the house. It was probably Eva who would know more than anyone else about Elizabeth's whereabouts. She did not tell Eva the details of the commotion that had occurred, she left out most of Elizabeth's personal attacks on her, but told her of the rest. Eva was upset. She had not heard from Elizabeth either which concerned her. She suggested calling Helmut, who still lived at home, but Claire did not think it would be right to do so at the moment.

Peter was silent. He went about his work at the hospital, where he was asked by his colleagues if he felt ill.

"Just a touch of the flu," he replied and left it at that.

On the third day after Elizabeth's leaving, Claire had a call from Gerda, asking if she could come to see her. Claire pretended to be busy at the moment. She did not want to air the situation with Gerda before things had become clearer. Gerda would not accept Claire's excuse and said that she would not take much of her time; there were things important to both of them which needed to be discussed. If Claire preferred, they could meet at the Lanner coffee house. Yes, Claire preferred that. She did not want Peter to have to participate in the conversation if he should happen to come home during Gerda's visit.

When Claire came to their rendezvous, Gerda was already waiting and it was clear that she was somewhat nervous. Gerda noticed the strain in

Claire's eyes and felt greater sorrow for her than for herself. Claire ordered her usual cup of coffee with cream, a *mélange* as it is called here, and waited for Gerda to start the conversation.

"First of all, I wanted to tell you that Elizabeth is staying at our house. From what she has told me, she did not inform anyone where she was, nor did she want me to tell either, but I did not think that it was right to keep you in the dark about it. Whatever your feelings about the situation may be, I know as a mother that you would want to know."

"Thank you" was all Claire said at that moment, tears filling her eyes. She really had no intention of letting Gerda know how deeply she was affected, but it was difficult to hide. Gerda continued:

"I did not approve of Elizabeth's staying at our house, but I could not turn her out either, you understand that?"

"I am grateful to you," said Claire.

"I understand you are upset about the situation our children have put us in and I want you to know that it has been an unexpected, and may I add undesired, surprise for us too. However, I feel there is little use in lamenting about facts that can't be changed. Let's see what mending can be accomplished. I know you may feel that Helmut has brought shame upon your family. I am truly sorry for that, but I want you to know, that Helmut is a responsible young man, even if you cannot agree at the moment. He was always a loving and attentive son to me, so I know he will be a good and loving husband also. I also wish they had waited a little longer to make such an important life decision, but I know that he and Elizabeth have been deeply in love for some time. I feel our blessing for their future would be wiser than our criticism. Can't you and Peter forgive them also? Don't you remember that we were also young once?"

At that reminder Claire managed a faint smile.:

"I appreciate all you are saying, Gerda. If you came to let me know your feelings, I am grateful. I can also assure you that we will deal with the situation in an appropriate manner and with as much grace as we can manage, and we will accept facts which can't be changed. You should also know—and I beg you to keep this just between the two of us—that the reason for our argument with Elizabeth was only due in part to the sudden announcement of marriage and motherhood with which she confronted us. It went far beyond that. She hurled accusations against Peter—and more so against me—that hurt us deeply and which Peter could not bear. He told her then to leave. Peter loves that child with all his heart, and she broke it. It will take time to heal and this hurts me more than Elizabeth's condition. I can accept that she made a decision for which she, in my mind, is not mature enough, but, as she pointed out, it is her life. Yes, I do remember that I was about the same age when I thought I knew what I wanted from life. But, Gerda, what do you think, were we not more adult than today's youth at that age?"

Gerda said:

"Does not every generation judge the previous one in that way?"

"Perhaps you are right."

Claire asked Gerda to let her know how things at home were progressing. She did not think it right for Elizabeth to stay at the Engebrecht's home and suggested that Eva would be the best mediator. She told Gerda that she had complete confidence in Eva to do the best for Elizabeth. Both women felt that their meeting had accomplished something, and they could trust each other to work things out for the best. After all, they would be family. At that, neither Claire nor Gerda knew how their husbands would feel about it. Gerda was just as aware of the animosity between Fritz and Peter as Claire was. Time would tell.

Eva found a tearful but unrepentant Elizabeth, who after some prodding agreed to stay with Eva for a while. Eva had asked some time ago if she could use the cottage behind her parents former home in St. Johann which had remained vacant since Dr. Kriegë's death, for her occasional stays in town. The big house was occupied by a younger physician who had come to serve the town after Peter had left for Salzburg. Claire was very satisfied with that arrangement. She knew that Eva would be most likely to find the right way to deal with the problems that had arisen with Elizabeth's emotional outburst on that evening at their home.

Peter still refused to talk about his once-favorite daughter, but Claire said that would not help in making the best out of a situation which could not be changed. Peter said if she wanted to deal with it, he would not object. If financial resources were needed, he would trust her to spend what was required.

"But, do not expect anything else from me, especially a blessing."

Claire went to see Hanna and Anton, who already knew some of what had happened. In a village like Kammerbach, secrets have almost no chance of survival, even for a short time. Since they did not know of Elizabeth's outburst against her parents, they did not see the situation as tragic. Of course, they thought that Helmut Engebrecht may not have been their choice of husband for their granddaughter, but Anton said that he knew him as a dependable sort of worker from his summer jobs on the farm. If he loved Elizabeth he would find a way to provide for her too. Hanna was more reluctant to show approval, but did not like Peter's scorn either. Claire did not mention what had really happened at their house. How could she!

Elizabeth's pregnancy caused more pity than consternation. Traditional morals in rural areas are somewhat influenced by the examples of nature around them. Mating happens everywhere. They knew that sometimes prospective brides had even to prove first that they were capable of producing an heir before being accepted into a family where the future depended on the certainty of procreation. Claire also had the feeling—and that may have been just part of the self-consciousness which had overcome her late-ly—that Hanna looked at her in a way that said: "Who are you to judge?" Of course, Hanna did not say that, and if she thought it, one would never know. However, Claire felt surrounded by that question from now on, when in the past she had never thought of herself as morally deficient. Now she remembered her own early life in St. Johann, where people did not exactly welcome the new Mrs. Peter Burghoff. It seemed now that only Dr. Krieger and Frau Mayer, Peter's housekeeper, had shown her warm acceptance. Franz Hinterberger, the bishop, of course, but he was Peter's friend and confidant. In those times she had been so completely enrapt in her love for Peter, occupied by the care for her young children, while still living those post-war years with deprivation, social and political insecurity, that not much else mattered, especially not the gossip within the community. It had never occurred to her what the content of that gossip may have been, but now she realized that it had spread to her children. To all of them, or only to Elizabeth? How about Eva? Tony and Chris were probably spared by distance in time and space and their attendance at a school removed from the local environment.

Why had the girls never questioned her or Peter before? She remembered Eva's impassioned pleas for her love. At one time, the child, about ten years old, had asked her if her own mother had been a bad person. When Claire asked who would have said such a thing, Eva said that she had heard it from a girl at school. Claire told her that her mother was a fine person, but very ill, and when people feel pain, they often hurt other people without wanting to.

"But she did not love me...I know that," Eva had said, and Claire had assured her against her own opinion that Marlena had indeed loved her daughter.

That was it and she did not remember that neither Eva nor Elizabeth had ever mentioned anything of the past or what they may have heard at school. Why now? Should she talk about it with Eva after all? Claire wished she could find a way to loosen Peter's stubborn silence in that matter. Whom else could she confide in? She felt very alone and sad, but what saddened her more than her own distress was Peter's grief. All she wanted from life at that moment was to see Peter happy again. She would try her utmost to achieve it.

A wedding had to be planned. Elizabeth refused to let her mother be involved. Why did she hate Claire all of a sudden? Why did she play the injured party, when it was she who had offended her mother? She was young and confused, proud, and feeling guilty also. In no way would she apologize to her mother, which Eva had suggested when she had finally told what had happened on that Sunday evening. Eva had been shocked, to put it mildly. She scolded Elizabeth and told her, as their father had, what an ingrate she had turned out to be, and asked her how she could have forgotten the loving and caring of their mother during all of their lives. Elizabeth tolerated Eva's chiding, but did not repent.

It was now up to Eva to act as an intermediary and to help with all the necessary things in preparing the wedding as soon as possible. Father Grumbacher was willing to set a date at the earliest possible time considering the necessary proclamations on the church portal. Eva talked to the Engebrechts and Gerda was only too willing to help with preparations. She also sought Claire's advice, whom she kept informed, but Claire was not involved in other than in financing matters. Peter was sarcastic about that, but was mostly silent about the affair and said only that he would not attend the ceremony. Of course, Claire talked him out of that. Would he want to give credence to the gossip already going around?

The wedding was held at the Kammerbacher church, with Father Grumberger officiating. The bishop's presence halted most of the unfriendly gossip, but since the invitation included all of Helmut's and Elizabeth's friends from the area, there was much support and rejoicing over the couples matrimonial union anyway. The banquet was held at Boehmer's Hotel Zur Post, with eating, singing, and dancing all night long. Helmut's band had to perform without him conducting it. They did an outstanding job and all seemed to be in the happiest mood, including the couple being celebrated. Both were indeed a feast to the eyes of the observers, the handsomest pair the countryside had seen in a long time, a vision from the fairy tales, where bride and groom looked so lovely that all the old women had tears in their eyes, and the old men smiled approvingly. Instead of the usual white gown and veil, Elizabeth had chosen a floor length Dirndl dress of exquisite, pale blue silk over a white blouse of finest linen, its high neckline and billowing sleeves edged with lovely lace. She did not wear any jewelry, her blonde curls were held in place by a wreath of the same field-flowers as were in her bouquet. Helmut wore the traditional festive costume of the region of the Pongau, with leather breeches, and *loden* jacket over a white, pleated shirt

Before leaving the church after the ceremony, Helmut and Elizabeth surprised the congregation with a musical rendering of their own. Helmut was handed his guitar by one of his attendants, and he and Elizabeth sang a duet of a sentimental folk song, familiar to everybody, but all said they had never heard it sung so movingly and beautifully. Their voices matched in perfect harmony, and if this was symbolic of their future life together, it was a good omen.

Claire was very emotional, and that was expected from the mother of the bride, although in this case it went much deeper. She had not spoken to Elizabeth since that fateful Sunday, or rather, Elizabeth had not spoken to her. Peter might have relaxed his fierce stand somewhat, if his eyes had not met his old foe, the father of the groom, standing in the vicinity of the couple,

Fritz Engebrecht with—in Peter's estimation—a smirk on his face which he found insulting and intolerable. Claire saw nothing but her beautiful daughter and her very handsome man. She did understand–she remembered all too well how she would have fought the whole world for her own—her Peter, not less handsome, but more so. She squeezed his arm on which she had leaned and he returned that gesture with that special look of his deep blue eyes which made her still swoon after all these years. *May Elizabeth find the same happiness—nothing else will matter.*

After the eating and toasting had subsided, the bridal couple went from table to table to greet their guests with thanks for coming to celebrate their union. They also stopped at the table of the Burghoff family, which included Kurt Boehmer who was by now Eva's official fiancé. Elizabeth just extended a happy smile to everyone, but Helmut bent down to kiss Claire and whispered into her ears,

"Please, do not worry, I will take good care of Elizabeth."

Claire, feeling the young man's cool lips on her cheek, and hearing his sincere voice, was very moved, and her eyes filled with tears. She said only: "I know that you will."

Tony and Christopher were not participating in the dancing afterwards, but followed the younger crowd outside from where one could hear much laughter and merrymaking. Claire tried to cast glances after them, because she noticed too many girls in their presence. She did not have to worry—not yet; the boys were just interested in a little fun and diversion, which did not really include girls. Both of them were preoccupied with their upcoming journey to Italy with the bishop. Tony had now been at the farm for almost a year, where Grandfather had worked him harder than he had expected. He felt that he deserved a vacation, and so did Christopher, who had still a few exams before him. Neither of them were aware of the special tension between their parents and Elizabeth, but found their sister unusually distant. They attributed it to wedding dithers and did not pay much attention.

Paul and Melinda Thoene did not attend the wedding because Melinda had not been feeling well. It was unusual for them not to partake in the Burghoff's celebration, and Elizabeth whispered to Eva:

"You see, there is more to my suspicions. Aunt Melinda may have heard something disturbing also." Eva answered sadly:

"Elizabeth, don't spoil your big day with thoughts that are unworthy of you."

"All I want to know is who my real father is. You know yours could not be him, the timing is all wrong. Uncle Paul knows the secret, and I will find out one of these days."

There was nothing more said, and Eva avoided all future conversation related to that subject. She believed with all her heart that Claire, her "real mother" as she always called her in her mind, was pure and innocent and she never wavered in her love for her. Eva was glad when the wedding was over.

Helmut had some prospects for a job with a big construction company whose president he had met at a festivity where he and his band had provided the musical entertainment. During a conversation they had about folk music Helmut confessed that he was seeking other employment, the band was just his hobby. Now, with the prospect of getting married, he was looking for a "real job." After some further questions, Mr. Eberharter had told Helmut to stop by at his office in Salzburg, maybe he could find something suitable in his company for the young man, whose open manners he liked. Helmut did not hesitate to take Mr. Eberharter at his word. He had no experience in construction—neither the manual work, nor the technical. Mr. Eberharter had a hunch, however, and he had always trusted his hunches when employing new people, that Helmut could nevertheless provide good service to his company. He thought the young fellow had a winning way. He conversed with ease, was neither a loudmouth or a braggart, nor shy or timid. After more talks between them, he decided that he was going to try Helmut as an intermediary in negotiations the company had with various authorities over permits, etc., and with the unions. Mr. Eberharter felt he could train Helmut well for such a job to the satisfaction of both. Helmut found the offer interesting and hoped that he would not disappoint his employer who had such confidence in him. He did not know if he had the talents which Mr. Eberharter sought.

After the wedding the couple went to Salzburg for a day or two of honeymooning, but Mr. Eberharter was proposing an immediate apprenticeship, making sure that Helmut became familiar with the company to the full extent. He was pleased that Helmut was an attentive student and saw a good future for him. Helmut was also happy that he had found a promising position so soon despite his own father's prediction that he was "nothing but a musician." Elizabeth was quite happy and content, reverting to her old self, namely the charming, pretty, sweet, smiling, golden-haired female, as everybody always had described her. It was not clear what had possessed her to confront her mother the way she had. It must have been fear, the knowledge of her own wrongdoing—only a psychiatrist might have found the hidden reasons that made her act so contrary to her previous disposition. Despite some feeling of shame, she still believed that she was in the right; she would never apologize. Maybe there would come a time she would speak to her mother again, but the bond between them was broken and it was not her fault. Such were Elizabeth's thoughts. Children are cruel—they can break their parents hearts without regret. They may sin themselves, but would never forgive their parents for any conceived trespass.

Chapter 24

Now it was up to Eva to prepare for her wedding. She and Kurt had decided to postpone it for a little while after her sister's, but Christmas seemed a good time. They would like to make it simple, which would suit them both better than a grand affair.

North of Salzburg is the small village of Oberndorf, where once, on a snowy winter's night in 1818, the carol "Silent Night, Holy Night" was played and sung for the first time during Christmas mass at the old Nikolaus Church. That church had to be torn down in later years because of a constant danger of flooding from the river Salzach, but a small chapel was erected on the spot to remember the composers, Franz Gruber and Joseph Moore, whose simple song has captured the hearts and emotions of so many around the world since then. That's where Eva and Kurt planned to be married, with only their immediate families in attendance. Claire and Peter thought that it was a lovely idea, because it was so very typical of Eva, who shunned attention. Kurt was much like his betrothed in many ways. It was what had brought them together in the first place: "One heart and one soul"—the same likes and dislikes, with only little differences. A good match, all their friends agreed.

In the meantime, Tony and Christopher had left with their protector and benefactor, the bishop, for their month-long journey to Italy. Claire and Peter received postcards periodically—probably written upon the bishop's urging—reporting about their itinerary, but not much more. Claire missed her sons; this summer seemed unusually lonely without their youthful and always lively presence, yet she was happy that they could experience the classic cities of antiquity under the knowledgeable and wise guidance of Franz Hinterberger, whose watchful eyes would see to it that they did not stray either.

Peter was very busy. Claire spent time at the farm, and also often with Melinda, whose health did not seem to improve after a bout with the flu a few weeks ago. Claire was concerned, but Melinda reassured her, smiling, that she soon expected to be her old self again. Claire talked to Peter about her impression of Melinda. He did not respond, as if he had not heard what she said. That was odd, but she did not continue to probe. He was probably preoccupied with some problem at the hospital. He could become very sparing of words if he had a patient's serious condition on his mind, and Claire would not think of demanding a response.

When Kurt Boehmer was in town, Claire and Eva joined him in the search for hidden treasures at Waldegg, "treasures" meaning anything which could be identified as having historic value in contrast to stored-away junk. With help from other historical societies, they found enough to justify arranging it for exhibition in a small museum. Old ledgers and even older letters gave evidence that Waldegg had once been an important holding of the Salzburger Archbishoprie and had passed into the ownership of Count Christopher von Schwertberg around fifteen hundred. In the middle of the sixteen hundreds a Baron von Burghoff was first mentioned, and although dates were not clearly marked, the Burghoffs descended from about that time. The once extensive holding shrank in divisions to various descendants; the name Burghoff was used at the Waldegg location on a genealogical chart of its owners dating to 1746. The old fortress had seen many important visitors and distinguished guests through its lifetime, including a Danish king, a Swedish prince, and several clergymen from Rome on their way to meet with the Prince-Bishops of Salzburg. These events had to be pieced together from various entries in yellowed documents, were not yet complete or authenticated, and needed much more work. Napoleon and his French army had passed through the area also on their conquering forays to Vienna and Moscow, but that Napoleon slept at Waldegg was probably only a popular rumor, no clear verification had turned up so far, except for Anton Burghoff's memory of his grandfather's story that he had seen the French emperor when he was a child.

Claire was waiting anxiously for her sons' return from their sojourn in Italy. Four weeks was a long time for the mother; the boys thought it had passed only too quickly. They were enthusiastic about their experiences, and could hardly wait to tell it all. Franz Hinterberger joined the family at their first back-home get-together, the day after their return. He too wanted to hear what effect their visits to the ancient cities, churches, medieval abbeys, and museums had had on his charges. Tony and Christopher could not praise their experiences enough, telling of churches even more grandiose than the Salzburger Dome, more like Vienna's St. Stephen and the Karlskirche, they observed. So many other sights, such as Florence's famous Uffizi museum, were overwhelming, Michelangelo's "David" imposing. Rome was their favorite, because they had had the chance of a private audience with the Pope under Bishop Franz's sponsorship. He gave them his blessing individually; they were enthusiastic about the Vatican museum, the Tivoli Garden, and—oh, the Italian food and wine!

"Wine?" interrupted Claire.

"Of course," said the bishop, smiling benevolently. "Remember, when in Rome do as the Romans do!"

After recalling some anecdotes, funny happenings, and their problems with the Italian language, when they found out that their of eight years of Latin studies were only good enough to read the inscriptions in churches and cemeteries, but not for conversing with people on the street, especially the girls, who pretended not to understand them at all. Tony said that did not matter that much, since both he and Christopher had been inspired to study theology and become priests anyway.

"What?" Peter and Claire said simultaneously.

"Why does that shock you?" asked the bishop. "It's an honorable calling, is it not?"

Claire turned red in the face. Did their best friend, the bishop, betray them by persuading her beloved sons, who were just about to enter the adult world with all its promises, to leave it all behind for a "religious calling?" At least that was as she could see at the moment. Peter had remained silent, but uneasy.

Then the boys exploded in laughter, and Tony cried out:

"You did fall for our joke, we were not so sure if it would work when we thought it up only yesterday."

Everybody joined in the laughter, although Claire did not feel comfortable to have been caught in a situation which could have created such a dilemma. She had seen a different future for her sons than in a devotion to the church. Franz, the friend, took her arm, and said gently:

"Do you think that I could have ever hurt you by even suggesting taking your sons away from you? But if they really had found a religious calling, would it be so bad? Look at me, I am perfectly happy…happy in my service to the church, and, I would say, successful as well as happy in my love of the secular world. Do you think that I am missing out on anything?"

"Yes, I do," said Claire with firmness in her voice. He knew what she meant, and smiled at her.

"Well, if I had met you when I was young…." and he did not continue. Claire's face got even redder, and she turned towards the others, who had surrounded the boys with more questions.

The time had come for the two young men to embark on their intended University studies in Vienna. Peter accompanied his sons to introduce them to his former landlady, Frau Jandasek, at her home in the Waehringerstrasse, within walking distance from the venerable institution on the Ringstrasse. Frau Jandasek, older now and white-haired as Peter had expected her to be, but remarkably agile for her sixty-five years, was beside herself that she would be able to take care of the sons of her former student-boarder, the "Herr Doctor," who had been her favorite, as she said, gushing all over. She could not stop admiring how handsome his sons were, just like the "Herr Doctor" in his student days. It made Tony and Chris a little uncomfortable, and they were wondering how their quiet and reserved father could have tolerated so much adoration. It was just Frau Jandasek's temporary excitement, and she calmed down soon enough.

Peter had said very little, just that he hoped that the boys would not be too much trouble for her. By that time her daughter, a woman in her forties and more reserved than her talkative mother, had entered and taken over to show the young men—as she called them, and Peter realized all of a sudden, that he too must try to consider them as such and stop calling them "the boys"—their respective quarters, which were simply furnished, but comfortable rooms, each with a large desk as main focal point, flanked by still empty bookcases. It reminded the boarders quickly what was expected from them, namely studying diligently. A bed piled high with down covers, a wardrobe chest, and one other chair besides the one in front of the desk made up the rest of the furnishing.

"No partying here," Tony observed and Chris nodded, but they had not expected it. They had already discussed joining a fraternity to which Peter had only a frowning response. In his time, he had not cared for the activities of these student associations, which were involved in constant feuds, mostly politically motivated and inspired by the consumption of much beer. He had mellowed with time, and many of his old friends had fond memories of those good old student days in Vienna, called *burschenherrlichkeit*. He was going to wait and see before limiting his sons in their recreational activities. They needed to make friends in their new environment, so different from the rural life they had known up to now.

Peter became quite sentimental when thinking about the changes that the departing sons not only would experience themselves, but that would also involve him and Claire. When they had left her that morning, she had bravely tried to hide her tears and emotions, but Peter knew how she felt. The same as he, and maybe a little more so. He would have to think about something to cheer her up. The estrangement from Elizabeth, and now the parting from the boys, was a great strain on his beloved wife. On his way home from Vienna he hatched a wonderful plan, but it had to be kept secret for a little while until the details were worked out. In the meantime, he stopped at the fancy flower shop which had served his sentiments a long, long time ago. Fall was not the time for white lilac, but roses were in abundance, and he purchased the biggest bunch he could safely carry home.

Heidi Karner had come from Bruck for a visit with the Burghoffs nearly every year, with her children when they were little, and now more often
alone since her sons had grown into adulthood and independence. One was
married, and Heidi showed proudly, as grandmothers are apt to do, the pho-
tographs of an adorable little girl. Claire was always glad to see her childhood
friend, and the few days of their visit passed only too fast. Heidi was the only
one beside Peter that knew Claire's story, but they rarely mentioned it, since
there was always so much else to talk about. At this visit, however, Claire
could not help but let Heidi know about Elizabeth's angry outburst. Heidi
had been informed about the girl's sudden marriage, and was somewhat surprised that she had not been invited to it; then Claire told her all that had
happened. It made Heidi just furious that Peter and Claire had permitted
Elizabeth to continue that unjustified scorn of her parents. She said that she
would go and see Elizabeth and set her straight, but Claire asked her not to.

"What could you say to her? That her mother seduced her father, who
was at that time married to another woman, while she was also engaged to be
married to an upstanding soldier, a decorated war hero? And when that inci-
dence resulted in a pregnancy, her mother lied to her parents and friends,
and disappeared to deal with the consequences of her action. That she lived
for a while in the home of a lesbian doctor, that she pretended to be honorable and decent, and deceived even a kind and good man who offered to
marry her, including the child. Dearest Heidi…would that sound better than
the accusation Elizabeth threw at us already?"

Heidi had tears in her eyes:

"You are much too hard on yourself, you are the most virtuous, honest,
moral, and truthful person, I know. If I could find fault with you, it is that
you love too deeply and without reservations. You loved that ungrateful child
more than yourself from her embryonic beginnings and you were willing to
carry the burden of shame all by yourself in order to spare distress and pain
to the other human being you loved so deeply, namely her father. Claire—
don't do that to yourself. You do not need to feel guilty about anything, the
least of all that you have given birth to her and your love. I am still angry at
her, but it is probably true, that only Peter, you and I—and probably Paul—
would really understand. Did you tell Paul about Elizabeth?"

"No, how could I?"

"He is part of Elizabeth's fantasy, yet he does not know the true story?
Don't you think you owe him that?"

Claire did not answer—she did not know what would be right; she did
not want to impose her life story on anyone.

Peter had struggled with the same anguish. He was hiding his grief in a
cloak of silence, yet his past upbringing urged him to confession, and he
finally decided to tell the bishop about Elizabeth's accusations and how he

felt helpless in countering them; how he still felt guilty for what he had done to Claire. His friend, saddened by Elizabeth's behavior towards her parents, felt nevertheless that Peter did not need to agonize over it, but to ascribe her outburst to her own feelings of guilt and to her youth which could not deal with such emotions.

"Talk to Claire about it, don't hide your pain; share it with her, she must be hurting even more, watching you suffer in silence."

"That is exactly why I am so troubled. I know how much Claire is undeservedly enduring."

"It will be less, when you share your feelings with each other, not by assuming responsibility or guilt, but by loving and understanding. You are torn inside because you feel telling Elizabeth the truth would be worse than her imagination? Do not apologize—if there was ever need for penance—and I am not suggesting in the least that it is so—you and Claire have done your share of that. Your daughter was lucky enough to grow up so much loved, nurtured, and protected, that she cannot grasp a different world, one of sorrow and despair, where every day could have been a final one, where one grasped for every bit of the happiness which was so rare. While I am angry at Elizabeth too, I feel we have to be patient with her."

Peter was glad to have shared his distress with the bishop. He was right—it was important to gain some perspective, to be patient, even with one's own feelings—it was unthinkable that all these years of loving that child could have turned into a cross one had to bear.

This conversation with Franz Hinterberger had happened weeks before Peter accompanied his sons to Vienna, and he had to admit that his heart was slowly healing; he felt more at ease again. He had shared with Claire what Franz had said, and she was glad about it too, although Elizabeth remained distant and all the news about the newlyweds came only through Gerda, who was thoughtful and trying sincerely to make amends for the lack of communication. Helmut had told his mother about Elizabeth's falling-out with her parents. Gerda was very disturbed by it and told him that she was certain Elizabeth had been unfair in that respect. Of course, she had heard all kind of gossip herself—the village is a gathering place for such—but she had known Peter and Claire almost as long as she had known Fritz, her husband, and she had always held them in high regard. They were very honorable people, fine and decent, and if they had some kind of romantic encounter during these awful years of war and sorrows—who was entitled to judge and throw the first stone? Elizabeth wondered who her father was?

"Silly child...tell her to look in the mirror and figure whose gentian-blue eyes she inherited, the color of Peter and Hanna Burghoff's eyes, that is."

And when Elizabeth's child was born, it also had those deep blue eyes, and she said to Gerda that they were just like Helmut's.

"No, darling, Helmut's eyes are the color of forget-me-nots, like mine and Ingrid's. Yours are the color of the Burghoff's." Elizabeth blushed and was quiet.

Chapter 25

Before Elizabeth's child was born, the Burghoff family faced other challenges. Eva was preparing for her wedding at Christmas. Claire helped whenever she was asked, and was enjoying it. Peter was loosening his purse strings in a generous gesture, and the two women were busy shopping. Eva's desires were very moderate She looked for transportation from the city to the "Silent Night" chapel in Oberndorf by horse-drawn carriages or sleighs if there was snow, which was likely at that time of year. Eva, in all her reserve, was quite romantic, and she could picture with great emotion the ride through the snowy fields and meadows, in sleighs decorated with evergreens, the bells around the horses' necks ringing through the still landscape. Claire agreed, it was going to be just wonderful. She too saw herself in one of those sleighs, wrapped in a furry blanket, holding Peter's hand and looking into the handsome faces of their two sons in the opposite seats, red cheeked from the winter cold, riding toward a happy family celebration. It was going to be a highlight in their lives!

The festivities after the ceremony would include only the closest family members on both sides, a dinner held at Salzburg's Goldener Hirsch, one of the best restaurants; a special festive menu had been set up to emphasize the importance of the occasion. Background music would be provided by a string quartet from the Music Academy, festive decorations should be according to the Christmas theme. Eva had it all planned in detail. The wedding would take place on the Sunday before Christmas, after which she and Kurt would retire to their little cottage in St. Johann, then spend Christmas Eve as it had always been, at the Burghoff farm, with a visit on Christmas day to Kurt's family at their place, the Hotel Zur Post, in Kammerbach, for which—unbeknownst to the couple—Kurt's parents planned a little surprise bash, only inviting a number of their intimate friends, respecting Kurt's displeasure with large scale festivities.

Claire and Eva had fun furnishing the cottage in the garden of their house in St. Johann, where Eva and Kurt wanted to stay for the next year or so until their career situations developed further. The city's school administration had asked Kurt to review the high school's present curriculum for teaching history, and make proposals for updating where advisable. Eva thought of teaching—either grade school or kindergarten, she was not too sure where she would best fit in.

The main house was still occupied by the doctor who had replaced Peter a few years back. The cottage was in good condition, but needed some better furnishings. Eva preferred good old country style to the contemporary mode. There was good furniture now being built in the old style new, carved or painted, but Eva was looking for genuine antiques. She and Claire studied how to recognize such and then drove around the countryside to find it. It was not as easy as they had thought when starting out, but here and there they found something to their liking. The cottage was small, and not much was needed, but it should be authentic and pleasing. They had almost overlooked one trunk, found previously in Waldegg, which they had set aside for the future museum. Eva said the museum should get it eventually, but in the meantime she would like to display it in her home. That was settled with Anton and Hanna, who could hardly believe that Eva would want something from the abandoned storage rooms at Waldegg.

"Why not buy some fine new things?" Anton wondered, but Eva only laughed, and when the old trunk was cleaned up it looked very appealing.

The months before Christmas went by so quickly for Claire, that she hardly thought of complaining about getting only a few letters from her sons in Vienna. They had matriculated at the University according to the requirements in their respective fields of study, and seemed to be busier than they had expected. Little time for fun and games, was their main complaint, not home sickness or the pace of the metropolis. Peter thought about how differently they reacted in comparison to his own experiences when he first went to Vienna. He always thought of himself as the "country boy." Claire laughed about that. She used to know him then and he had not appeared a "country boy" to her. She remembered how that medical student had impressed her with his intelligence, his fine looking appearance, his quiet, distinguished demeanor. If she had known how he felt about himself, she herself might have been less shy in his presence and their relationship could have had a different beginning. But who could say? She was perfectly happy with how their life together had turned out, even including the bittersweet memories of perceived abandonment.

During all that time she was kept very busy, helping Eva with the wedding preparations, and shopping for presents for the family Christmas.

Winter came early that year, and there was very heavy snowfall in the surrounding mountains, much to the delight of the skiers, not only the native ones, but the hotels had plenty of reservations from winter sport tourists who came flocking in an unusual pre-holiday throng, a boon to the local economy. The business people hoped there would not be an early thaw to end all these great expectations. They did not need to worry, the snow lasted, and the country scenery was indeed as lovely and romantic as certain Christmas cards had ever pictured it.

Tony and Christopher came home in mid-December on their Christmas holiday from the University and Claire was happy to have her house lively again. Kurt was back also. He had finished with all his studies and his dissertation and had received his doctor's diploma; it was going to be a final homecoming for him. He hoped to be able to stay in the province in the future. He loved the mountains, he was an accomplished mountaineer and skier. His medals for winning at the FIS (Federation Internationale de Ski) competitions were many and were proudly displayed at his parents' home in Kammerbach.

With all the snow, the temptation was great for the young fellows to visit some of the upper slopes, but Kurt hesitated because of the nearness of the wedding and the preparations for it. Tony and Chris pleaded with him to come along for at least one day of fun in the snow, and Eva also encouraged him. She said it would be the last time he could enjoy bachelorhood, the next time she would be coming along. The best slopes, with the newly erected ski lifts, could be reached by a short drive from St. Johann. When the young men left in the morning, it was snowing heavily. The skiing weather reports announced a good amount of powder snow atop a solid base; skiing should be good. Indeed, it was so all day long. By four in the afternoon it was getting dark. It was still snowing, and intermittent fog shrouded the slopes. Tony and Kurt skied together when they decided that it would have to be their last run. Christopher had already removed his skis and was waiting at the ski hut. It had been really great skiing the whole day; they were tired but it was that comfortable feeling of tiredness after good exercise in fresh air. Kurt saw a couple of friends who were going for one more run and he could not resist the temptation to join them. The boys said that they had just about enough for today, but encouraged Kurt to go ahead, they would get a cup of hot chocolate in the meantime. About one half hour passed, and when Tony saw Kurt's companions return, he asked for Kurt.

"He was ahead of us, is he not here?" There were a great number of skiers now gathered at the lodge, but they could not see Kurt. He had probably met someone outside. Kurt did not show after another half hour, and the boys became concerned. They talked to the ski patrol, and two men went outside. It was very foggy now and one could not see more than a few feet ahead. They went up on the lift to search for life, but there was no sign of

Kurt. Snow was also falling heavier and heavier and obscuring all traces. The station became alarmed and organized a large search party, including Tony and Christopher, but there was no sign of Kurt on the normal downhill run. Maybe he was sidetracked in the fog and had lost his way, which was difficult to believe because he knew the area well. The party had penetrating search-lights with them, and they also called through the night. They continued half the night without success. In the meantime Tony called home and Peter drove immediately to the ski resort. He promised to call Claire upon his arrival, but driving through the heavy fog took him longer than expected and Claire was nearly frantic when she did not hear from him.

Eva was at the cottage in St. Johann and Claire could not decide if she should inform her or wait a little longer. The waiting was terrible and while she gave a prayer of thanks that her sons were accounted for, she was in great fear of what could have happened to Kurt. During daylight hours they could probably find him easier, than at night and in the fog. Was he injured, lost in the mountains? The latter seemed unlikely, Kurt knew the area. She began to pray fervently for his safe return. God had listened to her so often in the past—he must hear her now, please God.

Peter finally called. The three of them were going to spent the night at the lodge and wait for daylight, when the search would continue. They were worried, of course, but they all had reason to hope to find Kurt then. That's what he said on the phone, but in reality he was more pessimistic. If Kurt had been hurt and could not move, he would have a difficult time surviving in the freezing cold unless he found or built some shelter. Kurt was experienced, he would know how to protect himself. While Peter speculated and hoped against hope, Tony and Christopher were agonizing about the situation. If they had only insisted that Kurt did not go on that last ride up the slope, just a word that they should leave now would have prevented Kurt from going once more. Or if they had gone with him, they always kept an eye out for each other. Peter tried to calm them down, but he was not very convincing, having a heavy heart himself.

In that season of longest nights, it seemed to Claire that it took forever until daylight came. Now she had to call Eva, she did not dare put it off any longer. She said she did not know the details, but Kurt had apparently had an accident. Claire would come to St. Johann, and they could decide together if they wanted to wait to hear from Peter or drive up themselves. Eva said nothing at first, and Claire did not know if she had heard her, but then Eva said only:

"I will wait for you here."

Since Peter had their car, Claire had to call a taxi, which was not so easy to come by on that snowy winter morning but she finally succeeded. Eva greeted her ashen-faced and with a tremor in her voice. They had not heard from Peter, and Claire suggested they wait until his call came. By noon there was still no call. The telephone company had told them the phone lines to the ski hut were down due to heavy snowfall. It also looked very dangerous or nearly impossible for them to drive up themselves, because the roads could not be cleared fast enough to make them passable for cars. The town was quiet; the traffic had stopped there too. The two women looked out the window; the garden was deep in snow. They saw the doctor from the main house leave and fight his way through it on foot—he probably had to make a house call—but no one else was to be seen on the street, not even the children for whom such a time normally would mean lots of fun. Such desolation—nothing happened to divert the women's mind from the one great worry about Kurt. They did not even think of talking about the wedding. Eva finally decided to call Kurt's parents in Kammerbach They had expected him to be home the night before, but he sometimes stayed on the mountains when he was skiing and it got late, and they had not been overly concerned. Even now they tried to calm Eva, and said everything would turn out fine; Kurt had been in difficult situations before, he knew how to take care. Eva was ready to grasp at every straw of hope, although in her heart she felt desperation. She feared the worst, and the inability to act, to go to Schladming herself, was making it unbearable.

Adolf Boehmer, Kurt's father, was not as calm as he pretended to be on the phone with Eva and in front of his wife. Immediately after he hung up, he looked for the number of Colonel Albert Schoenberg, the military commander at the garrison in Salzburg, who had been a guest at his hotel for many years and was well acquainted with the family. Adolf explained the situation at the ski resort above Schladming, and asked if they could expect any help from the military by sending a helicopter to help in the search. This was not an unusual request, helicopters often helped recover injured or lost climbers from the mountains. Colonel Schoenberg promised immediate action, even offering to have Adolf picked up to come along. Fortunately it had stopped snowing and the sky had cleared somewhat. The crew at the ski hut had temporarily stopped their activities when the copter arrived, and one of the rescue team went with them for a search from the air. They had a general idea where to look, because Kurt could not have strayed too far during the time he was missing, and indeed they saw something which appeared unusual at the bottom of a rocky snow bank to the right of the usual downhill run. They directed the ground crew to the spot, because the copter could not land anywhere near it. After a difficult climb, the rescuers managed to reach the area. The tip of a ski stuck out from the snow to pinpoint the area of the accident and they started digging.

Kurt's body was found under about a foot of freshly fallen snow. Piecing together the probable course of events, the examiner declared that Kurt had deviated towards a cliff in the heavy fog last night, which would have been easily avoidable in good weather during the day, had jumped the cliff and landed safely, but because of the steep slope he had reached great velocity and had hit an unseen tree. He had suffered a broken neck and had died instantly. The copter took his body back to Salzburg with Adolf and Peter. Tony and Christopher were to follow with Peter's car as soon as the roads were passable, which happened just before darkness fell that day. Peter called Claire from the hospital, where he would be detained for a while before he was able to take a few days leave to attend to the sad family affairs. Adolf was taking care of his part—arranging for the funeral. He was in control—used to handling such business—yet he acted with a broken heart. Kurt, his oldest, had been his pride and joy despite his refusal to continue in the family business, or perhaps even because of it. None of the Boehmers had gone beyond a high school education, but his Kurt had even received a doctoral degree. All of Adolf's steady summer guests at the hotel had been given yearly progress reports on Kurt's academic achievements. He had been so proud of him, even when he had chided his son for refusing to take over the hotel after him, it had only been half-hearted.

The news spread quickly through the village and had reached Waldegg before Peter could inform them. He had driven to St. Johann and when Claire and Eva opened the door they saw in his face that their prayers had failed. He told them in a few words what had happened and stressed that Kurt's demise was so swift that he could not have been aware of the situation or have suffered any pain. He had died happy and in anticipation of marriage to the woman he so deeply loved.

Claire's tears were streaming down her face and Peter had to hold her tight, for her knees would not hold up. His other arm reached out for Eva, yet she withdrew silently to her bedroom. So they spent the next hour, while Peter tried as calmly as possible to tell the story from the time he had arrived at the ski hut. He was shaken himself. How often he had had to tell such news to loved ones of patients, and he had always felt touched. Still it is different when it hits your own. Words are useless—only holding and touching gives some comfort. Eva could not be comforted. She refused to open her bedroom door, she wanted to be alone. No crying or wailing came through the door, only stillness. Claire made a pot of hot tea and fixed a few sandwiches. Peter had not eaten anything since he had left the night before, and neither had Claire nor Eva, she remembered all of a sudden. They ate a little, and felt somewhat better for it, but Eva still refused. Peter and Claire had to go back to their house in Salzburg and wished to take Eva along, but in a calm voice—which concerned her parents more than if it had been crying or lamenting—she said that she wished to stay at the cottage for a while; she would be in touch with them over the phone, and they could inform her what

plans the family had to deal with what had to be done. Peter and Claire had no other choice than to respect the poor girl's wishes, and left.

On the way to the car, they saw Dr. Hoerbiger, the tenant of the main house and informed him of the situation. He expressed his condolences, and offered to look out for Eva if there was any need. He suggested that he could prescribe some tranquilizers. He would knock on Eva's door later in the evening, to see if she needed anything that he or his housekeeper could do for her. Peter and Claire felt grateful for his attention and left. The boys finally arrived late at night with Peter's car. They were exhausted, physically and emotionally; not much was said and they went to bed immediately. So did their parents.

The funeral services were conducted on the day the wedding celebration should have taken place. It was beautiful weather, clear and cold, and the snow glistened in the sunshine. The winter scenery was that typical "Winter Wonderland," just as Eva had hoped it would be on that day. It was inconceivable that nature could be showing itself in a glorious display when hearts were filled with sorrow and sadness and the future looked dark and dreary. Eva performed her role silently and automatically. She did what was expected from her. She ate her meals. She took Dr. Hoerbiger's medication. She chose what she would wear to the funeral services. She did not ask any questions. She appeared to her family as if she were a ghost. Elizabeth had called her on the phone, excusing herself for not being able to attend the funeral; because of her late stage of pregnancy she had been advised by her doctor not to risk slipping in the snow. Without showing any regret or emotion Eva said:

"It's all right, Lisa, take care of yourself," and she hung up and refused to accept any other phone calls.

The funeral was a public event. Kurt was mourned not only as the son of the prominent Boehmer family, but he had many friends who came from various areas; some of the Mountaineers came from Tyrol; the skiers included members from many clubs. Salzburg's historical society had sent members with whom Kurt and Eva had worked when researching Waldegg's history. Colonel Schoenburg and the helicopter crew also arrived, and, of course, nearly the whole population of Kammerbach. The tragedy of the day which should have been the wedding day of the well known and well liked couple had touched many who would otherwise not have paid that much attention. The church bells in Kammerbach rang for an hour in the morning, and again for one hour before the funeral. Ringing the bells costs money, and such long ringing showed that a member of a wealthy family had died. Peter knew that there was more to its meaning in the old superstitions, but he had forgotten it. He just mentioned it to Claire and the boys when they were standing around looking helpless, where one does not know what to do or say. The funeral procession to the church was long, the music with its mourning recitals was painful to Eva. She had asked Adolf Boehmer to refrain from that part of the ceremony, but he said tradition required it. So she had to suffer that as well as Father Grumbacher's long and weary sermon and the long service as well. The people attending liked it, and also the wake held at the Hotel Zur Post, the Boehmer's place, where food and drink was provided.

It was a fine funeral was the opinion of the people. Claire had heard these words, *What a waste, that he died so young*, a number of times before their own family returned with Eva to Waldegg, and she thought about the meaning of "waste." She could not see it as such. Kurt's life had not been a waste. It was a great pity that it ended so soon, before he could continue to share his talents, his love, his life but his life had not been a waste. Just by being he had given his parents and his friends, so much joy. He was a loving son, a true friend to many, and he had made Eva happier than she had ever been. This was not a "waste." It would have been if Kurt had never lived at all. They all can build on the memory of his existence and the way he had touched them and find themselves rewarded by it. These thoughts made Claire feel a little better, and she hoped that in time Eva would remember her happiness with Kurt more than the pain of losing him.

The family spent the Christmas holidays together at Waldegg as they had been doing nearly every year. It was evident that it lacked the usual joy and happiness, but Hanna prepared the same dishes and baked the same sweets as always. There was the baked fish with potato salad on Christmas Eve before they all boarded the big horse drawn-sleigh to take them to the church in Kammerbach for Midnight Mass. Eva did come along, thinking wistfully how different the bells on the horses sounded this night than how she had imagined they would sound on her wedding day. While Claire's eyes filled with tears during Mass, Eva was dry-eyed and numb, not showing her pain.

The traditional meal on Christmas day, consisting of roast goose and red cabbage, with potato dumplings, salads, sachertorte, husarenkrapferln, spitzbuben, ischler-baeckereis, and on and on; everything was the same as always—yet in just a few days so much had changed. All tried their best to put on a brave face, and Peter even joked with the farm hands who lived at Waldegg and were traditionally invited to join the family on Christmas day, when they received their presents. The family exchanged also presents, but in a quiet way, without the usual expressions of exuberant surprise and delight.

Melinda called to express her feelings over the tragedy that had befallen the family. She had just returned from Vienna, where she had spent much of the last few months "researching for a new book," as she explained. Paul had commuted from his office in Salzburg to Vienna as often as he could, and the Burghoffs and the Thoenes had not seen each other for a while.

"Please come over to Fuschl for New Year's Eve," Melinda said, almost pleadingly. "I know you don't feel like celebrating at this time, but we need each other as friends, and I have missed you so much. And, please, persuade the children to come along also. My niece Annemarie and her brother Alex are here with us for the holidays, and I think it would be nice for all of them to meet."

Claire thought it would be good to see their friends—she had missed them also, but she was not sure how the rest of the family would feel about it. She was surprised that Peter did not seem to be reluctant as he so often was when it came to accepting an invitation, but was rather anxious. He asked how Melinda had sounded on the phone, another thing that Claire wondered about:

"I am certain she was sincere when she urged us to come."

Eva begged not to be included, although normally she liked the Thoenes very much, especially Melinda. She said she needed some peace and quiet, and time to think all by herself and she would prefer to stay in St. Johann for the next few days.

Tony and Christopher had expressed a desire to go back to Vienna as soon as possible, where they could find diversion from their ordeal by immersing themselves in their studies. They had no intention of going skiing again this season, and just being idle around the house was not to their liking either. Claire and Peter saw them maturing before her eyes. Their "happy-go-lucky" attitude when they arrived prior to all that happened, had changed. They were still feeling guilty over their part in the accident, although Peter had tried to make them see reality. They had done nothing to cause that misfortune; they had not been negligent in any way; they were grateful for their father's admonition, but they remained depressed. Claire expressed Melinda's wish to join them on New Year's Eve and added her own hopes that they would. In that case they knew they could not refuse. Besides, they really liked Uncle Paul, who had been such a great pal to them during their boyhood years. They had not seen him for a while and would like to tell him about their Italian experience, expecting a good conversation with him.

It started out to be a very pleasant evening. The young people took to each other quickly. Alex was in his third year of studying law, and his sister Annemarie studied music in the family tradition. They were very "Viennese," as Christopher observed, which meant easy-going, fun loving, and with that certain drawl in their speech that made them so appealing.

Melinda looked especially beautiful, wearing a soft flowing silk gown, a Christmas present which her father had recently brought her from the Orient. Claire thought she was slimmer than ever—her skin paler than ever, and her makeup a little heavier. She looked almost like a two-dimensional, exquisite painting against the yellow brocade wall in the living room. Her appearance was not lost on Peter either. Claire observed with amazement that her Peter could not seem to take his eyes off that lovely creature.

Champagne was flowing freely, an array of tidbits of various kinds were served, from the traditional hearty smoked sausages and herring in wine sauce, to imported oysters, smoked salmon on little pieces of toast topped with caviar, goose liver paté, various gelatin-covered specialties, and the best local cheeses. It was a feast after all, despite Melinda's invitation to an informal get-together of friends who had not seen each other for a while.

Paul had been rather quiet, but more of the excellent and expensive sparkling wine loosened his stance a little, he became more relaxed and conversation between them flowed freely and with great warmth.

As the evening wore on, Peter expressed a desire to hear Melinda sing one of his favorite songs—Schubert maybe? She suggested one of Schuman's Totenlieder, but he said it did not fit the happy atmosphere of the evening. Both he and Melinda stepped up to the piano and looked through some sheet music, their backs turned to Claire and Paul, who had again that sad expression on his face. Claire looked at Peter and Melinda with some surprise. Peter had his arm around the lovely woman's shoulder in a tender embrace. She was looking up at him, then leaning her head against his chest. Claire would have never expected to have reason to be jealous, but it hit her with force—this could not be her Peter? He had said so often that no other woman could ever even slightly interest him? She had believed that for all these years—was he after all just like other men, who could have their heads turned by a beautiful woman? A sharp pain filled her heart, she stood up and was going to interrupt that tender tête-à-tête, but Paul held her back and said softly:

"Have another glass of champagne, Claire."

By then Peter had returned to his seat on the sofa next to Claire and was holding her hand in his. Melinda started to sing—some haunting melodies, some happy, easy tunes—very charming, but her voice had a little edge to it. Claire noticed that Peter's eyes were fixed on her, while squeezing Claire's hand affectionately. Claire was confused and troubled—the champagne clouded her thinking and feeling. Paul looked at her reassuringly with his warm brown eyes, and the sad smile she had noticed before.

Fireworks across the lake interrupted Melinda's singing, and they stepped up to the window with the view of the lake. The night sky was dark, but the snow lighted up the surroundings and provided a romantic scene. The young people had joined them and when the clock struck midnight they toasted the New Year with good wishes for the coming year, each of them with different hopes in their hearts.

The Burghoffs spent the night at the Schlosshotel in Fuschl where Paul had made reservations for them, since the Thoene's visitors were already occupying the guest rooms, which at other times were always ready for the

Burghoffs. It would not have been far to drive to their Salzburg home, but with so much champagne in their systems Peter preferred not to, especially on those icy roads at night. When they said good-bye, Claire overheard Paul whispering to Peter:

"Tell Claire." Peter looked questionly, but Paul repeated: "Yes, do it."

Claire's heart pounded, her stomach was in knots—was it the wine or was it fear—what was it that Peter would have to tell her? What was it that she did not know, what terrible thing was going to come her way? Everything became blurry in her mind. Could Peter have betrayed her? Did Paul know something that she did not? *Oh God, help me*—the pain was too great to bear.

Peter was silent until they reached their quarters at the hotel, and after the boys had said their goodnights, he said he was very tired and assumed that she was too. They had better go to bed and get a goodnights sleep.

"Oh no, Peter," she said, feeling suddenly very cold, "Paul wanted you to tell me something, I want to hear it."

"Tomorrow, darling, I will tell you tomorrow," he yawned and was almost undressed and ready for bed.

"No, not tomorrow, I want to hear it right now," she insisted, and Peter looked surprised. That was not like Claire, what was the matter? Too much excitement in the last few days, too much food and wine tonight? He started to embrace her and kiss her good night as was his daily habit, but she turned him away and insisted they talk. He was very tired, he went to bed, pulled the bed cover up, and said almost hostilely:

"All right, if you have to know tonight," Peter was annoyed, but continued:

"Melinda is dying. The doctors in Vienna, where she has spent these last months, have told her to go home and face the inevitable. I have known about it for a long time. Paul had consulted with me about it and I recommended the Vienna clinic of Professor Sauerbrunn as the best I know. Paul asked for absolute confidentiality, which also included you. Only tonight he released me from my promise. I wished I could have prepared you better for such news, but you insisted."

Peter was still angry. Claire went to the bathroom, and was sick—sicker than she ever remembered that she had been, and it was not all a result of the eating and drinking that night. Peter finally got up and brought her back to bed, where she cried herself to sleep in his comforting arms with agonizing feelings of remorse, guilt, and anguish about Melinda's fate, and the tragic death of Kurt, just days ago.

Chapter 26

The New Year did not start well for Claire, she felt physically and emotionally drained and exhausted. The official report Peter provided to everybody was that she had the "flu"; he took care of her and saw to it that she had a good rest. They spent a few days alone together, and that was the best medicine for them both. Peter had not noticed, but he too was in need of decompression after the stress of the past weeks.

They called Eva in St. Johann, who said that she was feeling better, having slept much lately, probably as a result of Dr. Hoerbiger's prescription. She said he had been very kind to her and was fortunately not overbearing but understanding of her need to be left alone. His housekeeper had brought some freshly cooked broth and little pieces of roast chicken over, but did not invade her privacy either. Eva was grateful to them. Claire wanted to know if she did not want to come to Salzburg for a few days, but she said that she would do so as soon as she was ready.

"Give me a little time," she pleaded. Peter went back to work also, and the boys were off to Vienna.

Claire had lonely days now. She called Gerda to find out how things were with Elizabeth. She felt almost humiliated that she had to find out about her daughter's condition indirectly, but since Elizabeth had rebuked her once for inquiring by saying rather brusquely that she was doing just fine and would announce the birth of her child in a timely fashion, she did not call her again. Gerda knew how difficult the whole situation had become and was troubled by it—for the sake of both mother and daughter. At present, it seemed better to ignore Elizabeth's behavior. It would certainly pass once the child was born. Gerda had offered to come and help out after the baby arrived, but Elizabeth refused that also, saying that she had all the help she needed from a young woman whom Helmut had hired to make it easier for her. It looked as if Helmut's job was going well, and he could already afford some luxuries. They had rented a small house in Linz, where he was now headquartered, and were doing well.

Peter had provided Elizabeth with a trust fund as her inheritance, from which she could take monthly benefits. He told Claire their finances were somewhat strained at present, because of the funds he had set aside for the boys' education and Elizabeth's share. The farm was yielding just enough right now to pay its way—expenses for wages grew faster than the income from their production. Taxes were out of sight—but his income from his practice kept them comfortably secure. She did not need to worry about money matters, he just wanted to explain how things stood. Claire had never inquired about their finances. She was content with their standard of living, often even remarking how their lives had improved in that respect over the last ten years since Austria had become a free nation again. Claire had never been demanding, but rather modest in her own needs, and Peter's explanation did not worry her in the least. Peter found his wife very remarkable in that respect also. He had often listened to colleagues' complaints about their wives' spending habits and pitied them.

Claire was in a quandary as how to deal with Melinda. She would like to help in any way she could, but what would Melinda really want? Peter suggested waiting a little rather than bombarding her with pity. He said that Melinda would eventually come to his hospital and be treated by Dr. Nussbaum, the best there was in Salzburg to treat her type of cancer. He added:

"And I will give her my personal attention in many ways; I hope that you will understand that?"

Claire still felt ashamed of her silly behavior on New Year's Eve, but Peter was secretly flattered. She had never before shown jealousy. She had no grounds—she was, had been, and would remain forever his only love, there could be no doubt.

The Christmas and New Year's holidays over, life took on a more normal appearance again. Eva had been at the house in Salzburg several times for short visits, had borrowed some of the books in Peter's library, but had not commented on her future plans. If married to Kurt, she would have looked for a temporary teaching job until Kurt was settled with a position to his liking. Her parents thought that it would benefit Eva, if she continued with these plans, but they did not want to push her into making any decision. One evening, Peter came home and told Claire that Eva had called him at the hospital and asked if he could spare a few minutes to give her some advice. They had agreed to meet the next day, again at Peter's hospital office. Claire wondered why she would not come to the house and so did Peter.

Eva had her reasons, which had nothing to do with her parents, but with the hospital environment she wanted to experience. She told Peter immediately that she was convinced teaching was not her calling. She saw her life now in a different way. Since she did not plan to marry ever, she was looking for a vocation that could at least fill partially the void that Kurt's death had left in her life. The more she had thought about it, the more she became convinced that the medical field would suit her best. What was her father's opinion about that? Peter was delighted and suggested that she go to the dean of the medical school at the University in Vienna to find out how much credit she could receive for her years at the Teacher Seminary, and then proceed accordingly. He would support her financially towards such a worthy goal. Eva said she did not intend to go so far as becoming a doctor—she had thought rather of a nursing career. Peter was somewhat disappointed because he knew Eva had a good mind, and could handle the difficult studies for a medical degree. Eva countered that she was not afraid of studying, but rather was anxious to go to work and to care for patients. She had discussed it with Dr. Hoerbiger. (*Dr. Hoerbiger?* Peter wondered, *how did he get into the picture? And before she talked to me?*) Dr. Hoerbiger had said that there were good nursing programs available.

"What do you think, Papa?"

Peter was quiet for a while, then said he would discuss it with the head of the nursing staff at the hospital, run by the Franciscan Order of nuns (augmented by lay nurses), and see what she would suggest. Eva was satisfied, and Peter called next day on Mother Veronica who was only too willing to help. She had great respect for Dr. Burghoff, and would be delighted to talk to his daughter Eva about her desire to become a nurse. In her own mind she wondered if the child really felt a calling or was it just a reaction to the loss of her fiancé, as it sometimes happened.

Eva appeared promptly for the scheduled appointment with Mother Veronica, where she indeed found all the answers she was looking for. Seeing that the young woman was serious and determined, she offered to help her. Their order could—considering the many basic science courses Eva had taken at the teachers college—accept her with the prospect of finishing the course within two years, while at the same time allowing her to learn and perform some nursing duties at the hospital under the supervision of the medical staff.

That was exactly what Eva had hoped for. Her parents smiled when she told them enthusiastically about her interview with Mother Veronica. It was typical of Eva since childhood: she was clear thinking, always sure of herself, and determined. Not that they would have wanted to dissuade her, but it would have been unlikely that she would have changed her mind. They were happy for her too—although Peter would have loved to see her follow in his footsteps. Eva's only request was that she could stay at the cottage, and also keep her room at the house in Salzburg. Both were granted gladly. It meant that Eva would want to be independent in a way, but also keep in close touch with her parents, with Claire mostly in Eva's mind.

On January thirteenth, Elizabeth gave birth to a daughter. Peter called the hospital in Linz and talked to her attending gynecologist, who assured him that mother and daughter were doing well. Both were in excellent health. "Grandfather" Peter brought the report home to his wife, "Grandmother" Claire. They looked at each other happily, and laughed loudly: did their new title not make them feel old at all? As a matter of fact, they both wondered if they should not prove that they were still as young and fit and capable as they once were! And that was how they celebrated the birth of their first grandchild.

Elizabeth let it be known that she and her family would come to Kammerbach for the baptism of the child as soon as the weather would thaw a little, which was at the beginning of March. Their visit was very short, since Helmut had to be back at his job, but at least a family visit had taken place for the first time since their wedding. Eva took part in the baptismal ceremony, since she had been asked to be the child's godmother. The baby was named Eva-Johanna-Gerda, and would be called Hannerl. Great-grandmother Hanna Burghoff was pleased about that choice, and so was everybody else. Claire held the baby in her arms and remembered with great emotion the moment when she had held her firstborn, Elizabeth, and all the bittersweet memories of that time overwhelmed her.

Paul was missing that day. The Thoenes had planned to attend, but Melinda had had a reaction to a medicine she was taking, and Paul did not want to attend the festivities without her. Peter went to church with the family for the baptism, but remained silent. The other grandfather, Fritz Engebrecht, however, had to show off his glee over the event, which affirmed the connection to the esteemed Burghoff family. Peter cringed, Claire ignored it, but saw that Gerda was embarrassed by Fritz's behavior. Helmut behaved a little awkward with all the fuss but was attentive to Elizabeth, as Claire observed with satisfaction.

Eva had started her nursing training, and was apparently glad over her decision. It kept her quite busy and Claire saw little of her. Peter caught glimpses of her at the hospital, but they avoided closer contact, so there could be no suspicion that Eva would get special treatment as daughter of the chief of staff. Mother Veronica had told him that the training of the nurses was quite rigorous. He thought that it would be good for Eva and would take her mind off the tragic events of her recent past. As usual, Eva kept her feelings private, but she occasionally told Claire not to worry about her, she had regained her balance.

Claire turned her attention again to the Waldegg history project, but it was not as satisfying as it had been when Kurt and Eva were around, who would share her enthusiasm. She was working by herself now and her job consisted more or less of getting final approval for the museum from the authorities, as well as from the Burghoff family, whose privacy would be infringed if the museum were opened to the public.

In the end, it was worked out to everybody's satisfaction. The townspeople were proud to see their heritage now documented, and the Burghoffs felt their contribution was an obligation to the past. The so-called museum was accessible through an old stairway to the tower from the outside of the still standing wall. It consisted of three rooms containing old furniture, with pictures on the walls, as well as framed documents and weapons, including an almost complete suit of armor, which had only a few metal parts missing, which did not detract from its overall display. A massive wooden table which had apparently seen heavy usage was set with some eating utensils of heavy tin and pewter tankards and plates, ledgers, old books, letters, yellowed documents of all sorts were kept under glass on other tables. Gobelins and other tapestries were hung on the walls. One room served as a former kitchen with an open hearth and displayed heavy iron kettles as well as other kitchen equipment, not too much different from many kitchens still seen today in very old farmhouses in remote areas. Kitchens seemed to have undergone less change through the centuries in some places than other parts of farm life. Peter was not as impressed by the museum as the townspeople, but when it received the official designation "Cultural Monument" on a metal shield, affixed ceremoniously on the tower wall, he smiled benevolently, as he did also when he was presented with a copy of a discovered document, officially calling one of his ancestors "Baron Konrad von Burghoff," which would allow today's Burghoff descendants to use that aristocratic title also. When told, Anton grinned his jovial smile, Hanna said that she had always known about it. Some of the old townspeople had told her that when she had come here as a young bride, and Anton's mother had told her also. Only Anton's father had shrugged his shoulders and had said "*Firlefanz—that title does not buy us anything.*" Peter seemed to have inherited that attitude. Claire felt a little more impressed—she did not have to pretend modesty, after all it was not her family genealogy, and she said to Peter, who still called himself a country boy, that in her heart she had always known that he was very special.

Claire decided to go to Vienna for a couple of days to visit her mother, whom she had not seen since her and Peter's visit last fall. Rosemarie had been in fine spirits and ostensibly happy for which Claire was glad, but she had mixed feelings at the same time. It was clear to her now that the strained relationship between her parents when she was growing up contained a hidden story of which she had not been aware. The coolness of their relationship may have not been entirely her father's fault. Her mother had probably never loved him, and he had turned away to his studies and his books. How sad!

Peter had told Claire before she left to ask her mother, who was by now an experienced traveler all over the continent, for advice about the appropriate wardrobe for an Italian vacation.

"What are you talking about?" Claire said.

"Didn't I tell you? It must have slipped my mind," he answered jokingly – "We are going to take off for a month-long vacation in May; would you like that?"

Of course she would, but she could hardly believe that Peter could leave behind all his obligations and duties as he always saw them. He countered:

"Don't you think we deserve to take time off? You have always been selfless throughout the years, always giving and caring—" and Peter would have gone on, but Claire interrupted him:

"I am so excited. "Where are we going? Just the two of us, Oh, Peter, it will be glorious."

"I think so too. We still have to decide on details, I will leave that up to you, you are better at planning. My part was to free myself of my hospital obligations for a whole month. The only request I have is that you include a visit to La Scala in Milan. I need to find out if their productions are really better than those at the Vienna Opera house, as some claim." Claire said that she could hardly wait, but Peter cautioned:

"There is just one reservation that I have: if Melinda's condition deteriorates, we have to postpone our trip, you do understand?"

"How can you even ask?"

Claire's joy was dampened. She had a difficult time since that New Years Eve, thinking about the tragedy that had befallen their friends. The Thoene's city apartment was just a few blocks from their home in Salzburg, and she tried to see Melinda as often as possible without making a nuisance of herself. Melinda needed distraction but also much rest, and Claire relied on Paul to let her know when she was wanted. When the days were warm and sunny, Claire suggested a ride out into the country, which Melinda always enjoyed. She was too weakened by her medication to do the things she always had loved to do: playing the piano, writing, and entertaining. She never complained, never cried or lamented her fate—at least not in front of others. Paul called her a saint. He was very much affected and was grateful for Peter's attention and advice. He frequently invited him to join him for lunch when he knew that Melinda was in Claire's company. The four had been good friends for a number of years now, but the misfortune of Melinda's illness had brought them even closer. The bishop joined them at times, and just his presence and his compassionate manner brought a spiritual quality to their conversations.

Claire took a morning train to Vienna and had a very pleasant lunch with her mother and August, who both seemed to be leading a very contented and happy life, looking younger than their age. *Love can do wonders*, Claire thought, thinking of the visits with her mother at the time of her father's funeral. She did not forget to get advice about a traveling wardrobe as Peter had suggested; Rosemarie said to travel light—it would be warm and pleasant at that time of year.

"But my Salzburger *dirndls* would be out of place, wouldn't they? I have never added much else to my wardrobe."

Rosemarie agreed to accompany Claire to do some shopping in the afternoon. Not many summer fashions were exhibited yet, however, and they decided to visit an old acquaintance, a seamstress who had sewn most of Claire's clothes a long time ago, when that was still preferred to buying off the rack. The woman, not much older than Claire, was still in the business of sewing for her "refined" clientele, and was delighted to see Claire again. She had some good suggestions, and when taking Claire's measurements she said with admiration that these had not changed very much since then. Miss Kopetzky still had the old records to prove it. They decided on materials to make up a basic suit (a style that always had been Claire's choice) of raw silk and a couple of blouses to go with it, a white, loose-fitting, sleeveless linen dress for hot days, with a simple cover-up of the same white material for cooler evenings, and a silk shantung fitted dress in Peter's favorite color of cerulean blue (since he could not remember the famous "reseda" color) for more formal occasions. She thought Peter would approve of her choices—all very conservative, except for one of the blouses, the material of which was a geometric print of many colors. If she needed anything else, such as clothes for beach wear or silk scarves, she should purchase those in Italy, Rosemarie suggested, as well as sandals of the fine leather for which the Italians are well known.

All in all, it was a pleasant and successful shopping trip, which ended with dinner at the Rathauskeller, where August and the boys met them. Claire was so proud of her sons: so handsome—resembling Peter so much, it was almost like looking at him when she had first met him, except for the color of their eyes. Everybody said they were the color of hers, but she thought they had inherited Anton Burghoffs stone-gray color, only the blond locks were definitely Peter's. Chris was as tall as Peter, Tony had a more stocky figure, strong, solid—she could not take her eyes off her sons.

They chatted amiably. August asked all the important questions about their studies, but was always tactful enough not to be more inquisitive than young people cared for. Since the bombed-out building where she used to live was quite near, they passed it on their way home. Indeed, a new building had been erected, modern, ugly, lacking any style, just a concrete box with tiny balconies interspersing the boring facade. She thought, "What if had I to live here—and had to be glad that as a bombing victim I was even given the right to another apartment?" How lucky her life had turned out to be.

On the way home on the train the next morning she had similar thoughts. August had asked her last night if she missed her old hometown, Vienna. People who had had to leave it for any number of reasons seemed to desire to come back and many were doing so. Claire did not; she had never missed the city or the people—her old friends had dispersed—some had died in the war; but it reminded her to write to the Woerners in Nuremberg. They had visited them in Salzburg a couple of times, and it had been a very joyful reunion, but they had looked worn and old, especially Georg. They had had a difficult time reestablishing themselves after the war, and, it was odd that they, who were not natives of Vienna but true Germans, were homesick for that city which had not even been too hospitable to them when they first arrived. Claire thought she felt differently because she had raised her family in the country; that was where she belonged, Vienna had no special pull on her. It also occurred to her that even when she was only a teenager on summer vacation, she felt that she rather belonged to the country, despite her appreciation and pride in the cultural and historical aspects of the place she was born.

Her thoughts strayed into different directions. She remembered that she had forgotten to mention to the boys, as well as to her mother, that the title of Baron for the descendants of the Burghoff family had been brought up again in the old papers, displayed now in the museum at Waldegg. Would her sons have been impressed? Probably not, just like their father. She smiled at the thought of what Peter would say when she told him about her seamstress who still conducted her business of sewing, but only for her refined clientele, and since she was making a couple of outfits for Claire to wear on their Italian sojourn, it meant that she considered her to be refined!

Three hours on the train passed pretty fast while looking out at the lovely scenery. She took the bus to her home and expected Peter still to be at the hospital. Indeed, he called a little later and was glad to know that she was back. He asked her about her visit with her mother and the boys. He sounded a little distracted and she asked if he was feeling well.

"I asked Eva to come home earlier tonight, as I won't be able to make it for dinner, and I don't want you to be alone," he said

"I'll be happy to see Eva, although I thought, that she wanted to go to St. Johann tonight. I hope that you won't be too late?"

"I don't know—please don't wait up for me."

Claire was disappointed, but she knew if Peter was needed at the hospital, she had to be patient. Eva came, and was also tired and rather short on words. She wanted to hear about Tony and Chris, but then excused herself to go to bed. Claire read for a while, and made it also an early evening, but when she heard Peter coming in at midnight, she was wide-awake. He was not in a talkative mood either, so her stories about Vienna, mother, the boys, and the seamstress had to wait.

Peter was up early and had left for the hospital before she came down, with Eva close behind him. All alone for breakfast, she felt lonely, and her first impulse was to call Melinda, but it was too early. Melinda was never up before ten o'clock. The housekeeper was also off today. Only the old gardener was doing some spring-cleaning and she envied him his garden work. She missed her garden from St. Johann, where she had planted flowers and vegetables. She would not need to plant these in order to supplement their ration supplies anymore, but flower gardening would be gratifying. However, in their present house the gardeners would not like any interference.

She felt lonely and bored and decided to take a walk through town, get some fruit and flowers from the open market at the old town square, maybe buy a sandwich and eat her lunch at Mirabell Garden, if it should warm up enough by noon. Spring was in the air; she bought a bunch of violets and sniffed their fragrance with pleasure. When she passed Paul's office, she decided to peek in to see if he could accompany her on a stroll through Mirabell, something they sometimes did together. Paul's secretary said that he had not come in that morning, nor had he telephoned; she assumed he was still at home. Claire almost wished that she had stayed another day in Vienna, but nobody needed her there either. She started to feel sorry for herself—a husband, four children, friends—but no one needing her or wanting her today. She went home rather than going to Mirabell, put the flowers in a vase, and the fruit in a basket on the kitchen table. She busied herself with dinner preparations, although it was still early for that. She was restless and could not find a reason for it.

In mid-afternoon, the phone rang. Peter wondered if she was at home. He would like to come home for a cup of coffee. He could seldom take a break like that, and Claire's mood immediately changed in happy anticipation. He probably felt sorry to have been so short yesterday and in the morning, barely giving her a chance to let him know that she was back. When Peter came, he looked drawn and tired. They sat down together at the kitchen table with the freshly brewed coffee giving off a fine aroma, and a plate of *anis-zwieback* to nibble on.

Then Peter told her about Melinda's sudden downturn. He had spent most of yesterday at the Thoene's, consulting with Dr. Nussbaum, Melinda's specialist. She had had a bad night, her pain was increasing, and he had discussed with Paul and Dr. Nussbaum the latter's suggestion to transfer Melinda to the hospital. Paul would prefer that she was taken care of at their home, if at all possible. Dr. Nussbaum was against it, but Peter tried to persuade him. He would arrange for twenty-four hour nurse attendance, would also make himself available at any time, day or night. He wanted to get Mother Veronica to give Eva time off to tend to Melinda. It was all now arranged, and they hoped to keep Melinda comfortable at home. Peter said that he had little hope that she would recover from the setback. Paul was very distressed and in need of medical attention himself. Peter was taking care of that. Claire was anxious to offer her help in any way, but Peter said the best thing for her was to be understanding and patient with him and all those involved. Claire promised to remain calm, but when he left she went to bed; she felt very sad and the tears flowed until she fell asleep.

The situation did not improve during the next few days, and Peter said they would probably have to postpone their planned trip south. Of course that was all right with Claire, how could one even think of leaving when dear friends needed one. She called her seamstress in Vienna to ask her to send all her things without a fitting, as she was unable to come to Vienna. She was sure everything would fit just fine. It was also a proving time for Eva, who had been so fond of Melinda. Claire thought that the past year had put a great burden on all of them—the psychological upheaval, starting with Elizabeth, than Kurt, and now Melinda.

She prayed that God might spare Melinda from suffering too much pain. Peter said that was his job and Dr. Nussbaum's. Claire could not help thinking it was true that doctors felt that they did God's work, even her usually humble Peter. At the same time, she knew that Peter was selfless and devoted to the care of his patients to the utmost, so she prayed for him too. She was surprised and glad when she got a call from Paul saying that Melinda was feeling better for the moment and would like to see her that afternoon if she were free to do so. She would be there in an instant, she said, and ran almost all the way to the Thoene's home.

She did not know if Peter was there, or Eva, and neither were, only the nurse and Paul. Melinda sat propped up in her bed, dressed in a lovely lacy white gown, roses on her bedside table, which made Claire immediately regret that she had come in such a hurry that she forgot to bring flowers. Melinda greeted her with a sweet smile, saying that she had missed her, but her jailers kept all visitors away. Claire used all her strength to behave herself as she normally would: calm and controlled, loving, but not mushy. Melinda was advised not to talk too much, so Claire did the talking. She could finally tell somebody about her visit to Vienna, the boys, and her mother, who was happy and in love in her golden years! She asked Melinda if she had heard from her family lately, and heard, that her brother had announced he would visit soon. She also asked that Claire should tell her if she looked well enough—she would like to have a little more makeup, but nobody seemed to know how to help her with that. Claire immediately jumped at the chance to suggest that, if Melinda would like it, she would like to come once a day to help her with that.

"Claire, that would be so nice. You understand that I want to look presentable, resembling my old self rather than the ghostly appearance I see in the mirror." That was settled. When Paul left the room for a while, Melinda took Claire's hand and said softly:

"Claire, you will take care of Paul, won't you? He can't manage by himself—he'll be needing you and Peter; please, promise."

Claire was startled, but caught herself quickly and replied in a lighthearted tone:

"Of course, Peter and I will take care of you and Paul, whenever you need us."

"No, Claire, you know what I mean—I don't have to spell it out, do I?"

Claire could hardly contain her tears. Paul came back into the bedroom with Dr. Nussbaum, and Claire said:

"So long, I'll see you tomorrow." Melinda smiled.

When Peter came home that evening, Claire told him about her visit with Melinda, and what she had said. Peter only said:

"I know, she asked me also."

Claire visited Melinda the next morning with the intent of helping her with her makeup, just a little lip and cheek color would do, and Melinda was too jittery to apply it herself. She did not feel as well as the day before, and said barely more than "Thank you" to everyone. Claire promised to come again the next morning before Melinda's brother was expected, but by that time Melinda was not interested in makeup—she was medicated to lessen her pain, and had lost much of her awareness. She smiled faintly at her brother, and drew her last breath the same evening.

Even though all her family and friends had been prepared, the reality of her death was a heartbreaking blow, not only to Paul but to all who had been close to her. Death seems to be appropriate for an old person, but if a beautiful woman in the prime of her life is stricken down by such an unmerciful illness it causes distress beyond the normal grieving.

Paul and Melinda's brother Victor had the blessing of some distraction in having to take care of the necessary formalities, such as burial arrangements, etc. Melinda had wished to be cremated, and her family in Vienna expressed the desire to have the urn interred with a memorial service. Paul had no objections. His brother-in-law made all the arrangements. Paul was only capable of just giving his approval to all his suggestions, being overcome with grief. The local mourners expressed their condolences, Peter and the bishop urging Paul to avail himself of their offer of assistance in any way. Paul thanked them all.

The memorial services were scheduled for a week later, and the Burghoffs, Eva included, as well as the bishop, drove to Vienna for that occasion. Tony and Christopher also attended. They had all met Melinda's niece Annemarie and nephew Alex at New Year's, and now the rest of her large family, father, uncles, aunts etc. Most of them were members of the upscale musical and theatrical establishment connected with the Opera and the Burgtheater. Melinda's brother, the father of Annemarie and Alex, was a prominent lawyer. Not all attendants were upper class, many of the servants who had known Melinda throughout her life came to pay their respect as well as former schoolmates, teachers, and acquaintances.

The services were held at the Ruprechtskirche, Vienna's oldest church, which Melinda had always been so fond of. It has a Romanesque nave and bell tower, gothic aisle and choir, and stained-glass windows dating back to the fourteenth century. The urn burial took place at the Central Cemetery, Austria's largest with five hundred thousand graves, where the famous (the musicians buried there include Strauss, Schubert, Brahms, Beethoven, and others) and the wealthy, as well as the poor, find their final resting place. The Viennese love lavish funerals, and many spend their life's savings for that last honor. Funerary monuments come in all styles, from the grand to the bombastic. Melinda's urn was buried in the family vault of the Moell's, where her mother also lay. Victor told Paul that the family had agreed that he could choose to be buried there also. Paul felt a little offended—since he had his own family, the living as well as the dead, in Carynthia—but true to his gentle nature, he just nodded without making any comment. He had always respected Melinda's family, but was not inclined to accept the sometimes patronizing ways they showed, probably unintentionally, but nevertheless resented by Paul. This was not the time to deal with it.

Paul was going to stay a while in Vienna on business. Peter, Claire, Eva, and the bishop returned to Salzburg on the same day, after a short visit with Tony and Chris. Peter was especially anxious to return to his duties at the hospital, where there were patients and doctors waiting to consult with him. It would take his mind off the tragedy of these last few weeks that had affected him and Claire. He had to deal with the seriousness of life and death often enough, but even in his profession one could not get used to it. Eva was also eager to return to where she felt that she was needed and useful.

Claire and Peter also went ahead with their holiday plans, since Paul had insisted that business would keep him occupied and away from home for the next few weeks. He had long postponed an invitation from a London publishing house and now felt himself to be ready more then ever, to keep his mind on a different keel.

Chapter 27

Peter had decided that they would travel by car with no fixed itinerary. A travel guide and map would suffice to lead them on their way. However, the unplanned route had to include visits to Milan's La Scala, Florence, Rome, and a week on a Greek island. With her new clothes still packed as they had come from the seamstress in Vienna, Claire added just a few necessities for comfortable travel, a simple skirt, a couple of blouses, and a sweater. Peter believed in traveling light. Claire suspected that his conventional suits would not be comfortable in the warmer climate, yet to avoid his protesting against new clothes, she let him believe he was well covered as far as his wardrobe was concerned. And for a while it was indeed just right.

They stopped in Tyrol with Uncle Greiner's family, because it had been Hanna's wish that they see them. It was a very pleasant visit, but Peter noted wistfully that Uncle Karl was no longer as tall and strong as he remembered him and he thought of his own parents, who were also getting on despite that they somehow seemed to him to be ageless. Children, no matter what their ages, don't see the decline in their elders—or avoid seeing it, because such reality would cause discomfort. He vowed that upon their return from vacation he would have a heart-to-heart talk with them about their future. Both his parents were in good health but most likely overburdened by the demands of everyday living.

They also visited BurglMayer-Steinbrenner, who had invited them every time she came to visit her parents in Kammerbach and stopped by to see the Burghoffs. She was part of Claire's memory of the days at the beach, and had also been an elementary school classmate of Peter's. Burgl and her husband owned a first class tourist hotel at a popular ski resort just south of Innsbruck, where even at this late season some hardy skiers still ventured on the icy slopes.

Burgl was overjoyed to see her friends from Waldegg and showed them around proudly. Beside the main house; her holdings consisted of several additional tourist lodges, all built in the regional style of architecture and very handsomely furnished. Burgl's husband had died a couple of years ago in a climbing accident, but her son Eric, two years older than Eva, very serious and capable, was following in his father's footsteps and was a great help to Burgl in running the extensive hotel business.

Burgl's daughter Inge came around to greet her mother's guests, who were charmed by the lovely eighteen-year-old girl, and her open and engaging manners. Claire asked why she had not seen her at Kammerbach, did she not visit her grandparents?

"Oh, yes, I am there every summer during my vacations from school, since my mother is so busy here. For some reason she does not want me to get mixed up in the hotel business," said Inge laughing, "but my grandmother keeps me close to the farm. She thinks I could profit from learning to do farm chores, although I always tell her, that I don't intend to become a farmer."

"What do you want to become?" Claire inquired

"If I only knew—most likely I will study at the Art Institute in Innsbruck in the fall, and hopefully find out if I have a little talent in that field."

Burgl said that Inge was very good at all kind of handicrafts. She pointed out some ceramic plates mounted on the walls in the foyer which Claire praised as very accomplished art work. Inge blushed over the compliment but said she had a lot to learn, she was just a beginner.

When Peter and Claire were leaving, Claire made a strong plea to Inge to visit them at Waldegg in the coming summer. She said their sons would also be coming home, and the young people could join up for beach parties on Kammersee.

"Do you remember those days, Burgl?"

Burgl nodded smiling, but Inge said she rarely went to the beach, as it was too boring. When Grandmother gave her time off, she ventured to the city of Salzburg and the museums there, which she just loved.

"Even better," Claire said, "you can visit us at our home in the city." Inge promised cheerfully. She liked Claire instantly and admired the handsome Dr. Burghoff, who had just stood aside, smiling.

When they continued down the road in the car, Claire again mentioned, what a lovely girl Inge seemed to be, so that Peter said:

"Claire, are you thinking what I think you are thinking?"

"Of course not, Peter. By the way, what did you think that I was thinking of?" They both laughed, neither one saying anything, but Claire was thinking…!

From Innsbruck they took the road over the Brenner Pass, enjoying magnificent mountain scenery on the way, staying at roadside inns before descending into the lower lands of the Italian countryside. They were enchanted by the lake region of Lugano, where spring had progressed further than in their alpine homeland. Here, trees and shrubs scented the mild air with an intoxicating fragrance. They stopped at romantic places, took a boat ride on Lago Maggiore, visited gardens along the road, and at last headed towards Milan.

A sightseeing tour of the city itself was not on their itinerary, but an evening out at the opera at La Scala was a must. Puccini's *Tosca* one night, and Mozart's *Figaro* the next, made Peter admit that the worldwide fame of that musical establishment was justifiably compared to Vienna's. He could not make himself admit that it was better, but he praised both productions here as the finest he had ever attended.

Florence was just as the travel guides described it: an art connoisseur's dream. They visited all the sights, such as the Duomo, the magnificent gothic church of Santa Croce with the tombs of Michelangelo, of Galileo, and many other important historical figures, the Pallazzo Vecchio, and, of course, the Uffizi with its extensive art collection. They walked across the Ponte Vecchio with its famous shops. Peter saw an exquisite gold pendant at one of the jeweler's shops, a copy of an antique original, and while Claire was browsing at a leather goods store, he purchased it to surprise Claire at a later occasion.

Nearly overwhelmed by so much sightseeing, they now decided to take a more leisurely drive through Tuscany, rich not only in culture but also landscape, with medieval castles and churches throughout. They passed through Pisa, Siena, and finally continued along the coast towards Rome. Wherever it seemed most pleasing, they stayed a few days. Rome was their last visit to a city. After seeing all the important sights there, St. Peter's, of course, and the Vatican museum, the Tivoli Gardens, and more, they garaged the car and boarded a ship to take them to the Greek island of Kathere. This last part of their holiday was to be devoted strictly to relaxation, to digesting the impressions of the past weeks while they were immersed in a culture with reminders of antiquity as well as of the Renaissance, which had rekindled in both of them memories of their school days and the lessons in the history and languages of those times.

It occurred to Claire that, while very much impressed with what they had seen, they had forgotten their own museums in Vienna.

"Peter, did you often go to the museums during your student days in Vienna?"

Peter said:

"Not too often, I must confess, but I went occasionally. I also went to some of the galleries, like the Albertina where so many of Dürer's artwork can be found. My excuse? I was concentrating more on music, and whenever I could afford the time, my destination was the Opera or the Musikverein."

"We are rightly enthusiastic about what we have seen here, but can you remember which paintings by Rubens, Rembrandt, Tintoretto, etc., we have at Vienna's Kunsthistorisches Museum?"

"No, but I remember many paintings by Peter Bruegel, which I liked especially, and other Flemish masters, as well as Dutch, Italian, German, (Lucas Cranach, e.g.), but you are right to remind us to also pay more attention to our local art treasures."

"Does that mean we are going to take more vacations from now on than in the past?" Claire asked.

"Well, maybe we can squeeze in a few days here and there, but don't count on as much as we are having here. Maybe after I retire?"

"Retire? I can't believe what I am hearing; are you thinking about that already?"

"In a way. I can see that Father is getting too old to carry on alone, and Tony is not yet ready to take over. My contribution to Father's work is very limited, as you know, since the hospital needs my full attention. In about four years from now, when I am sixty years old, I will have given the hospital fifteen years of service; I think it will be the right time for them to look for a successor. There are a good many fine doctors around who would qualify to take over my position."

"I am surprised, Peter, that you could give up your medical practice so easily, when it was paramount in your life since the time you became a doctor."

"There are two things I have to correct here: I am not giving up my medical profession, but I am going to limit it to consulting, so I can give time to Waldegg, the other: you were always 'paramount' in my life."

"Really?" teased Claire, "I remember when in May of the year 1937, that a certain young doctor made it quite clear to me that establishing his medical practice was 'paramount' over all his other plans. If he even had any other plans, he did not tell me so."

These were some of the discussions they now had. It was a great luxury to have the time for it and they both conceded that it was probably the first time in their life together that they had experienced the leisure to be alone with each other, with no interruption by duties to family or to work. Even Peter, known to be not much of a conversationalist, could talk at length on various subjects. They talked about their past and their future, and about the children, of course, always their principal interest.

Elizabeth's attempt to put up a wall between herself and her parents, was still hurtful, but not as intense as a year ago, when they had been looking desperately for an answer to that conflict. They had resigned themselves to accept Elizabeth's doubts until, hopefully, she would find her own resolution. It was Eva who now most required their loving understanding. She seemed to be reconciled to Kurt's death, finding either consolation, distraction, or direction in her nursing career. It was hard to tell if she just appeared so, or if she had found some inner peace, because it was not Eva's way to show emotions openly.

The "boys"—Peter and Claire always smiled, talking or even thinking of them. Pure joy! A little worry here and there in the parental fashion, but mostly great pride and confidence. They had been rascals at times during their adolescence, but despite some scratches and bruises, physical as well as emotional, they remained hale and hearty. Peter especially expressed great hope for their futures, Tony as the "Squire of Waldegg," Christopher practicing medicine in his father's footsteps, hopefully in their home region of the Pongau. That was all Claire could wish for herself, but her thoughts went further, hoping the boys would find the right mates to fulfill their lives with the love and devotion that their parents felt for each other.

They talked also about their own parents, and Claire was still in wonderment that her mother could have found the happiness of her youth at her advanced age. She was now nearing her mid seventies and still acting like a blushing bride. She asked Peter if that was not a little out of place—medically speaking—Peter laughed:

"Medically speaking—and emotionally also—there is no age limit for feeling love and passion if health is also present. I sincerely hope that the two of us will go on to be the same forever."

The days on the sunny shore of that Greek Island were an experience all on its own. Climate, scenery, people—a world away from their alpine homeland. Sometimes they felt as if they were just dreaming. When they arrived by boat with no reservations for accommodations, they were a little concerned and sorry not to have planned ahead, but the man at the tourist office sounded so confident that they started to trust him. They really had no other choice. Language was a great barrier for positive communication at first, because the man was only helpful in English and a little in French, but not in German. Claire remembered a little English from school, but Peter was completely lost. However, the fellow, whose profession was tourism, was not at all disturbed. With gestures and broken English, and his evaluation of the customers' status, he promised just the right accommodations: a villa right on the sea, with a great view, and lots of privacy. Since these customers never asked the price, he had no problems. He led them around the village on foot, with the help of a young boy to carry the luggage, they went up steep streets, around tight corners where the houses were situated so close to each other, that you almost had to squeeze through between them. Peter was already worried. A few steps down again, and there they were: A house, gleaming white, as all the others, but standing alone on top of a rocky ledge. The entry was not noteworthy, but upon entering the marble foyer, the view of the deep blue sea captivated the visitors. At that point Peter and Claire hardly cared about the rest of the accommodations, but they turned out to be satisfactory too. No great luxury but clean, a good bathroom next to the bedroom which opened onto a large balcony with the best view of the sea. They were enchanted. The proprietor, an elderly lady, seemed too distinguished to be asked for service, but a servant turned up soon enough, and it was conveyed that they would get breakfast every morning, but would then be on their own. They would find a restaurant not far away. If they needed anything, they should ask for it. Claire laughed. They should have brought a Greek-German dictionary with them. Although Peter had had years of classic Greek language instruction at school, the modern Greek language was lost on him. In Italian it was easier to find similarities to Latin, and both he and Claire had managed pretty well in Italy, not speaking but understanding and, above all, reading. All that made no difference. The language was not as important than it had seemed at the outset. The people they met in the house and in the streets and the restaurants were friendly and helpful, not that Peter and Claire needed much attention. They absorbed the new impressions with great pleasure. They loved their veranda, where they breakfasted every morning and also spent the evening hours in their lounge chairs, watching the stars above and inhaling the fragrant scents rising from the garden below. They took walks along the shore, swam when tempted by the coolness of the sea, and marveled at the clear water, where you could see down to the bottom.

Greek food was…different. All the fish dishes were excellently prepared, only so many olives, so much olive oil and the strong cheeses made from sheep's milk, and especially the heavy wines, caused stomach upsets sometimes. However, they learned to avoid these and to enjoy the rest.

After swimming one morning, and after too large a lunch at the restaurant, they took a siesta in the shade on the balcony. The sun was extremely hot at that time of day, and resting felt luxurious. Peter fell asleep, Claire mostly only dozed and became restless after a while; she decided to walk down the beach front to where they sold fresh fruit at a kiosk.

Peter had a dream similar to the dreams he had so often. They always dealt with losing sight of Claire. This time, as sometimes before, he saw her swimming out into the sea; she was going further and further out, and he could only see her head occasionally bobbing out of the water. He tried to follow her but could never reach her. He finally woke, looking for his wife and feeling distressed over not finding her right next to him. He stood up and stretched; where could she be? He looked over the railing of the balcony; there were people at the shore. He could not see any swimmers. She would not have gone for a swim without him? That nagging fear of losing her in his dream lingered. Then, further down the road he noticed a figure walking towards the house: Claire! There could be a hundred women walking beside her, and he would still recognize her without even seeing her face. The way she moved and walked with long measured strides, her head held high, gave her an appearance of elegance—a woman who knew where she was going both physically and emotionally—no meandering or wobbling even on that uneven walkway at the beach. Peter's heart swelled with pride and relief. He compared her with the marble figures of the Greek goddesses one encountered everywhere here. Fortunately not as cold and lifeless, he smiled to himself. Still in the grip of his recent dream of fear of losing her, he continued the thought that he also often harbored: why had that lovely creature chosen him—the simple country boy? What lucky fate had caught them together after all the seemingly unbridgeable obstacles?

By that time, Claire had returned, carrying a basket with fruit, cheese, and bread. With the bottle of wine cooling in the landlady's cellar, they would have a delicious supper:

"Don't you think so?" she asked Peter, who took her in his arms, saying only:

"Don't ever leave me, Claire." She laughed, teasingly,

"Why would I ever want to leave the best husband and lover I could find anywhere?"

That night Peter gave her the precious gold pendant which he had secretly purchased in Florence. It looked marvelous around Claire's slender, sun-tanned neck, and she vowed never to take it off, even though she had previously avoided showy jewelry.

Just two more days, and then it was back to their life of work and duty. As much as they had enjoyed those wonderful days, not only for the travel experience, but more so for their time together, they also longed for their home, the family, the routine of life. They had many obligations: Eva, Paul, the boys coming home for their summer vacation should be great. During the long drive back from Rome by a different route, they stayed only one more night on Italian soil, then entered Austria, passing the border town of Traviso.

Chapter 28

The air here seemed to be different and so did the smells and sounds, although it may have been only the change of scenery that made it feel that way. However, the architecture of the homes was so obviously different and noticeable, even after only a few miles inside Austria. The smallest house was kept meticulously neat here in contrast to the *dolce far niente* style of its southern neighbors. With all the appreciation of the cultural experiences and the luxurious and delightful vegetation in those southern lands, Peter and Claire talked about how good it felt to "come home," to their homeland. Once an empire and the cultural center of the European continent, plunged into two world wars, some said due to its own malfeasance, and paying the price for its mistaken beliefs with the lives of millions of its citizenry. It was now a shadow of its former stature. It may have lost in size, but it had not lost its distinction of having been the main contributor to the arts and sciences during its two-thousand-year history. Claire was reciting in that vein with some emotion, when Peter interrupted:

"Now, Claire, are you remembering your social studies class, or are these your own patriotic feelings?"

"Probably a little of both—I know I have often been quite critical of our country since the war and its aftermath, but today I feel generous. Don't you also think we can be proud of much of its accomplishments and of our heritage?"

"Of course, I too feel patriotic at times, but I am leery of exaggerations that often lead to chauvinism, which we can observe not only here but in so many places around the world."

Returning from a foreign country, it was logical to succumb to the temptation to compare. It felt good to have the leisure to have conversations like that before everyday life would dictate less philosophical exchanges. In

Greece and Italy it had been summer already, but here in the alpine region the lilacs were still in full bloom. So were the luscious meadows, where the haymakers had begun the harvest only in the lower valleys. At higher elevations the thick green grasslands, painted with yellow, blue, and red flowery accents, were a delight to the eyes of the passerby, as well as nutritious and delectable to the grazing herds of cattle.

They arrived at their home in Salzburg late at night, hoping to find Eva there, but a note on the kitchen table told them that she was spending the night in St. Johann. The air in the house was stale and Claire opened the windows to let the cool night breeze fill the rooms. The scents from the pines and other evergreens in the garden were boldly refreshing, and Claire felt like filling her lungs with the clean, healthful air. It was good to be home!

Peter had poured himself a cool glass of beer, a brand from the brewery across town, and looked through the last edition of the newspaper to catch up the happenings which they had avoided hearing about during their vacation.

"Peter, for some reason I feel so thankful—not for anything specific, but in general. For our life, for you, for our safe return—I could go on. I think I would like to go to church tomorrow. It is Sunday you know, are you coming with me?"

"Well, could we not sleep in instead? Work will start early on Monday morning, I have to remind you." Claire did not answer, and Peter continued reading the newspaper.

"I see there will be a performance of a Mozart mass at the Dome, and the bishop will give the sermon on the occasion of the beginning of the confirmation season. We should probably go after all," Peter said.

A musical performance at the Dome, with his friend officiating, could get Peter to church more easily than appealing to his religious obligations, thought Claire. Peter had his own standards, and they were impeccable, but did not always conform.

It was a lovely Sunday. The singers at the Dome were excellent. The music well performed and Peter was also elated by the bishop's sermon on the theme of the meaning of the "Holy Trinity" delivered in his usual style: intelligent, sensible, crisp, elegant, and short. Peter loved it. He remembered the often tedious, long-winded, thundering sermons he had had to attend during his school years. Claire also liked Franz Hinterberger's sermons, which were always uplifting and this Sunday was no exception. To have him as a friend, was another reason to give thanks today. God had filled her life with many blessings. The afternoon was spent at Waldegg, where Peter's parents were expecting them.

After reporting on their travel experiences they brought out the gifts they had brought back: a Rosary, blessed and handed to Claire by the Pope in person for Hanna, and several bottles of Chianti for Anton.

Peter's father was apparently anxious for a conversation concerning the farm. It was that time of year when farm work seemed to be piling up, and every hand was needed. It was more and more difficult to recruit experienced farm workers. The old ones were wearing out, and the young people were drawn to city jobs. Anton was aware that machinery would have to replace more and more what men used to do, but he felt himself to be getting too old to deal with all those necessary changes. Peter knew that he was not of much help either and suggested that they might have to replace Laszlo with a younger manager, who would be better versed in the modern technology which was replacing the old ways of running the agricultural business.

"How could we propose that Laszlo retire without offending him?" Anton said that would not be a problem. Laszlo had mentioned many times lately that he would like to return to his homeland if it were not for his obligation to Anton, who had been so good to him when he was a refugee in need. Peter and Anton decided to look into neighboring farming communities first to find a suitable replacement for Laszlo.

Hanna also complained, which was very unusual for the always strong and independent woman, who had performed all the household duties at Waldegg with exemplary finesse, beside overseeing her own holdings, which included the sawmill. She would still command the household affairs, but much of the paperwork and bookkeeping would have to be turned over to someone else. When Claire volunteered to help out, Hanna was more than pleased. Of course, she had hoped that Claire would do so, but now it was all set. They agreed to keep the young secretary who had already done the correspondence for Hanna and Anton, but Claire would be in charge now and would oversee her.

Claire was also happy about the arrangement. She had been thinking for a while as to how to fill the spare time that her own shrinking household now offered. With the children away, a husband fully occupied with his profession and a housekeeper still in attendance—on which Peter had insisted—she had plenty of free time on her hands. She would spend two mornings a week at Waldegg and was looking forward to it. She had never told Peter before, but her secret desire had always been to live on the farm. She had not expressed her feelings in that regard for his sake; she had not wanted to influence him, knowing how devoted he was to the medical profession. When he had mentioned recently that partial retirement in a few years and moving to Waldegg was in his mind also, she truly rejoiced. That was where they both belonged, Claire thought, with a guilty feeling at the same time, however. It was where Peter belonged, and she with him, of course; but would she be able to fulfill her duties as a "farmer's wife" with her city upbringing and her knowledge of farm work only from observing others doing it?

When she told Peter about her concerns, he only laughed:

"I don't see you as a farmer either, but for your sake I will make an exception in my acceptance of the title of the 'Lord of Waldegg,' and pronounce that you are very well suited to preside over our estate as 'her Ladyship of Waldegg.'" She was happy with his assurances, and looked forward to their future.

Eva also returned to Salzburg in the evening to welcome her parents back from their sojourn. She was in good spirits, saying that a stay at her cottage in St. Johann was always uplifting. She had started to plant a little garden there, where Claire had once had one when their family was young. It had been neglected for a while when she moved away, and Dr. Hoerbiger, a bachelor, had not paid much attention to it either. Now, Eva reported, he even came by to offer help with digging in the ground, which she had happily accepted. Dr. Hoerbiger was busy too, his practice was doing very well. The windows of his study looked out over the garden though, and he had said he appreciated the improved appearance, and that it was good to see lights in the windows of the cottage at night; it made him feel less isolated. Eva reported all this just to show that she had been busy as she said. She had missed her parents but had not been lonely.

Claire listened with heightened attention. She planned to go with Eva when she had a free day to go there. Maybe Eva could use her help? Eva said she would like to spend as much time there as she could, since it was also a good place to study in peace and quiet. Peter said only:

"Better than here at home?"

"Well, St. Johann is my home; I grew up there, and I love the cottage. You do understand, don't you?"

Peter just grunted approval, as he was busy with his mail, but Claire said warmly:

"Of course, we understand that, especially now in the summer. I miss my old garden also. Maybe in the winter when there is heavy snow, you will prefer not to commute as much and we'll see more of you here in the city?"

"Perhaps," Eva said.

At night, when they were alone, Claire asked Peter what he thought of Dr. Hoerbiger. "He seems to be a decent fellow, a good doctor, I hear, but I don't know him that well. He approached me some time ago, and wanted to know what we plan to do with the house in St. Johann. The location was very good there for his practice, but he was looking into the future. He would like to get an option to buy it if we ever wanted to sell. I told him that we had no such plans at this time."

"We would not want to sell the place as long as Eva is happy in the cottage which is part of the property. Don't you think so?"

"I always had it in mind to keep the place for Chris if he should decide to settle down here also."

"That could take a few years, don't you think?"

225

"Indeed—probably five or six years until he is finished at the University and a couple more for hospital practice—yes, it would be quite a while."

"And if Eva should leave?"

"Well, let's wait and see what happens in the future. We are not going to make a decision regarding the house presently, right? Especially since the rent we collect from Dr. Hoerbiger is providing welcome funds to supplement our other family expenses." Claire was concerned:

"Do we have financial problems? I am sure we could economize in a number of ways, such as to let Frau Petersky go, I am sure I could handle our household by myself."

"No," Peter smiled, "but I told you that keeping up Waldegg is not much of an income-producing undertaking these days. Labor expenses are up, together with taxes. Income from cattle sales is down, production of dairy products is regulated by the government to avoid overproduction; the same applies to our grain harvest. Interestingly enough, father's tree farm and his other horticultural experiments, which we once considered just a fancy hobby of his, are very promising. He is providing ornamental trees and shrubs to every new building project, public and private, in and around Salzburg, and has earned a good reputation in that field."

"I shall have to learn a lot, once we are living there, I know so little," said Claire. "I want also to see how the people working on the museum project are doing. I thought we would have the official opening this summer."

Claire did not have to worry about too much leisure time once the boys came home from the university, although they stayed only a few days at the Salzburg house and then moved to the farm. Grandfather Anton had urged them to come since he could use all available help, and they were really looking forward to some open-air activity after the long school year when they had been cooped up in the big city. Tony was especially eager to start with the farm work again; Chris was not as eager, but willing enough. They had helped every summer since they were old enough, sometimes even exaggerating their contributions in their memory. Peter was happy to see his strong sons using their muscles for the good of the farm instead of idle loafing. Claire was less enthusiastic and always reminded them also to relax and maybe go down to the beach?

"Don't you remember, Peter?"

"Yes, I know, but then we had plenty of workers in the fields. I was more of a nuisance to them at home and mother thought I should not injure my hands for my future profession as a surgeon."

"And how about Chris?"

"Chris will take care of himself, don't worry about him, Claire. He already declared that surgery would not be his field."

"Don't doctors need healthy limbs for other faculties also?"

Claire did not want to give up, but it did not matter, since Chris had made his own choices already. He mostly helped his grandfather in his horticultural endeavors, digging, pruning, and planting, he liked that.

In August, Burgl Mayer-Steinbrenner came with her daughter Inge to stay at her parent's farm for several weeks. Claire was pleased to see them, and Burgl came to Salzburg frequently to meet her. They went shopping, usually ending up with coffee at one of the charming *konditoreis* and a nice chat. It occurred to Claire that she really did not have many female friends, at least not close friends, like Heidi who lived too far away. She had had a great affection for Melinda, and the two had shared a close friendship which had sadly ended only too soon. She did get along very well with Gerda Engebrecht, but had little in common with her other than their grandchild Hannerl. Gerda was a good person, but her interests were limited, and after the few occasions when they exchanged family news, there was not much else to talk about.

Burgl was a little more sophisticated, had a good education and great business experience. Claire felt comfortable in her company, although admitting to herself that none of these women were like Heidi. She knew a number of ladies in the community, wives of doctors from the hospital whom she had met at various social functions, even having had them in her own home at times, but neither she nor Peter were inclined for much socializing; therefore her acquaintance with most of the ladies remained just that. She concluded that she really did not miss such female friendship very much either. Her family had provided all the human companionship she ever craved. Paul Thoene and Franz Hinterberger, whose friendships she truly cherished, were a much treasured addition.

Before the mothers, Claire and Burgl, could arrange a "casual" meeting between Inge and the boys, knowing that the three would not be very open to any suggestions, the situation came about naturally when the three met at the lake one Sunday afternoon. Despite Inge's declaration that she had better things to do when in Salzburg, the hot August sun demanded some cooling off. The boys had been of the same opinion. Sunday was a day of rest, strictly adhered to in these rural areas, and not much was going on otherwise. They leisurely strolled the short distance down from Waldegg, when they overtook a young girl, wearing country-style overalls, who had come from the side path leading from the Mayer farm. A friendly greeting between them led to a casual conversation. The girl was quite pretty and obviously not shy. Tony asked her where she came from and she said she came from the Mayer farm. In an open and friendly manner she asked where the young men were staying.

"We are spending our summer holidays at Waldegg," said Tony.

The waters of Kammerlake were indeed refreshing, and a number of summer guests crowded the beach. The three of them took advantage of a nice spot to put down their towels. When the girl shed her clumsy overalls, the boys noticed with delight that, like from the cocoon of a caterpillar, a very pretty butterfly emerged. Aware of the boys' looks or not, she immediately went into the water and with great elan and sporty self-confidence she swam quite a distance out into the lake. Tony and Christopher mused: she did not seem to be a simple farm girl after all. Who could she be? It was a long time before they found out. Inge stayed in the water for some time and did not pay any attention to the pair of young men, who were trying to close in in a nonchalant way. She too acted uninterested, although she was not. Finally tired, she swam back to shore. At the boat ramp she ran into a girl she used to know and found it quite convenient to get into conversation with her before returning to her towel. From the corner of her eye she had spotted the young men there already for a while, but pretended not to be eager to join them. She almost overplayed her game, because Chris was ready to go home to watch a soccer game on the television, and Tony, a little hesitant, agreed. Inge finally came over and sat down on her beach towel.

"Did you not love the water?" she started the conversation, and they talked a little of this and that, when all of a sudden, Inge was struck with a suspicious thought:

"Say," she started slowly, "are you two by any chance brothers?"

"Indeed, we are," Chris volunteered.

"And do you have a mother...."

"Yes," Tony interrupted her with a laugh, "we both have."

"Very funny—I know a mother who said she had two very nice sons; her name is Claire Burghoff—but that could not be your mother." Tony acted embarrassed:

"I did not mean to be such a clown, I am sorry," and Chris added

"Yes, our mother is Claire Burghoff, how do you know her?"

"Our mothers are friends from a long time ago, when they played together here on the same beach. She told me about it when she and your father visited us a few months ago at our place in Tyrol. She even invited me to visit her in Salzburg during my vacation here, but my grandparents, the Mayers, keep me so busy, and insist that I become a farmer, that I do not have any time. My mother meets yours often when she goes shopping in Salzburg. What a coincidence that we met here, is it not?"

Inge was so sincere and open and both boys were quite taken by her. They all stayed a while longer, Chris forgetting the important soccer game on the television, and they had a very pleasant time together.

When they mentioned the encounter to their mother, she could not have been more pleased to hear that Inge had impressed them. Now she could invite the girl without appearing to conspire, which was what she had in mind, however. She thought how she would have hated it if her mother had done so, but then Claire defended her plans by believing that she had only Tony's best interests in mind. Inge would be such a good match! Not only was she a lovely person, of good background, solid farm stock, intelligent, pretty, but also the heiress to quite a substantial neighboring farm. Her son seemed already to have a very good first impression. Claire was all excited, but when she confided it to Peter he warned her to stay away from any kind of matchmaking. Nevertheless, in the back of his mind he thought Claire's idea might have some merit.

Yet complications arose. Why had she not foreseen it? It happened that both Tony and Chris found lovely Inge worth their attention, and a competitive spirit arose between them, which had happened before only when both were involved in the same athletic event. Inge seemed to enjoy their attention without choosing a favorite. Peter said only:

"I told you so," and laughed.

The summer went on, with the three young people dreading the day of departure from Kammerbach. They spent much time together. Grandfather Anton was already complaining that the long evenings the boys spent at the Mayer farm made them too sleepy the next morning and not as fit for heavy work. He was not too serious in his grumbling as he remembered having been a young man once himself, he sighed with a smile.

Claire suggested to Hanna that they give all of them a "going back to school" party on the second Sunday in September and to include all the family members, including the Mayers. It could be a garden affair, and she would arrange for everything. She had hinted to Hanna that young Inge was worthy of the Burghoff's courting, and this aroused Hanna's interest enough that she agreed.

Claire took care of all the invitations. Eva had to change her hospital schedule, but was quite eager to come. However, she immediately asked if it would be all right to ask Dr. Hoerbiger to come as well. Claire was taken by surprise. She had known that Eva and Dr. Hoerbiger had developed a friendly relationship, but inviting him to a family affair? She agreed, of course. She had met Dr. Hoerbiger a few times when she helped Eva with her gardening projects. He was a nice young man of rather scholarly appearance, tall and lean, with a reddish-blond shock of unruly hair above horn-rimmed glasses through which warm hazel eyes always seemed to be searching for an answer, pleasant in his demeanor, quiet and reserved. He had always been very polite towards Claire, but had immediately retreated into his house when she found them together in the garden. Eva explained that he was extremely busy, sought out by more patients than he could handle, and was already looking for a partner. She seemed to know a lot about him, but why she would want him to join their family gathering, Claire did not know.

Hanna said to Anton: "We have been neighbors of the Mayers for so many years, and this is the first time they have been invited to Waldegg. I hardly know Helga Mayer, and have seen her mostly at funerals or weddings. She is such a cold person, don't you think? I am not sure I like the idea of having them here, but Claire said that the children have become friends; she also likes Burgl Mayer, so we'll try to be hospitable."

Anton said that he had known Thomas Mayer since their childhood together and had found him to be a good man. Not long ago, at a meeting at city hall, they had a lengthy conversation in which Thomas had brought up his dilemma of getting to be too old to continue with the farm work much longer. Since he had no family members who would take over, he was considering selling the place if he could find the right buyer. He seemed to be depressed over the situation. He had hoped, not having had any son as successor, that his grandson Eric would finally take over but the boy was entrenched in the hotel business in Tyrol and had no interest in farming. Anton told him to let him know if he became serious about selling.

"Why would you want to know?" asked Hanna.

"Well, that farm is a very productive piece of land, I would not like to see it go to strangers, maybe even to a corporation. You know what those people do to our land: they develop it into tourist places."

"Anton, how could you afford to buy such a large piece of property?"

"I was planning to talk to Erwin Selzer, the banker down at the Savings Bank, and see what kind of mortgage would be available. I was also thinking that you might want to sell the sawmill. It's probably worth quite a sum, what do you think about that?"

"Forget it! I have taken care of that mill since we got married, and I have plans for it at my death. It will remain in the family. I am not going to be your banker." Hanna was a little agitated.

"Well, it was just an idea," Anton sighed, "I'll have to talk to Peter about it though."

"By the way," he added, "you also asked me if I thought that Helga Mayer was a cold woman? I don't know her that well, but I know that some people think the same of you. Every strong woman with a mind of her own and a will to defend it, is often called 'hard.' But I know, in your case it is just a shell, underneath which it is all softness and sweetness," and with these words he approached her and tried to embrace her. With a laugh she wiggled out and said:

"Still the old charmer, trying to bewitch me? It won't work, I am too old for your games now."

"Old? You are old? Since you brought it up before, I also remember the time when we were first married. To me you look the same today and I love you as much as I did then. Maybe I have not told you that often enough lately, but I want you to remember it always."

Hanna tried not to show her tearful emotion over his words—after all, she had to keep up her reputation as a "hard woman."

The party was held. The Mayers came; Eva brought Dr. Hoerbiger along, and since the Engebrechts were related to the Mayers also—Fritz was Thomas Mayer's nephew—they were invited as well. Gerda came with her daughter Ingrid, but Fritz could not make it due to a previously scheduled hunting party with some people from Vienna. Peter sighed with relief.

Paul, of course, was present also. Since his return from London the month before, he had been a frequent visitor to Peter and Claire's home. It was not only the pledge they had made to Melinda to look after him, it had become quite natural that he was included in all family affairs. He was indeed a best friend.

Hanna paid special attention to Inge, who was gay and bubbly, and she had a good first impression of her. Tony and Chris were obviously charmed by her and she did not seem to favor one over the other, but enjoyed their company. To Claire's surprise, the reserved Dr. Hoerbiger had a very good sense of humor and entertained the party by telling some very funny stories. He normally gave the impression of not being anything but a serious "medicine man." Now she could understand why Eva seemed to feel so comfortable having him around, and Claire was grateful to him for that.

Gerda had news from Helmut and Elizabeth, whom she had visited a week before in Linz: Helmut had been promoted, and Elizabeth was expecting again. Claire could not help but feel a little twinge in her heart for having to hear about her daughter's condition in a roundabout way. This was now the way it was between them, and Peter had recommended her to accept it without letting it bother her. Of course, he did not exactly adhere to such good advice himself. Elizabeth's estrangement was still painful to him but he did not want Claire to know it.

At parting, everybody talked about a reunion the next year, but Inge invited Tony and Chris to spend Christmas vacation at her family's Steinbrenner Hotel in Neustift, one of the popular skiing areas in the Stubai Valley, south of Innsbruck. She looked to her mother for support and Burgl said emphatically that they would be very welcome there. Claire had already started to regret her attempts to acquaint the young people with each other. She shared her sons' vacation time with Waldegg every summer, because they had done this since the boys were little, and besides, Waldegg was home for all of them anyway. But Christmas was always her own feast, and they normally spent only a couple of days with Peter's parents and the rest at their home, first in St. Johann, and then during the later years in Salzburg. Now a young girl they barely knew wanted to take that away from her. She said, rather coolly:

"I know how terrific the ski slopes in Tyrol are, but they are quite challenging around here too. Maybe you would like to visit us here during your Christmas vacation?"

Inge laughed and said:

"If Mother lets me?" Burgl said nothing, but Tony said he had never skied in Tyrol, and it sounded very tempting.

Claire did not want to remind them of last year's Christmas vacation with its tragic ending on the ski slopes, but she could not help thinking about it. At that time it seemed that her sons' taste for skiing had vanished, but youth can forget so quickly!

Two weeks after Inge's departure, the boys also left for the university in Vienna. Eva was very much occupied with her studies and work at the hospital and spent more and more of her free time in St. Johann. Peter was, of course, fully involved again in the pursuance of his profession, and Claire was feeling lonely. The bookkeeping for Hanna's affairs was not very time-consuming; the people from the historical society had nearly finished with their Waldegg Museum project, and did not need volunteers anymore. Elizabeth was living too far distant, and did not want her mother's involvement anyway.

Paul suggested that Claire should turn to her writing again, and he helped her in discussions of subject matter, and she in turn helped him with decisions regarding the sale of his property at Fuschl. Since Melinda's death he had been there very seldom. It had been a lovely home for them when she was alive and they had entertained many artist friends, from Melinda's musical genre to Paul's writers and poets. When Paul wanted to invite people whom he needed to see on business or socially, he now preferred to do it at a restaurant or club. He had maintained the apartment in the city, where he was comfortable and which was close to the Burghoff's where he felt more at home than anywhere else. Peter and his friend Franz found the addition of Paul into their midst most welcome, and when they spent an occasional evening together at the Burghoff's, Claire was included and her voice listened to. For an outsider it may have looked like a disproportionate male preponderance in that group of friends, but none of them would have thought so. What they had in common was a great respect for each other; in addition, the three men admired Claire, each in his own way. Peter, of course, loved and adored his wife with a great passion, and they all knew that Claire bathed in the recognition of her husband's unquestioned devotion which she returned in equal measure. She would have been surprised, however, to know the innermost feelings of the other friends, whom she also loved—in a different way.

Paul, with the sensitive soul of a poet, had loved Claire from the moment had he met her a long time ago, during the painful days of the last battles in an unfortunate war. She was so alone then and in such need of a friend. He had offered her his heart and his hand, not knowing much about her past, and she would have made him the happiest man if she had accepted. When she could only return his friendship, he did not question that either, but knew that his feeling for her would last a lifetime. He had married the exquisite Melinda, loved her, pampered her, and was grieved by her leaving him. He had yearned to become a father, but her illness, known to him for quite some time, had prevented it. He was grateful for their life together of not too many years. Paul's feelings for Claire had never changed, but she would not know it, nor would anyone else. With an honest heart, a true and honorable gentleman, he could include Peter in his admiration of both, and their friendship became the sustaining element of his life.

Franz Hinterberger never hid his admiration for Claire, and had told his friend Peter at one time that if he had had the fortune to meet Claire—or someone like her, he added to be sure that his friend did not misunderstand—he may have had second thoughts about accepting the church's dictum of celibacy and found another calling. There had been times when he truly envied his friend. Such a confession did not disturb Peter, who accepted it as a compliment, as well as an understanding of his own actions in the past involving Claire. The bishop too was an honorable man and always acted as such, but a man, and despite his vows to the church, he could not prevent himself from having dreams, for which he had to pray for forgiveness afterwards.

Claire would never have been aware of all of this. She had never been a flirt. Seducing a man never came to her mind—well, except that one time when she had thought of testing Stefan's single-mindedness, but it had been merely a weak attempt. As long as she could remember, there was only Peter in her life. He filled it completely, in every way.

Christmas came around faster than anticipated. Everybody was rushing to get ready for that most important holiday of the year. Tony and Chris said they would be home by mid-December, but planned to stop in Linz on their way for a short visit with their sister Elizabeth, whom they had seen so seldom since her marriage. They had been aware that there had been tension between her and their parents, but did not speculate much about it, assuming that it was because she had become pregnant before it was acceptable. Both had thought at the time that she had been foolish to accept family responsibilities at such a young age; they would certainly want to remain bachelors as long as possible. It was bad enough to be dependent on your parents' approval for so many things, but to have to consider a wife's wishes too, was not wanted in the near future. A couple of years ago girls were not uppermost in their minds, their career goals were. Life in Vienna and fraternity parties had not changed too much about that; female companionship was a welcome distraction from studies at times, but not to be taken too seriously.

Elizabeth was happy to see her brothers, and Helmut was a most thoughtful host, eager to show them how well he provided for his family. They all enjoyed the visit, and little Hannerl was admired as was expected, but on their way from Linz to Salzburg the boys reaffirmed their conviction that they would take their time before making commitments of the size their sister and Helmut had.

Claire had great plans for the season. It was to be a wonderful time, especially since last year's Christmas had been such a sad time for the family and not the joyous occasion it is meant to be. She even suggested that Anton and Hanna should spend the holidays with them in Salzburg, instead of the traditional celebrations at Waldegg, thinking that it would spare Hanna the effort of preparing the feast. She was wrong; her suggestion was nearly an affront to Hanna, and she reacted very coolly towards Claire. Peter was also on his mother's side, and she had to admit to herself that she had been rather selfish in trying to overturn "tradition." She continued, however, to make plans for the time between the holidays, when the boys would be at home. She would have some parties. Maybe she should suggest that the young people invite some of their old friends from school for a New Year's Eve party with dancing? Asking Eva's advice, she got only a half-hearted approval, and Peter expressed no opinion at all. *Well*, she said to herself, *they are still too busy to be in a holiday mood, but that will change*, and she continued with her preparations.

The first evening at home with the boys was most joyful. *One really had to stop calling them "the boys,"* Claire said to herself, *they were a couple of very attractive young men*, Tony very outgoing, somewhat boisterous and a little rough at the edges, Christopher more restrained, showing a little more sophistication. Peter observed this and wondered if Chris was putting on a little show, or had he really become more influenced by Viennese culture and society? When he and Claire exchanged views about their grown-up sons, he told her of his observation of Chris, in comparison to Tony who had remained the "country boy."

"A country boy just like you?" Claire teased her husband.

"Yes, a son of the soil, that's me!" Peter said with emphasis.

Claire would have never called him that herself. His soul may have been attached to the land, his country upbringing, his roots, but his demeanor was that of a sophisticate, a nobleman if you will, one of the landed gentry. Peter would have frowned at her descriptions, she knew that, therefore did not mention it to him, but said, that it was very likely that both his sons represented their father's personality, and he mused about her observations.

It had snowed a little already, promising a white Christmas. Not too soon and too much, hoped Claire, otherwise they would certainly run off to the ski slopes again. Her wish was granted; it did not snow enough until a couple of days before Christmas Eve, but then very heavily, so everybody was pleased. Tony and Chris were at home every evening, sometimes bringing an old school friend along, and it was a jolly time, with Claire relishing her sons' presence. Just then a letter came from Tyrol, reminding them that there was good skiing in Neustift, and that they had promised to visit. Claire had forgotten about the girl, Inge, consciously or unconsciously—she did not want to share her sons' time with her. Tony seemed to be genuinely pleased about the renewed invitation and suggested that he would like to accept.

"We could go there right after Christmas Day. What do you think, Chris?"

Before Chris could answer, Claire said firmly that she expected them to be at home on New Year's Eve, as she had planned a party. Tony was agreeable, as was his nature, but he did not give up either.

"All right, then we'll have another week before we have to go back, I'll let them know that we are coming the day after New Year's."

To everybody's surprise, including Tony's, Chris said:

"Count me out, Tony, I don't think I want to go skiing. You go ahead and give Inge my regards." Then, a little hesitantly, he added:

"Mother, I hope you won't be angry, but I have promised to attend another New Year's Eve Party in Vienna."

Before Claire could swallow her disappointment, Tony asked:

"What's this, you did not mention anything to me before?"

"Yes, I know, I did not want to talk about it, because it was only I who was invited and I did not want to hurt your feelings."

"Well, go on, don't keep us in suspense," said Tony

"I told you that I have seen Annemarie Moell a few times during the past months, and she has invited me to a large New Year's Eve bash with the Moell family and their friends. I thought it would be quite nice to meet all Aunt Melinda's family. We met Alexander, Annemarie's brother, at last years New Year's Eve at Uncle Paul's home, you remember?"

With that he addressed himself to Claire also, hoping for her understanding. Claire could not hide her disappointment, not only over Christopher's plans, but also over Tony's. She had been looking forward so much to their presence at home. She realized in one quick and painful moment that her sons were ready to go their own ways, not tied to her apron strings anymore, as Hanna, the wise and experienced mother-in-law, had forewarned her some time ago. She said a little slowly and softly:

"Yes, I think I do understand. You just go ahead with your plans."

Tony immediately wrote his answer to Inge Steinbrenner, that he was looking forward to skiing in Tyrol and to seeing her again. Chris could not make it because of prior plans.

Christopher came into the kitchen later that evening, where Claire was busy with dinner preparations. He had a very soft spot in his heart for his mother, and regretted to have disappointed her; he said that he would return for the balance of his vacation if she wanted him to.

"If you stayed on in Vienna, what would you be doing there alone?" she asked.

"I have a lot of studying to do before the semester ends, I could do it then."

"Tony does not have to study?"

"Ah, Tony—he has different requirements, and is also less ambitious, as you know."

Yes, Claire knew—she became wistfully aware that it was easy to plan for your children when they were little, but now she would have to face the fact that most of the time they would make their own plans. Tony would probably prefer to spend New Years Eve in Tyrol also. Maybe her idea of celebrating at home was not so great after all. It was thoughtless of her not to consider that Paul might not be in the mood either, nor Eva, both remembering the sad time last year. Claire decided to cancel all her plans and let the holidays approach without much fuss. At least Christmas would be spent in the old tradition, and the weather was also cooperating with enough snow to provide the "Winter Wonderland" scenery. At Waldegg, the horse-drawn sleigh would be readied with the soft and warm fur blankets in which they would ride to Midnight Mass at the Kammerbach church. The presents for the family were already wrapped and hidden away and the kitchen was filled with the sweet aroma of the old-time goodies baking. It was going to be a good Christmas, Claire was sure of that.

Chapter 29

Eva was hardly ever at home, only when her workload at the hospital did not give her time to catch the train to St. Johann and she did not want to drive her car when the snow conditions made it hazardous to get back and forth. She was very conscientious and would not put her patients in jeopardy by coming to work late or not at all. A few days before Christmas, Eva called to ask if it would be all right to bring Dr. Hoerbiger along to Waldegg. At first Claire did not know what to say. Their Christmas celebrations were always strictly reserved for the family. What reason did Eva have to bring a stranger home? So she said she would ask Hanna, but assumed it would be all right. Eva said Dr. Hoerbiger had no family of his own, and she would feel bad if he were alone at that special time of year.

"I remember that your father used to be on call even at Christmas time, Is Dr. Hoerbiger off duty?"

"Yes, this year he has a substitute doctor who would take his calls."

"All right, I'll talk to your grandmother and let you know."

First she discussed Eva's phone call with Peter, who thought it would be all right.

"But it is such a family affair."

"Well, Paul is going to be with us too, did you not ask him?"

"That is different. He is family, is he not? Especially since we promised Melinda to take care of him."

Hanna had no objections to Eva bringing her friend, and so Dr. Hoerbiger was invited and he gratefully accepted.

Christmas Eve and the following day went by very pleasantly. All the old customs and traditions were observed, including the dinner with all the usual trimmings on the evening of the twenty-fourth, the musical renditions and

237

the singing of Christmas carols. Dr. Hoerbiger's contribution was a pleasant baritone voice, which made him even more sympathetic to Peter. Everybody went to church at midnight, and stayed up afterwards for the exchange of gifts and drinking of good cheer. The mood was not exuberant, but comfortably cheerful.

The big feast occurred the next day, when the dining table was laden with many delicacies, and some of the farm hands and household help who received their yearly gifts joined in.

In a quiet moment later in the day Eva asked Claire if she could talk to her privately. Claire had been wondering before about Eva's solemn behavior. Was she all right? Was she thinking of the time a year ago, when her dreams were so cruelly turned into ashes? Was she reliving that sad event? Eva smiled when she saw her mother's concerned frown:

"It's nothing bad, Mommy, but I need your advice. Dr. Hoerbiger has offered me a position as the nurse in his office when I am ready!"

"That is nice, would you want that? Your father could probably find something more challenging for you, don't you think so?"

"Of course, I thought of discussing this with him, but William made me another offer as well."

"Yes?"

"He asked me not only to join his practice, but also his life—to marry him!"

"Eva! Is this not too sudden?"

"Not really, Mother. I have known him now for quite a while."

"Yes, yes, but how do you feel about it? What did you say?"

"I said I would think about it—and I have! I will accept!"

"Eva, tell me—do you love him? Does he love you? He is quite a few years older than you, is he not?"

"Mother, you ask too many questions all at once. Yes, he is ten years older, but I like that, he is old enough to know what he wants."

"And he wants you? I repeat: does he love you?"

"Of course, Mother, or he would not want to marry me, would he? Did he tell me that he loved me? Not in so many words—you know how men are usually shy about saying such words." *Do I know*, thought Claire; even her beloved Peter had some inhibitions in that regard. He could show it a hundred times before the words would come to his lips.

Claire was still concerned about Eva. She did not seem joyous enough, did she have reservations? Eva assured her that she was happy, only she was a little cautious this time. She did not want to tempt fate. Claire understood.

"Do you want to talk to your father?"

"Not today—I planned that for New Year's—can I bring William to the house then?" she said, laughing happily. "He is very formal and wants to ask for my hand in the proper manner."

Since Claire's plans for a New Year's party did not seem to work out, she canceled it altogether and asked Hanna's opinion about spending the holiday at Waldegg. Hanna was delighted; in the past few years they had been left alone more often because the younger generation chose to celebrate on their own turf. Anton and Peter also liked the idea. Hanna went ahead preparing the usual dishes for that occasion, which meant special preparations for the pickled herrings, the jellied meats, like pig's head and various other specialties in aspic, as well as smoked meats and fish. Claire could not help thinking that only twenty-some years ago they had suffered from lack of food as a consequence of the war and its aftermath. Now that time seemed to be eons past, at least for the survivors. It should be a happy time now, but there was much concern among the population about the communist threat from the recuperating Russian nation. The division between East and West Germany, and the Berlin blockade were regarded with sympathy as well as with fear for Austria's own future. However, New Year was always a reason to celebrate. The past year had not been a happy one for the Burghoffs with the tragic deaths of Kurt Boehmer and Melinda Thoene, but the hope for the New Year was better.

Claire had told Peter about her conversation with Eva, and he was pleased. It was comforting to know that his daughter would be in good hands. He had not previously given much thought to Dr. Hoerbiger, whom he had just considered as a distant colleague who was renting his building in St. Johann after he had left there. He had heard about him, of course, in talks with other medical acquaintances, and the last few personal contacts when Eva had included him in family gatherings had shown him to be a congenial fellow. Claire had reservations—not about Dr. Hoerbiger, but about Eva. Was she really in love with the man, or had she been so lonely and he so available, that she had just succumbed to the inevitable?

New Year's Eve turned out to be very pleasant, everybody was in a good mood for that special evening. Paul—Uncle Paul—they all called him so, in his usual charming way was the favorite of everyone, even Hanna, who was slow to warm up to "outsiders" as she called all those who were not family. Tony was especially gay, and had an exchange of fun-filled stories with Dr. Hoerbiger, as they tried to outdo each other in witticisms, Anton came up with some of his own rib-ticklers from the past, and even Peter cracked some jokes. The Burghoffs and friends celebrated New Year's Eve in the appropriate manner. After toasting the New Year at midnight, Tony, encouraged by Anton, went down to the village to get reacquainted with other young farm people in their frolics of the day, and Eva expressed a desire to join him. Anton and Hanna, as well as Claire, retired, and Paul had already fallen asleep on the sofa.

That was when Dr. Hoerbiger approached Peter and had the expected exchange with him. William felt it was his duty to let Eva's father know where he stood, his background, his financial status, and his future plans. No father could have been more pleased over the solid proposal of marriage to his daughter. Unusually for him, Peter became, however, somewhat emotional, and wanted to know also of William's feelings for Eva, conveying his own strong convictions about the marriage commitment. He wanted to be sure William knew everything about Eva's past, including her mother's. William said that Eva had told him everything, and that he loved her deeply. He was nearly thirty-five years old and was fully aware of the solemnity of his action. He was also sure that Eva loved him. Peter sighed in relief that this conversation with William had gone so satisfactorily. He told him Eva would have an appropriate dowry. Considering the drinks consumed that evening, Peter and William seemed to be of clear mind and their apparent happiness was genuine and not just a result of consumed spirits. They went outside for a while, stomping through the snow which glistened in the light of the moon. The night was clear and crisp and the stars were shining brightly. The two men had a very good feeling about each other, and about the world in general. It was good to be alive.

It was a late New Year's morning for everybody, only Hanna and Claire were busy in the kitchen to prepare the feast for the day with the help of the old kitchen factotum, Luise. Hanna and Luise were, as usual, in a fracas and Claire found much humor in their verbal exchanges. Hanna was always in control of her servants and handled them with authority, however Luise had a special position. She had been at Waldegg since she was a very young girl, had first been the nursemaid to the children, had tended to them and had served Hanna through thick and thin; Hanna had taught her everything she knew, including how to stand up for herself. Hanna trusted Luise completely, and the girl, a mature woman by now, returned that trust with complete devotion. Never married, she considered the Burghoffs her family. Both Hanna and Luise had grown old together and had shared so much of their lives, that Luise had also adopted an authoritative manner; though she never overplayed her role as the servant, she would argue with her mistress over kitchen and even family matters until Hanna stopped it.

Most of the time Claire found their arguing more comical than serious, and this was so on that first day of the New Year. She had learned to be very careful with Luise, who had strong opinions and was not shy about expressing them. It was important to be accepted by Luise, otherwise her disapproval could be hurtful. Of course, the family took her moods in stride. Peter was used to it since he was a little boy. He had always been her pride and joy, feeling she had raised the boy herself. She was the one who had most strongly disapproved of his marriage to Marlena. She had even disliked the child Eva and was very suspicious of Claire in the beginning. Only when she saw Peter's happiness in his new life, had she grudgingly accepted her.

Today's dispute was over the choice of soup to be served. Veal broth with tiny dumplings or fried biscuits as the garnish? That's what made Claire smile when listening to the two old women. If a stranger who had no knowledge of their special language had heard them, he would have thought a serious fight was under way.

Dinner was served with much fanfare. Despite the eagerness of the guests to dig in, since their appetites had been challenged by the delectable scents emanating from the kitchen, Peter made them wait a little while by announcing the engagement of Eva to Dr. Hoerbiger. It was joyfully received by the family, and toast after toast followed, until Hanna protested that the food was getting cold. This New Year's dinner and merrymaking lasted the whole afternoon, and Claire admitted that that party was even better than the one she had planned originally could have been. Although they missed Chris, it was a happy time.

Tony was up early next morning and eager for his skiing trip to Tyrol. *Or was he excited to see Inge*, Claire wondered, but Tony did not say. The rest of the family returned to their respective jobs, only Claire felt somewhat left out. She must find a vocation. Paul's suggestion to take up writing again looked better every day but it was difficult to get started. She called Paul for help and he had a number of ideas. The important thing, he said, was just to sit down and write about anything that came to mind—it would develop into something she would enjoy doing. He assured her that she had a talent in that direction. She felt a little better, and Christopher's phone call, that he had decided to stay in Vienna for the rest of the vacation, did not upset her too much. When she questioned if he had had a good time at the Moell's party, he answered hesitatingly, that it had been all right. Claire told him of their celebration and Eva's engagement, and that they had had a really wonderful time at Waldegg, and could not help but to have some satisfaction in her voice. Chris noticed; he was sensitive enough. He apologized to his mother for not having been there. However, he was not really sorry. It was true. The New Year's Eve party at the Moells had been a disappointment in some ways. He had had no idea that it would be so formal. He looked out of place, dressed in his dark blue "go everywhere" suit, when all the gentlemen were wearing evening clothes (in tails) and the ladies' dresses were so décolleté as to almost make him blush. Annemarie had been beautiful and charming, and had introduced him to a number of the guests by whom he was supposed to be impressed, either by their titles or their governmental positions or their other accomplishments. Except for Alexander and the girl he was with, there were only elderly people present, and he was as bored as Alexander also seemed to be. Annemarie tried to be gay, but despite the champagne, which was flowing freely, the whole atmosphere felt superficial to Christopher. Annemarie's mother was loud and overbearing, and when meeting Chris, she scrutinized him openly, asking about his background, and commenting:

"So, you are from the provinces, studying in Vienna? Do you like the big city or does it overwhelm you?" Chris answered with "Yes" and "No," until Annemarie dragged him off. She was somewhat embarrassed by her mother's questioning, but she was used to it. Her father, Melinda's brother, remembered meeting Chris before in Salzburg, and was more jovial, but no more sincere. The evening was not what he had expected, but Annemarie made up for it. She was beautiful—just like Melinda. She had indeed a resemblance to her, but more than that she copied her aunt's somewhat exotic look, had her dark hair pulled straight back into a chignon, and wore a gown of oriental silk, just as Melinda would have. Chris was impressed. Before he left, she asked him if he would come to a recital the next weekend, where she would have a major part playing her cello. Of course he would, and that's why he had decided to stay in Vienna for the rest of his vacation. He went to the recital; Annemarie was certainly the star performer, and he felt privileged by her attention. After all, he was only a "country boy." He had inherited his father's modesty.

Tony had a good time in Tyrol also. With many tourists from all parts of the continent, mainly Germans from the northern regions of their country where they lacked the mountains for skiing, but also the Dutch, the English, and the Americans. It was an international crowd of ski enthusiasts.

Inge was an excellent skier, but also much fun off the slopes, perky and cheerful, genuine, unpretentious, and very pretty on top of all that. She looked as fetching in her ski outfit as she had in her bathing suit on the beach last summer, Tony thought. Well, almost, he reminded himself immediately! In other words, he was becoming very taken with her, and she responded in a charming manner, not a tease or a flirt as the girls he had met at fraternity parties had been. How tragic that the vacation days were so few. Both looked forward to the summer in Salzburg. Like his grandfather and namesake, Tony knew instinctively that he had found the girl he wanted to marry, and—like his grandfather—he did not think that she would refuse, even though she had repeated again in conversation, that she would not want to be a farmer. Tony was a practical thinker: she had said nothing about not wanting to be a farmer's wife, he thought. Besides, he was no ordinary farmer or cowherd, he would become the "Squire of Waldegg." Tony had no inhibitions, he was proud of his background, his family, and of himself. Well, the latter needed improvement—he was not as studious as he should have been, but he promised himself to make up for it in the coming months. It would be such a long time until summer, but Inge sent him off with a really warm goodbye kiss, and that had to last.

The two young Burghoffs now changed roles at their students' quarters at Mrs. Jandasek's in Vienna. The formerly "Take it easy" Tony became serious about learning and attending all his lectures, as well as seeking advice from experts in his field of agriculture. Peter would have been proud of him, had he known. Christopher, on the other hand, was sidetracked by an enchanting young lady who was not only a fine and talented musician, but who also knew the arts of beguiling, bewitching, and captivating a young men's heart, though never giving away her true feelings. Christopher fell for it with the naïve innocence of first love. His studies suffered, but his social life was enhanced, and he was traveling in a world foreign to him up to now. Paul Thoene could have advised him, but Paul had no idea, and neither had Peter. Tony was concerned, but did not think it was up to him to take Chris to task.

In the meantime, back home things were progressing as expected. Elizabeth gave birth to a healthy boy at Easter. Claire drove with Gerda to visit, and it was a joyful and pleasant occasion. The child was named Siegfried, and big baby sister Hannerl accepted the newcomer as if he were just another doll, only a little more lively. She was an adorable, very pretty child, and reminded Claire so much of Elizabeth. She remembered how loving her Elizabeth had been and her coolness now hurt even more. She did not let on, and she was grateful for Gerda's presence, who was always so tactful and understanding. Gerda was prouder of her son than of the babies, whom she admired but did not gush over as most grandmothers are inclined to do. Helmut had succeeded in his life and his job, despite his father's disapproval of him as a young boy, and he showed himself to be a loving and attentive husband and father. Gerda observed this with great satisfaction because Helmut's father had been no example for the boy in that respect.

Elizabeth did also a fine job as a wife and mother, and so the grandmothers could leave for home with a good feeling. Elizabeth promised a visit on the occasion of Eva's wedding in July, about which she was very happy. The sisters had been so close at one time, and Elizabeth seemed to miss her.

Eva was planning for the wedding. Her lovely gown which had been intended for her wedding to Kurt, was still in the box. At first it seemed only practical to use it, but when Eva lifted it out of the box, her heart felt pangs of pain and memories. She put it back quickly, and asked Claire if she would mind if she did not use that dress.

"Of course, darling, you need to find another one," was all Claire said. She understood. Eva played with the idea of wearing something like Elizabeth had at her wedding, but Claire talked her out of that. There had been a reason for Elizabeth's wedding costume: they had had a traditional country-style wedding. Eva's would be in town. William was not from the country either, he was city bred. It would be inappropriate for him to wear the Salzburger or Pongauer traditional costume.

The wedding was going to be small and private, but when considering everyone who would be offended if not being invited, it grew larger and larger.

July was the chosen time, when Tony and Chris would have returned home. Willy had no relatives that needed to be invited, except for an old aunt living in the city of Steyr. He called her on the phone, as he did ever so often since she had always shown an interest in him and had sent him little packages on occasion during his student days. She said to her regret she would not be able to undertake the journey because of old age and ill health. William's parents had died when he was quite young and he had gone through schools and studies on stipends from a church organization. He wanted to invite the rector from his upper school who had been very generous to him all his life. Since he had become a popular doctor in the small town of St. Johann, friendships had developed which also must be honored with an invitation. The same applied to Eva's friends from her earlier school days and the new ones from the hospital, and also the family friends from Kammerbach. It became a social event in St. Johann after all, and the local newspaper reporter, though not personally invited, took part by taking pictures not only of the couple, but everybody noteworthy around, like Bishop Hinterberger.

It was a warm and sunny day, but it had cooled off enough in the late afternoon so as to leave all the guests comfortable. The birds—a couple of blackbirds especially—already sang their evening recital from the old linden trees in the churchyard, accompanying the guests walking towards the old gothic church. Inside the church a quartet of local musicians provided the country touch with guitar and zither recitations.

With all the Burghoffs present, there were four generations sitting in the first row, from Anton's white head down to Hannerl's pale blond locks. Eva looked as lovely as a bride should. This dress was very different from the one at home in the box. It was of fine, white, cool linen, embroidered around the neckline, with a long veil with pearl accents, simple, yet very becoming to the dark-haired young woman. The newspaper account said of the wedding that the bride had been exceedingly beautiful. She was indeed. When Eva and Elizabeth were small, their contrasting looks had always been remarked upon by others, and most of the time the blond curly-haired one got more praise for being lovely. Elizabeth was still judged as such, but today, everyone commented how lovely Eva was.

Dinner for all invited guests was at the biggest hotel in town. The revelry and dancing lasted till the early morning hours, as was the custom all over the Salzburger land on such occasions, in towns or villages alike, and the consensus of the guests was that the Burghoffs had given a fine wedding for their daughter Eva, and had honored Dr. Hoerbiger appropriately by that.

The newlyweds went on their honeymoon to the place they had already had in mind for a while: to Eva's cottage in the backyard of Dr. Hoerbiger's medical office. It had now been completely furnished with good country antiques and was charming in every respect. The flowerbeds were in full bloom, the entry porch encased in climbing fragrant roses. Eva said to William:

"Does it not look like the little house in the magic garden from a fairy tale?"

"Yes," William answered, "and the princess and prince who live in it shall be happy for ever and ever."

In later years when they became a family, they moved from the fairy-tale cottage into the big house, which Eva's father had given to them as a wedding present and they continued to live happily ever after there also. *It gives one great pleasure to see that there are sometimes happy endings to stories, especially when they happen to such deserving people.*

Chapter 30

Tony and Chris had taken up their places at Waldegg. Christopher was concentrating on working in Grandfather's greenhouses and his lab. There were now two experienced nurserymen employed to take care of the growing business, but Anton still found satisfaction and interest in his experiments with seeds and propagation. Tony had his eyes and hands on everything. He was so eager to learn that his grandfather wondered *what has gotten into that boy?* Hanna thought she had the answer, but she did not say so. She observed Tony on his way towards the Mayer farm nearly every evening. Tony and Inge had a marvelous summer, working hard, but finding enough time to be together.

Christopher's summer was less exciting. Annemarie accompanied her mother to the fashionable spa in Gastein, but they also planned to come to the "Salzburger Festspiele," the yearly event in the city that drew visitors from around the world to the presentations of music and drama. Everybody who was anybody tried to come to these events. Many, of course, came out of genuine appreciation of the artistic presentation, others just wanted to be seen.

Claire's mother and her husband, August, had attended nearly every year and took the opportunity to visit Claire and her family. It had always been a pleasant visit. Claire was amazed to see the change in her mother since her marriage to August Klemperer, and wondered that her life with Claire's father must have been quite different from the impression she had had as a child. It was good to see her happy now.

Chris had a letter from Annemarie—her letters, however rare, made his life this summer at least bearable, he thought—in which she announced she was coming to Salzburg with her parents. They would stay at the Hotel Bristol and would like to entertain him and his parents for dinner on August fifth, at eight thirty; Peter said:

246

"To me that sounds more like a summons than a gracious invitation, I am not sure I will be free that evening."

"Ah, Peter, you know you can make yourself available," suggested Claire. When Peter looked into Chris's pleading eyes, he gave in,

"Of course, tell Annemarie we'll be delighted."

It had been a hot August day, but it finally cooled off somewhat in the evening. Claire had pondered what to wear, knowing that the Hotel Bristol catered to a wealthy, international clientele. Then she decided on her white, sleeveless linen, the one she had worn on her trip to Italy where it had served her through many occasions. Yes, and the turquoise blue silk shawl. The men wore their dark blue summer blazers and light colored slacks. The two men in her company thought Claire looked gorgeous, but when she entered the grand vestibule she noticed immediately, that they were all underdressed. The elegance of the public was evident, and the Moells were attired accordingly, but the Burghoffs were impressive just by themselves. Claire could see that her handsome husband and equally good-looking son had already caught the eyes of some of the ladies.

The introductions proceeded; Claire and Peter remembered having met Annemarie's father, Arthur, before, when he had come to Salzburg to visited Melinda at the end of her life. Her mother, Beate, an impeccably coiffured reddish-blonde, heavily bejeweled, immediately took over the conversation, first talking about their recent visit to Gastein's spa, where the most interesting thing seemed to have been a princely visitor from an Arab country, who had been seated right next to her while gambling at the casino. She asked if the Burghoffs went there often, and what Dr. Burghoff thought about the radon treatments at the spa. He answered with a smile, that they had never visited the casino in Gastein, and that the radon treatments would not be harmful in small doses. Beate returned a cool smile. Then she turned towards Claire:

"I understand that you are Viennese; whatever made you leave our wonderful city?"

Before Claire could answer, Beate added;

"Oh, of course, I know! When we women are in love, we will follow the man of our dreams even to purgatory."

"Is that where we are right now?" asked Peter in a friendly tone.

"Of course not, Salzburg is very charming, but I confess I think it is still somewhat provincial; when you venture a little outside: cows, cows, everywhere...."

"Yes, that is so, but is the filet mignon here not delicious? I expect dessert with some delectable white stuff—called whipped cream—for which we are also beholden to those bovines of the countryside."

"You are so right, Doctor, we city people are not nearly as grateful to the peasantry as we should be for providing us with all that." Beate laughed out loud, as if she had just said something very humorous. Arthur raised his glass, and said:

"We enjoy the Salzburger Festspiele every year, and should give credit for its cultural contributions. A toast to Salzburg and its fine citizenry, like our friends here." And he continued:

"Yes, our dear parents also took part in these festivals for many years—even in the days before the big stage was built it was a great place for the performing artists of many generations. I assume you know about the Moells? My father was the famous Theodor Moell, whose works are probably in your library, are they not?"

Claire said:

"I am afraid not, but, of course, the name is very familiar to us, I remember it even from my school days."

"Where did you go to school, Mrs. Burghoff?" Beate was talking again.

"I went to the *Rainergymnasium*, and then to the university."

"Oh, we must have some common acquaintances from those days, I went to the Oberschule for Young Ladies in the same district. We are certainly of the same age."

Oh no, Peter said to himself, *she must be at least ten years older*; he was becoming somewhat irritated. Claire said that she had lost track of most of her schoolmates during the years. Arthur was ready to continue with his family story.

"My mother was a talented singer who would easily have made it to the Opera stage, if she had not sacrificed her career for the sake of raising five children. My poor departed sister Melinda inherited much of mother's talent and looks. Well, the five of us followed in the footsteps of our distinguished parents, I must say in all modesty. My older brother, Andy, and my sister, Leila, are actors at the Burghtheater, you must know them;" Claire nodded and Arthur went on:

"My other brother, Bruno, left Austria in 1938 because he was married to a Jewess, and you remember how that was then. They went to England first, but now they are in Hollywood, where he is doing very well as a movie director. Melinda was the youngest, the favorite of our parents, I must say. They spoiled her a lot, but she was very special. Well, that is the way of the world—the best are taken from us." He sighed, but was eager to continue:

"Only I did not conform to the artistic bent in our family, but I can see that the tradition and talent was passed on to our daughter Annemarie. She will go far—unless she is foolish enough to follow the example of her grandmother and have five children. That would prevent her from achieving fame and glory, would it not?"

Annemarie was visibly annoyed and rolled her eyes. Claire was becoming uneasy herself. She found Arthur pompous but could have put up with it, if with his last words he had not turned towards Christopher, whose face had turned red. Peter was very, very, quiet. Arthur continued:

"I became a lawyer, as you know, and the family was lucky for it. It is always I who has to keep order in the family, to remind them of their obligations, and to keep them out of trouble; financial troubles I mean, because these artists have never learned how to take care of their money. They are all well off, thanks to me, I can proudly say."

Peter was getting a little edgy—he had to listen to an overbearing loud-mouth beating his own drum, when he could have been at a concert at the Mozarteum. Arthur continued:

"I have talked enough about my family" (*You said it*, thought Peter), "and now it is your turn. You are a doctor, practicing medicine here in this city? Good clientele? I suppose wealthy visitors must also get sick during the festival season, and then there are the tourists in the winter? Profitable?"

Peter fumed, but for Christ's sake remained calm.

"Yes, I perform surgery at St. Marcus."

"But farming is your background, Christopher told us?"

"Yes, my father still runs the farm and we keep some of those cows you see on the meadows outside the city." Peter smiled at Beate.

"How big is the place?"

"Fairly large. Waldegg has been in the family for generations, and we follow tradition just like your family. Our son Tony will take over one of these days. Our daughter Eva, who is studying to be a nurse, just got married to a physician in St. Johann. Another daughter lives in Linz, she is married also and has two children. Christopher is studying at the university in Vienna, but you know about him already. My wife and I are enjoying our family and our friends. One of them is known to you, Paul Thoene, at whose house we met your children Annemarie and Alexander more than a year ago. That's about it for our family, Mr. Moell."

And before Mr. Moell could think of more questions, Peter said:

"This was a fine dinner and we thank you for inviting us. It is getting rather late, and I have an early surgery scheduled for tomorrow morning. You will excuse us, won't you? It was a great pleasure to meet you and your lovely wife." Peter turned to Beate and bowed to kiss her hand. Before the self-impressed Arthur Moell could say much, the Burghoffs departed. Beate, over the clangor of the many bracelets on her arms, looking admiringly after the departing Peter and said, "What a handsome man!"

"A peasant," said Arthur, gnashing his teeth.

Annemarie was unhappy. *That meeting did not go well*, she thought. Chris was also distressed. He had the uncertain feeling that things were not quite right. He could not blame his father. Annemarie's father had been rather boorish, and her mother was silly and overbearing, but that was not the girl's fault. They could have paid more attention to her. She was the important subject that night, and somehow it did not feel right. On the way home neither Peter nor Claire let on how they felt, they just talked about the next few days and asked if Chris would stay in town and see Annemarie. He just mumbled something and they let it go.

Once alone, Peter asked Claire how she had enjoyed the evening, she had barely said a word. Claire laughed. "I enjoyed not having enough time to say any thing. The Moells did it well, did they not? But I liked your little speech in answer to Arthur's inquiry about our family."

"God, I hope Chris will see the light before it is too late. I don't think much of the girl either," Peter sighed. This time it was Claire, who was calm and reassuring:

"Don't worry about Chris. Tonight he got a few lessons to think about. By the way—did you know that Annemarie was coloring her hair black? Why is she doing that at her age? Probably to imitate Melinda's look." Peter wondered:

"How do you know?"

"I could see it, underneath she is probably a mousy brunette."

"You women can see much more than we men. I would never even have guessed it," and he sighed again, remembering only too well his own failings a long time ago. He had been lucky in the end, but Chris must be prevented from such a serious mistake, if he could only make him see it. Next morning he sent a fancy flower arrangement to the Moells' suite at the hotel, thanking them again.

Chris had a call from Annemarie and he spent a couple of days with her in Salzburg. He returned to Waldegg without saying much about it when the Moells left the city. They had not made any attempt to visit with Paul Thoene, who had chuckled, amused, after hearing about their visit from Claire. Claire said Peter was worried about Chris's infatuation with Annemarie.

"I do not know too much about the girl, but I am familiar with her background. I know her ambitious mother, who has great influence over her. I think Beate is thinking more of an Arabian Prince as being suitable for her daughter. Forgive me, but Chris would not live up to her expectations. I would guess the affair will be over soon."

By the end of the summer, another little family get-together at Waldegg was planned, and Elizabeth announced her visit with her two children. They stayed at Helmut's parents' home, but spent much time at Waldegg. Little Hannerl was already walking and her brother Siegfried was a strapping baby.

One afternoon, Elizabeth was playing with her children in the garden when Paul joined her, coming up the footpath from the lake. Fond as he always was of children, he took Hannerl in his arms and danced around with her. Finally out of breath, he sat down next to Elizabeth and said:

"You don't know how much Hannerl reminds me of you when you were a baby."

"Uncle Paul—when did you see me first?"

"Oh, right after you were born—I was present at your baptism, as you know." Somewhat hesitantly, Elizabeth slowly asked:

"Uncle Paul, are you my father?"

Paul was cuddling baby Siegfried, and, half absentmindedly, did not pay too much attention to Elizbeth's seriousness when she asked that question. He answered lightly:

"I wish I were, and your brothers' and Eva's too—you know how much I enjoy children."

Before he even had finished his sentence, Claire and Eva approached them, coming from the house. Claire said:

"Ah, Paul, I am glad to see you. We were expecting you, but I did not see you drive up."

"No," Paul said, "I came on foot from the lake, where I had left my car earlier." To Claire's astonished looks, he continued:

"I met with Frau Wagner earlier."

"Frau Wagner, the forester's widow?"

"Yes—well, I may just as well tell you my news. I am buying her cottage; I don't want to spend another summer without a daily swim in the lake as I am used to from childhood. When I heard that she might be selling the place after her husband's death, I could not resist the opportunity to live near the water's edge again, and besides that, it is so near my friends at Waldegg."

Claire, surprised and overjoyed, went to Paul and hugged him warmly while Elizabeth winked at Eva, as if she were saying: "You see?"

Eva ignored that look, thinking: *Does she still not giving up on her suspicions?* Claire said:

"Oh Paul, Peter will be so surprised—he should be here any minute, I can't wait."

"Peter won't be surprised—it was he who put me in touch with Mrs. Wagner in the first place."

Just then Peter joined the group and was anxious to hear the details of Paul's meeting with the widow Wagner. Paul said that they were near agreement, at least about the purchase price, but the details would be worked out by Paul's attorney. As it turned out, Frau Wagner was very distressed about having to leave the home she had lived in with her husband for so many years, but was unable to keep it up, to pay the taxes, etc. Her son in Saalfelden wanted her to move in with him, but she was really worried about that. When Paul offered to have her to stay on as his housekeeper, at least temporarily until she could decide how to continue with her life, she was only too happy to sign the deal. She even included her two dachshunds, Schatzi and Waldi, her husband's trusted hunting companions. They would be so much happier to stay on too and she would take good care of everything.

Paul added that he would undertake minor remodeling, but on the whole the location, on the lake and near the woods, was very much to his liking, and he thanked Peter for giving him the lead.

Elizabeth listened, but in her heart she remained suspicious that she still did not know the whole story about her own life's beginning, and vowed that one day she would find out. She still thought that Paul had had something to do with it.

September came around, the time when Tony and Chris usually prepared themselves to go back to the University in Vienna. Inge had already left for Innsbruck, where she planned to continue at the Art Institute. Tony asked Peter when he could come to the city to see him for a talk, not involving Claire for the time being. Peter wondered what was on Tony's mind, and asked him to come to his hospital office. Tony arrived, somewhat ill at ease, and while Peter's concern increased, he came right out with what he had to say.

"Father, I have long thought about it—as a matter of fact, the whole summer —and I have come to the conclusion, that I think I am ready to stay on at Waldegg for good. I do not want to continue with my studies in Vienna."

Peter was surprised.

"What brought that on? I thought you enjoyed the studies at the agricultural college?"

"Yes, I did, but I do not know how much I can still profit from continuing there. Grandfather not only needs me, but can give me more practical experience than they would teach me anywhere."

"Well," Peter said, "I think I should talk to your grandfather about it. I agree with you that he needs you, but that should not necessitate your cutting your education short."

"Father, believe me, I have thought about it. What good will more class work do me, when I am so anxious to get hands-on experience. This summer gave me special ideas as to how I want my future to be."

Peter saw his son's seriousness, but could not help another question:

"Does it have anything to do with that girl—the Mayer's granddaughter?"

"Inge?" Tony asked. "In some way, yes, because I want to marry Inge one of these days—not tomorrow, but I have decided she is the one I want to bring to Waldegg as my wife."

"And she has already agreed to that?"

"I have not asked her, but I am pretty sure she will consent."

"What I heard her say at one time is that she was not interested in farming, she is an artist, or something."

"A ceramicist—but does that mean she could not be both? At any rate, this is not the question now. She is back at school, and I want to stay at Waldegg. What to you think?"

"I have no intention of forcing you to go back to school if you don't want to, but I want to discuss your ideas with your mother and your grandfather."

"Of course," Tony said, and felt relieved that the conversation had gone so well. He had known that his father would listen to him, but had not been sure he would not have more objections. Mother would be easily persuaded by his father, and Grandfather already knew of his plans, but Tony had his promise not to reveal them until he had talked to his father.

In a short time all was settled, and while Peter and Claire still had some reservations, they helped Tony with his move to Waldegg. They admitted to themselves that their reluctance might have something to do with the recognition, that another one of their offspring was going to leave their home for good. The "nest" was emptying fast.

Christopher was lonelier than they, returning now to his room at Frau Jandasek in Vienna without his brother. However, he was looking forward to seeing Annemarie again. He had written to her several times, and she had sent a couple of postcards from her travels with her mother, saying she was looking forward to seeing him.

For the first few weeks, Christopher was busy at the university with setting up his next course selections. With some of the preliminary state exams behind him, his further study would require intensive medical courses. These would be difficult, taking much of his time for studying and laboratory work, and therefore he was not really worried about not hearing much from Annemarie, who had said she was very much involved with her classes at the conservatory also. She did invite him to another recital, where she shone with her cello solo. Afterwards she was surrounded by many of her admirers, so she had little time for Chris. He understood, yet was somewhat hurt by her apparent indifference. She promised, however, to call him soon. He waited impatiently. Finally, her call came, and they planned an outing together to the Vienna Woods the next Sunday. They had to bundle up for their stroll from Nussdorf up the Kahlenberg, because, although it was a sunny day, the November wind was blowing hard. It was good to reach the restaurant and settle down in the warm, cozy dining room. The view through the expansive glass windows was lovely. Quite a number of people had also braved the chilly weather, which was a good excuse to warm up with a hot toddy or hot chocolate, whatever their taste. The atmosphere was filled with laughter, and Christopher also felt in a cheerful mood. Annemarie was bubbly and looked fetching in her high-necked white sweater, her dark hair in gentle curls around her shoulders. Her cheeks were red from the wind and the swift ascent from the village. Chris felt silly that he was reminded of one of his beloved childhood fairy tales, namely "Snow-White," the beautiful girl with skin as white as snow, hair black as ebony, and lips as red as blood, but he mentioned it to Annemarie anyway. She laughed but said the comparison did not fit her well at all. Snow-White was too sweet; she would rather be compared to the wicked "Queen of the Night" in Mozart's *Magic Flute*, if they had to stay with classic tales. Their conversation was light and of no importance. Annemarie was sparkling, but, to Christopher's distress, she tried to mock whatever he said to compliment her. At one point she asked out of the blue, if it was true that his father was a baron, and if Chris would inherit the title. Chris answered honestly that he had never given it much thought. It was never discussed in his family. He thought that after the end of the monarchy in Austria, the Republic had done away with all aristocratic titles.

"Then the Burghoffs probably do not even have that title if your father never uses it," Annemarie said.

"I think it may exist, but father would be more proud if I followed him in achieving the academic title of Doctor rather than worrying about the baron."

"And how long will this take?" Annemarie wondered.

"Another four or five years—maybe longer—depending which direction I decide to go. My father chose surgery, but I can't yet say if I will do the same. There are so many areas in the field of medicine that excite me."

"Four, five or more years?…I thought so." Annemarie said.

Christopher, not yet twenty-two and still quite naive, had no idea where Annemarie was heading. After a while she seemed to be bored, and suggested they get back before the afternoon turned dark. They took a short cut through the woods, and immediately caught the train into the city. Annemarie did not want Chris to accompany her further than the station, from where she had just a short walk home, and she said she would call him again soon.

Christopher felt that the afternoon, having started as a lovely fall outing through the Vienna Woods, had turned into a cold November evening, and he could not explain what had happened. He found out a couple weeks later, when he happened to see Annemarie on the Ringstrasse arm in arm with a young man he had seen previously at one of her recitals. He stopped to greet her, but she just waved in passing, and did not interrupt her conversation with her companion. A few days later he received a note from her, saying that she had so many engagements in the coming months that she would be unable to see him for a while.

Well, Christopher was young and inexperienced, but not so naive that he did not understand. He was hurt, and he wished Tony were still sharing his quarters at Frau Jandasek's. He was lonely. Just a few more weeks of school and he would go home to Salzburg, go skiing, celebrate Christmas with the family, and also New Year's, he promised himself—no fancy party in the big city with shallow people in superficial conversation.

When Christopher arrived home for his Christmas break, Claire was anxiously expecting to hear about his time in Vienna, since he had not written much lately. Chris reported on his progress in his studies, asked his father a number of medical questions, but never mentioned Annemarie. His parents did not mention the subject to him either. It had apparently passed beyond concern.

Chris and Tony went to Tyrol together for New Year's, and Chris felt happy and exhilarated for the first time in months. The skiing was great, Inge and her family very pleasant, the tourists in a holiday mood which was very contagious. Chris got lots of attention from the young females on the slopes and in the lodge, which he did not seem to notice—at least not openly. Tony and Inge announced their engagement to everyone's heartfelt approval, and a summer wedding and a reunion in Neustift were planned.

The one nearly as happy as the young couple was Anton, who saw the succession of Waldegg in the proper sequence, enlarged by the Mayer holdings Inge was to inherit, which would indeed make them the owners of the largest property around. Peter was, of course, still the legal owner of Waldegg, and could change his heir at will, but that would be most unlikely. His son held the same respect for the proper succession as it had been for generations.

Hanna was also satisfied. Inge's bloodline stemmed from farm folk close to Waldegg for generations. She still considered Helga, Inge's grandmother, a cold person, but granted her to have taught her granddaughter enough about running a farm, that she could expect cooperation from Inge when introducing her to the way Waldegg had been run under her reign. She had to talk to Anton, as well as to Peter, about living arrangements for the future, when Peter and Claire would also move to Waldegg, as it had been planned at one time. She had been thinking that she and Anton should make room for the young people—it always had been that way—and should fix up the old house that Laszlo had left. Their new manager lived in the village with his family, an arrangement they all had agreed upon. These days, the farming help wanted more freedom just like other employees in business had, which meant they showed up in the morning for their duties at the farm, and left at the end of the day for their own homes in town or village. It took some adjustment for Hanna and Anton, since in the old days their farm hands had been part of the family and had lived on the premises. That only applied now to fewer and fewer of the older workers.

Anton agreed. In his heart he felt some regret in leaving the house where he was born, and where he had spent all his life, but that was as it should be. His own father had not lived long enough to have had to make room for the next generation, but three generations should not live under the same roof. He consoled himself with the realization that they would not really leave Waldegg, but just move across the expanse of the orchard—one could even see the main buildings from there.

Anton and Hanna made an inspection of the old house. It would take some work, but it could be made quite livable.

"Or," he asked his wife, "should we move into the *senioren-home* in Kammerbach?"

Hanna gave him one of her looks, without saying a word.

"I was just kidding. No, we are going to build ourselves a honeymoon cottage that will rival Eva's in St. Johann. Yes?" he said, smiling. Hanna smiled also. It would work out just fine.

When they had the chance a few weeks later, they told Peter what they had decided to do. Peter had to confess that he had not thought about it yet. In the first place, Tony was not even married, and he nor Claire were ready to leave Salzburg either, but he had to admit that his retirement from his position at the hospital was not too far off. He planned to talk to Claire about it. To his surprise, Claire had already been thinking about the situation. For years it had been her dream to live at Waldegg, but she realized that even by further remodeling of the existing structures to make more room, it seemed not right to live in such an extended family circle, no matter that they all loved each other and got along so well. However, when she heard of Anton and Hanna's plan to move to the old house, she did not feel comfortable either. Hanna and Anton should not have to move. As much as she would have loved to live at the "castle," she thought it would be only fair to let the old folks live out their lives in their old home. Peter appreciated his wife's consideration and he told his parents that he expected them to stay on, and that he and Claire would remodel the old house for themselves. In order not to let them feel that he and Claire had sacrificed their plans on their account, he added that he would still need some additional rooms because he was going to continue a consulting practice and it would be very difficult and costly to do that in the main building.

Anton and Hanna were very satisfied with that arrangement, and so was Tony, when told. He had also been talking to Inge, after he had showed her all the living areas, as well as the rest of the unused part of the castle. They had been secretly wondering what extensions could be made. Inge was not very concerned; she was easy-going, gay, and happy. They would manage just fine, even if they had to squeeze in somewhat. But now, with Tony's parents' idea there was no such situation to deal with.

After a few sentimental moments over the loss of her dream of living at the "castle," and a talk with the architect who was working on Paul's hunting lodge, Claire even became excited over the new adventure of remodeling the old house in the orchard. The architect, Gerhard Schroeder, an old friend of Peter's school days, pointed out, however, that it would be probably more cost effective to tear the building down and build anew. Peter ruled against it. Although he had no sentimental attachment to it, he liked the feeling of the old structure with its massive walls, the arched ceilings like those in the main house, and especially the location of the house at the far end of the orchard, open to the south with an unmatched view of the lake and the high-rising mountains in the background. Although the area was not suited for wine growing in general, the massive grape vine along the south wall of the existing house produced not only a substantial harvest of luscious fruit in the fall, but was also very decorative in the spring when the first delicate green leaves appeared, and in the fall when they had turned into shades of bronze and orange. Whatever plans Gerhard Schroeder came up with, that vine had to be saved.

Claire, of course, had her heart set on a number of other things she wanted to include in the house plans, like saving the massive hearth in the kitchen, covered with precious ceramic tiles as old and artistic as those she had found at the castle. Gerhard Schroeder agreed, even though the preservation of the old with the demands of combining with the new technology, especially when it came to plumbing, heating, and lighting, was a challenge. Of course, they had installed electricity many years before, and the wires ran on the surface of the walls, but that all had to be changed. The bathrooms were rather primitive also, and despite the antique appeal of the old large bathtubs in the cold and unheated large rooms, Claire opted for a completely modern version with built-ins and the newest fixtures, as well as a few luxuries for occasional pampering.

The kitchen would be the focal point of the home. It was already a very large room, divided between the work area and the sitting room by the tiled back of the kitchen hearth. Claire had great ideas about the furniture and decor here, helped by a catalog from a local furniture maker of fine quality products, many carved in the old traditional styles, but enhanced by modern techniques to make them more comfortable.

This kitchen-eating-sitting room combination would be where they would mostly gather with family and friends. Across the hallway another large room would become a library-parlor combination, if they had to entertain more formally. Even in Salzburg that had not been too often, because neither Claire nor Peter cared for it. It would also contain Peter's newest stereo equipment where he could indulge in the enjoyment of musical selections undisturbed. Adjoining the library, Peter would have a smaller office for consultation with patients and the practice of minor medical procedures. He would deal with major surgical tasks at the hospital in the city as before, where his privileges to do so would continue.

Upstairs, two bedrooms were planned, each expansive and each with its own bathroom. The guest room was large enough to accommodate either single guests or a family with children. Claire and Peter's bedroom did get special attention. It was large, with windows on two walls, and a door on the third, opening to a roofed balcony, providing a sensational view of the glorious mountains. Claire had no definite plans for the furnishings here, but they would certainly include some of her antiques which her mother had passed on to her when moving in with her new husband, but also the big old bed she had shared with Peter all these years.

All the work done to the old house required Claire's special attention and she enjoyed it even when complications arose because the county's architectural approval had to be secured. Thanks to Claire's research into the past of Waldegg and its consequent designation as a historic landmark, the authorities under whose jurisdiction such specification now fell, wanted to be consulted more often than the architect or Peter appreciated.

Before the planning was even half completed, there was the summer wedding of Tony and Inge in Tyrol, an event enjoyed by the whole family. Anton and Hanna used the occasion to visit Hanna's family for a few days, which became more sentimental for Hanna since most of her siblings had passed away, and only Karl, her older brother still teetered on. Of course, there was the younger generation to get better acquainted with, nieces and nephews, and cousins. It hurt her to see that most of the old family farms had given way to hotels with their extensive tourist attractions, like swimming pools, tennis courts, even a golf course. She had heard about it, of course, but seeing it was more painful. Karl's grandson kept only a small farm for raising Hanna's beloved Haflinger horses. She knew that farming, as she had known it in her youth, was on its way out in many places in Salzburg also, but Tyrol was probably leading in the changes to accommodate the tourist trade. This had become Austria's most profitable export, and the scenic landscape of both provinces was more suitable for tourism than to farming in the old style. Cattle were still grazing the alpine meadows and producing some of the best quality milk products not only for home use, but competing successfully with Swiss products for export. Agricultural production had increased in other Austrian provinces, thanks to modernized farming methods, so that the country could not only feed itself, but could sell grain and other farm products to the world. Of course, Hanna knew only what she had heard discussed between Anton and Tony, and did not fully understand how the government exercised its influence by dictating what and how much a farmer was allowed to produce. Just thinking about all the regulations she heard of made her angry and defiant in her votes on election day. These thoughts were going through her mind on her way to the wedding of her oldest grandson in Tyrol.

Chapter 31

The wedding was the sensation of the Stubai valley. Mainly a skiing resort, it also hosted a large number of summer guests, some of whom came to engage in mountaineering, others to take the invigorating mountain air for health reasons, others just to wander through the woods of the lower regions in the valley and enjoy the fantastic vistas of the majestic mountain ranges. Therefore, there was a large crowd taking part in the wedding ceremonies beside the family visitors, and it must be admitted that mother Burgl and her son Eric had planned the very traditional and folksy feast and all its hoopla with business considerations in mind. The tourists always loved these country-style feasts with the display of old traditional costumes, music, and dancing; and even Peter, who normally looked like a conservative statesman, joined in some of the rollicking, kicked up his heels and danced a few. Claire and Peter left next morning, since Peter was expected at the hospital, but it was told that the party lasted another full day before the last of the guests left. Paul accompanied Anton and Hanna back home.

Tony had a special surprise for his bride when they arrived at Waldegg. He had rummaged around Waldegg's abandoned storage areas and found just the perfect place. It had housed an old horse carriage, not worthy of keeping or repairing; he had cleaned it out and turned it into a perfect pottery shed. He even had gone to Salzburg and visited a well known potter there who had helped him purchase the most important equipment: a potter's wheel and a kiln, basic paints and glazes. He had put up storage shelves, installed good lights—only the details as to an artists own taste needed to be added. Inge was not only surprised, but overjoyed. Claire was pleased to see that her son, despite his young age, already knew how to please his wife. Anton's and Peter's traits were clearly showing in their offspring.

Hanna and Inge had a good talk about sharing responsibilities. Hanna pointed out, that it was Peter and Claire who should be reigning in Waldegg, but they had decided to skip the succession in regard to living in the house itself, so it would be up to Inge to take over all the household chores. However, if Inge wanted Hanna's help for a while, she would be only too pleased to continue for the time being. Inge was perfectly satisfied with that arrangement. Actually, she had been prepared to ask Hanna for it herself, as her mother Burgl, as well as her grandmother Helga had suggested. Helga had warned her that Hanna was a stern woman, but very accomplished in running Waldegg, and it would be only to Inge's benefit if Hanna would show her the way she had been doing it. Inge found Hanna very likable—she reminded her very much of her own grandmother and she found it rather amusing that both had so much respect for each other, but did not seem to especially like each other. Claire remained in charge of Waldegg's books, but Anton's tree business was handled by another book-keeper.

The calendar of the year of 1969 registered two more births for the Burghoff clan: Eva bore a healthy redheaded boy in October, who was named Heinz after Wilhelm's father, and Elizabeth became the mother of a third child in November, also a boy, named Gunther. The traditional singing at the family gathering on Christmas Eve was embellished by the sounds such new babies are capable of, and were very appropriate for the celebration of the birth of the one whom Christians all over the world remember at this time.

Claire was sentimentally aware of being a grandmother to four young children. Where had the years gone, since she had the first child herself at about the same time of year? How different were her circumstances then, alone with no happy family around. Then she looked at Paul who was sitting in an easy chair, looking dreamily at the Christmas tree. Was he remembering also? He had been her friend then as he was now, and tears welled up in her eyes. Peter noticed it, without knowing the cause, but he came and stood behind his wife, his hands holding her shoulders in a calming motion. She leaned her cheek against them, and felt the weak moments of these somewhat sad memories passing. How unbelievably lucky had her life turned out since then, how could she have even in her wildest dream imagined that Peter would be a part of it again—and his family and their children, and now even grandchildren.

Peter's thoughts were slightly different when observing the gathering of family members. He looked at his parents and remembered his boyhood days when his brother Hans was alive and they had celebrated the feast in that same room, which had changed little since then. He loved its coziness despite it being large and really needing all the people now present to fill it up adequately. Way back there had been only his grandparents here, but later in the evening the more close servants always joined in and jostled with the boys, until Hanna reminded everybody of the solemnity of the occasion.

Anton also looked around the family gathering with an observant eye. He felt satisfaction, because he saw the orderly continuation of Waldegg and the Burghoff family. His son Peter had done well and had raised a remarkable family, not without the help of a good woman, he said to himself, observing both Peter and Claire. Peter had been lucky, just as he had been with finding Hanna—how long ago—was it really more then sixty years? Tony did well also; that granddaughter of old Mayer was a good choice, and a darnn pretty girl to boot, he observed with the keen eye of an experienced connoisseur of womanly charms and virtues. And Chris—well, he would find himself a good wife too, he would also honor the name of Burghoff. It's in them—the Burghoff men. At that moment he had completely forgotten that his beloved Peter had failed once upon a time in that respect, and he did not even remember it when he looked at Eva, who happily tended to her little redheaded baby.

Was Hanna also lost in emotional thought at this occasion? Not really— she had too much thinking to do about the material needs of her family, about food and drink, and also about the feast tomorrow. Claire would help, of course, but it was still up to her to organize it. While his parents looked frail and aged to Peter, Hanna did not intend to show any weakness before finally collapsing into her bed later that night.

Paul was keeping his thoughts and feelings to himself that evening. He would not have shared them even with his dearest friends, Claire and Peter. He was grateful to be everybody's "Uncle Paul" and part of that wonderful family. The painful little twinges in his heart were his alone to keep and cherish.

The younger generation avoided introspection—they just enjoyed Christmas, and were looking forward to New Year's Eve, to be celebrated right here at Waldegg. Burgl Mayer-Steinbrenner, Inge's mother, and the old Mayers and Helmut's parents, Fritz and Gerda Engebrecht were coming, as well as a few boyhood friends of Tony and Chris. Waldegg had not seen such a large party within its walls for a long time, but Tony had thought that it would be a good time to introduce his wife Inge to a number of people who had not attended the wedding in Tyrol.

By the spring of the following year the remodeling of the old manager's house was finished, and Peter and Claire were very satisfied with the results. All the difficulties that had arisen were only structural headaches for the architect and the builder, Claire had to compromise only a little in her vision and was very happy. Happier than she would have thought to have been a few months ago, when it became clear that she would not be living at the "castle," as the Kammerbacher people continued to call it—despite Peter's repeated reminder to them: "It's just an old farmhouse like yours." Of course it was not, and the plaque affixed on its old walls said distinctly that it was a historic site and a National Monument, with a marking on its plaque which said, that in case of war it would be protected and not attacked. Peter always laughed, when he saw that notation. As if bombs made any distinction as to their targets. Why were the Dome of St. Stephen and the Vienna Opera house hit along with so many other cultural monuments?

Claire was still busy with the interior furnishings, and they did not intend to move in before Peter's official retirement from the hospital when he turned sixty. A successor had been found for him, so it was time to wind up his business. Peter harbored some regrets about it, but tried not to show it. After all, he was not retiring from his profession, just from his place at the hospital. Colleagues had asked for and had been getting his assurance that he would be available for consultation for many years to come. He gave them an invitation to visit his new home at Waldegg, just about an hour's drive from the hospital in Salzburg.

Claire used the occasion to give a splendid party which spilled over into the lantern-lit orchard between their new home and the main building. It was a very lively gathering of the medical staff, and many were surprised to see the extent of the estate. Peter had always described it as just the farm of Waldegg where he came from. Some native Salzburg people had, of course, known of Waldegg, but had never really associated it with Dr. Burghoff.

Chris had come home to help with the move. Unlike during his younger years, he did not spend all of his vacation at home these days. He had been asked by one of his professors to help in a research project, which was an honor he could not refuse, so he had spent most of the summer in Vienna at the clinic. His parents accepted with some sadness that they would see their youngest child at home less and less. When Chris moved his belongings into the large guest bedroom at the new house, he too was sad. Had he now become a guest? At the same time he realized that he would indeed spend less time at home, that he was in the process of building his own career.

The transition to their new life went very well for Peter and Claire. They were suddenly aware that this was the first home they had had all to themselves. It was just like being newly married: an unencumbered honeymoon couple. It was a good time. Peter was often home for days in a row, which had not happened before. They could take lengthy walks together, even sleep-in some mornings. Claire had never been an early riser, but Peter had always had to be up at dawn. His old habits soon caught up with him, and while Claire was still asleep, he would go across the orchard and visit with his mother in the kitchen for breakfast. Hanna treasured these mornings when she once again had her son to herself, and they discussed many things for which there had been so little time before. Then Peter usually went off to seek out his father or Tony, and their Waldegg business became a common ground for planning and discussions.

Claire insisted that she would do without housekeeper or gardener from now on, and had only engaged cleaning help, but she still found much leisure time left to do as she pleased.

Peter was called often enough for consultation or to help with a difficult surgical procedure, which not only kept him financially independent but also kept his scientific interests awake.

It was a good life, a very good life. Peter and Claire held hands on their walks through the woods, along the lake, and were happy. They were thankful for their health and the other good fortune in their life. Ah—it was wonderful, to be young again! That is how they felt and it gave them great pleasure.

Of course, life always provides just a little reminder that too much happiness needs to be curtailed somewhat under even the best of circumstances. Gerda came over with news which her son had just told her. His company had accepted a proposal to bid on a giant project in the U.S.A, and he had been offered the chance to lead a group of engineers to explore it. He could be gone for a long time, years maybe, and he had decided to take the family with him. Fritz had said nothing, just stared, Gerda reported, but she was very concerned about it. She told Claire about it in Peter's absence, and both women shared their anxiety. In a way, it seemed to be a great opportunity for Helmut. The salary he mentioned was very substantial and it was easy to see that to refuse such temptation was difficult, but the children were so young, and Elizabeth was too. Such a move would not be an easy undertaking, would it be not wiser for Helmut to go alone, and send for his family later, when he was settled? Such were the thoughts of the two mothers, who finally admitted to each other that it did not matter what they felt about it, the children would do what they thought best anyway.

Gerda left and Claire could hardly wait for Peter to come home. She looked out over the fields for a rider and his horse. Peter inspected the land on horseback, rather than by car, not only for the convenience of being able to go where the roads did not, but because he enjoyed riding as he had in his youth. Tony and Chris did the same, Anton once had too, but now it was easier for him to climb onto a tractor than on a horse.

Finally, she got a glimpse of Peter on his way back, but she knew he would take care of his horse first, so she went to the stables and said that she had something to tell him. He could not imagine what could be so important that it could not wait until he had cleaned up. He went to the fountain to cool his face in the sparkling spring water, and Claire even followed him there. She quickly told him Gerda's news, and Peter held his face under the spout once again. When he had cooled himself enough, he said only that it was up to Helmut and Elizabeth how and where they wanted to live. They certainly would not want any advice from them, and besides, what advice would be appropriate? He, Peter, would not know what was best. He wished, however, that the news had come from Elizabeth directly, and not over the grapevine. Claire reminded him that Gerda was not grapevine but family, and he conceded. His anger was only covering up new pain that Elizabeth was inflicting on them. He saw the tears in Claire's eyes—why was this child of theirs continuing to hurt her mother who had suffered so much on her account? Peter felt so protective of Claire that he forgot his own discomfort at the news, and he talked to her calmly, trying to make her feel that it was good news that Helmut had really turned out to be so successful. Who could have foreseen that when he had appeared to be only a "good-looking, good-for-nothing lad?" Helmut had worked himself into a respectable position, not to mention the income which would provide them with security and prestige. Claire started to feel better—where would she be without Peter, who always had the right view on things? Thank you, God, for Peter.

She did not pass on the news until Elizabeth found it in her heart to inform the rest of the family herself on a visit to the farm. By then, Claire had prepared herself emotionally to accept the fact of her leaving the country. In her heart she hoped it would be only temporary, but somehow she felt she knew it would be for a very long time. She did not show her trepidation; she wished Elizabeth all the luck for this great undertaking and so did Peter. Elizabeth was disappointed that her parents took it so calmly. She was still the spoiled little girl, expecting the world—at least her family's—to turn around her. Hanna was the only one who expressed real concern, especially for the babies' sake. Taking them half around the world into the unknown!

"Grandmother, we will be living in California, one of the most civilized places on this planet. They have the best of everything there in living conditions, the best doctors and hospitals for one, not to mention the luxurious lifestyle available to anyone."

"You saw too many Hollywood movies, they don't show you the real world. I have read stories about exploitation of farm workers, who definitely don't live in luxury."

"Do they here in Austria?"

"Elizabeth, I admit that I don't know if it is right for you to leave here. I sincerely hope that everything will turn out just fine, and that we will see you back in a couple of years, as Helmut says."

"Maybe sooner, Grandmother."

Elizabeth's brothers looked on it as a great adventure, and wished her the best. Elizabeth and her family were leaving in November.

"At the worst time of the year," Hanna lamented, "the children will catch colds."

"Mother, the winter climate in California is as mild as in the Mediterranean. November there will be like spring here."

"Yes, and no snow at Christmas, what will that holiday be like?"

It was not easy to convince Hanna, that Elizabeth's going away was a good thing. Claire had similar thoughts, but kept them to herself, as also the occasional tears of heartache.

Happy news and sorrows seem to follow each other in no particular sequence. Inge announced she was pregnant. It was hard to tell if Tony was the happier or Anton. The old man acted as if he had achieved all the goals of his life. Yes, the succession for the Burghoffs was secured, this was important to him and he planned to celebrate accordingly.

"Bring out the best plum brandy I have saved for such an occasion," he told Hanna. She made sure, however, that the bottle disappeared after his second potion. By that time he had fallen asleep in his chair anyway, happy and content.

Work in his greenhouses still occupied Anton these days, but he complained he was getting tired quickly. Peter urged him to have a medical checkup, but Anton refused, saying he already knew what the doctor would say to him: "Anton, face it, you are getting old." Peter thought his father was probably right. He was eighty-six years old, had been healthy all his life—slowing down was normal—and even a medical examination would not prevent it. He knew his father's blood pressure was only slightly raised, his heart rate normal, therefore he did not insist on the examination, but he recommended him to take it easy. It happened automatically. Winter passed, and during the early warm spring days Anton enjoyed sitting on the bench outside the kitchen and letting the sun warm his bones. From there he could hear the lively sounds from the kitchen, where Hanna commanded in her usual manner. She was only two years younger, he thought, but as busy as ever. Well, Hanna knew that was not true of her either; her reign over the kitchen staff was now more from her easy chair than with her former hands-on participation. Anton looked out over the garden. The blooming fruit trees in the orchard obscured Peter's new house somewhat. Yes, he approved, it had turned out just fine, and especially now, framed by the cherry blossoms, it had a special dream-like quality. He felt himself getting drowsy—he thought he should not have gotten up so early that day—maybe he needed another nap. Walking through the kitchen, he asked Hanna to tell Peter to come and see him. Hanna asked:

"What for—he'll come when he is done with his work."

Anton was cranky: "I want him here now, tell Seppl to get him." And he went slowly upstairs to his bedroom.

Hanna could not find Seppl, who was the boy—no, the man. He was Peter's age—who had been with the family since her son was an infant. He was retarded, but could look out for the boys well enough then, and they had kept him in the family ever since. He was not much good for farm work, but did lots of household chores, such as bringing wood into the kitchen, fetching things when needed—they always said that they really could not do without him, but dependable he was not. Sometimes he just disappeared somewhere in the hay and slept until he felt like coming around again as he had today. Hanna called, but Seppl was not in hearing distance, so she let it go. When neither Peter nor Anton appeared at lunchtime, she sent the kitchen girl upstairs to call Anton to come down. The girl came back and said the master was sleeping in his chair, and she did not want to wake him. Then Peter passed the kitchen door to go to his house to have lunch with Claire, Hanna told him that Anton wanted to talk to him. So Peter went upstairs, and found his father still sleeping—except it did not seem so—yes, Anton had fallen asleep, but it was for good.

Peter had, of course, expected it would happen—it was the way of life—but at that moment the realization hit him hard. He sat down near his father and had the conversation that Anton probably was thinking about too. Peter needed that time for himself to recover enough to face his mother. When he finally came downstairs, Hanna looked at him, and instantly knew:

"He is gone, is he not?" was all, she could stammer, then slumped down into her chair.

Yes, Anton was gone, and despite all his descendants who were there to mourn him, he left a big gap in the makeup of Waldegg, which was felt by everyone. They realized how difficult it would be to fill his shoes.

In early summer, another Burghoff was born. He was named Karl Anton, and filled the place with happy sounds, which Grandmother Claire could hear from her kitchen window. Great-grandmother Hanna watched the child in his crib which had been set outside to enjoy the fresh air under the trees in the orchard. Netting prevented insects from bothering him, but let him watch the movement of the leaves in the wind above him, which seemed to give him so much pleasure as he gurgled happily while watching it.

Uncle Paul joined in the admiration of the newest clan member on his frequent visits to Waldegg. One could hardly call it visiting—he was considered family and his presence was expected. He had not retired from his business completely, but had hired a staff which could take care of it without his daily advice. He had made a good move with the purchase of the forester's lodge on the lake. The remodeling to fit his style and needs had turned out well, and the widow Wagner took good care of him. The dachshunds accepted him as their new master and accompanied him everywhere, also on his daily walks through the woods with Claire.

Claire loved exploring all the trails and paths around their property, sometimes with Peter, but often alone or accompanied by Paul, Schatzi, and

Waldi. On one such stroll through the woods, a little beyond where the foot-path ended and a clearing opened, she discovered a small structure, over-grown with ivy and thickets. It looked as if it had a turret, like a chapel. It took some effort to push the vines aside, but then she noticed a glassless win-dow through which she could glance into the inside. Indeed it must have once been a chapel, she could see some overthrown, banged-up benches, peeling frescoes of saints, partly covered with mold—all forgotten by time. It was not so much the building that intrigued her, but the lovely setting of its surroundings. At one time it must have been a larger clearing, but it was now overgrown; large boulders were lying around, as if they had just rolled off the towering mountain wall above; a small creek rambled between them, finding its way to a mossy pond. The sunshine filtering through the needles of the surrounding pine trees added to the enchanting setting. Claire thought it was like one of those paintings one was likely to call 'kitsch," but in real life would touch one's soul. Peter had to see it, and she could not wait until he could find the time to come.

Peter finally came with her, but it was on one of those cloudy, windy days, and the romance that Claire had described was not there. However, she insisted that they should do something about the place. Peter looked at the building. It was fairly sound, but the inside was just in shambles. What did Claire have in mind? By that time she was so swept up with the idea, that she tried her best to get Peter's promise to restore the chapel, because she felt in her heart that it was a very special place. She argued that it was on Burghoff property and it was therefore their responsibility

It was not often that Claire asked for something. She had made sugges-tions here and there, when they were building their house, for instance, but had never insisted. It was different this time and Peter, still in doubt, let him-self be persuaded to think about restoration.

Paul had also accompanied Claire to the place. It was again one of those perfect days and times when the sun came shining through the gaps of the overhanging trees, leaving dancing shadows on the granite boulders and the brook, and he was no less enchanted by that scene than Claire had been. He composed a poem in his head to do it justice, and by the time they returned and found Peter, Paul presented the jingle, not a poetic masterpiece, but it rhymed and amused Peter. He acted as if Paul and his poetry had him con-vinced finally to take up the chapel project, but he said that he would first ask the bishop's advice.

In the meantime, Claire had searched the church records of Kammerbach with regard to historical information, but there was none. The new priest—after father Grumberger had passed on—had absolutely no knowledge of it; Hanna had never heard of it; nor had other old timers whom Claire sought out. However, she had the feeling that there was something familiar about it, and Eva also thought so. Therefore they looked into the available papers on the history of Waldegg and found a mention that Napoleon's soldiers had camped one night around the Old St. Johannes chapel in the forest with no further description. This must have been it. It did not say that the soldiers had damaged it, which was unlikely anyway because the French were mostly Catholics too, and would not have willfully destroyed a sanctuary. There were no records of a battle fought there, although at a not too far distant place, at the Salzach-Klamm, the French had encountered fierce resistance from the Austrians. An elaborate chapel, built on a rocky rise, with memorial markers with the names of the fallen Austrian soldiers is there today. It is often used for weddings now, and the area is also a tourist attraction. A hotel built right next to it takes advantage of the visiting romantics and the history buffs.

Peter reminded Claire of all that. Would she like to see "her chapel" turn into a tourist attraction on their home grounds, especially with the increasing interest in the Waldegg museum, with which she had already been involved? No, of course not; if Peter had reservations, she would forget her plans. Peter had already talked to the bishop, and Franz thought the restoration of another part of Waldegg would be very appropriate and would find approval from the locals, as well as the church.

It did not take much to clear the site enough to make the approach to it easy, but not so as to invite a tourist crowd. The chapel was small, it had probably been used only as an occasional retreat for Waldegg family members when they desired a private hour of prayer. The structure had a vaulted ceiling and gothic window openings. The fresco remnants could not be saved, they had been mostly washed away by wind and rain entering through the glassless windows, but one of the workers found a notation of 1743, which seemed to be the date the artist had put on his work. The prayer benches may have been fancily carved originally, but were brittle and decayed and fell apart.

Restoration was not too difficult. No architectural committee was needed, just a few good workmen and some money. Stained glass windows were commissioned by the museum's committee and financed by donations from the Waldegg and Mayer estates. The Burghoffs tried to keep it a family project, though the consecration by the bishop was public and a community affair. The chapel was designated to the memory of Hans (Johann) Burghoff, and therefore kept its likely original name of "St. Johann Chapel." In order to keep the area from being overrun, Peter installed a gate, which would prohibit any vehicular traffic through the Waldegg pastures to the forest which surrounded the chapel.

Hanna was very moved by the effort that Claire had put into the project. She had always appreciated and respected Claire, but there were reservations which she had been unable to overcome. She admitted Claire was a very good mother, a loving wife to Peter, who so adored her, that Hanna would never mention any criticism of her daughter-in-law in his presence, but she could not completely forget the circumstances of her entering Peter's life. She knew Claire as a moral and upstanding person, however there had still been these little doubts that never let her love her completely. Claire had felt that unreachable reserve and had attributed it to a mother's reluctance to share her beloved son's affections. No matter how much she herself liked and appreciated Inge, she still felt sometimes as if she had lost a part of Tony to her. So she understood Hanna. When it was obvious that Claire deserved all the credit for the restoration of the chapel in the forest and that it was she who had proposed its dedication to the memory of her son Hans, Hanna embraced Claire for the first time; and her thanks and tears came from the heart.

During the restoration of the chapel, which took nearly two years from Claire's discovery to the consecration by the bishop, Claire and Peter made various pleasure trips for which they had previously had so little time. They went to Vienna often, usually to a concert or to the opera, which Peter considered his reward for having to abstain for so long from his passion for music because of lack of time. On these occasions they frequently visited their son Christopher, of course, who had involved himself completely in his studies, so that Peter reminded him not to become estranged from life's other pleasures. Chris reminded his father that it was rumored he had done exactly the same, when he was a student. At least, that's what Frau Jandasek said. Peter laughed:

"That woman still exaggerates my virtues. I admit that I was also very serious about my studies, but I was not as smart as you are and had to study harder."

His parents insisted, therefore, that Chris accompany them to these cultural events whenever possible. Claire felt vain enough to feel very special in the company of the two most handsome—as she put it and meant it—men in the audience. At one event at the opera, they encountered Annemarie Moell in the foyer during intermission, who greeted them, especially Chris, with such enthusiasm that Claire's heartbeat increased with worry about the effect on her son. But Chris seemed to be genuinely indifferent, and she soon found out why. After the performance when they had coffee at the hotel he told his parents, that he was seeing a former classmate, named Renate Koenig. She was the daughter of one of his professors, and they had many common interests. Christopher had decided to specialize in Neurology. Renate was working on a degree in Psychology, her father's specialty. Claire said with some hesitancy:

"Well, why don't you invite her to visit us in Waldegg, when you come the next time?"

"Yes, one of these days I may just do that." Chris said lightly, and Claire was set at ease. It did not sound too serious—for some reason she wanted Chris to take his time. She talked to Peter about it, wondering why she had not felt the same way about Tony. Peter laughed:

"Because there you were the matchmaker, remember? Do you have similar plans for Chris?"

"No, of course not, but…" and her thoughts were trailing off.

They occasionally visited her mother also, who was still as happy as ever with August Klemperer, who, though not ailing, seemed to be aging visibly, Claire felt. Her mother did not seem to notice. She was lively and active for her age of seventy-five, lovingly caring for the love of her youth, *making up for lost time*, Claire thought.

Two years later, August died quietly. Claire arrived at her mother's home with pity in her heart for her mother, and she said so. Rosemarie was not as disconsolate as she had assumed. She said there was no need to pity her; she had been blessed with the fulfillment of her maiden-dreams in a loving relationship whose memory would endure forever. How many women could say the same? She would remain as close to August in thought as if he were alive. He had enriched her life beyond expectation. They had both known that the day would come when they would have to part again. They had used the time they had together well, and only pleasurable memories filled her heart. Claire was speechless—again, her mother had surprised her with her ability to accept the unchangeable with serenity and dignity.

August had bequeathed the lovely house to Rosemarie for as long as she chose to live there. Then it would become the property of his two children. Rosemarie would also inherit all his personal belongings and financial investments, which were substantial; she could live a very comfortable life to the end of her days. She did so for five more years.

Christopher had come to the rededication of the chapel, bringing Renate along and announcing their engagement to the family. Claire was surprised to see how different Renate was from his onetime love interest, Annemarie, the very pretty and exquisite flirt. Renate was of average looks, although smartly dressed, serious, apparently very intelligent, but…Claire did not want to think it but it always came to her mind: Renate appeared to be cold.

"Yes," Peter said, "like an Ice princess."

"Oh, I want Christopher to be loved and cherished." Claire cried out.

"Don't judge by appearances, underneath that icy surface may burn a quiet fire—I trust Chris is no fool," Peter countered.

The wedding took place in Vienna, after Christopher's promotion to the doctorate. Renate had already received her own. It was not an elaborate affair, nor a country feast as his other siblings had celebrated in the province, but was dignified, with the closest family members and friends of the couple present. It was obvious that Renate's family was distinguished and refined, but Claire thought they all showed the same aloof manner as Renate. Her father was a professor as Claire's father had been, but in the medical ranks, which paints its members as being more worthy than those of other academic backgrounds. Professor Koenig appeared to think of himself as very special; no wonder that Renate was infected by it, especially since she was following his career example also.

These were Claire's thoughts during the wedding, and she cried a little. It did not disturb anybody; mothers, especially mothers of sons, are supposed to be teary-eyed at such events. Peter pressed her hand gently, assuring her that everything was just fine. When she observed Christopher's behavior after the ceremony, which showed such happiness and joy, she relaxed. His happiness was all that was important. She only hoped that his natural charm would not be infected by the increased feeling of self-importance which seemed to prevail in the Koenig household. Anna Koenig, Renate's mother was very dignified also, and performed her role in the wedding and at the reception afterwards at the Hotel Sacher in style. She showed only great warmth when addressing Christopher, which made Claire even more uneasy. They were not trying to lure her son away from his family with their sophisticated manners? She compared Anna Koenig to the mother-in-law of her son Tony, Burgl Steinbrenner, or Gerda Engebrecht, Elizabeth's mother-in-law. Both were friendly, warm, and sincere. They were Claire's friends. She would not want to have to consider Anna Koenig as a competitor for her son's affection.

Not one of his wife's thoughts entered Peter's mind. He observed the family, their friends, and came to the contented conclusion that he himself had chosen right by going back to his country roots instead of making his career as a surgeon in the big city as his professor had once suggested.

One thing Claire was not aware of: Anna Koenig was so consumed by fear of showing how difficult it was for her to perform the dignified role here, that she could do it only by freezing up and praying nobody would notice her jitters. She succeeded, but it was a pity that the two mothers did not get to know each other for a long time. Not until the baptism of the twin daughters of Renate and Christopher, but that was some time later.

When the Burghoff clan, including Tony, Eva, and Wilhelm,—Inge could not make it to the wedding because of the late stage of her pregnancy and it was too strenuous for Hanna also—returned by car to Salzburg, the younger people were discussing the event and made very positive comments about Renate, who was so visibly in love with Christopher, and so charming. Peter and Claire looked at each other. Renate charming? What did we miss?

The second child born to Tony and Inge, was also a son, Hans Peter, just about two years younger than his brother Karl Anton and joyfully received by all. Inge's mother, Burgl, had moved back to her ancestral lands. Her son, Inge's brother Eric, had married and was successfully and capably running his tourist hotels in Tyrol. Her parents, the Mayer's, had moved into the retirement home in Kammerbach, which they had endowed with funds in previous years. These funds were to be used to add a new wing to the existing building where they now lived in comfort. Burgl had purchased a little house in Kammerbach, suggesting her parents spend the rest of their years with her, but they preferred the carefree living which the retirement home could provide with their live-in medical staff. They could visit Burgl any time, and feel more independent than they would sharing her home. They also felt that Burgl might want to remarry one of these days, and a separation now would be less awkward than later. Indeed, there was a prospect in Burgl's life. At least she had plans in that respect, even though the "prospect" had no idea.

In the meantime, she visited at Waldegg often and was a great help to Inge in caring for her two strapping boys. Hanna did not mind the intrusion. She remembered that she had always thought that Burgl would have been a good choice for Peter. A homegrown girl, who understood the land, the animals, who could competently ride any horse. Claire had some respect for horses—but she never trusted them enough to ride one, although Peter, who loved to ride, had often urged her to do so. Well, Hanna admitted, it had all turned out for the best, but Burgl was welcome company in her kitchen.

She forgot, that it was really Inge's kitchen now, but Inge was satisfied with the arrangement. Burgl's presence at least gave her some time to devote herself to her pottery. She had crafted some very fine pieces, and had added a few for display in the folk museum of Waldegg, and had found to her delight that they pleased the tourists enough to want to purchase them. Tony would not allow it. He jealously guarded every piece which he considered his talented wife's artwork, and only for their own enjoyment and use. They did not need an income, he said. At least, not yet, he joked, but with the new farm regulations, restrictions, and ever-increasing taxes, they might just throw in the towel one of these days and go into the tourist business too. Of course, he was not serious, but it became more and more of a challenge to be profitable in the agricultural business. The nursery, offering special plants not easily available from ordinary nurseries, did exceedingly well on the other hand, Grandfather knew what he was doing, producing only the rarest and best, which was in demand all over the country now.

Claire had never made many friends in the village. The people had respect for her, even liked her to a degree, but she was not one of them. Many referred to her as the "Baroness of Waldegg," although she had never even once used such an image herself. They did not even call Peter "Baron," he was more of a country boy to them. This did not apply to the city-bred

Claire. She also had the bearing of being someone special, not a country girl. Claire was not aware of anything like that, but felt the reserve of the women throughout the time she lived at Waldegg. She could remember it also from St. Johann, although then it was for different reasons: she had been considered an intruder. She was friendly and kind to everyone, and wondered sometimes, why in return she was treated politely, but not cordially, by the locals. For instance, when she was shopping in town and approached a group of women who were in lively conversation, she noticed that they stopped talking, greeted her politely, smiling and commenting on the weather or something banal like that, but it was evident that they did not want to include her in their previous gossip. Not that Claire would have been interested in it, she just noticed the women's behavior. She talked to Peter about it, who put his arms comfortingly around her and told her not to pay attention. She was very special and the village folks, as nice as they were, just did not understand that. Claire was only halfway satisfied. She was sure that she was not special and had never been, but just had not assimilated enough of that certain local image. She could not talk in their vernacular, her educated speech patterns showed through even when she tried to be "folksy." Peter admonished her not to do that but to remain herself; she was just perfect in his eyes, and he continued in that vein to disperse her feelings of discomfort.

Paul had just entered the room, when he heard Peter talk about Claire being perfect. He smiled and said he fully agreed, whatever she was perfect in. Peter explained what they were talking about, and Paul said that he would agree with Peter: Claire was perfect! So the discussion ended on a humorous note.

Paul came often, and the three of them spent many evenings in animated conversations which they enjoyed equally. Not exactly equally. Paul would, of course, never reveal his deep love for Claire which had existed for such a long time. Way back, when she was sitting across from him at his desk in his office in Velden, he had not only been impressed by her writing ability, but had been magically drawn to her. Not that she was of exceptional beauty, but she had an aura that captured his heart. It had made him propose to her only a few months later, at Christmas, during an emotional time in their lives, although he knew almost nothing about her past. When she declined, confessing only "sisterly love" for him, he was not deterred, and repeated: "Claire, marry me" often afterwards, hoping that she would at some time relent. When Peter appeared on the scene, Paul was finally aware of the futility of his hopes. You can't just stop loving someone, he told himself, but you can learn to adjust to the inevitable. He had settled for friendship, and it was not difficult to include Peter for whom he had learned to have the greatest respect. It had been a wise decision that had allowed him to remain a part of Claire's and Peter's life even if it had differed from his dreams. His marriage to Melinda was full of tenderness and compassion, and he mourned her loss deeply. The Burghoff family, including the children, grandchildren and other relations, became his family, and they treasured that kind and generous man's affection with the same feelings for him.

Bishop Franz Hinterberger was also a very welcome guest at Peter and Claire's home, which they had named "House Elizabeth" in memory of a dear and emotional past. The bishop was especially close to Peter, with whom he shared so many childhood experiences, dating back to boarding school. If the female villagers kept themselves distant from the "Baroness," there were others, like Paul, who admired her greatly, and that was the case with the bishop also. When he was asked to perform the marriage ceremony for his friend Peter to that lovely young woman, Peter had told him what had happened between him and Claire in those perilous hours of the last state of the painful war. He was overwhelmed with compassion, and a sensation that he had not previously experienced. Having been a priest for many years, he had witnessed happiness and sadness—more of the latter in those years of turmoil, war, and death, but a feeling, unknown to him before, entered his heart. Compassion turned to love—a feeling that applied not only to his friend, but also to this young woman, and he had to struggle with that for all the years to come. He was a priest, loyal and devoted to the teachings of his church, and trained to defy temptations, even those that are just in one's mind. The church's teachings had an easy answer to his feelings: they were the work of the devil who would stop at nothing to gain possession of his soul. Franz did not accept that axiom. He was a honorable man, and the vows he had given to become a priest, a servant to the church he loved, were ingrained into him and he would always be true to them. Human emotions could be controlled by prayer and meditation, and he practiced these very often. Franz sometimes told Peter that he envied him, and Peter accepted such utterances as compliments, never sensing their true meaning. Claire never did either, Franz made sure of that. When they felt honored, as did the rest of the family, by the presence of "His Eminence," Franz was humbled just the same by the affection bestowed on him by these friends. Peter loved him as one could ever love a friend. Claire was more shy about her feelings towards him, being aware that Franz knew all her secrets; therefore, Franz had a special position in her heart, aside from her admiration for him.

Peter and Claire talked often as to how very pleased they were with the final outcome of their house. Every room was carefully furnished to fit its purpose and to provide the intended pleasures. For Peter, it seemed to be a peaceful retreat after a long days work, but he also enjoyed its comfortable luxury where he could relish undisturbed privacy with his beloved wife, listening to music, or just meditating. When friends, such as Paul or Franz or others whose company he liked, joined them, he truly appreciated the effort that Claire had put into making it a home to be proud of. Peter and Claire both felt equally that this home was finally the one that was truly their own, not in the sense of possession, but reflecting them, their taste, their personality. Claire, especially, remembered the days, when just a roof over her head was enough. When that roof became a house in St. Johann with enough room to have children join their life, but without real comforts, she still thought herself to be lucky and was content. When that functional domicile was exchanged for the elegant residence in Salzburg, supplied to the head of the hospital, it never became a home in the real sense, despite that they occupied it for nearly fifteen years. *They were tenants*, she always thought, and she had looked forward to the time when they would move to Waldegg and live in the "castle." That dream had not been realized, but better things had happened: their own, very private castle—just Peter and Claire living there happily forever and ever. Was it not a fairy-tale?

Their quiet privacy was occasionally interrupted by the laughter—sometimes cries also, of course—of a ever-growing bunch of little children. Burgl stopped by sometimes and Claire was glad to see her. When Paul was there, Peter and he left the ladies and went into the library, claiming they would probably like some privacy. Burgl often protested, but the men did not listen. Burgl's move back to Kammerbach had indeed other motives beside her being homesick for the playgrounds of her youth, before she got married to that Tiroler, Steinbrenner. Yes, she wanted to be near her aging parents, as well as near her daughter and grandchildren, but that was not all. When the Burghoffs went to the wedding of Tony and Inge in Neustift, they had also brought "Uncle Paul" along, whom Burgl found very charming. He was a widower. She too had lived alone for nearly ten years already. Burgl had been a good businesswomen, she was smart and aggressive and knew how to get what she wanted. She wanted to get to know Paul Thoene better. He must be tired of living alone, just as she was. She was financially well off, no one could accuse her of looking for a man to support her. She herself had much to offer, and not only financially. They were compatible in age, she considered herself good looking and in fine physical condition. So went her thoughts and even further. However, Paul Thoene did not seem to notice her efforts to seek his company, so she had to become more aggressive. She stopped by his house one summer evening, pretending to have taken a stroll along the lake. He was polite, and they sat for a while on his patio in the light of the early moon. His eyes glanced across the lake to the windows of "House Elizabeth" where the lights had been just turned on. Paul said lightly:

"It is getting dark, maybe we should turn in."

Burgl had hoped it would sound like an invitation to come inside, but his activities were more like taking leave of her. *Well*, she thought, *maybe next time*. A few days later she came with a freshly baked cake which he accepted hesitantly. Burgl said that he had liked the same cake before when he ate it at Waldegg, so she thought it might please him. Paul answered that he was pleased, of course, but his housekeeper, Frau Wagner, already spoiled him with too many sweets, and he had to watch his weight. He was friendly, but not exactly in the way Burgl would have hoped. She continued to seek his company and it started to annoy him. To avoid her, he stayed for days in his apartment in Salzburg, and Claire missed him at Waldegg. She told Peter, who happened to have to go to a medical meeting in Salzburg the next day. He called Paul there and asked if he would have lunch with him. Paul seemed eager to do so. After they enjoyed a fine goulash and a glass of beer, Peter asked Paul why they had not seen him lately. Paul was only too happy over the question, and said that Burgl had been seeking him out so often that it had become a nuisance, and he had sought relief in the city for a while. Peter could not help himself but laughing loudly over Burgl's naive attempts to lure Paul with her baking talents. Peter had known Burgl since their days in elementary school, and he had always liked her She was a good girl, rustic and simple minded, definitely not in Paul's class. Paul rejected Peter's notion that his social standing was above hers, but admitted he did not know how to handle a woman in whom he had not the slightest interest, but who he was bound to meet regularly on his visits to Waldegg. She had spoiled his joy in living on the lake and the visit to the friends he cherished. What should he do? Did Peter have some advice?

Peter had—but he told Paul to come right out and tell her so, or he would do it for him, because they missed Paul a lot at home. Paul promised. It was really silly that a man his age should need to hide from a pursuing female. Peter said:

"That comes from being so damned charming. Look at me—no woman is chasing me!"

"You are lucky, Peter," Paul said, and it contained a hidden meaning. He always called Peter lucky. When Peter told Claire the reason for Paul's absence, she was dismayed. How could Burgl be so foolish as to think that Paul could be interested in her? Claire felt almost jealous, and that was silly. When, a long time ago, Paul had written to her about his marriage to Melinda, she had hoped that he would be happy, just as she would have felt for a brother. When she met Melinda, she was glad to know that she was the right choice for Paul. But Burgl? However, was Burgl's daughter not good enough for her own precious son Tony? That was very different, Claire told herself. She became somewhat confused, she did not want to analyze her thinking further. The fact remained: we have to free Paul from that enamored lady! Claire did not think of it as being humorous as Peter had.

By the way, Burgl was not so insensitive as not to notice Paul's cool demeanor and short greeting when they met again. She went back to Neustift for the three following summer months to help her son with the business, and his wife with their new baby. During that time she met a visiting tourist from Germany who owned a sausage factory, had never been married, and who fell in love with the charming—and rich—widow from Tyrol. It was a happy ending, which shows that these can happen anywhere, if one just looks for them.

Chapter 32

Nineteen seventy-five was the year of Peter's sixty-fifth birthday, and Hanna urged him to make the transfer of Waldegg to his eldest son official. Peter had hesitated, thinking that Tony should be older before taking on all the legal responsibilities. Anton had not made him the official heir until he was fifty. Hanna said that those had been very different circumstances. Peter had not been actively working and gaining experience on the farm, while Tony had, and on top of that he had education in the field also. Did he not do an excellent job in managing all of Waldegg's affairs, including the tree and nursery business, to the extent that Peter had hardly ever had to interfere? Tony could continue to have his father's advice, but now, with children of his own and a wife who was also a farmer's descendant by birth and therefore well trained for her position—Peter noticed the hint in her voice, regarding Claire's background—Tony should be acknowledged as the "Esquire of Waldegg."

Peter talked it over with Claire. After all it concerned her also. Basically it would not change much, but Peter wanted to be sure that it was set up in a way to do justice to all of them. Inge had brought a substantial inheritance of her own into her marriage with Tony, however, that was all tied up in property, mostly land. Peter was willing to turn over the landholdings of Waldegg to Tony, but requested a share of the agricultural income, leaving Tony the rest. The other children had been endowed with trust funds, which would be increased by Peter and Claire's own estate holdings when they died. Peter wanted to make sure that Claire would have no financial obligations should he die before her, but instead be well provided for to live comfortably for the rest of her life. She had just recently inherited some money from her mother's estate, but he wanted to be certain that his estate would also contribute appropriately to her security.

He contacted Dr. Knoebel, his father's old attorney, who was most famil-iar with Waldegg's affairs, and asked him to draw up the necessary documents, to be presented at the family's birthday celebration for Peter. All were present, except Elizabeth. She sent congratulations to her father's birthday, but was not able to make the long journey for family reasons, claiming her little boys were too young, and she could not think of leaving them behind. She wrote seldom, Helmut had more frequent contact with his mother. From each letter it appeared that they were very happy in that new land, and were even planning to apply for citizenship. Claire was sad—she had foreseen that the parting could be for a long time. She longed to see her grandchildren, who, judging from the photos they sent, looked quite handsome curly-haired blondes, and were described as having blue eyes the shade of cornflowers. Claire knew those so well! When she suggested a journey abroad to see Elisabeth and her family, Peter did not want to hear about it. He did not ever say so, but his sorrow over his so much loved child and her denunciation of her parents, had never left him. Only once, he had remarked to Claire about Elizabeth:

"I think we loved her too much," to which Claire replied:

"Can one really ever love too much?" Peter apparently thought so.

The birthday celebration went on in the usual manner, but was high-lighted by Peter's announcement of Tony's succession and Hanna's forth-coming ninetieth birthday celebration. With the growing family, there seemed to be more and more birthdays to be celebrated, therefore they decided at a family council, that only those ending in zero or five would get special attention from now on, except for the younger children, of course. Now, Hanna's would be a great event, even though she had objected, con-sidering that her siblings were dead and there were barely a handful of her old friends still alive who could join in a birthday party. However, a couple of nieces and nephews from Tyrol, who were in their seventies themselves, showed interest in coming to honor her, so she gave in. She gave strict orders to the kitchen staff as to the food preparation for a couple of days of festivi-ties, told Inge what dishes to choose and how to set up the great hall for din-ing. Since they all insisted that her birthday was to be celebrated, she said, it had to be in the grand style—the best china, the best linen, silver, all the old treasures on display.

The mayor of Kammerbach had already announced the attendance of the village officials as well as the community band. Father Leutzinger, the successor to the previous village priest Father Grumbacher, also had a spe-cial program in mind, and when Bishop Franz Hinterberger offered his assis-tance, his excitement found no end. A performance of the Kammerbach's children's choir would be part of the program also and much more.

The closer the time came and the more preparations were in progress, the more Hanna grumbled about all the commotion. They—Eva was mostly responsible for that—had called the florist from St. Johann to inspect the house, so he could plan the floral decorations.

"What else? Maybe a merry-go-round and a clown for entertainment," Hanna said.

Peter was on her side, but once the floodgates had been opened, there was no stopping. Kammerbach and its citizens would honor the ninety-year-old matriarch of Waldegg as they felt to fit the occasion. Claire helped Hanna with her personal preparation; she was going to wear her old, silken, traditional dress, including the fancy headdress which Anton had once ordered to be made for her specially when they were invited to the arch-bishop's investiture. The archbishop had been born in a neighboring village and he and Anton had been childhood friends. Hanna's outfit had been cost-ly and splendid and she remembered being admired for it in those days. She wore it very seldom later on, especially since she grew in size through the years and could not fit into it anymore. However, in the last dozen years or so she had lost enough weight and she always thought it would be a very proper dress to be buried in, but it would now serve at her ninetieth birth-day party as well. Claire brought it out from storage. It was musty and the silk showed some breakdown in the folds, but it was still lovely, and careful professional cleaning would most likely restore it. Hanna also dug out her old jewelry that had been stored for so long, antique brooches, pendants, rings, bracelets. After the celebration she would turn it over to her daugh-ter-in-law, she told herself. She had no use for it anymore, the children should enjoy it. She had kept on with her life after Anton's death, she thought, but it was not the same. What good times she and Anton had when they were young, a good life, filled with love! Yes, she missed Anton very much, but soon they would meet again. She believed that firmly, and was looking forward to it.

A few months ago, Peter and Tony had suggested making it easier for Hanna by fixing one of the downstairs bedrooms for her, so she did not have to climb the stairs. Claire and Inge prepared it so that it was a comfortable sittingroom-bedroom combination, and Hanna was satisfied with it. However, on the day before the celebration, she gave that room over to one of the guests, and asked to be helped upstairs to her old bedroom. She said that she wanted to sleep with Anton that night in their old bed. Peter and Tony heard what she said, and were not sure if she meant it in jest, or if her mind had started to slip, but they helped her up the stairs, and Claire saw to it that she had everything. A long time ago they had installed an electric bell for them if they should need help. It had never been used, but Claire now pointed it out to Hanna again.

"Claire, turn off all the lights. I am tired. I am going to go to sleep now," Hanna said. Claire did as she was told, but as so often, she had premonitions, and later, at midnight, she wakened Peter to come with her to see if Hanna was all right.

"Of course, she is," Peter said, "she would use the bell if she needed something."

"She never did before, I don't think she trusts its electrical workings."

Claire was right—and so was Peter. Yes, Hanna should be looked after, and no—she did not need anything anymore! Hanna had gone to sleep with Anton, as she said she would!

The consternation of the congregated well-wishers can be imagined. Some had come from quite a distance to celebrate Hanna Burghoff's birthday. The florist was at work decorating, and some of the musicians had already come, before the sad news could reach any of them. After a quick consultation with Claire and Tony, Peter decided to ask everybody to stay on and celebrate the memory of Hanna, as she surely would have liked them to do. The intended congratulatory speeches needed very little change—they had been composed in praise of Hanna's lifelong achievements and were just as fitting as an eulogy. Food and drink were already prepared and could serve a wake just as well. The sadness of the occasion was soon overshadowed when friends and family members told happy and amusing stories of Hanna's life. She would be missed, but after all, she had a long and good life, was what most people attending the wake said.

Shortly after the funeral Dr. Knoebel asked the family to assemble for the reading of Hanna's will. She had dealt with distributing her estate in a fair manner, leaving the bulk of her investments to Peter. To Claire's great surprise, she was to take over the sawmill and receive the earnings from it until her death, when it would become part of Waldegg. Hanna had added that Claire had earned her special respect and was an exemplary wife to her beloved son Peter as well as a loving mother to her children. Eva, Tony, Chris, and Elizabeth; all were remembered with special bequests. She also did not forget to leave a substantial sum to the church of Kammerbach. Hanna had been a wealthy woman. Her absence from the household at Waldegg was felt for a long time, and the family as well as the servants talked about that. Everybody had always turned to her for advice and direction. Peter missed his early breakfasts with his mother, but even more the loving attention she had always bestowed on him.

The Burghoffs added a number of new members to their ranks in the following year. Gretchen was born to Tony and Inge, Lilly to Eva and William, and the twins Tessa and Christina to Christopher and Renate. Four little girls: it seemed that Hanna had exercised some influence from the heavens to even out the distribution of females in the family. That is what some folks said. Claire had her hands full as a grandmother also. Peter's contribution was more in good advice than in hands-on help. He enjoyed a visit with the babies, but was not the cooing type. He shook his head when observing his friend Paul cuddling the gurgling infants. Paul enjoyed every minute of it, it did not seem to matter to him that they were not his own, though the family considered him as their very own, and he responded with much loving attention.

Chapter 33

The following years passed in relative tranquility for Peter and Claire. They enjoyed their home, their family, their friends, the seasons, but most of all, they enjoyed each other. Peter continued to care for Waldegg, kept his surgery-consulting job at the hospital also, enjoyed shop talk with his son Chris on his visits to Waldegg, and also with his son-in-law Wilhelm. Claire liked to work in her garden, or to visit Eva. Paul had again encouraged her to continue with her writing and was of valuable assistance in that respect.

After the birth of the youngest of the four girls to the family, there seemed to be a pause in the proliferation of the Burghoffs. Peter commented that it was good for the sake of the world's threatening overpopulation, but Inge warned him that she and Tony still had plans. They heard less from Elizabeth since Helmut had now moved his family to Australia, where he had bought a sheep farm; he reported extraordinary things about the extent of their holdings, which were to be counted in thousands of sheep. Elizabeth had mentioned that the scenery was disappointing, lots of dust with a constant danger of drought, and when it finally rained, the mud was unbelievable. They were very happy, the family thrived, and their life was a good one.

One day Claire met Fritz Engebrecht when she was shopping in Kammerbach, and he was somewhat friendlier than he used to be and talked mostly about the children. He did not criticize Helmut, as he had done when his son was younger, and he seemed more relaxed in general than she ever remembered him. He could not, however, refrain from saying again how his life had mostly been unfair, and even now in his old age he had been deprived of another pleasure, namely of seeing his grandchildren grow up. Claire reminded him that there had been many lucky happenings for him also, he just forgot to count his blessings. When she said that, he looked at her with such a sad smile that she felt embarrassed and sorry. After all, one cannot tell somebody that he should be happy if there is no joy in his heart.

Knowing that Peter had no special fondness for Fritz, she did not mention their meeting until a few weeks later, when the notice of his passing was received. He had died of a severe heart attack; Gerda told them that he had been ill for a while. Claire had difficulty in persuading Peter to attend the funeral, but then he finally saw how improper it would be to stay away and he made his appearance at the church services. Helmut could not arrive in time due to difficult air travel connections, but he stayed with his mother afterwards for a few days to help her settle affairs. On that occasion he visited Waldegg and brought greetings and detailed information about his family back home in Australia. He looked exceedingly well, handsomer than ever, Claire thought, grown in stature, with tanned features under the curly blond mane, quite a "hunk," as some would say. His demeanor was that of a serious family man, proud of his accomplishments and self-assured. Peter and Tony asked many questions about farming in Australia, and Peter was delighted to hear Helmut's knowledgeable assessments. Tony said jokingly if the state of agriculture in Austria continued to make it hard for the farmers, he might join his brother-in-law in Australia one of these days.

"Without me and the children, of course," said Inge.

Helmut mentioned that Elizabeth had adjusted very well and that she was a remarkable homemaker; she also managed to bring a lovely rose garden to life even in the desert. Claire was so happy, she could hardly contain herself, and Peter also smiled all the time.

Gerda's daughter Ingrid offered her mother a home with her in the city of Salzburg, but Gerda had other plans. There was not much money in Fritz's estate, but a pension from his school director's job would suffice to keep her modest lifestyle intact. She had always been the enterprising one in the family, and had a plan again, this time just for herself. She found a small shop in Kammerbach, and—having acquired some knowledge in that field—set up a business dealing in antiques, small items at first, including art treasures she found in the countryside: paintings, a spinning wheel, and similar things. She told Claire that her life was filled with excitement, and she was content. Claire had always liked Gerda, even in the olden days when they were supposedly competing for attention at the beach in Kammerbach, but now she appreciated her even more, since she was also the grandmother of some of the Burghoff's descendants. Helmut had inherited his mother's traits, she thought, and wondered how the grandchildren they had in common would do in life.

The following years continued to be good times for Peter and Claire. Freed from many of the old responsibilities and with time to enjoy their various inclinations, Peter listened to his favorite music for hours, went fishing with Paul, and mountain climbing with Franz and a few other friends.

Claire's garden grew well, to the delight of all who stopped to smell her roses, and her writing became almost an obsession when the weather kept her indoors. It went especially well while listening to Peter's music selections of Mozart, Schubert, and many other classical pieces on the stereo.

Paul was always available to both his friends with encouragement for Peter's music and Claire's writing. Claire and Peter roamed through their beloved countryside regularly, sometimes in the company of one or two of their friends, and often took excursions by car to events in the big cities. Vienna was, of course, the main attraction, although Claire was not as emotionally attached to the city as Peter thought. Not all the memories of that time in her life had been happy ones.

Christopher and Renate had professional success, and their family life seemed to be quite congenial since the girls were normal and healthy. There was a time when it had worried their grandparents that Renate had decided to continue her professional life a couple of years after the twin's birth, with Christopher's approval. Renate had a good reputation as psychologist, and did not want to give up her practice. A nanny was hired to take care of the two little wildcats, as they were called then. In reality they were two very spoiled infants, who topped the usual reputation for that period called "the terrible twos." Renate had her professional ideas about raising children which differed one hundred eighty degrees from the one practiced by previous generations, where "children should be seen, but not heard." Renate practiced permissiveness to the extreme, convinced that to raise children to become well adjusted, happy adults, they had to be given all the freedom to make their own choices. Peter and Claire were aghast, but since Christopher fully agreed with his wife's psychological arguments, they abstained from criticism. Renate's mother shared Claire's opinion, by the way, and that brought her and the senior Burghoffs closer, resulting in a very cordial relationship between them.

When Tessa and Chrissy were about four years old, and several nannies later, on one of his visits to Waldegg Christopher finally came to the conclusion that Tony's Gretchen and Eva's Lilly, the same age as his twins, were happy, uninhibited little girls in contrast to his wildcats, and he asked if Inge would consider letting his children visit them during the summer months. He and Renate were beginning to be concerned that the twins were not well enough adjusted for kindergarten the next year. They thought that country air and the freedom they enjoyed at Waldegg would be beneficial to them, whereas in the city they had only occasional strolls to the park to let them enjoy nature. Inge hesitated for a moment, but her usual friendliness overcame her doubts and she consented under certain conditions. The main one was that the twins would be treated in the same way as her own children, had to listen when told to behave, and would be punished for infractions. Renate said they would, of course send a Nanny along to help take care of the girls. Inge said no to that. She had help with the children from a young woman from Kammerbach, who was very good with them. Tony added that she seemed to be like Luise in her young years, who had taken care of Peter and his brother Hans. Luise was long gone, of course, but her memory was still alive for Tony and Chris. Renate had some misgivings, but Chris convinced her that the girls would survive.

They did indeed; after some temper tantrums, which to their surprise were ignored, they adjusted rather nicely, and by the end of the summer they did not even want to go home. Another year, another summer, and they were ready to enter school, only now being called the twins instead of the wildcats.

On one of their travels, Peter and Claire visited the Woerners in Nuremberg, who had previously come to Waldegg several times, but had been missed lately due to Georg's health. It was not the hoped-for happy reunion because of Georg's plight with Parkinson's disease. He suffered with the limitations it put on him and Lieschen told them privately that he really felt degraded by the loss of function. He could not hold a cup of tea or spoon his soup without spilling it. It made him resent the situation and he was angry most of the time. Nevertheless, he told Peter—who had heard it before— that Claire was very special, and if he had not already been married way back when she first came to his office, he would certainly have married her. Lieschen just laughed about it, saying:

"Why do you think she would have wanted you?" to which Georg had no answer. Well, it only showed that they had not forgotten Claire and the good times before that dreadful war!

The Woerners were about ten years older than Claire, and this visit made her think about their own aging. Both she and Peter had been fortunate to have been healthy all their lives and they were still in good physical and mental condition, but eventually they would have to consider the inevitable. Not yet, she said quickly to herself. They still enjoyed their life and each other in all its aspects.

Just around Peter's seventy-fifth birthday, they had a surprise visit from Australia. Helmut had mentioned before that he had promised Siegfried a trip to Europe after his graduation from boarding school in Sydney. The slender young man of eighteen with shoulder-length curly blond hair and lovely blue eyes, showed up one time, unannounced, but to everybody's delight. The only problem was that he did not speak any German, and only Tony, Chris, and the older Burghoff boys, Karl and Hans, had some background in English learned at school. Nevertheless, there was communication, translation, and interpretation, and Siegfried was inundated with questions. He was a friendly and very likable young man; "very handsome" were the female's comments, but Grandfather Peter was shocked by his appearance, referring mostly to his hair and his blue jeans with holes at the knees, and a tee shirt with some weird pictures of wild looking rock stars on it. He told Claire to buy some decent clothing for the fellow. Claire laughed. She was more informed than Peter about young people's dress codes these days. Siegfried had indeed the proper wardrobe for his plan to join his idols. When he said that music was his main interest, Peter asked what he liked. Not having heard the names that Siegfried listed, he asked about Mozart, Beethoven, Brahms—Siegfried hesitated with an answer at thinking they were friends of his grandfather.

Siegfried could stay but a few days, after which he wanted to see Vienna, and then go back to London, where he had an introduction to meet some rock musicians. Paul, who listened to all of Siegfried's stories, and was a main translator since he was fluent in English, offered to take him to Vienna and make him familiar with the music scene there. So, after a few days of excitement over the visitor from "down under," they left. Peter confessed he was very disappointed to see a possible talent go to waste, Claire was less concerned about that. She would have loved to keep that lovable sweet boy here forever. He reminded her so much of...yes, sweet, lovable Elizabeth.

Chapter 34

I was a hot and muggy summer Sunday afternoon. Heavy dark clouds looked threatening between the mountain peaks, a storm had been brewing for several hours, but did not seem to break. Peter and Claire walked along the path between Waldegg's wall and the gully which extended further into the fenced-in pasture for the horses. They heard behind them the ringing of a bicycle bell and, turning around, saw their grandson Karl racing towards them, calling out:

"Hello—Grandpa, Grandma...beware, the storm is coming, you had better turn back."

Peter smiled proudly, looking after that handsome, strapping next-in-line of the Burghoffs.

"How dear he is to be concerned about us," said Claire.

"Yes, they are fine specimens, these three boys," said Peter, and added quickly with a smile:

"And, of course, Gretchen too."

At that moment he noticed his horse, Zeus, still grazing in the meadow, when it should have been in its box at the stable. He told Claire to heed Karl's advice and go back, while he would look after the horse. Claire watched him as he jumped down the incline and climbed over the fence. "Agile as ever, he has not aged in forty years," she said to herself, smiling while turning towards their house. The first heavy drops fell as she was entering. "He'll get wet," were her thoughts, as she rushed to close all the windows. She should have done it before; a strong wind made it difficult and a thunderous, deafening bolt of lightning nearly caught her off balance. "That was close," she said, seeing the storm unfurl through her bedroom window.

Claire usually liked to watch thunderstorms, they seemed to release the tension in the air, and the aftermath was as if nature had taken a cleansing and refreshing shower; everything smelled so fresh and aromatic. Now she wished that Peter had returned. He had probably taken shelter with his horse and was waiting for the downpour to subside. One hour passed, the rain was only a trickle now, but Peter had not come in. He was most likely attending to Zeus, because today, Sunday, not many of the stable hands were around. When she became uneasy, she threw her raincoat on and ran to the main house, where she found Tony and Inge in the kitchen. Tony said not to worry, his father was probably checking if doors and windows down at the stable were closed. After another while, he also put on raingear and went out to check for himself, and Claire went back to her house. Within the next half-hour she heard the sirens of the fire department, and the pit in her stomach grew bigger. When Tony entered, his face chalk white, she stood up, trembling, sensing bad news. Tony himself was shaking, but he went towards his mother, putting his arms around her, saying:

"Mother, you have to be strong."

"Tony—is your father...hurt?" she stammered.

"Yes, father is..." he could not continue, but his face said it all

"No, no, no—he is not..." and Claire fainted.

In the meantime the village doctor arrived, and the captain from the fire department, and tearful Inge telephoned all who had to be informed. When Claire gained consciousness, she screamed that she wanted to see Peter, but was gently held back by the doctor.

"Later," he said, but she became angry.

"Now! I have to be with Peter."

"Mother, they had to take him away." Tony tried to calm her, but was barely in control himself. Claire started to cry uncontrollably, and Dr. Maurer found it necessary to sedate her. When Eva and William arrived a couple of hours later, she was half-asleep, and they put her to bed. Then they talked about the terrible accident that had caused Peter's untimely death. He had reached his horse just when the first lightning bolt struck—and it had struck him directly. He had been killed instantly; the horse was badly burned and had to be shot by the fire department people. Peter was burned beyond recognition, and they took him to the morgue immediately.

The news of such tragedy striking Waldegg spread quickly, and nearly the whole community went teary-eyed to bed that night. Christopher arrived on the last train, and the family gathered at Claire's house, all in great pain over the loss of their father, but mostly concerned as how to deal with Claire. The bishop came, and so did Paul, and nobody was hiding their tears. Eva stayed with Claire in her bedroom, in case she awakened. Tranquilizers should be used only sparingly, Claire's pain would have to heal naturally. That was rhetorical, medical advice. Claire's pain did not heal quickly. She could not be prevented from crying incessantly, her body shaking to exhaustion.

Eva could not persuade her to make personal preparations for the funeral, she refused to make any decisions at all. With Eva's help and a dose of tranquilizers she finally summoned enough strength—mostly half unconscious—to attend the church service. People came from far and wide to attend, not only those from the nearby communities, but also from St. Johann, Salzburg, and Vienna, wherever Dr. Peter Burghoff was known. The flowers were mountainous, the music during the services performed by a symphonic contingent from Salzburg. Bishop Franz, who had known the deceased longer than anybody else present, gave the eulogy in an emotional show of grief for his dear friend. Claire attended, stony faced under her black veil, giving some of the ever-present busybodies reason to call her the coldhearted baroness, despite the stories told in the village by some of Waldegg's service people, that Claire Burghoff was grief-stricken and under medical care. Tony, Christopher, and Eva were aware that the funeral had developed into a grand affair, although it was not of their own doing. They knew their father would have shunned such public display, but it could not be prevented, considering Peter's social standing. Most people were impressed. People in the country love a lavish funeral and would spend their life's savings to be assured the best one they could get. Claire was oblivious to most that surrounded her. She felt good about the music—it was Peter's music—but her mind was numb. She did not, and could not, think and acted only automatically.

After the services there was a gathering of friends and others who had traveled from afar at the two hotels in town, and the usual wake continued there. The Burghoffs went home. Claire went to bed, where she stayed, refusing nourishment or company for many days. At first, the family accepted her wishes, but soon it became obvious that Claire could not go on in that fashion without endangering her own health. She did not eat, did not speak, ignored all who implored her to regain her composure. The medical team that was consulted did not want to make predictions, but felt that Claire had lost her will to live. They suggested she be constantly attended by a nurse and also by her family. Eva spent two days a week with her mother, and so did Paul, Franz, and the household of Tony.

Christopher came from Vienna as often as possible. Claire's continued refusal to eat—she only took sips of cold tea—and speak and her apparent physical decline became of grave concern, and after a while Christopher saw the urgent need to find an outside specialist to help deal with his mother's situation. He consulted Dr. Murgl, a psychiatrist from the clinic in Salzburg who had been an associate physician at the hospital when Peter was the

Primarius there. Dr. Murgl, not being a family member and with no emotional ties, would be able to give an unbiased diagnosis. He approached Claire, who did not acknowledge him at all—he thought she was too weak for that. She allowed him to take the usual vital statistics; however, she remained completely uninterested. Blood pressure and heart rate were dangerously low. Dr. Murgl sat back and said nothing for a while. Then he talked to Claire in a serious but cool manner about his findings. He expressed his sympathy for her loss. Peter's departure was painful to many, but, of course her grief for him could not be compared and no one should suggest otherwise or deprive her of expressing it. However, did she think Peter would have approved of her obvious refusal to keep on living? Was she not acting very selfishly? Did she not consider the pain she heaped upon her family over and above their own suffering and grief for their father? He told her that on his way in that day he had met a little girl outside her door, who, her deep blue eyes imploringly searching his, asked, "Please, doctor, make Grandmother well again."

"I promised to do the best I could, but, Mrs. Burghoff, this is up to you. I cannot do it by myself. The nature of your illness lies deep within your soul. I can show you the way you need to follow, but you have to go it on your own."

Claire had gazed past the doctor and he did not know if she had listened at all. Still after mentioning the child's plea, Dr. Murgl saw a little tear run down Claire's cheek, a hopeful sign that he had struck a nerve, although she did not say a word. He continued:

"Of course, there are things we could do to prevent your further physical decline, and I will propose these to your family. We shall order your transfer to the hospital in Salzburg, where you will be fed intravenously for as long as you refuse to take food the normal way. It may help to make you feel stronger, but I believe that mending your soul will have to be your own decision. Consider what Peter would want you to do—I believe he should be your inspiration. I will talk to your sons, goodbye, Mrs. Burghoff."

When Eva came back later, Claire asked her pleadingly:

"No hospital, please, I will try," and from then on she took little bits of this and that, some soup, toast, tea, very sparingly, but at least she tried. She still did not say much, because whenever she tried to say something, she began to cry.

Franz and Paul took turns to be with her, reading to her, or talking quietly. They were tireless in caring for their friend, a woman they both adored, yet could not find ways to soothe her pain. She looked so frail, buried in her pillows, a shadow of her former lovely womanly appearance. Only slowly she improved. Was it the threat of hospitalization or Dr. Murgl's reminder of what Peter would want her to do? His admonition had some results. She did get up from her bed for short stays in her old rocking chair, but she was easily exhausted. Christopher still saw it as an improvement of her condition.

It was December and Christmas was near. The family was still subdued, but for the children's sake some of the old preparations were made. Claire did not know of it. She looked out of her window one stormy, dreary day, saw the trees bare of leaves, and shivered, although there was a nice fire in the fireplace. The nurse had left, and Claire waited for Inge's kitchen-maid to bring her hot chocolate, as she had done recently when Claire's visitors were expected. Claire began to look forward to that, barely being aware that she did so. The bishop was late today. The weather was miserable; it would not keep him from coming? Claire went to the window and looked down the road, but could not see any approaching car. Marie had come with the tray of hot chocolate and a plate of freshly baked cookies and left. Just then she heard footsteps coming up the stairs and a knock on the door. Franz had arrived. Claire was still standing at the window, and he was surprised. He came towards her and, as usual, took her hand to kiss it. While he bowed his head, she stroked his hair, and said softly:

"You are late, I feared you would not come."

Franz was moved—it was the first time that she had reacted to his coming, and in such a tender way. He took her arm and guided her to the sofa, where they sat down and he poured the chocolate into her cup.

"I am sorry that I was late today—but not coming? These visits here with you are the most precious moments of my otherwise lonely existence, you should know that."

Claire said nothing, but tears came into her eyes, and then she whispered: "I have been so ungrateful—to you, and everybody else, I am so sorry."

"Just get well, dearest Claire, you know how we love you."

He wanted to say: "How I love you," but that he did not dare. They were sitting watching the flames in the fireplace, nothing further was said. It was cozy and warm in here, while the wind howled outside. Then Marie came again to pick up the tray, asking if anything else was needed. There was not, it was peaceful and soothingly quiet, and when the time came for the bishop to leave, she said:

"Thank you for understanding, my dear friend."

Claire felt an unexpected desire to be well again, and to be part of her family. All of a sudden she missed seeing her grandchildren. No, the pain in her heart would never go away, but she would have to learn to live with it. Peter would want that, and God in his grace had surrounded her with people who loved her to help her fulfill his wishes.

Here, the story of Claire could properly end. But since her life continued to be of importance to others as well, we'll still follow it for while.

Chapter 35

Christmas without Peter was difficult, but Claire thought of those before her. Hanna had surely missed Anton the same way, yet she had not let her sorrow spoil the joys of the season for the others around her. Claire could do no less. She helped Inge with preparations as long as her strength held up, practiced Christmas songs with the children, playing the piano for them. Uncle Paul joined them there frequently. He had brought a collection of songs from other countries; they wanted to include the foreign workers they now had at the farm in their celebrations this year. Some were from Greece, some from Turkey and the Balkans. The children were delighted that all these countries knew "Silent Night" in their own language, and therefore they mostly practiced that beloved Christmas carol.

Christmas Eve was therefore not much different this year at Waldegg than before, except in Claire's heart. It was difficult for her to try to be as joyful as this holiday demanded. Of all the children, it was Karl Anton whom she saw often wistfully looking at her. He sensed her grief and that moved her greatly. That boy grew more and more in the image of his grandfather Peter, she observed with great warmth.

Her own children were occupied with their offspring, but gentle Paul was always there, trying to provide her with comfort and support in his quiet way. *Dear, dear Paul*, Claire thought. *How fortunate am I to have a friend like him. I am lonely without Peter, but I am not alone. Paul knows how I feel.*

The months passed into a new year, and Claire learned to cope. She involved herself in many projects, writing was one of her favorites. It went well, especially since Paul was so encouraging. She hoped that his evaluation of her talent was strictly professional, and not due to his devotion as her friend, but time would tell.

Eva was of great help and support to her in many ways. She was not only a daughter but her mother's true friend, and she accompanied her when shopping in the city, or to social or business meetings. Claire visited Gerda, who appreciated her advice in the acquisition and sale of her antiques. Yes, she also had fun on the occasion of Burgl's visit with her new husband, the sausage maker from Bavaria. Burgl had hit it right, she was very happy and sparkled in her new role. They had brought several baskets filled with samples of all the varieties of sausages, all with the name of "Josef Sauerbrunner's Finest" imprinted on their casings, and indeed, they were excellent, as you would expect from a fine Bavarian sausage maker. His business was booming, and Burgl, the experienced manager, was contributing much to Sauerbrunner's enterprise.

One day, over coffee, Burgl confided to Claire:

"You never knew that at one time I had my eyes on Paul Thoene, but fortunately I caught myself quickly enough to realize that I had nothing in common with that man. He is certainly nice, and all that, but not my type at all. He can look sincere like a puppy dog, but there is no passion in that man."

Burgl went on in that vein for a while, and Claire could hardly contain herself from laughing out loud. She said, referring only to Burgl's puppy dog comparison:

"I would not call him that—more like a well bred setter with an elegant coat and those eyes which say that they believe in you unconditionally."

"Well yes, but I am glad nevertheless to have seen the light in time, although it would have been nice to live near all of you. But we are not that far away, it's only two hours drive to Munich, and we are living in Gruenewald, a lovely suburb. I hope you will come to visit us."

"Yes, I would like that," said Claire. Then Burgl mentioned Peter, and the conversation trailed off, because it became too painful.

Burgl had turned the house in Kammerbach which she had once purchased into a tourist *pension*, and it was doing well. Burgl had certain talents, that was evident.

Claire told Paul about her conversation with her, and they both had a good laugh, but she left out the puppy dog comparison. Paul was only too happy to see that Claire had regained much of her old ways. She had always had a good sense of humor, and it was refreshing to see it return.

Later that spring, Paul fell ill, first with a bad cold, which then turned into a case of pneumonia. Claire was beside herself when the doctor told her it was serious. She insisted on taking care of him, and stayed with him during the crucial times day and night. Paul recovered, but it took a while before he regained his strength, during which time Claire tended to him with much care and affection, just as he had shown towards her during her illness. It caused, of course, some tongue wagging in Kammerbach, despite Frau

Wagner's, Paul's housekeeper, assurance that there was no reason for it. What would village life be if gossip could not spice it up a little? Especially when it concerned outsiders. Paul Thoene was definitely one, and the baroness too. Her living in the province for forty years or more did not matter. Someone even thought the two had known each other before she married Peter Burghoff, rest his soul. The subjects of the gossip did not know anything about it, which is often the case. It would not have mattered.

When Paul was feeling better, his visits to Waldegg became more regular again to the children's delight. He had an uncanny way of communicating with youngsters, awakening their interest in the world around them, be it music, literature, or science, Paul knew enough in nearly every subject, and they even bragged to their friends in school of having an uncle who knew "just about everything."

Paul and Claire's relationship with the bishop had changed somewhat since Peter's death by not having the previous get-togethers at "House Elizabeth." Peter was missed, and the evenings of music and conversations just did not seem to come together as they once did. Franz came to see Claire, and sometimes she drove to Salzburg to meet him there. She always felt strengthened in her spirits after these visits, not that the churchman preached or prayed with her. There was communication on a different level which was not definable They often attended services at the Dome, hearing an inspiring sermon or a fine concert, or they would walk through the Mirabell Garden, smelling the roses, listening to the birds singing —not much needed to be said between them. It was peace and comfort to both.

They were not aware of being observed by the curious Salzburgers, sitting on the park benches along the walkways every afternoon, as was these elderly women's regular habit and recreation. They found pleasure in their idle gossip and excitement when it dealt with the celebrities who were visiting Salzburg regularly in the summer months and during the festival season. And all, of course, knew the old bishop, who had always been well liked. Some said they also remembered the lady, a doctor's wife who had often strolled through the park in her younger years.

The history of Salzburg was combined with the history of the church for hundreds of years. Its bishops reigned, sometimes with, sometimes without approval of the secular powers. Some of them were saints, such as St. Bonifacius, or St. Virgil in the eighth century. Some were of princely rank and often ruled in the capacity of worldly rulers. The importance of all of them to the country, the church, and to the culture of the region—good or bad—was very remarkable.

As it is with many people, these Salzburger matrons at the Mirabell Garden did not know all of the history of their beloved city, but they knew that it was the Archbishop Wolf Dietrich von Raitenau (1587), a typical

Renaissance Prince with great ambitions, who had charged the Italian architect Scamozzi with the construction of a cathedral to be bigger than St. Peter's in Rome. At the same time the archbishop commissioned the building of the Mirabell Palace for his mistress, Salome Alt, by whom he had twelve children. For financial reasons the size of the church was later reduced, but other palaces, such as the Bishop's Palace and other churches were built. The Mirabell Garden was added at the beginning of the eighteenth century, and it enchants visitors to this day with its fountains, statues, and landscape, a truly lovely place to spend some time sitting in the shadows of the old tress or strolling among its manicured lawns and carefully tended flower beds. Was their bishop following in the footsteps of his predecessors as far as their liaisons with the ladies were concerned?

"Don't be silly," said Frau Gruber, "the bishop is an old man."

Frau Kretchmayer said:

"Well, I don't know—did you read that interesting article in the *Salzburger Nachrichten* the other day, that old age is no obstacle to romance?"

"But that does not go for Bishop Hinterberger, he always had such a solid reputation, not like Father Kleinschmitt—you remember him?"

The ladies laughed, recalling the stories, people used to tell, saying they knew where the Father had spent the night. His trusted dog would wait for him at the doorstep of that particular home, where he apparently dispensed good will and heavenly blessings.

One of the younger ladies added with some admiration of the bishop's companion:

"The woman is pretty enough for any man to fall in love, don't you think so?"

"Yes," said Frau Gruber, "and it is also true that 'there if no fool like an old fool.'"

They continued with their speculations, not in a mean spirit, just passing time in pleasant idle talk. Another couple walking by would be next in line for their scrutiny.

The bishop and Claire did not know of the ladies' speculations, but even if they had, they would not have paid attention. They enjoyed their visits together to that lovely place, smelled the fragrant flowers, and occasionally even held hands—two old friends, feeling comfort in each other's company.

Another year passed with relatively little change in Claire's life. She had passed her seventieth birthday without much fanfare, on her insistence. She did not care to be reminded of birthdays past and present, nor was she concerned about her age at all. She was healthy, felt fine, and took care of herself, enjoying some of the luxuries she had frowned upon when she was younger. She joined exercise classes, let Paul teach her the art of sailing on his boat, had body massages and manicures in Salzburg, had her hair done at an exclusive salon there, but rejected the recommended hair coloring. She liked her gray hair, it suited her. She had no desire to look younger, she just wanted to be satisfied with her appearance. Vanity was foreign to her personality. She chose her clothing with care, she could afford the best, but was never excessive in any purchase.

Eva was more than ever in awe of her mother's dignity. In her opinion, if any of the Burghoffs deserved the description "aristocratic," it should be Claire. Her father had been rightfully proud of his wife in every respect. Was it a tragedy that their life together ended prematurely, or was it a fitting finality to an ultimate relationship?

Sometime in early April Franz mentioned to Paul and Claire that he had been told by a member of his church council about an interesting tour to Spain for the study of churches. The tour was conducted by a professor from the University of Heidelberg, and Franz's colleague had been highly impressed when he attended the year before. Franz said that he planned to participate this year and suggested that Paul and Claire join him. Paul had an important meeting of publishers in London scheduled at the same time and regretted he could not attend. Claire also hesitated.

"Going to church daily for three weeks is probably more than I can endure," she said, but Franz explained that it was not a religious excursion. It was mainly for the study of the architecture of these churches, many of which had their origin in, or were built upon the remnants of, mosques, dating from the time when the Arabs had conquered and occupied these lands. Franz was interested in the historical aspects. Claire's interest was stimulated, but she could not decide until Paul and her family tried to persuade her.

"It would do you good, Mother," said her children, "You need some change in your daily routine. The month of May should be a great time for a visit to Spain."

Yes, she thought with sadness, *just as it was in Italy and Greece, so many years ago.*

Franz brought the travel brochure, and she finally agreed to join him. The group was limited to twenty people; they would travel by bus, all arrangements were made in advance. Franz found out that most participants were mature individuals, professors, architects, some retired; a few came as couples, others were single like Claire and Franz. It sounded better and better, and Claire was looking forward to that journey more and more.

It was indeed a well planned tour, conducted by a lecturer who was very knowledgeable in church history, but more people in the group seemed to be interested in the human history of all the sites they visited, and gathered around the bishop, who was an expert on that subject.

Salzburg has a great number of churches, many in baroque style such as the Dome, but also in gothic style. However, they could not compare with the myriad of churches in all major and minor towns throughout Spain.

They came in many styles, some of which Claire did not appreciate, but she was in a minority with her judgment. The architects in the group marveled about almost everything, and she noticed that some people just mimicked the opinion of those who they thought were experts on everything. She called them "intellectual snobs," the bishop called them-people who needed attention," and he was willing to divide his evenly.

Claire probably felt somewhat neglected, but more than that, she was getting tired of the daily excursions; they were strenuous. The bishop, who had been besieged day-in, day-out by those who took advantage of his patience—as Claire saw it—admitted himself to be fatigued also. Occasionally the tour leader left an afternoon free of guided trips, and Claire and Franz took the occasion to sit leisurely in a park, watch the people, and cool themselves near one of the many lovely fountains, to just relax, before they gathered with their group again at the evening meal. Claire admitted that she missed her home very much. The itinerary also included a two-day visit to Morocco, to provide the group with a break in their routine, and everybody was looking forward to that. Claire and Franz and another elderly scholar decided to forgo that visit and stay in town. They watched the others board the ship for the crossing, and then returned to the hotel. Claire decided to take care of some personal needs, neglected during the somewhat hectic schedule, went to the beauty shop and later would meet Franz for lunch.

It was so nice to be alone, she thought; alone, of course, meant including Franz. She was weary of all the people whose endless chatter was at times annoying. She said to Franz that the meal shared with him alone was so much more pleasurable than the group dining, and Franz said he was glad that she found his company to her liking. They then took a siesta during the next couple hours, when the southern sun was beating down, and decided later to take a walk along the cliff shore of the Mediterranean, where the gentle breeze brought comforting relief from the heat of the afternoon. This was wonderful, and a calm of mind and a soothing serenity settled over Claire. Franz also loved the quietness, but more than that, he felt how happy Claire's company made him. He looked at her and remembered the day when he first met her, when she stood before him and he had married her to his friend Peter. Her sincere loveliness tugged at his heart then, and it grew, but he had kept his feelings buried deep within his soul.

He looked at her face and, as always, was captivated by its beauty. Fine lines and creases at the corners of her eyes and of her lovely mouth had added a charm of maturity which made her doubly desirable. After all those years of denial and longing in his heart, he could now touch her hand without qualm or fear of impropriety; he did not have to pray lest he forget his vows or worse, betray a friend.

Such scruples had never affected Claire. She never had any thoughts of other men but Peter. However, her loneliness since his death was very difficult to bear, and she felt so very comforted by the nearness of the man she so greatly admired. They were sitting on a bench, looking out over the sea, watching the seagulls. Franz put his arms around her shoulders, and she leaned her head against his chest. It was strange to hear his heartbeat—she had never heard another men's heart pumping but Peter's, and she had to smile at herself over her wonderment. How silly.

Out of nowhere, a little kitten jumped upon the bench they were sitting on and, as these felines are prone to do, snuggled up first to Claire, then inspected Franz's lap, where she decided that it was a comfy place to rest. It was an adorable creature, and Franz patted its soft fur tenderly. Claire watched in amusement and noticed, as if for the first time, the remarkably fine shape of this man's hands, now cuddling the kitten between them. She wondered why she had never consciously seen these hands. How many times in all these years had she shaken them, had seen them in church holding a chalice or a monstrance, watched him play the violin at their home and heard only the sounds of the instrument which he played so skillfully and with such emotion? How come she never noticed these hands just by themselves? She felt a desire to touch them, and felt almost envious to see them caress that little kitten who started to purr contentedly.

Claire suddenly felt a cool breeze and shivered in her light dress. Franz suggested that they return to the hotel before she caught cold. Neither of them was hungry, and they decided to skip supper. Claire went to her room, decided to take a shower and then finish reading the novel on her bedside table. Returning from the bathroom, she slipped into her robe, actually an old silk kimono that had seen better days, but since the tour guide had suggested they travel light, she had found it most suitable to tuck into the suitcase. She felt refreshed now and settled down into the comfortable lounge chair to read, before turning in for the night. However, she could not concentrate on her reading. From somewhere in the distance she could hear a guitar playing a Spanish rhythm, and then a man's voice softly singing an accompanying melody. Claire felt restless, lonely, and wished the tour would end and she could go home. She had been away more than two weeks and suddenly felt homesick. Of course, she would stick it out, just like all the others. Recognizing that did not make her feel any better. Then there was a knock at the door and she heard Franz's voice calling her name. She opened the door, and he asked if she had possibly changed her mind about supper. She invited him to come in, but said she was not in the mood for food, however a cool drink and his company would be very welcome.

"You will have both in an instant. Let me call room service. Would a pitcher of Sangria be all right?"

They had tasted that Spanish concoction of fruit and wine several times during their tour, and found it rather enjoyable.

"Yes, very much so. And now excuse my appearance, I had not expected a visitor. I will change quickly while you wait on the balcony."

"Please don't, that gown is very becoming—you look just lovely—as a matter of fact, more beautiful than ever," exclaimed Franz.

"Ah, Franz, you had better put on your spectacles before making such reckless statements." Claire wanted to sound lighthearted.

"I don't need spectacles to see what's in my heart."

They both went out on the balcony, settling on the two-seater bench. When the waiter from the hotel brought the fragrant sangria its fruity aroma mixed well with that of the orange blossoms drifting in from the garden below.

"I am glad you came in, Franz, I was feeling very blue, ready to go home."

She watched him pour the sangria into the glasses, and again his hands captured her attention. Why did she never noticed them before? And what did it mean to her now? She thought of Peter. The pain of his loss would never go away, nor the feeling of a void in her heart. And yet, there was still room for other emotions. She yearned to be held, to be loved; was life passing her without that comfort she once treasured?

The birds in the garden below had stopped singing their revelry and dusk settled over the land. The guitarist Claire had heard before, strummed on his instrument for a while, and then sang a melody, which was passionate and haunting at the same time. Claire asked Franz if he could make out the lyrics, since he was quite versed in the Spanish language. He stepped up to the railing of the balcony to hear better, and listened for a while. When he turned around, he smiled:

"I could not catch every word, but enough to tell me that it is a song of love, longing, loneliness—you know, the universal theme, known to all who love or have loved."

Claire had stepped next to him, asking:

"Have you ever?"

"Ah, Claire, you should not ask...." He noticed, that Claire was trembling, and he put his arm around her. Their eyes met, and Claire, on an unexplainable impulse, not thinking, just feeling, whispered almost soundlessly:

"I love you, Franz." And her lovely, old silk kimono slipped from her shoulders. Wicked, wicked Claire!

Much later that night on the balcony, they relaxed in comfortable lounge chairs under the starry heavens, enthralled by the wonders of the firmament as it appeared on that moonless night. They sipped on the champagne which Franz had ordered to celebrate their journey together, as he said.

"Is it at all possible to count the stars we can see here tonight?" Claire wondered.

"There are more of them than grains of sand on all the beaches of the world," Franz said. "And this is the number of those we can see, what we don't see is infinitely greater than that."

"Tell me about God, Franz, I always believed in His existence, and I am convinced that He guided my life, but the older I get, the more I would like to know. They call you 'a Man of God.' Tell me, what do you know about God?"

"What a difficult question—and I do not know the answer. I am quite certain of the divinity of an omnipotent, infinite, timeless, changeless, eternal power, but I cannot describe it to you. It is not of human comprehension. I have often struggled to define it, but I came to the conclusion that it is not for us to know, just to believe. And that I do with every fiber of my being."

They were quiet for a while. It was a sweet stillness which engulfed them in a meeting of two loving souls searching for answers to the ultimate question.

Franz held her hand in his and trembled.

"Claire," he said, all of a sudden with a heavy voice, "I love you," and he dropped the glass he had been holding in the other hand. Claire looked at him, startled. In the darkness of the night she could barely make out his face, but his head had dropped to his chest. Claire cried out and ran to call for help. When the hotel doctor arrived, he ordered immediate transportation to the hospital with the diagnosis of a severe heart attack. Claire stayed with the bishop the whole night. He regained consciousness just long enough to recognize her anxious presence. He tried to smile and said:

"It is all right, dearest, I am very happy," then turned his head and exhaled his last breath.

Claire could hardly grasp what had happened. She must have dreamed it—but it became reality soon enough. She was shaken and in pain, but was able to get hold of herself enough to give appropriate directions. She ordered the transfer of the bishop's body to Salzburg, and informed the diocese and her family of their return. She packed her and the bishop's belongings and boarded the train on which his body was also transported home to Salzburg. Only when on the train and alone in the passenger compartment, did she give way to her grief. It was a sad ending to their journey together, but the memory of beautiful moments with a beloved friend would carry her through the rest of her life.

The bishop's funeral was, as expected, a grand affair, which the Church celebrated with all its known formality. Claire and her children had honorable positions in the procession, since he had made his wishes clear as to the station of the Burghoff family in the event of his passing. Claire felt strange when she observed all the pomp and heard all the speeches honoring their bishop. She remembered listening to his heartbeat on the little bench on the beach in Spain. She wanted to say to the mourners:

You may extol the virtues of His Eminence, your bishop, and praise his strength and his faith, but it is I who really knew him, the man and his soul, tender, loving, and vulnerable.

She was immensely proud that he had been her friend through these many years, knowing more about her life than anyone else here, and loving her despite her shortcomings. How blessed she was. Would she miss him? "Oh God, it will be between you and me to know how much."

Something strange happened in the days and weeks that followed. She felt that Bishop Franz was always near, she listened to his advice and they continued their last conversation about God, the stars, and the universe. She relived the sweet moments of understanding his love for her. It was calming and she was content.

When Paul returned from London two days after the funeral, he was shocked and distressed. He even blamed Claire for not informing him in London so he could at least have been back for the funeral. Claire countered that she did not know how to reach him.

"How about calling my office, they certainly knew how to get hold of me!"

Claire admitted she had not even thought of that in all the turmoil she found herself in and the confusion surrounding it all. She was also surprised at Paul's displeasure with her—the first time that he had ever talked to her like that. He asked about the details of the incident of the heart attack. Claire mentioned that Franz had been kept quite busy during their tour in Spain, with tireless lecturing and explaining, but on the day when it happened, he had seemed to be relaxed and in very good spirits. She told about their leave-taking from the tour group, who went to Morocco without them, the leisurely walk along the coast during which Franz had shown no sign of fatigue, not even during the last minutes of their inspiring conversation.

Paul wanted to know more:

"Was he excited about something?" and he went on and on, until Claire started to resent his questions, when they began to feel like an interrogation, and fell silent. Paul said:

"I blame myself for not going along; maybe I could have prevented this from happening."

Now it was Claire's turn to become angry, and she said in a cool tone of voice:

"I am quite sure your presence would not have changed anything. The time for Franz had come—it is as simple as that. And, by the way, he was content. With his last breath he said...." And Claire stopped. She never lied, but to tell the truth now was not right. Franz's last words were very personal, and most precious to her. Paul pressed on:

"What were his last words?"

"I don't remember exactly, they were just a few, and hardly audible. I think he meant to say that he was happy."

"Happy? He must have known his condition?"

"No, he tried to smile, and I think his mind was still continuing the conversation we had only a few hours before."

"What about?"

"About God, the universe, infinity, the stars above. Paul, I am sad and in pain also, your questioning is making me feel worse."

"I am sorry, Claire, but I am extremely upset. I think that if I had been to the funeral and participated in the solemnity of the ceremonies and the churchly pomp, my soul would have had time to quiet down."

Claire understood and they talked about how funeral services do have a specific purpose—not for the deceased, but for those left behind, whose mind can be distracted from feeling the pain by all the commotion. Actually, what neither of them knew was that the bishop had had problems with his heart long before that trip. Only his doctor and Peter had known; Peter had told him to avoid stress and strain, and he took medication prescribed by his physician, but he had kept his condition to himself.

A short time after that, the Burghoffs, Claire and her children, and also Paul were called by an attorney to attend a meeting to listen to the reading of the bishop's will. Its content surprised all of them.

To his godson Christopher, he bequeathed a prayer book of special significance. It had been given to Franz Hinterberger on his investiture as bishop by Cardinal Anninger, who had been his benefactor throughout his theological studies. The Cardinal had met the young man already during his school days at the Jesuits' boarding school, had observed his diligence and sincerity, and his unbending religious conviction, and liked his handsome appearance and personality as well. He knew that priests could be so much more effective within their parish when they had that kind of appeal rather than being stern faced sermonizers. Franz Hinterberger did not disappoint the Cardinal, who continued to watch over him and was eventually influential in his becoming a bishop at a rather young age. When that happened, he presented to the newly installed bishop a rare volume of an old collection of prayers and philosophical essays from the eighteenth century. The book was bound in finest red leather with gold inlays and tooling, and had been given to the Cardinal as a present by the previous Pope himself in recognition for his contributions at an ecclesiastical council. Much history was contained in it. The bishop added the latter explanation about the prayer book, so its meaning was understood by Christopher. In his dedication he wrote: "To my godson Christopher, whom I love as I would have loved my own son."

To Peter he left a page from an earlier manuscript of Mozart's opera *The Magic Flute*, a rare find, which had been given to the bishop by a Salzburger wealthy merchant; on which occasion was not mentioned, but it was authenticated as original and was in Mozart's own handwriting. Tony was mentioned to receive it as Peter's heir according to a codicil from the bishop.

To Eva, the bishop bequeathed an original oil painting by Defregger, well known for his renderings of farm family scenes, this one depicting an old woman surrounded by several youngsters in prayers before their meal.

To Claire, the bishop left an antique gold and sapphire ring. Attached to it was a personal sealed note with an explanation. He said it was his mother's, who had given him the ring when he was still a boy, long before he became a priest, but shortly before her death, with the admonition to give it to his future wife. Since he never married, he wanted it to be given to the woman he most admired in all his life, Claire Burghoff.

Claire put it on her finger. This ring and her small wedding band—once almost forgotten in the rush of the day at that time, but treasured ever since in all its simplicity. She would wear both now forever, as she did also the pendant that Peter gave her in Florence. It was the only jewelry she ever wore.

The bishop remembered Paul with a walking stick, elaborately carved and with a handle of ivory and silver, which he had once purchased himself on a trip to the Orient.

The rest of his estate went to the church, as was expected; he had no other heirs.

Paul stayed away for a few days, then returned to Waldegg to resume his cherished role as "Uncle Paul," and being his old self, warm, loving, compassionate and advisor to young and old. Claire depended much on him. Although he had sold his publishing business shortly after the bishop's death, he kept himself busy reading manuscripts, which were sent to him. With his suggestions and editorial advice, Claire published a volume of short stories, and was working on a novel, giving her and Paul enough material for debate and argument, which they both equally enjoyed.

From now on, Paul would never go without his fancy walking stick, although he would deny the need for one. Despite his progressive hip pain, resulting from his shorter leg, he would not admit to being incapacitated. He and Claire wandered, as in all the years past, through the countryside, but more often now they took the car and drove to more distant places. A favorite afternoon excursion was a ride up the Gaisberg located just adjacent to the city of Salzburg, providing a magnificent view from its nearly two thousand feet elevation. They went to Hellbrunn with its many fountains and water works, or rode through the countryside to enjoy the scenery of many lakes, and historic places. They treasured each other's company. Claire had found that inner peace which old age can bring, if one's life's goals have been nearly met, when one has learned to accept the inevitable and that which was fated. She could now visit Peter's grave, which had been a daily routine for her since his death, without the anguished pain in her heart. She could find pleasure in reading Elizabeth's short letters, and not fret over their scarcity. She felt herself to be so very lucky to have children and grandchildren of whom she could be proud, to love and be loved. She was healthy and grateful for it. She could face the rest of her life with confidence and without trepidation.

On this sunny afternoon in late fall, Paul and she were once again on top of the Gaisberg, never tiring of the lovely view over the city below. Today a haze lay over it, and the rich colors of the changing leaves of the beech woods and maples nearby reminded them of the end of a lovely season, which would probably soon bring a halt to their excursions. Winter would also have its pleasures, sitting by her fireplace, reading, writing, and doing some needlework. Claire was deep in thought —sometimes she liked to dwell on the past, not in morbid recollection, but to think of the good things that had come her way, and the fortunate events that had graced her life.

She walked towards the edge of the rocky ledge, where the view was wide open and reached beyond the city towards the mountains. Paul observed her from the distance. He could never cease to think of her other than with great love in his heart. He had loved this woman from the first time he met her—how many years ago? Forty-five or more? From some distance one could even surmise that it was a young woman who stood there—slim and elegant of appearance, in a light gray dress, a pink shawl flowing in the wind, the last rays of the sinking sun putting a golden shimmer onto that still lovely, serene face.

Paul came close, and when she met his gaze with that sincere look of her dark gray eyes, he said it once more, with a tremor in his voice....

"Marry me, Claire..."

With a sweet smile she took his hand and placed it against her cheek:

"Ah, Paul...you know, I..."

"Yes, I know," Paul said, and took her arm.

They walked slowly back to the waiting car.

The End